continued . . .

Death on the Mississippi

"Lovers of historical mysteries should rush out for a copy of *Death on the Mississippi*, the delightfully droll debut of Wentworth Cabot, newly hired secretary to the celebrated author Mark Twain. Twain lights up the pages as he gives his lectures, mourns his impecunious state with disarming honesty, tells a fantastic tale of hidden gold to his young clerk, and generally suffers fools none too gladly. Cabot is alternately dismayed, baffled, and awestruck by his new boss's behavior as they set out on a riverboat lecture series in the company of a New York cop and, most probably, the killer the cop seeks. There's a good plot, a bevy of suspects, lots of Twain lore, and even a travelogue of life on the Mississippi in the 1890s. *Death on the Mississippi* is thoroughly entertaining."
—*Alfred Hitchcock's Mystery Magazine*

"Adventurous . . . Replete with genuine tall tales from the great man himself." —*Mostly Murder*

"Exciting . . . deftly dovetails flavorsome riverboat lore, unobtrusive period detail, and a hidden treasure with an intricate mystery—all to give peppery, lovable Sam Clemens a starring role in a case worthy of the old inimitable."
—*Kirkus Reviews*

"A well-done historical. This catchy adventure features a treasure hunt and showcases Clemens's knowledge of the river as well as his legendary gift of gab . . . Recommended."
—*Library Journal*

"A thoroughly enjoyable period mystery with Clemens and Cabot forming an uneasy alliance that possesses elements of Holmes and Watson as well as Wolfe and Archie. A very pleasant debut that will have readers eagerly awaiting the next entry." —*Booklist*

The Guilty Abroad

A Mark Twain Mystery

Peter J. Heck

BERKLEY PRIME CRIME, NEW YORK

THE GUILTY ABROAD

A Berkley Prime Crime Book / published by arrangement with the author

PRINTING HISTORY
Berkley Prime Crime mass-market edition / October 1999

All rights reserved.
Copyright © 1999 by Peter J. Heck.
Excerpt from *The Dumb Shall Sing* copyright © 1999 by Stephen Lewis.
This book may not be reproduced in whole or in part,
by mimeograph or any other means, without permission.
For information address: The Berkley Publishing Group,
a division of Penguin Putnam Inc.,
375 Hudson Street, New York, New York 10014.

The Penguin Putnam Inc. World Wide Web site address is
http://www.penguinputnam.com

ISBN: 0-425-17122-1

Berkley Prime Crime Books are published
by The Berkley Publishing Group,
a division of Penguin Putnam Inc.,
375 Hudson Street, New York, New York 10014.
The name BERKLEY PRIME CRIME and the BERKLEY PRIME
CRIME design are trademarks belonging to Penguin Putnam Inc.

PRINTED IN THE UNITED STATES OF AMERICA

10 9 8 7 6 5 4 3 2 1

To my friends in phosphor,
especially the gang on GEnie.

Historical Note and Acknowledgments

The historical Samuel L. Clemens, on whom my fictional detective is broadly modeled, lost his fortune in the early 1890s. After a series of bad investments—capped by the failure of the Paige typesetting machine, an unsuccessful rival of the Linotype—he was nearly bankrupt. He moved his family to Europe to economize, and spent much of the latter part of his life abroad, earning money to repay his debts by touring and lecturing. Thus it seems natural to take him to Europe for an adventure or two. I have chosen 23 Tedworth Square, in which he lived a few years after the nominal date of this adventure, as the home base for his London visit.

I also wanted to show him in the context of his family, from whom his financial troubles in later years forced him to be absent more than he would have liked. I have brought the whole family together to give the girls a chance to become characters in their own right. (Those interested in Twain's family life would be well advised to seek out Clara's book, *My Father Mark Twain*, which includes many letters and photographs illuminating this part of his personality.)

Twain is viewed as one of the prototypes of modern skepticism, and many of his remarks and writings on spiritualism and other supernatural phenomena amply support this image. The account of his visit to a medium in *Life on the Mississippi* is characteristic of his reaction to his own time's equivalent of "New Age" beliefs. However, at Livy's urging, he did attend séances after Susy's death in 1896, in hopes of communicating with her spirit. The experience seems to have done nothing to change his mind concerning supernatural claims.

Gaslight London is of course the home turf of one of the greatest of all fictional detectives, Sherlock Holmes. Twain himself was no admirer of A. Conan Doyle's stories, going so far as to lampoon Holmes in "A Double-Barrelled Detective Story." Still, it seemed appropriate to pay some homage to the Holmes canon in a book set not only in London, but touching one of Doyle's own obsessions, the spiritual world. So I have borrowed Inspector Lestrade (whom I have promoted to chief inspector, in accordance with the Peter Principle). I hope his performance here is in harmony with his character as drawn by his creator.

Researching these books is always enjoyable. As before, I have borrowed many of Mark Twain's own stories and sayings, which readers familiar with his work will recognize. The serendipity of research always turns up something amusing; this time it was the Hartford air-gun factory, which was later converted to bicycle production and may well have built the bicycle that Twain attempted to tame in his Hartford days. And I found Clara's description of her father as a "bad, spitting gray kitten" an irresistible image.

Of course, Mark Twain never became a detective (although his skeptical attitude and sharp mind would undoubtedly have made him a good one). But, given that fictional assumption, I have tried to make his character as authentic as I can. In the process, I have accumulated far too many debts to previous Twain scholars to acknowledge in this brief space. As always, any errors or distortions of fact are my own fault. But I hope I have been able in part to capture the spirit of a writer who was one of the key influences on my own growth and outlook on the world.

Finally, special thanks are due to my wife, Jane Jewell, my first and most demanding reader, who has contributed to the improvement of this book (and of its author) at every stage.

The Guilty Abroad

Abroad

+>=<+ +>=<+

A Mark Twain Mystery

≈ 1

I had been in London only three days, in my capacity as traveling secretary to Mr. Samuel L. Clemens, a well-known author under his pen name "Mark Twain." It was my first journey out of the United States.

I don't know whether Mr. Clemens or I was happier to be in London. My employer (an old hand at foreign travel) was enjoying a long-awaited reunion with his wife and three daughters, who had been living abroad for some time. He had set aside all work for a few days in favor of spending as much time as possible with his family. That left me free to see the sights of London—and I had been doing so with a vengeance.

Today I had visited the British Museum. All morning and most of the afternoon, I had gazed in awe at a thousand treasures I had previously seen only in books. Those illustrations were now plainly exposed as shoddy counterfeits, compared with the originals. The Elgin Marbles alone were worth crossing the ocean to see. But at last, the guards began to announce that the museum was about to close, and I was forced to drag myself away.

I walked out onto Great Russell Street, in front of the museum, in the waning sunlight. The curbside was lined with people trying to hail cabs—and the drivers clearly knew this for a spot where they would get good business this time of day. After surveying the tangle of horses, carriages, and would-be passengers, I decided there was no point in fighting the crowds here. The weather looked fine—evidently a rarity for an October day in England. I decided to walk to nearby Euston Station, perhaps half a mile away, where there was a large hotel in addition to the train station. There, I would have a far better chance of finding a hackney coach to take me out to Mr. Clemens's rented apartments in time for supper.

I had just turned up the street toward the station when a woman's voice behind me called out in an American accent, "Why, Mr. Cabot! What a surprise to see you here!"

Standing on the street corner in a foreign country, three thousand miles from home, the last thing I expected was to hear a familiar voice call my name. I turned to discover the smiling face of Martha Patterson—or, as she was now known, Mrs. Edward McPhee. I had been told that the world is a small place; now I understood what that expression meant.

"Good heavens, Miss Patterson," I said, removing my hat. "I mean, Mrs. McPhee . . ." My voice trailed off. It was certainly a shock to find her in London; a shock, and something of an awkward sensation, as well.

I had first met Martha when we were passengers on the Mississippi riverboat *Horace Greeley,* during the lecture tour for which Mr. Clemens had first engaged me as his secretary. She and I had become friendly—or so I had believed. She had introduced herself to everyone aboard the boat by her maiden name, and I had foolishly believed that she had taken a fancy to me. But at the end, we learned that she was married to Slippery Ed McPhee, a gambler and confidence man whom Mr. Clemens had known during his early days on the river.

But what on Earth was she doing here in England? She politely ignored my sputtered exclamations and merely stepped close to me, smiling, and said, "What are you doing in England, pray tell? Are you still working with Mr. Clemens?"

"Yes, I am," I said, somewhat regaining my composure. I still found her flashing eyes and bright smile hard to resist. "He's over here to see his new book through the press, and visiting his wife and daughters. I was just on my way to join them for dinner.''

"Are you staying nearby, or do you need a ride? Edward is bringing a carriage around, and we could take you home.''

"Oh, there's no need of that,'' I said, not certain I wanted to share a cab with Slippery Ed McPhee, despite the presence of his charming wife. (Or was it perhaps *because* of her presence?) "I was planning to walk up to the railroad station and find a cab there. I'm going all the way out of town, to a place called Chelsea.'' Even had I felt comfortable accepting a ride from them, I could hardly impose on them to take me so far out of the way.

"Why, how fortunate that we met,'' she cried, clapping her hands. "That's the very place we're staying! Now you must ride with us!''

I was at a loss what to say, and at that exact moment a carriage pulled up a short distance away and a curly-haired fellow with a broad hat leaned out and shouted in a broad western accent, "Here we go, Martha!'' It was Slippery Ed McPhee, and no other.

"Hello, Edward, look who's turned up in England,'' said Martha, taking my hand and pulling me toward the waiting carriage.

McPhee squinted in my direction for a moment, then his mouth fell open with surprise. "Well, fry me for a catfish! If it ain't young Mr. Cabot. Is my good old buddy Sam over here, too?''

"Yes, Mr. Clemens is here with his whole family,'' I said, deciding that further resistance to Martha's invitation would be undignified. "Your wife has offered me a ride out to Chelsea—if that's not inconvenient to you.''

"Why, no, easiest thing in the world,'' said McPhee. "Good to run across another fellow that talks regular American. These here limeys swallow half their words.'' He gave a loud laugh, ignoring the icy stares of nearby spectators.

"Really, Edward, one shouldn't make such remarks in public,'' said Martha as she accepted my assistance mounting into the carriage. "These people have spoken English far longer than we have.''

"Well, you'd think they'd've learnt how to talk it better by now," said McPhee, chuckling, as his wife settled into the seat beside him. She gave him a fond smile, as if he'd said something quite clever. I clambered up and took a position in the facing seat. The driver snapped his reins, and the horse started off toward the sun, which was already brushing the chimney tops to the west.

After thanking McPhee for the ride home, and exchanging a few more pleasantries, I said, "I must say, I never expected to see the two of you in London. What brings you to this side of the Atlantic?"

McPhee's expression turned serious. "Well, son, I have to say that when Sam gave me that talking-to back on the river, it got me to thinking. 'Ed McPhee,' I says to myself, 'maybe it's time for you to get a fresh start in life. Time to walk the straight and narrow, for a change.' So I made up my mind to do just that. Of course, I couldn't have done it without this little lady, here." He patted Martha's hand. His wife blushed, and waved her hand as if to dismiss his compliment.

"Oh, you give yourself far too little credit, Edward," she said, smiling again at her husband. She turned to me and continued, "But you must understand, Mr. Cabot, it's difficult to start with a clean slate in a place where everyone knows you, and where some of them hold your past against you, however much you've changed."

McPhee nodded and gave a snort. "The lady's got it dead to rights," he said. "At first, I thought about heading to New York, or maybe even California. But then I thought of all the fellows from my old line of work that had moved to all those places, and I just knew it wouldn't be long before bad company come looking for me, wanting to go out on the town and raise a little hell. It's mighty hard for a man to look an old friend in the eye and just turn him down cold, especially if that old friend's still in the same old business."

"Edward's given up cardplaying entirely," Martha explained, a proud look in her eye. Her husband smiled foolishly, as if this were the greatest of accomplishments.

As before, I found it puzzling that a woman so obviously intelligent and ladylike could enjoy the company of a crude specimen like Slippery Ed McPhee. And yet, they seemed to be happily married, and I had never seen any sign of friction between them. In the circumstances, all I could think of to say was, "Why, my congratulations to you."

Privately, I wondered—could he really have turned over a new leaf? For his wife's sake, I hoped he had, though it was hard not to be skeptical. It was easy for him to claim that he'd started a new life, but he might just be running from the consequences of the old one—with the police in hot pursuit.

"It must be quite an alteration in your life, Mr. McPhee," I continued. "I can hardly remember seeing you away from the card table in all our time on the river."

"I got to say you're right," said McPhee, shaking his head. "But I'm proud to tell you, I ain't dealt a hand of monte since we set foot in England, and nobody over here seems to know how to play poker right. But that's all by the by. I reckon this is the last place any of my old crowd is ever going to show up and try to rope me into some sort of crooked business—that's why I come over here. And then, first thing I know, here's Mr. Cabot, and now you tell me good old Sam is here, too. We'll have to get together and have a laugh about old times on the river."

I was not at all certain Mr. Clemens wanted anything to do with Ed McPhee, even if his reform was genuine, but I refrained from telling him so to his face. For all I knew, my employer would be pleased to hear the news that McPhee had found an honest way of life, and would do what he could to further the fellow's attempts to amend his life. It would not be the first time Mr. Clemens had helped someone who was down on his luck.

Our driver (a self-important little Cockney with an extravagant beaver hat that had seen far better days) took us a short distance south along Bloomsbury Street, crossed Oxford Street, then slanted to the southwest along Shaftesbury Avenue in the direction of Piccadilly. He picked his way carefully, as the streets were full of carriages and pedestrians: Londoners making their way home after a long day's work.

To an American eye, London seems to resemble Boston in the rambling layout of its streets. In both cities, many of the prominent streets began as winding country roads leading to small towns now incorporated into the modern city. In sheer size, however, London is a better match to New York. But London's antiquity sets it apart from anything in the United States. For someone who grew up (as I did) in a town like New London, Connecticut, where the oldest surviving buildings are just over two hundred years old, it is a heady experience to visit a city possibly ten times that age.

"Just imagine," I said, with a sweeping gesture. "These roads once felt the tread of Roman legionnaires, and before that were perhaps the paths that the Brythonnic tribesmen led their herds along. Every stone has seen the passage of millennia of history."

Our driver turned around with a disdainful look on his pockmarked face. "You're way off the mark, guv'nor. This 'ere's Shaftesbury Havenue, and there's not a single buildin' more'n ten years old. They knocked down me sister's 'ome to make the streets wider, and moved 'er and the brats off to a new place, willy-nilly. That there big posh theater is right where she used to live. That's always the way of it—move out the 'umble workin' folk so the rich don't 'ave to see 'em on their way to the play'ouse." He punctuated this sentiment by spitting sideways into the street, and turned back to his horses.

I was somewhat taken aback by this response, but McPhee took it in stride. "Jimmy's a wonder," he said, clapping the driver on the back. "The little rascal knows his way around this big ol' city as well as Ed McPhee knows his way around a deck of cards—and that's saying a Missouri mouthful. He's been driving us ever since we come to town."

"Well, that must be valuable knowledge for a driver," I said, impressed in spite of myself—I had seen McPhee dealing cards. "Do we pass by anything of particular historic interest on our way to Chelsea? I'd appreciate your pointing it out to us, if we do."

Jimmy turned around and looked at me again, as if deciding whether to trust me with his hard-won gems of knowledge. At last, he seemed to have determined that I was not about to set up in competition with him, and he nodded. "I'll do that, guv'nor. But we're goin' the wrong way to see the real 'istoric parts of Lunnon. Most of what we'll be goin' through was open fields and country villages not all that long ago. Nothin' Roman 'ere."

"How long ago was it open fields?" asked Martha.

"King Charles's time, barely two 'unnerd years since," said the driver, waving his hand to show his opinion of such freshly settled areas. "Oh, I won't say there's not a fine old 'ouse 'ere and there, but there's nothin' out 'ere like what's in the City." I wondered idly what he would have to say about New York or Boston, which could not have been much more than frontier villages at the time he spoke of.

Nonetheless, I was well enough entertained by the sights he did point out. " 'Ere's Piccadilly Circus," he said as we entered a large open area where several broad streets converged. He pointed to a large winged statue of an angel, rising above a public drinking fountain. "That statue's made from haluminium—cost a bundle, it did. There was haluminium cups for drinkin' when it was first put up, but they didn't last long. I know a lad what clipped one, and 'e stayed drunk three days on what 'e 'ocked it for."

Around the base of the fountain sat a number of garishly dressed women. "Those are the flower girls," said Jimmy, without further explanation. From the look of them, I did not think they sold many flowers.

We continued southwest on Piccadilly Street, originally an ancient road leading west from the walled City of London. There were a good many grand homes, almost mansions, along the way. Those overlooking the Green Park to the south had a fine view of Buckingham Palace. Evidently this was one of the most elegant of addresses during the early years of this century. Jimmy pointed out one house that had been occupied by Lord Chancellor Eldon, who amused himself by counting long and short petticoats from his drawing-room window. " 'E counted a lot more short than long," said Jimmy, cackling merrily.

At the corner of Green Park, we passed the mansion of the Dukes of Wellington, and an equestrian statue of Wellington as the victor of Waterloo. "That's the new statue," said

Jimmy. "The old one was so ugly that some claimed the Froggies 'ad it put up in revenge for losin'." We all laughed heartily at this anecdote, and Jimmy turned around to grin at us as he guided his team—a nicely matched pair of grays—onto Knightsbridge Road. His previously sour countenance was much improved by the grin.

We followed Knightsbridge Road a short distance to Sloane Street, then turned south until we reached King's Road. "In me grandsire's time, nobody but the Royals could travel this way," said Jimmy. "Heverybody else 'ad to show a copper token to ride 'ere. But now it's free to all." We followed the road west into the heart of Chelsea, where Mr. Clemens had taken apartments for his stay in the London area.

When the carriage pulled up in front of my destination, I was ready to leap out and send Mr. and Mrs. McPhee on their way, but before I could open my mouth to thank them, Slippery Ed stepped to the pavement and offered his wife his hand. "Come on down, Martha—I can't just drive right by old Sam's door without stopping in to say a word or two. Wouldn't be the neighborly way to act."

And so, with the two of them behind me, I walked up to the door, knocked, and waited. To my surprise, Mr. Clemens himself opened it. He was still wearing an overcoat, and had evidently just arrived home himself. He looked up at me and said, "Wentworth, why are you knocking? Why didn't you just come on in?"

Then he saw who was standing behind me. "Jesus H. Christ!" he said. "I should have known better than to let you out on your own in a strange city, Cabot. Couldn't you bring home an alligator or a skunk, or some other sort of pleasant companion, instead of Slippery Ed McPhee?"

At Mr. Clemens's rude greeting, Slippery Ed McPhee's jaw dropped, and he fell back a step. Then he let out a loud guffaw and said, "Sam! If I didn't know what a joker you was, I'd think you didn't want to see me and my missus! Why, you haven't changed a bit since you and me was both pups on the river."

My employer glared out the half-open door, blocking the entranceway. "Ed, I can't say I expected to find you here," he said. "What the hell are you doing in London? As if I couldn't guess . . ."

"Well, I'll bet you five bucks you *can't* guess," said McPhee, a sly grin on his face.

"He means to say he *would* bet you, except he's given up gambling," said Martha McPhee, who had stepped forward to take her husband's arm. "What a pleasure to see you again, Mr. Clemens! We're staying not far from here, so when I chanced to meet Mr. Cabot outside the museum, I thought the friendly thing to do was to offer him a ride home."

"Given up gambling?" said Mr. Clemens. "I wouldn't buy that yarn if it was printed on the back of ten-dollar bills and stuck between Exodus and Leviticus. I'd sooner expect a fish to give up water, or . . ."

Martha put her hands on her hips. "Really, Mr. Clemens, I'm disappointed in you. I know as well as anyone that Edward has had his faults in the past. But it is hardly charitable to hold those old ways against him when he has made a genuine attempt to change his life."

Mr. Clemens was about to say something in reply when a new voice came from behind him. "Who is there, Sam? Do we have company?" It was Mrs. Clemens, who stepped up and looked over his shoulder.

"It's just Wentworth, and a couple of people who gave him a ride home," said my employer, trying to maintain his position in the doorway. "I reckon they'll be going now." At this, I did my best to maneuver closer to the door so I could step inside quickly if Mr. Clemens decided to close it in McPhee's face.

"Howdy, you must be Mrs. Clemens," said McPhee, removing his hat and giving an exaggeratedly low bow. "It's a pleasure to make your acquaintance—I've known good old Sam since before the war, but this is the first chance I've had to meet his pretty little lady."

"You flatter me," said Mrs. Clemens, obviously amused at the compliment. She looked at her husband. "Perhaps you should introduce me to your friend?"

"Not quite a friend," muttered Mr. Clemens, but he stepped to one side and said, "Mrs. Clemens, may I present Mr. and Mrs. McPhee—they were on that river cruise last summer. I think I told you about that trip, Livy?" He raised his eyebrows and gave his wife a very significant look.

Mrs. Clemens seemed puzzled for a brief moment; then she smiled. "Yes, you did," she said, turning and nodding to the McPhees. "Good afternoon, Mr. and Mrs. McPhee. So—the notorious Slippery Ed has come to London! Are you two here to see the sights, or are you traveling on business?"

"A little of both," said Martha, taking the conversational lead again. She stepped closer to Mrs. Clemens, putting herself between me and the door, as she continued. "We're enjoying the sights, and I'm doing some library research. And we plan to go up to Scotland, to discover our families' history—I'm a Patterson originally, and of course the McPhees were Scottish, too.''

"A Patterson?" Mrs. Clemens looked more closely at Martha McPhee's face. "There were Pattersons living close to us in Elmira, New York, where I grew up. Do you have family there?"

"Not that I know of, Mrs. Clemens," said Martha. "I grew up in Chicago, and my family came from Baltimore before then. But I suppose it's possible they were related to the Pattersons you knew."

"Perhaps you'll learn that on your visit to Scotland," said Mrs. Clemens. Then she looked at her husband. "But we shouldn't keep you standing on the porch all this time. Why don't you invite your friends inside, Sam?" By now, the sky was beginning to darken.

"Oh, we couldn't intrude," said Martha. "I know you must all be getting ready to sit down and eat, and we should be getting home to supper, ourselves."

"Still, I insist you step inside at least long enough for a cup of tea, or a glass of lemonade," said Mrs. Clemens, beckoning to them. "After all, we owe you that much just for giving poor Wentworth a ride home. I'm sure he'd be hopelessly lost if not for you."

At that, Mr. Clemens found himself speechless—as did I. Hopelessly lost indeed! With a sigh, my employer admitted defeat. He stepped aside and waved us all through the door, although he sent a particularly evil glance in my direction as I passed him. I rolled my eyes and shrugged in response; I was as puzzled as he at Mrs. Clemens's open invitation, after she knew what visitors stood on her doorstep.

Inside, we sat in the gaslit front parlor as Mrs. Clemens rang for a servant to bring us drinks. We were joined there by Mr. Clemens's oldest daughter, Susy, a fair-haired young woman a couple of years older than I. Susy was bright and sensitive—she had spent a year at Bryn Mawr college—but I had the strong impression that she was unhappy with her present state of life. London seemed to bore her, a sentiment I found incomprehensible. Then again, I had not had the ex-

perience of seeing my family fall into financial difficulties, as
had the Clemens children.

Mrs. Clemens played the hostess in exemplary fashion,
even to a couple of dubious character—I knew that her husband had told her in detail about the doings of Slippery Ed
McPhee on our riverboat journey. These had included a suspiciously steady winning streak at poker, as well as his running a fraudulent "game" called three-card monte.

Mrs. Clemens showed the McPhees to comfortable seats on
the large davenport facing the mantelpiece. While we waited
for the refreshments to arrive, she engaged Mrs. McPhee in
conversation as if Martha were a proper young woman whom
Mrs. Clemens had just met at a church social. As I had seen
before, Martha was everything that her husband was not—
charming, well-spoken, and quite capable of holding her own
in the most respectable company.

Mr. Clemens sat next to the fireplace, swirling his glass of
whisky and soda, doing his best not to scowl at McPhee—or
me. Finally he broke into the conversation to ask, "Well, Ed,
your young lady says you've quit gambling. If it's true, I'm
glad to hear it. But I wonder—what are you doing to make
ends meet these days? It can't be easy for an American to
find work over here in London."

"Well, Sam," said McPhee, "what made me look at my
life and change my ways was when my sweet Martha found
out she had a gift, so to say. And that made me bound and
determined to see that she didn't hide her light under a bucket,
you know? This here young lady can bring help and conso-
lation and advice to folks all around the world, and durn if
I'm not going to see that she gets to do it. So I guess you
could say I'm working to promote Martha."

"A gift?" asked Mrs. Clemens, curiosity evident on her
face. She turned to Martha and asked, "What sort of gift is
that? Do you sing, perhaps?"

Martha blushed prettily, but it was Slippery Ed who answered. "Well, the young lady has what you might call a
spiritual gift—" he began.

"Damnation, I should have known it!" said Mr. Clemens,

setting down his class abruptly. "McPhee, have you gone into the spiritualism racket?"

"Well, it ain't exactly a racket—" began McPhee, but his wife cut him off with a gesture.

"I understand your concern, Mr. Clemens," said Martha McPhee. "I am sad to say that there are far too many fraudulent mediums and spiritualists, who do no more than prey on the unwary. Only the most naive would deny this. But there are dishonest and unscrupulous men in every profession. Quack doctors, greedy ministers—why, I'd wager there are writers whom you would consider frauds." She smiled brightly at Mr. Clemens, then continued. "But we do not blame the good ones for some of their colleagues' lapses. We should not throw out the baby with the bathwater."

Martha gazed sincerely at each of us in turn as she spoke. I found myself wanting to believe her, but I could not forget that this deceptively innocent young woman had concealed her true relation to McPhee in order to cultivate my friendship, then induced me to risk (and lose) my money on his monte game. Why should I suppose that she and her husband had really reformed?

Mr. Clemens was about to make some reply, but his wife shot him a look, and he fell silent while Mrs. Clemens said, "I certainly agree that we should not reject the truly gifted because of false claimants, Mrs. McPhee. But you still haven't told us—what exactly is the gift your husband says you have discovered?"

Martha McPhee lowered her eyes and said, in a quiet voice, "I have discovered that I can act as a sort of messenger between the living and those who have gone on before us." She sat modestly, with her hands folded in her lap and her eyes averted.

"A medium," said Mr. Clemens, scornfully. I could see that his worst suspicions had been corroborated. Seated next to him, Susy Clemens turned an inquiring look toward Martha—the first sign of interest she had shown in the visitors. I found my own curiosity piqued, despite my skepticism toward all claims of the "supernatural." I could not forget Eulalie Echo, the voodoo woman we had consulted in New Orleans, whose powers (real or not—we would never know for certain) had helped us bring a murderer to justice.

"Yes, I am a medium, to use the common term," said Martha, looking directly at Mrs. Clemens. Her expression and posture were dignified yet humble—there seemed no deception in her. Mr. Clemens snorted and stood up abruptly, going over to the sideboard to refresh his drink as she spoke. Martha glanced his way, shook her head sadly, and then fixed her gaze on Mrs. Clemens again.

"I can understand your husband's reluctance to accept that I might have been granted such a gift, Mrs. Clemens," she said. "It does appear to defy all normal logic, and Mr. Clemens clearly believes that the world ought to be a logical and rational place, without any intrusive ghosts or spirits. I have read his books. But tell me, Mrs. Clemens—have you never felt a hint of something from beyond, or had a sensation of the continued presence of a loved one who has gone on before?"

A sad, distant look crossed Mrs. Clemens's face. She nodded and said, "I have often dreamed of my mother—she passed away only a few years ago. And of our little son, Langdon, who died so young . . ."

"Yes, dreams can be communications," said Martha, in a quiet voice.

"If that's so, any drunk in the gutter, or a Chinaman in his opium den, can be a prophet," said Mr. Clemens. He had returned to his chair, and had become increasingly restless (pointedly consulting his pocket watch) while listening to this recital. I expected I would have to endure considerable talking to for having brought these unwelcome guests to his door. He stared at his wife and said, "You aren't going to swallow all that hogwash, are you, Livy?"

"I am not quite so ready as you to reject proofs of the spiritual world, Sam," said Mrs. Clemens, returning her husband's gaze with equanimity. "As you may well imagine, my husband and I have had this discussion before," she added, turning to the rest of us with a wry smile.

Mr. Clemens threw up his hands. "Yes, and with about as much conclusion. Say, Ed, instead of this stuff, why don't you just get out the cards and deal a couple of hands of monte? At least then we'd all know what we were getting into.''

"Why, I thought I told you, Sam, I gave up that rowdy way of life,'' said McPhee. "It's a deception and a swindle, and I don't mind saying I'm ashamed of myself for having done it all those years. But I'm a changed man, Sam. I done seen the light, thanks to little Miss Martha here.'' He reached over and patted his wife's hand, and she blushed again—very prettily, I thought. I would never understand why she had married Slippery Ed. He must have been old enough to be her father—if not her grandfather!

"I suppose it would be easier for us to evaluate Mrs. McPhee's gift if we'd actually seen her at work,'' said Susy Clemens. "As it is, how can we judge her when we've only heard of this gift secondhand?'' It was her first indication of more than a vague interest in the conversation—perhaps understandable, since she must have heard many of her father's old friends and acquaintances make fantastic claims of one sort or another.

"Yes, I suppose you're right, Susy,'' said her mother. "And at the very least, I think we should allow Mr. and Mrs. McPhee the benefit of the doubt while they're guests in our home.'' She said the latter with a significant glance toward Mr. Clemens, who made a grimace but said nothing.

"Well, young lady, if you'd like a demonstration, I reckon that's right easy,'' said McPhee, rubbing his hands together. "We've got a small group coming to our place for a meeting—quality folks, a real English baronet and an important doctor, and their wives—and we could use a few more to fill out the table. If you all want to come see what it's all about, we'd be pleased to accommodate you.''

"A meeting? Do you mean a séance?'' asked Susy Clemens. Her eyes were suddenly brighter as she turned to face the McPhees. By this point, she had abandoned all pretense of boredom and disinterest.

"*Séance* is the common term, yes,'' said Martha McPhee, smiling at Susy. "I prefer to call it a *sitting*—I'm afraid the other word has been tarnished by association with people whose motives have not always been aboveboard. But I will second Edward's invitation. I do not know whether what you see or hear will convince you, Mr. Clemens—frankly, I cannot know in advance what you *will* see. But I would welcome you and your family as visitors—no, as participants—in our sitting tomorrow night. And then you may draw your own conclusions.'' She settled back on the davenport, with a modest air.

''What do you say, Sam?'' said McPhee, again rubbing his palms together. The mannerism was beginning to annoy me, though perhaps the old cardplayer needed to do something with his hands. ''I'll reserve seats for the four of you—the missus and the little lady, and Mr. Wentworth here. That's four free passes—no charge, none at all. Are you game?'' He beamed at us, as if only a fool would turn down such a generous offer.

Mrs. Clemens looked at her husband, a thoughtful expression on her face. ''I can't see any harm in accepting the invitation,'' she ventured.

Mr. Clemens sat scowling at his now empty glass. ''No harm other than lending my name and reputation to one of Slippery Ed's schemes,'' he said at last. ''I can see the newspapers: 'Mark Twain Attends a Séance!' in eighty-point type. I don't want to give you that kind of implicit endorsement—you or any other medium.'' As he said this, he pointed directly at Martha McPhee, whose tranquil face belied any notion that his tirade might apply to her. I thought he was about to continue, but then his daughter's dejected expression caught his eye, and he paused.

Seeing her father hesitate, Susy seized the opportunity. ''Please, Father, I think we should go. I've always wondered what it would be like to hear the spirits talk.'' She went over to his fireside chair and put her hand on his shoulder, a look of hope upon her face, and Mr. Clemens was lost. As I had observed during the few days since my arrival, both he and his wife were concerned with Susy's low spirits.

''Damnation,'' he said, under his breath, but all his resistance was gone. He turned back to Martha. ''I'll come to your meeting. But only if you guarantee you won't use my attendance to promote your schemes in any way, and that I'm free to write whatever I want about the whole mess—or to write nothing at all. I'm not going to shill for you, and I want you to understand that if I see anything that looks like trickery, I'll expose it without hesitation.'' He slapped his hand on the arm of the chair to punctuate this point.

Martha's face never changed. ''Why, Mr. Clemens, I would certainly never expect you to compromise yourself. I think I can undertake to promise—for myself and for Edward—that we will make no representation of any sort concerning your attendance at our sitting. As I told you, I have no idea what, if anything, will occur tomorrow night, so of course I cannot anticipate what you will think of it. But I would hardly expect you to write anything contrary to your principles, and even less to keep silent about something you thought dishonest. I *have* read your books, you know.'' She smiled and shook her head at him, as if addressing her marks to a slightly dull schoolboy.

''Well, maybe you have,'' said Mr. Clemens. He looked at his wife, who smiled, then up at Susy, who positively beamed. Finally he looked at me. ''You know these two, Wentworth. They'd play Barnum himself for a sucker. Is there any reason to think they wouldn't try to hoodwink *me*?''

I looked at Martha and Slippery Ed, sitting next to one another on the long davenport, then turned to Mr. Clemens. ''Quite frankly, sir, I don't think Mr. McPhee would hesitate one moment to try to deceive you, if he thought it was to his advantage.'' McPhee bristled, but I held up my hand and continued. ''On the other hand, I don't think he has much chance of succeeding.''

Mr. Clemens chuckled. ''You give me too much credit, Wentworth—not that I entirely object, but it's not what I hired you for. Still, maybe you're right. And maybe it's even possible that Slippery Ed's turned over a new leaf—it wouldn't be the first time I'd been surprised. Well, if Livy and Susy want to go see this séance with their own eyes, I reckon they'll need a couple of gentlemen to escort them. But I warn you, Ed—if I see a single word in the papers, or anywhere else, that looks as if you're trying to exploit my name and reputation, I'll write an exposé that'll make you wish you'd never learned to read.''

"Why, Sam, I wish you'd learn to forgive and forget—'' began McPhee.

"I can forgive—that's no problem," said Mr. Clemens. "But a man who forgets a deliberate injury is nothing but a fool. And London may have its share of fools, but Samuel Langhorne Clemens ain't one of 'em. I remember the old days on the river—the time you got kicked off the *Natchez* for dealing bottoms, the time you jumped off a boat in midstream to get away from all the boys that wanted to tar and feather you, the times they threw you in the hoosegow in Vicksburg, and Memphis, and Napoleon, and St. Louis . . . There's stories enough to keep my typewriter rolling for a good long time, with nothing but simon-pure truth for fuel. One more thing—if I see one word about my wife or daughter, I'll make you wish I'd cut off your face the minute you stuck it in my front door.''

"There won't be no need for that, Sam," said McPhee, glumly. "I know how to respect a lady as much as the next man.''

"Then are we agreed?" said Martha, clapping her hands together. "You will all be there tomorrow night?" She was the picture of delighted innocence; she might as well have been planning a picnic in the park. Whatever my reservations about her "gift," it was hard to deny her talent—she rivaled any actress I had seen.

"We shall be there," said Mrs. Clemens. "Is there anything we should bring with us?"

"Not unless you wish to attempt communication with some particular spirit," said Martha. "Then I suggest you bring some object—preferably metal—which the person owned or used. A ring or a brooch, perhaps, that the person wore regularly.''

"Why metal?" asked Susy, a puzzled look on her face.

"Metal and stone retain the emanations better than other materials," said Martha. "They can serve as beacons, if you will, to guide the spirits back. But wood or even paper will serve, if the object was closely enough associated with the departed spirit. Clothing has generally been washed, which reduces its efficacy for this purpose.''

"And I reckon if the metal is gold or silver, the spirits just might take it back,'' growled Mr. Clemens. "I think we'll leave the jewelry home, thanks. I'll tell you one more time, Ed McPhee—you'd better not do anything to make me regret this!''

"No tricks, Sam—honest Injun,'' said McPhee, with such a show of sincerity that I was almost tempted to believe him.

3 ⌐

The next day, Mr. Clemens remembered some correspondence he needed to attend to, and so my plans to go back into the city had to be postponed. I briefly wondered whether I was being punished for bringing home McPhee and his wife, but if so, Mr. Clemens was punishing himself as well, since he spent the entire morning away from his beloved family, dictating letters. After luncheon, his wife handed him a thick sheaf of typewriter paper—chapters from his latest book, marked with her comments and emendations—for him to revise. We sat together the whole afternoon in his little office at the head of the stairs, he working at the typewriter (which he had brought all the way from America) and I turning my hastily scribbled notes into finished letters for him to sign and dispatch to various parties all over the world.

It was perhaps four o'clock when Mr. Clemens tore a sheet of paper out of the typewriter, put it on the growing pile of finished copy, and pushed back his chair with the air of a man who has finished his work for the day. I kept on writing—I needed only a few lines to complete the letter I was working on. He watched me for perhaps two minutes until he saw me reach for the blotter, and then he said, "Well, Wentworth, what do you make of McPhee's séance? Is it just one more of his damned swindles?''

I looked over to try to read his expression, but he was concentrating on loading one of his pipes. "I can't judge for certain," I said. "I suppose we'll all know better tonight, after we've seen it."

"Oh, I wouldn't be so sure of that," said Mr. Clemens. "Do you remember how Slippery Ed took your money at three-card monte? You knew there was some kind of trick to it, and you were keeping your eyes on him the whole time, and he still managed to sneak in the stinger. That old rascal has about as many principles as a snapping turtle. He'd cheat *himself* if he could figure out a way to make a profit on it. Hell, he'd probably do it anyway, just to stay in practice."

"I suppose you're right," I admitted, blushing at the memory of how easily McPhee had deceived me. "But he's not charging us admission, and he has given his promise not to use your name in publicity. I don't see how he gains any advantage."

Mr. Clemens snorted and waved his hand, strewing the rug with a small spray of loose tobacco from the still unlit pipe. "You don't think he's likely to keep that promise for five minutes, do you?"

"*You* don't?" I asked, surprised. "Then why did you accept it?"

My employer finished tamping down the remaining tobacco and looked for a match. "Because Livy and Susy want to see the damned séance. Did you see that little girl's face light up? What kind of father could tell her no? Mark my words, though: if McPhee tries anything crooked, I'll lambaste him as a fraud and an outrage, and publish it for the whole world to see. And if he's lied to me, it'll give me the moral high ground. If you want to get a reader on your side, there's nothing that'll do it faster than the righteous indignation of an innocent, trusting man who's been lied to. But if people think you go around looking for trouble, they pay you a lot less mind."

"I can understand that," I said, nodding. Then a thought occurred to me. "Do you mean to say you're *not* going to

McPhee's séance with the intention of exposing him?''

He chuckled. ''Even if I did, do you think it would make much difference? Old Barnum was right, you know. It doesn't matter how many suckers you wise up—the swindler just has to walk down to the next corner, and there'll be another one along by the time he plants his feet. No, I just think of it as gathering material I might be able to use sometime. And there's always the tiny chance that some of what goes on *won't* be a sham—that's the part I'm really curious about— though it's the last thing I'd expect.''

''I'd have thought that voodoo ceremony we saw in New Orleans would be enough to convince you,'' I said, remembering a hot night on the shores of Bayou St. John, with Eulalie Echo dancing to wild drum music, and spine-tingling voices echoing in the dark.

''Nobody who's met Eulalie Echo is likely to call her a sham,'' said Mr. Clemens. The pipe was finally lit, and the aromatic fumes began to fill the room as he puffed on it. ''For one thing, I think she's absolutely sincere in what she believes. I'd guess the ceremony we saw that night was made up—not the real thing at all. The point was to scare the murderer into confessing, not to get in touch with the voodoo spirits. But if there's any case to be made for supernatural powers, I'd pick Eulalie Echo as the best evidence I've seen for it.''

''Then why couldn't Martha McPhee have genuine powers?'' I asked.

''Ah, now we get to the nub of it,'' said Mr. Clemens. ''You still want to believe in that girl, don't you? Even after you found out she'd lured you into Ed's game—even after you found out she was secretly married to him.''

''I wouldn't put it quite that way—'' I began, but he cut me off with a wave of his hand.

''We could argue about that all day long and get nowhere,'' he said. ''She *is* pretty—and that smile of hers is mighty persuasive. But best we both go in tonight with open eyes and as few preconceptions as we can manage—we'll have plenty of time afterwards to argue about what we see. Promise me you'll keep a sharp lookout, and do your best to remember everything you see and hear—not just the parts meant to impress you. I know you've got a good memory, Wentworth, and I'll trust you to use it to full advantage. Between the two of us—and Livy and Susy, too; they've both got good heads on their shoulders—we've got a respectable chance of spotting any shenanigans. After we get home, we'll compare notes and find out what we think happened.''

"Fair enough," I said.

Mr. Clemens rose to his feet. "Good, then let's go have a drink before dinner. I've gotten as much done as I'm likely to, and you look like you're ready for a break, too."

Neither Mr. Clemens nor I said any more about the séance, but inevitably, the subject came up over dinner. Clara, the Clemenses' second daughter, had been in something of a sulk all through the meal, shoving her food around her plate, and saying very little, even when directly addressed. Finally her father put down his coffee cup with a loud rattle and said to her point-blank, "Clara, what the blazes is the matter with you? I know the English can't cook worth beans, but there's something else bothering you, or I'm a half-shaved monkey."

"Nothing's wrong, Papa," muttered Clara, peering down at her half-eaten beefsteak with a martyred expression.

"She wants to go to the séance, and so do I!" said little Jean, at twelve years old the youngest of the three Clemens sisters. "It's not fair that Susy gets to go and we don't!"

"Why, Mr. McPhee only offered us four admissions," said their mother, in a reasonable tone.

"He'd have let all of us in if you'd asked," insisted Jean. "I bet he'd let us in even if we just showed up, without asking."

"I'm certain it's not suitable for young ladies of your age," said Mrs. Clemens. "We'll tell you everything that happens, you know. You and Clara can play games and have much more fun than we will, sitting in the dark in a cold English house."

"Besides, there'll be nothing to see," said Mr. Clemens, gruffly. "It's all a sham—everything Slippery Ed does is a sham and an imposition."

"You took us to see Barnum's circus, and you said that was a sham, and we had a good time," said Jean, shaking her finger at her father. She turned and shot an accusing look at me, sitting next to Clara. "Mr. Cabot is going, and he's not even part of the family."

"Wentworth is going because I think a strong young fellow with a level head is good to have around when you're dealing with a perpetual fraud like McPhee," said Mr. Clemens. "I've heard tell of séances where the spooks tried to steal the ladies' purses, and something like that is right in McPhee's line. If I'd had the last word, we wouldn't be going at all. I've never heard of a spirit that could tell you anything worth the trouble of walking across the street to hear."

"Mama doesn't think it's a fraud," said Clara, quietly. This caused an awkward moment, for it was true—and a significant bone of contention between her parents.

"I have not made up my mind yet, Clara," said Mrs. Clemens. "Mr. McPhee may be questionable, but his wife appears to be an intelligent woman of some culture, and I think she may be sincere. It would be wonderful if they could really help us communicate with the spirits of those who have gone before us. If Mrs. McPhee is genuine, I should think everyone would want to know what she has to bring us. And if she and her husband are the frauds your father believes them to be, perhaps we will learn what their tricks are—and then expose them so that others won't be injured by them."

"It's still not fair," said Jean, sinking back into her chair.

"I'll tell you what," said Mr. Clemens, resting his chin on his steepled fingertips. "If you and Clara have questions you want to ask the spooks—"

"Why do you keep calling them spooks?" demanded Jean. "You wouldn't call them that if you took them seriously."

"Papa doesn't take *anything* seriously," said Susy Clemens, drawing a chuckle from her father and knowing smiles from her sisters. "Nonetheless, I think he has a good idea," she continued. "You and Clara can tell *me* your questions, and I'll be sure to ask them—and bring you the answers. And that way Papa can spend his time watching out for Slippery

Ed's tricks, instead of trying to remember your questions—or what the spirits say."

"It won't be the same as going ourselves," said Clara.

"No, but it's the best offer you're going to get," said Mrs. Clemens, in a tone that made it clear that there was nothing more to be gained by arguing the point. She looked up at the clock on the mantelpiece. "We've got just over an hour before we have to leave, so you girls decide what you want Susy to ask. We don't want your father to keep the spirits waiting—it would be terrible if they were cross at him, and wouldn't say anything!" At that we all laughed, and went off to ready ourselves for the evening.

We arrived at the address McPhee had given us a little before the hour of nine. It was a chilly, damp evening, and there was a fine mist beginning to descend, diffusing the glow of the gaslights along the way. *Exactly the sort of evening one should be going to see ghosts,* I thought to myself. A large, well-appointed brougham was in front of the building just as our driver pulled his horses over. A sharp-featured man stood on the curb beside it, reaching up his hand to assist a lady out. Another woman stood beside him, holding an umbrella. "Well, it looks like the rest of the suckers are on time," said Mr. Clemens, in a loud voice.

"Hush, Youth!" said Mrs. Clemens, jabbing him with an elbow. "I can't change what you believe, but I wish you would be careful what you say in front of the others. Some of the people here tonight may be grieving over a recent loss."

"All the more reason to warn them before Slippery Ed starts his swindle rolling," growled Mr. Clemens, but I could see that he was chastened—at least for the moment.

I alighted from the carriage and helped the two ladies out. The trio that had arrived before us had already gone up the step to knock at the door, and so just as Mr. Clemens came out of the carriage, the door to the building flew open, and McPhee's hearty voice rang out. "Welcome, folks! Come right in." Then, after a brief pause: "Hey, Sam—glad you could make it. Welcome, ladies—I guess that's the whole crew here, now.''

Inside, McPhee led us and the other fresh arrivals up a flight of stairs to a second-floor apartment, where a tough-looking fellow with his cap tilted over one eye stood beside the door, as if on guard. McPhee clapped him on the shoulder and said, ''I reckon this is the whole bunch, Terry. If anybody else shows up, don't let 'em in without my say-so.''

''Right-o, Mr. McPhee,'' said Terry, with a heavy Irish brogue.

''Mr. McPhee, is it? You're coming up in the world, Ed,'' said Mr. Clemens.

McPhee turned and laughed. ''Good ol' Sam—always ready with a joke! Come on inside, folks, and Miss Martha will introduce you all to each other.''

''Don't give your right name,'' Mr. Clemens said to me in an exaggerated stage whisper that brought a glare from his wife and a giggle from Susy.

McPhee steered us into a modestly furnished foyer, where he helped us hang our coats and hats in the closet. We then went through an inner door into a roomy, very decently appointed parlor dominated by a large round table. The gaslights above the fireplace were burning brightly, and there were watercolors of rural landscapes hanging on the wall. The room seemed warm and pleasant, even though there was no fire burning. The curtains were drawn closed.

In one corner was a large wooden table with several chairs around it, and several objects on its bare surface: three silver candlesticks, metal-rimmed spectacles, a large brooch, and several books—presumably objects belonging to loved ones whose spirits might be summoned. But on the whole, I thought the room looked far too ordinary to become a sort of annex to the next world. Had I come there for a social call instead of for a séance, I would have considered it a cheerful place indeed, though not really an elegant one. Martha McPhee was already there, of course, along with four others—two gentlemen and two ladies.

''Good evening, Mr. Clemens—I'm so pleased you were able to join us,'' said Mrs. McPhee, coming forward to greet

us. She was wearing a very plain white dress that effectively
set off her dark hair and bright eyes.

"Mrs. McPhee, you've found a very pleasant place," said
Mrs. Clemens, leaning on her husband's arm. She suffered
from a weak heart, and I knew it had taken an effort for her
to climb the stairs, but she managed a bright smile. "Do you
and your husband live here, or is this just your business address?"

"Oh, this is our home for the time being," said Martha.
"We were lucky to find such a comfortable place, and in what
we hear is a very good neighborhood. I'll show you around,
later, if you wish. But please, have a seat."

She turned to the others who had arrived with us. "You
must be Dr. Parkhurst," she said to the sharp-featured gentleman, who replied with a nod and a grunt, and then she
turned to face the rest of us. "Let me introduce you all—I
assume no one objects? Very well, as you all know, I am
Martha McPhee . . ."

Dr. Oliver Parkhurst was evidently a distinguished London
physician, and looked every bit the part—respectably dressed,
with dark hair just beginning to go gray, and the sort of face
that suggested insight and intelligence despite his gruff manner. He had come with his wife, Cornelia, a stout middle-
aged woman with an anxious expression. The other lady with
them was her younger sister, Ophelia Donning, a spinster. Her
hair was golden blonde, and she carried herself like a born
aristocrat. I would have guessed her age at no more than
thirty-five. Either she was considerably younger than Mrs.
Parkhurst, or one of the sisters did not look her age. All three
of them were dressed in conservative good taste, in keeping
with their stations in life.

Sir Denis DeCoursey was a tall, white-haired gentleman
with broad shoulders and piercing blue eyes. He wore a small,
immaculately trimmed tuft of beard under his lower lip, and
his well-worn blazer was a shocking bright red. He spoke
with an almost incomprehensible drawl. He was the baronet
of whom McPhee had spoken, and he evidently had inherited
very substantial properties somewhere in Kent. His wife,
Lady Alice, was a tiny little white-haired thing with a high-

pitched voice, full of energy. She was wearing a shoddy non-descript dress and a hat that must have been new at some point, though perhaps not in my lifetime. Had I passed her on the street, I might have taken her for a poor parson's wife. I was surprised—here were a real English baronet and his lady, and they were far less fastidious in their dress and appearance than a London doctor and his family!

The other man—pale, thin, and elegantly dressed, with a pale blue flower on his lapel—introduced himself as Cedric Villiers: poet, sculptor, musician, and all-around genius, to hear him describe himself. His hair was somewhat longer than the fashion, and swept straight back from his bulging forehead. He seemed only a few years older than I, and I wondered how he had managed to accumulate so many accomplishments in such a short time—if indeed he had! He sat toying with a thin ebony cane, its head carved to resemble some sort of fantastic serpent. He gazed out at the world with an annoyed expression, and barely condescended to glance up to greet us.

The last member of the group was Hannah Boulton, a woman just past middle age, dressed in heavy mourning; as we later learned, her husband had died not quite a year since. Her face was partly concealed by her veil, but it showed evidence that she must have been quite a beauty in her youth. Both the material and the cut of her dress were of the highest quality.

Of course, once Mr. Clemens introduced himself, he was the object of everyone else's curiosity. As always with a new group, he spent a few minutes ''in character'' as Mark Twain, entertaining the others with a few amusing remarks. It seemed to be a sort of professional obligation, though he never acted as if he minded it. The others seemed pleased to have such a famous man among them—with the possible exception of Cedric Villiers, who merely looked bored. That was apparently all the current fashion among British geniuses, since he did his best to maintain that appearance for most of the evening.

Perhaps inevitably, after Mr. Clemens had made a few remarks on general subjects, Sir Denis leaned forward and said,

"I say, Clemens, it's quite a surprise to see you here. I've read some of your books, and I'd have thought you'd not be all that keen on spirits and the other world, eh?"

"Well, I can keep an open mind about the spirits," said Mr. Clemens, leaning against the mantelpiece. "I can't say I've ever heard anything about the other world that made it sound very appealing. If the spirits are talking to us from Heaven, I reckon I'll see what I can do to get to the other place."

"Papa!" said Susy, feigning shock, and Mrs. Boulton appeared genuinely shocked. But Sir Denis gave a deep chuckle, and even Villiers's face betrayed a brief flicker of interest.

"There you go with your jokes, Sam," said McPhee, who had been bustling about the room, arranging chairs while Martha handled the introductions. I had tried to watch what he was doing, but it was difficult to keep an eye on him and still pay polite attention to the others as they introduced themselves. McPhee continued with a smile that seemed a bit forced. "Just you wait till you hear Miss Martha's spirits. I reckon they'll change your mind, if anything can."

"I'm from Missouri, Ed," said Mr. Clemens, shoving his hands into his pockets. "But I'll tell you before we start, I took all my money out of my wallet before we came here, so there's no point trying to steal it."

McPhee laughed again, and Mrs. Clemens gave her husband an icy stare, which he pretended not to notice—though he evidently decided not to pursue the subject any further. As for Martha McPhee, her expression of wounded dignity spoke volumes. Slippery Ed's nervous laughter faded into an uncomfortable silence.

Stepping forward, Martha McPhee said, "Now that we all know one another, why don't we begin our sitting?" She walked over to the large round table and rested her hand lightly on the back of one of the chairs. "Please take any seat you wish—it doesn't seem to make any difference to the spirits."

"What if I wanted that one?" asked Mr. Clemens, pointing to the chair Mrs. McPhee had her hand on.

She smiled patiently, like a teacher confronting a stubborn

schoolboy, and stepped away from the chair. "Why, of course, Mr. Clemens. Would you like to search under the table or have me roll up my sleeves, as well?"

Mr. Clemens had clearly not expected this response, for he muttered, "Oh, I reckon any old chair will do," and took the one nearest to him.

Martha McPhee smiled again, and stepped forward to the same chair as before. "Come, now, I believe we are all ready. Edward, when everyone is seated, will you see to the lights? And then I'll ask you to retire to the outer room to guard the door. We have exactly twelve in our circle, and anyone else would bring the total to thirteen. So please make certain no one intrudes until we are done here."

"It figures Ed would be the unlucky thirteenth," said Mr. Clemens, under his breath. But he took his place at the table, and the rest of the group seated themselves, as well. His wife sat to his left, Susy on his right, and I chose the seat between Susy and Martha. After a few moments of shuffling chairs, everyone was in their places, and McPhee began to turn off the gas. As the last flame went out, we found ourselves in darkness, and we heard McPhee cross the room and open the door; a brief shaft of light came in from the foyer, and then he closed the door behind him, leaving us in the dark—waiting for whatever spirits chose to come.

4

Sitting in the dark room, I was not entirely certain what was supposed to happen next. While I had a broad notion of the kind of thing that might occur at a séance (or "sitting," as Martha McPhee evidently preferred to call it), there was considerable divergence among the reports I had read and heard. Would the spirits speak to us directly? Would there be physical manifestations of their presence? Would we experience a genuine glimpse of the spiritual world, or was it all (as Mr. Clemens clearly believed) more of Slippery Ed's trickery?

"Let us hold hands," said Martha in a quiet voice. "Forming a circle will combine our separate energies, so that I can draw on them to communicate with the other side."

"Why don't they just get a telephone put in?" said Mr. Clemens in a stage whisper, followed by an involuntary exhalation that I interpreted as the result of a nudge to the ribs from his wife.

I stretched my hands out tentatively in the dark and grasped those of the women on either side of me, Martha McPhee to my right and Susy Clemens to my left. The thought went through my mind that, whatever Martha said about the "energies," having both her hands held would certainly limit her opportunities for deception. But I reminded myself that I would have my best chance of discovering what was really going on if I freed my mind of all preconceptions and simply observed the evening's events. Mr. Clemens had given me that advice on our first trip together, and it had served me well every time I had actually been able to follow it. I mentally put the issue of possible deception to one side, and resolved to pay close attention.

After a few moments, when all hands were presumably joined, Martha spoke again. "If we are successful in our attempt to converse with the other side, I shall very likely go into a trance, to provide a conduit for the spirits to communicate. Any of you can ask questions, but perhaps it would be best if one person were to take the lead. Sir Denis, I know that you have been at sittings before tonight. Would you be willing to make the first overtures to any entity that might appear?"

"Yes, of course," came Sir Denis DeCoursey's voice from across the table. "But I would hope that others will feel free to ask their own questions, once we have established communication. Are there objections to that?"

"I certainly have none," said Martha, "though I cannot say how the spirits may respond. They are often reluctant to answer questions they consider frivolous or hostile. If we are all ready, then, I will attempt to channel our energies. I feel that they are very strong this evening."

There followed a period of awkward silence—possibly five minutes, at a guess. Except for the utter dark, and the two warm hands I clasped on either side, it reminded me of a Quaker meeting I had once attended in the company of a Yale classmate of that persuasion. Someone coughed, and one of the women on the other side of the table gave a little nervous laugh. My ability to concentrate was just at the point of evaporating when there came a sudden loud rap. With the exception of Martha McPhee, I think everyone at the table jumped at the report; I know I heard several gasps. It sounded as if it came from the exact center of the table, loud enough that I think it would have been audible outside the door.

"Is there anyone there?" said Sir Denis, more calmly than I think I would have managed.

Barely had he said these words than a volley of knocks commenced, six or seven in rapid rhythmic succession. "Better let 'em in," said Mr. Clemens, but no one bothered to shush him. I cannot say what was in anyone else's mind, but I was at once exhilarated and, I admit, a bit frightened. All I could think was that it was of the utmost importance that I remember everything that transpired. If there really *were* someone there, attempting to communicate to us from beyond the grave, it would be mad not to heed every single syllable of what the summoned spirits might have to tell us.

"Do you wish to speak to anyone here?" said Sir Denis. This time the answer was a series of knocks from different quarters of the room, some of them nearly as loud as pistol shots, others much softer. While I had no idea of the cause, the effect was as if several different entities were answering the question at once.

Then came a voice that, had I not been seated next to her, I might not have recognized as coming from Martha's mouth. "Why do you call me?" she said. She spoke almost tonelessly, and her hand seemed limp, as well; I was quite ready to believe that she had fallen into some sort of trance. Indeed, had I not known better, I would have thought it was a man's voice I was hearing. Or was it a spirit? I felt a chill at the thought.

"First tell us who you are," said Sir Denis. "Some of your loved ones from your former life may be here, and they would gladly speak with you."

"My former life is a shadow of a dream," said the spirit voice. "Things are far different here, far happier. But I remember that when I walked upon that lower plane, I was called by the name of Richard."

Someone gasped, then said, "Richard? Can it be? This is your loving Hannah—oh, Richard, how I miss you!" I realized it was Hannah Boulton, the widow, speaking. Was this truly the spirit of her dead husband?

"Hannah . . . yes, I recall that name." The voice remained calm, though I must admit a chill came over me every time it spoke. I was almost persuaded to loose my grip on Martha McPhee's hand, though I held on for fear of breaking the circle and causing who knew what consequences.

"Surely you recall more than that," said Mrs. Boulton, pleading in her voice. "Oh, dear Richard—we were married twenty-eight years."

"Yes, Hannah—I could not forget that," said the spirit, in a voice still without emotion. I thought it would have been much more interesting to know if the spirit would have recalled the name Hannah, or their long marriage, without prompting. Judging from Mr. Clemens's audible snort, he was of the same opinion. But a grieving widow could hardly be expected to raise objections that occurred to more disinterested observers.

"Are you happy where you are, Richard?" asked Mrs. Boulton.

"We are all very happy. There is no pain or sadness here, only a faint memory that once I felt such things. We do not speak of such things among ourselves."

"Who else is there with you?" This time it was Sir Denis who asked.

"Many others beyond counting," replied the voice. "It is a great comfort to be among so many happy souls."

"It must be," came a familiar drawl. "Down here, pain and sadness are pretty much the standard topics of conversation." As he said these words, I could just barely hear Mrs. Clemens's warning whisper—"*Youth!*"—but my employer continued blithely, as if he had not heard his wife. "What do you all talk about up there?"

"We speak of our present state of happiness, and of the loved ones we have left behind."

"Aren't you sad that you are separated from them?" continued Mr. Clemens, still cheerful sounding.

There was a considerable pause, as if the spirit were deciding how to answer. "We are not sad because we know that we will soon be reunited with them," said the voice at last. "Our present separation will be but the blink of an eye compared to the long duration of eternal bliss together."

I expected Mr. Clemens to continue his cross-examination

of the spirit, but Mrs. Boulton spoke before he could get out his next question. "Richard, are you certain we shall be reunited? Will it be long?"

"We shall be reunited, Hannah," said the voice. "How long it will be in earthly years I cannot say—that is not within my ken, nor do we measure time as you do there. But have no fear, we shall be together in bliss." There was an almost imperceptible pause, and then the voice said, "There are others who would speak; I must bid you adieu for now."

"Richard! Wait!" sobbed Mrs. Boulton, but the voice came again, sounding fainter: "Adieu! Adieu!"

"Did he speak French before he was dead?" asked Mr. Clemens in a low voice, but before anyone could answer, there came the sound of a distant bell, tolling slowly. It could almost have come from some church in the vicinity, except that no church would be ringing its bells at this hour. Then came another loud volley of knocking from around the room, followed by the sound of a violin playing some eerie minor-key air. My first thought was that someone in another apartment was playing, but the sound, though soft and muted, seemed to come from directly above the table. It played for perhaps a little more than a minute, then stopped abruptly in the middle of a measure, leaving a pregnant silence.

"Is someone there?" asked Sir Denis DeCoursey, again taking the lead as Martha had requested. He was answered by two firm raps. Evidently taking this as affirmation, he continued, "Do you wish to speak to us?"

"Beware!" The answer was loud and sudden, and punctuated by four rapid knocks, seemingly from midair. I gave another involuntary jump.

"Why, are you going to play that fiddle again?" said Mr. Clemens. He was braver than I, to ask such a frivolous question in the presence of a voice so fierce sounding.

"That will be quite enough—the spirits are not amused with this kind of impertinence," said a woman's voice on the other side of the table. I could not identify the speaker, but her crisp English accent carried a heavy load of disapproval.

"Well, I don't want to be a bore. What kind of impertinence do you think would amuse them—Oof!" said Mr.

Clemens as his wife nudged him again, while Susy Clemens added her whispered admonition: "Papa!" (Still, I thought I detected amusement in her voice.) He muttered something it was probably just as well we couldn't quite hear, then fell silent.

The ghostly voice paid no attention to Mr. Clemens's gibes. "Beware, beware!" it said, and there was a distinct rattling and scraping, as if of heavy chains. "I come to warn you of great danger." Again, the words came from Martha's mouth, but it was not at all her natural voice we heard. This speaker seemed also to be a male, but the tone and timbre of the voice were distinctly different from the one that had called itself "Richard." I wondered how, if Martha was purposely producing the voices we heard, she managed to make them sound so different.

Taking the lead again, Sir Denis asked, "Is your warning for some particular person here, or for all of us?"

"All who live in that sad world are in daily peril, but my warning is for one soon to be bereaved," said the voice, ominously. The chains rattled again. "Hold not too tightly to the things of the world, for they will not profit you when you must cross to this side."

"Soon to be bereaved?" said a woman's voice—the same, I thought, that had admonished Mr. Clemens. "Can you not tell us more?"

Indeed, I thought, the warning was general enough to apply to almost anyone. With twelve of us at the table, one or another was almost certain to experience the death of a close friend or relative within some period of time that qualified as "soon." If the spirits had no better information than this to offer, there was not much to be gained by asking their advice.

"There is a wife among you soon to be a widow," said the voice. There were gasps from several points around the table, and I remembered that three of the women present were here with their husbands—not counting Martha McPhee, who showed no outward reaction to what her voice had just said.

"Pray tell us whom you mean," said another woman, an older-sounding voice. *Lady Alice,* I thought. "Is there no way to prevent this bereavement?"

There was a very loud rap, and the voice said, "What is destined cannot be changed. Cling not to the things of the world."

"Can you tell us who you are—or were?" asked Sir Denis. "We would know better how to understand your words if we knew from whom they came."

"What I was is less than nothing," said the voice, now fainter, as if more distant. "I have left behind the shreds and tatters of my life upon that plane. What I am now you would not recognize."

Mr. Clemens spoke again, in a more serious tone than before. "Why do you come to warn us, if you can't say who the warning is for, or what it means? Why have you come at all?"

"Poor deluded mortal!" said the voice, suddenly loud again. The chains rattled rhythmically as it continued, "You comprehend nothing. I tell you once again, beware—hold not too closely to material things. Beware!" The chains crashed loudly, as if dropped onto a wooden floor from a height, followed by sudden deep silence. I had an almost palpable sense of the spirit's absence. I also had a keen awareness that we had learned almost nothing from it. I wondered what else was to come.

A short period of silence was broken by music again—the sound of an accordion. The melody was more cheerful this time, perhaps a dance tune, though not one I was familiar with. Still, I found myself feeling somewhat lighter in spirit, after the lugubrious message of the previous spirit. I also thought to note a faint odor of incense—or was it merely one of the ladies' perfume I smelled? Again the music ended, although this time the unseen player ended on a proper cadence. As before, there was a moment of silence, and then Sir Denis asked if there was anyone present. He was answered with a veritable chorus of knocks, too rapid and numerous to count, from above, below, and from all sides.

"Is someone there?" said Sir Denis again. "Pray tell us who you are, and to whom you wish to speak."

The new voice replied by laughing, long and loud. Not a joyous laugh, but a *wicked* one—the laugh of someone rejoicing at the destruction of a foe, or at some ill-gotten gain. It made the hair stand up on the nape of my neck. What sort of spirit had come among us now?

"Speak to us," said Sir Denis again. "Have you a message for anyone here?"

The laughter was repeated, and then a voice spoke. "I have no message for you," it said. Unlike the previous voices, this new one was unmistakably that of a woman—although it was as different from Martha McPhee's natural voice as the others had been. For a moment, I thought I recognized it—but the person of whom I was thinking was thousands of miles away, and to the best of my knowledge still among the living.

"Why have you come among us, then?" asked Sir Denis.

"I come because I am compelled," said the voice, significantly. There were more rappings, interspersed with the high-pitched tinkle of what sounded like small silver bells.

"How compelled?" asked Sir Denis. "Is it we who have compelled you, or some power on the other side?" To this the voice responded only with a deep sigh. A silence followed, although I had a strong sense that the entity behind the voice was still present in our midst.

"If you have no message for us, will you answer a question?" It was Susy Clemens who broke the silence. I felt her grip on my hand tighten, as if to gather reassurance.

"I will answer what I may," said the voice, its tone somehow gentler. "There are many things I am not permitted to speak of. And you may not understand some of the things I am permitted to answer. There are realms beyond the ken of mortals."

"I can accept that," said Susy, in a quiet but confident voice. "Tell me, please, can you foretell the future?"

"Past and future mean nothing to us," said the voice. "We see many things, some that have already happened, some that may happen, and some that may never come to be. Which are which we cannot always say." The small bells tinkled again, sounding closer now.

When the tinkling had subsided, Susy continued. "Would you please answer a question for me and my sisters? Which of us will be the first to marry?"

I heard her father's soft chuckle as she finished the question. The female spirit responded with a gentle laugh, as well—it would have been a warm, friendly sound, had I heard it in any other setting than this. "The first to marry will be married the longest," it said.

"But which of us will it be?" said Susy, pressing the question. "Surely, it cannot be forbidden to tell me that."

"What is forbidden and what permitted is not yours to judge," said the voice, now not as friendly sounding. The silver bells began jingling in a slow, steady rhythm.

"Why can't you ever give a plain answer to a plain question? Papa thinks you're just a humbug, and I'm beginning to think he's right," said Susy, now sounding distinctly cross.

"You do not know whereof you ask," said the voice, distinctly angry. "You mortals cannot see what is before your faces. How should you presume to quiz those who can see more clearly? Why should I deign to answer you?"

An ominous volley of raps came from every corner of the room, growing to a thunderous crescendo, and the slow tolling of a distant church bell began again.

"Stop trying to scare the girl," said Mr. Clemens, sharply. "She asked you a polite question, and you dodged it. She asked you again, and you still haven't said anything worth listening to. If you can't give us good answers, why don't you just say so, without all the damned noises and mumbo jumbo?"

As if to spite him, the knocking continued just as loud, now joined by rattling chains. I braced myself for an outburst from my employer—or perhaps from the "spirits," who seemed to be building up to some sort of culmination. I cannot say exactly what I expected to happen—but surely it was not the sudden groan that came from across the table, followed by a piteous cry.

"Oliver! Oh, dear Lord, what has happened? Oliver, give me your hand again!" It was a woman's voice, obviously in utter terror, and there was no question of its being from any otherworldly source. This was flesh and blood, in deep distress. I opened my eyes, which had been tightly closed in concentration during the séance, and realized that I could dimly make out shapes and movement across the table.

A confused babble of exclamations followed. "What the devil?" "Cornelia, what is wrong?" "Oh, Oliver!" I heard chairs scraping back from the table, then the rapping and ghostly noises stopped abruptly, as if someone had thrown an electrical switch. "Somebody strike a light," said another voice, urgently. Someone was sobbing.

It was Mr. Clemens who was the first to find a match and strike it. In the wavering light I could see Martha McPhee sitting next to me, looking about her as if just awakened from a dream. Across from me several people were on their feet, frightened expressions on their faces. "Someone light the gas," said Sir Denis, leaning forward intently, his own match illuminating the tabletop.

Mr. Clemens reached me his matchbox, and I turned to find the light. But I did not need any more light than I already had to see the dark form slumped back in a chair on the far side of the table. There was more than enough light to recognize it as a limp human body. "It's Dr. Parkhurst," said Sir Denis. "Good Lord, the man's bleeding. It looks as if he's been shot!"

5

There was a chorus of gasps and shrieks at Sir Denis DeCoursey's announcement that Dr. Parkhurst was bleeding—and then, even as we watched, the doctor fell slowly sideways out of his chair onto the floor. Several of us were already on our feet, Mrs. Parkhurst was still in her seat, leaning sideways and imploring her husband to say something. Her sister, Miss Donning, recoiled as if in horror at the limp form on the carpet. I turned up the gas and lit it, then hurried back to the table to see what else I could do.

"Shot?" said Cedric Villiers, for once not looking bored. "How the devil could he be shot? I didn't hear any gun go off."

"With all that knocking and bell ringing, who could have heard it?" said Mr. Clemens, who had sat back down and put his arms around his wife and his staring daughter. He turned to look at Sir Denis DeCoursey, who was kneeling over the limp form. "Is he dead?"

"Youth!" said Mrs. Clemens, plainly shocked—at what, I wasn't quite certain, but her use of her habitual pet name for her husband struck an incongruous note to my ears. Then, after a moment, she said quietly, "Oh. I suppose it is an appropriate question, in the circumstances."

"He's just barely breathing. We must try to find a doctor, though there's not much hope with a head wound like that," said Sir Denis, and even from across the room I was inclined to agree with his grim prognosis. With the lights up, I could see quite clearly. Too clearly; I wanted to turn my eyes away from the grisly spectacle.

"Someone help me move him to the sofa," said Sir Denis. Cedric Villiers was closest, but he made a face, and so I stepped around the table to help. I took the legs while Sir Denis grasped the wounded man under the armpits, and between the two of us, we managed to get the limp bundle over to the nearby sofa. He was surprisingly heavy—Dr. Parkhurst had not looked that large when he had been standing on his feet. Sir Denis knelt down next to him, then looked up and said, "Someone fetch some water, and some cloths we can use as bandages. We must do whatever we can to give the poor devil a chance to live."

Lady Alice, who had stood up almost as soon as the lights came on, nodded and went off with a purposeful look on her face. Most of the others, I noticed, were doing their best to look away. Mrs. Parkhurst had now fallen on her sister Ophelia's shoulder and was sobbing loudly. She reached out toward her husband and cried, "Oh, help him! Someone please help him! Dear Oliver, don't die! Don't leave me alone!"

After a moment, Lady Alice returned with a basin of water and some towels, which Sir Denis used to swab off Dr. Parkhurst's forehead, then to try to stanch the bleeding. After getting a closer look at the wound, he frowned and put his ear against the doctor's chest, listening intently for a moment. His expression was grim as he straightened up and said, "I'm afraid there's no heartbeat. May the Lord have mercy on him."

At that, Mrs. Parkhurst began to shriek, "No, no!" Her sister wrapped her arms tighter around her, and now Hannah Boulton began to sob loudly. Mrs. Clemens and her daughter Susy both had shocked expressions, but neither seemed quite as stunned as the other ladies—of course, they had not known the victim.

Lady Alice's face was grim, but she went and touched Martha on the shoulder. "Mrs. McPhee, is there another room where we can take Mrs. Parkhurst and the other ladies? This is a rather terrible scene, I'm afraid."

Martha was still in her seat, blinking like a person just awakened from sound sleep. At Lady Alice's words, she started and rose to her feet. "Yes, of course, what am I thinking of? Please, ladies, come with me. Mrs. Parkhurst, may I take your arm?"

Still sobbing loudly, Mrs. Parkhurst let herself be led through a door, apparently into a bedroom, supported by Martha on one side and by her sister, Miss Donning, on the other. The other women followed them—although Susy Clemens seemed reluctant to leave. I almost would have traded places with her, had I any good excuse to remove myself from the grisly scene. When the door closed quietly behind them, Sir Denis said, "Now we must call in a doctor—though I fear there's little the fellow can do. And we need to inform the police."

"Good thinking," said Mr. Clemens. "Is there a telephone in the building?"

"I certainly wouldn't know," said Cedric Villiers, with a surprisingly indifferent shrug. "Ask that fellow out in the foyer—he's the one renting the flat."

Mr. Clemens was closest to the door; he stepped over and opened it. "Ed, you better come inside. We're in trouble."

"What, is the show over already?" said McPhee, getting up quickly from the red velvet-covered couch where he'd been sitting. I could see a deck of playing cards spread out on a small table in front of him—some sort of game. Apparently he had not given up cardplaying quite as completely as Martha had suggested. He took out his watch and glanced at the time. "Martha usually keeps things going a bit longer than this."

"The show's all over, Ed," said Mr. Clemens, in a weary tone. "Or maybe it's just gotten started. Somebody shot Dr. Parkhurst while the lights were out, and it looks like he's done for. We're going to need the police. And we might as well have a doctor, just in case."

"Shot? Police?" McPhee's jaw fell. "Sam, you wouldn't

pull my leg about something like that, would you? It ain't a bit funny, and that's the truth.'' His voice had nothing of its usual jovial tone.

''I fear he's got right of it, Mr. McPhee,'' said Sir Denis, and his sober expression emphasized the truth of his words. ''Here's the poor fellow on the couch.''

McPhee stepped inside the door and took in the scene at a glance. His face turned white as he saw Dr. Parkhurst's body on the sofa. ''Jesus, it looks like he got in front of a cannon.''

''Yes, I'd say he took at least a forty-caliber round,'' said Sir Denis. ''Now we need to fetch the constable.''

A cagey look crossed McPhee's face. ''Look here, I don't think we need to go bothering the cops about this little thing,'' he said, trying his best to regain his usual poker face. ''Poor man's dead and gone, and can't nobody help him, right? Seems to me we can settle things up without any big fuss.''

''It's way too thick for that, Ed,'' said Mr. Clemens, taking McPhee's elbow. ''Here's a respectable citizen shot dead, and that's murder in anybody's book. You can't just throw around a couple of bucks and make it right, as if you were caught with loaded dice in your pocket. We're in a foreign country, and the police play by different rules. Now, is there a telephone in this building, or don't you know the answer?''

McPhee wrinkled his brow for a moment, then brightened up and said, ''Well, there ain't no phone in here, but I seem to remember there's one at the tobacco shop two streets over—owner lives right upstairs from the shop. I reckon he'd let me use it if I tell him how it's an emergency. Why don't I just go do that? I'll only be a few minutes . . .''

''Let's not be so hasty,'' said Cedric Villiers, holding up his hand. ''I don't at all like the way this fellow acts. If we let him go, who's to say we'll ever lay eyes on him again?''

Mr. Clemens nodded. ''I guess you've got a point, Villiers. If we let Ed out the door, he's as likely to skedaddle as to go find a bobby.''

''Sam, you ought to know me better than that,'' said McPhee, puffing himself up like a rooster. ''Ed McPhee ain't so low as to run off and leave little Miss Martha all by herself when trouble starts. 'Sides, I'm the only one that knows his way around this here neighborhood. It'd take anybody else twice as long as me, with all these misty dark streets."

"What, are you daft? A yank know Chelsea as well as I?" said Cedric Villiers, sneering. "I'll wager I could walk blindfold to this tobacconist, or anywhere else within a mile of here. But I hardly think it's necessary to knock up the shopkeeper. There'll be a constable out on the streets, most likely over at the corner of King's Road."

"I don't doubt it," said Sir Denis. "But consider this— we've got a murder on our hands, and every man in this room will undoubtedly be considered a suspect. In fact, Mr. McPhee may be the only one of us with a sound alibi—at least we know he was out of the room when the shot was fired."

Mr. Clemens looked around at the rest of the company, his eyebrow raised in questioning, then shrugged. "Well, then, I guess Ed's the one that has to go. But just to be on the safe side, I say we send somebody to keep an eye on him. How about Wentworth, here? He used to play football—if that old potbellied card shark tries to give him the slip, I reckon my man can run him down and put a hammerlock on him."

"And how do we know they won't both abscond?" said Cedric Villiers. "As Sir Denis points out, everyone in the room is a suspect. Your man has as much reason as Mr. McPhee to run away."

"You can't be serious," I said. "I never saw that poor man before this evening. What reason would I have to kill him?"

"That's for the police to determine, isn't it?" said Villiers, fixing me with his gaze. "Your employer wanted to discredit the medium—it was obvious the minute you came in the room that you were not believers. Mr. Clemens has evidently had dealings with Mr. McPhee before, and it's plain they are not friends."

"That's preposterous," I began, but Mr. Clemens raised his hand, and I deferred to him.

"Fair enough, Villiers," said my employer. "I know Wentworth, and I know Slippery Ed, and I know damn well which one I'd trust in a pinch. That don't cut ice with you, and there's no reason it should. But the sooner we get the police in here, the sooner we can all get out—the ladies in particular. My wife and daughter won't stay the night next to a cadaver—not if I can help it, they won't. So we've got to send somebody. I say we send 'em both, and get it over with.''

Neither Sir Denis nor Cedric Villiers could think of any further objection, and so McPhee and I put on our coats and hats and went down the stairs to look for a policeman, or failing that, a telephone. As we came out on the street, something occurred to me. "Where's the other fellow who was here when we arrived—the Irishman? Did you send him home already?''

"Oh, Terry?'' said McPhee. "Why, once Martha started her show, he wanted to go wet his throat. There wasn't nothing I needed him for, so I told him to go ahead, long as he came back to straighten up when things were over. Martha usually runs just two hours, so Terry knew how much time he had. You can bet he'll be surprised when he gets back and finds that fellow dead, and cops all over the place.'' McPhee chuckled, as if amused at his assistant's probable discomfiture. He himself seemed to have accepted the necessity of informing the police of the shooting.

"I should imagine so,'' I said. "Well, if he can prove his whereabouts during the séance, he shouldn't have much trouble with the police.'' I looked around me, trying to see through the thick mist that now shrouded the streets in every direction, reducing the flickering gaslights to a nebulous glow and chilling me despite my coat and hat. It had been an eerie scene an hour earlier, when we were merely on our way to the séance, without any notion of what was about to happen. But the fog had thickened, and there was a definite sharpness in the air. After having heard the spirits' voices, I found the atmosphere downright macabre. Add to that the shock of knowing that a man had died violently, not ten feet away from me . . . I shuddered, in spite of myself.

Then I snapped out of my reverie; action was the best antidote to this sudden fit of apprehension. "Which way are we going?''

"Let's go thataway,'' said McPhee, pointing down the

street to our left. "Like that fancy boy said, the coppers usually lurk around over on King's Road, which is the next big street. If we don't find 'em there, we can cut back over to that tobacco shop for the telephone. And if *they* ain't home, we'll figure out which way to jump next."

"Very well, Mr. McPhee, lead the way," I said. After we'd gone a few paces I added, "I hope you'll remember what you said about not leaving your wife to face the police alone."

"Don't worry, sonny," said McPhee. "The days is long gone since ol' Ed could outrun a young sprat like you. 'Sides, you know I went right out of that room after I doused the lights, so there ain't nothing the law can pin on me, this time. I might have had something to worry about, back in my rowdy days, but I'm a reformed man. And you can go to the bank with that."

"I certainly hope so," I said. I meant it, too. I was undoubtedly a faster runner than McPhee, but in a fog this dense, he probably would not have much trouble if he wanted to evade me—especially if I let my attention wander. I made up my mind to keep a close eye on him. I thought the fog had gotten thicker even in the few moments we had been outdoors, and the air had certainly become colder. I buttoned up my collar, wishing I had brought a scarf with me tonight.

We came to a larger cross street, and McPhee said, "There's usually a cop over that way"—he pointed to the left—"at least in the daytime when the shops are open, so they can confiscate an apple or a piece of cheese when they're in the mood." He chuckled. "I reckon that's the first place to look."

"Let's hope we find him quickly," I said. "I'm freezing out here."

"Ah, that's the way it always goes with the police," said McPhee. "Smack-dab in your face when you don't want 'em, and never there when you could use a helping hand. It's downright aggravatin', either way. Enough to make a fellow lose faith in the government."

"I had no idea you had faith in government to begin with," I said as we walked down the cobbled street. I would have preferred going a bit faster, but there was no hurrying Mc-

Phee—and I certainly did not want to get ahead of him.

McPhee laughed, with what seemed false heartiness. "That's a good one, sonny. I guess if you hang around with ol' Sam long enough, some of his jokes are like to rub off on you. We'll make you into a reg'lar fellow, yet."

I wasn't entirely sure what sort of man McPhee considered to be a "reg'lar fellow," let alone whether I wished to be included in that class of humanity. However, I saw no advantage in contradicting him. We walked onward through the lowering fog. At last, in the diffuse light of a street lamp, I discerned a dark-clad figure with the characteristic rounded helmet of a London bobby. "There's our policeman," I said, then raising my voice, "Good evening, Constable."

"And the same to you," said a deep voice. Under the light, I could see the figure turn to face in our direction. " 'Ow can I 'elp you?"

"Let me do the talking," whispered McPhee, then before I could agree or disagree, he called out in a louder voice, "Everything's fine, just fine. But we got us a little problem we sure could use some help with."

That hardly seemed an adequate way to characterize a murdered man in his apartment, but I said nothing for the time being. However, I made up my mind to challenge any outright misstatements of fact McPhee might make.

The policeman had walked forward to meet us, and by now we were close enough to make out his features. He was solidly built, a bit above average height, with a square, clean-shaven jaw and large dark eyes. I would have guessed his age somewhere in his thirties. "What's the problem, then?" he said, eyeing us both up and down. "You two are Yanks, are you not?"

"You got that one right," said McPhee, adopting the hearty manner he employed when greeting strangers. "Ed McPhee's the name, and this here's Mr. Wentworth, works for my old partner Mark Twain—I reckon you've heard of *him,* even in these parts."

"Aye, that I 'ave," said the policeman, not obviously impressed. He pointedly ignored McPhee's proffered handshake.

"Now, what can I 'elp you with? Are you two staying 'ere in Chelsea?"

McPhee rubbed his hands together. "So we are, so we are, but that ain't the problem—in fact, that ain't no kind of problem at all. Awful nice place, as far as I can see, and I been all over the world, to Mexico and everyplace. But the problem is, I have some folks up to my place for a sort of meeting, quality folks, you understand, Mr. Mark Twain and Sir Denis DeCoursey and all. Well, one of 'ems took mighty sick. I reckon you ought to come take a look."

"Sick, eh? Well, I'd think you'd want a doctor for that, not a constable."

"Why, the fellow's a doctor himself—or was one, I guess is the right way to put it," said McPhee. I wondered how long it was going to take him to admit that Dr. Parkhurst was dead, let alone that he'd apparently been murdered.

"Was one?" said the policeman, lifting his eyebrows. "Just what is that supposed to mean, now?"

"Well, it seems as if the fellow had a little accident . . ." McPhee began. I could stand his equivocation no longer.

"The doctor is dead," I said bluntly. "In fact, we believe he's been murdered."

"Murdered, is it?" Now the policeman took a definite interest. "Now, I expect we'll go and 'ave a look at that. Just where did you say this murder was?"

"The place is right off Old Church Street there," said McPhee, pointing back the way we'd come. He gave me an exasperated look, as if to reprimand me for telling the truth before he was ready to let it all out, but I paid him no heed. The policeman needed to know what he was getting into.

"You wait right 'ere," said the policeman, in a voice that made it clear he was not issuing an idle request. He grasped the whistle hanging on a lanyard around his neck and blew three sharp blasts. From some distance away came a response—two whistle blasts, a pause, and then two more. The policeman nodded and said, "Right, then. There'll be one of the lads along in short order. We'll wait 'ere for 'im."

Sure enough, in perhaps two minutes, another policeman came into view, walking briskly and swinging his truncheon.

"What's the word, Albert?" he said as he saw his fellow.

" 'Ullo, Charles. These two tell me there's a dead man in Old Church Street, apt to be a murder," said the first policeman. "What address did you say?"

Before McPhee could answer I gave him the number. "The second-story flat, in the back."

"There you 'ave it. Tell the station I'm going with these two American gentlemen to see what's 'appened," said Albert, indicating us with his hand. " 'Ave 'em send me a lad or two to 'elp sort it all out. They'll want to send over a doctor, too, in case the bloke's still breathing."

"Aye, that they will," said Charles. "I'll report straightaway. Best be sharp, lad—if it's murder, like as not you'll be seeing the chief inspector this night." He nodded, turned, and walked off into the fog.

"Well, gentlemen, that's done. Now, let's go see what the story's all about," said the policeman. We turned and started the short trek back to McPhee's apartment through the chilly fog.

McPhee kept up a line of irrelevant banter the entire way. "I'm mighty glad we found you as quick as we did," he said to the policeman. "Sir Denis and his lady, and Mark Twain— he's my old pal from the river, known him for years—they said, 'Ed, we're in a heap of trouble, and no doubt about it.' And I told 'em, 'Don't you worry, boys, I'll fetch a bobby in and he'll get straight to the bottom of this mess.' And so I done it, just like I said I would. Any help you need to figure things out, Ed McPhee's your man." For his part, the policeman greeted this obvious attempt to curry favor with the silence it deserved.

We reached our destination soon enough. Cold and damp as it was, I almost wished I could stay outside rather than go back into that room and look at the lifeless body sprawled upon the sofa. But, to judge by my previous encounters with the police, we were in for a long interrogation. Probably even the ladies would be put to the question—even if none of them were suspects, they were certainly witnesses. Although none of us could have seen much in the pitch darkness of that sitting . . .

I wondered how long it would be before I could get back to my warm bed, and whether I would have any luck getting to sleep at all that night. Then I remembered that one of the group who had begun the sitting would not be sleeping in his own bed tonight. Poor Dr. Parkhurst was well beyond any thoughts of warmth and comfort, and I suddenly felt guilty wanting them for myself.

6

McPhee and I led the policeman up the stairs to the apartment where the séance had been held. McPhee opened the door, and we were greeted by a cloud of tobacco smoke almost as thick as the fog outside. Mr. Clemens and Sir Denis DeCoursey had pipes burning briskly, and Cedric Villiers was smoking a sweet-smelling cigarette in a long amber holder. I suppose that to tobacco addicts, the chance to smoke was comforting. The three of them had (very understandably) decided that the little anteroom where McPhee had waited during the séance was a more pleasant spot to sit than the larger room with the doctor's body. Villiers had taken up the deck of cards McPhee had been playing with, and was dealing them out in some sort of crisscross pattern on the table.

"Thank goodness," said Sir Denis, rising to his feet. "It's good to see you, Constable. We've got rather a sticky affair here."

"I'll do what I can, sir," said the policeman. "But I'm afraid you'll all 'ave to wait until someone comes from the station—the inspector or 'oever takes 'is place. If we've really got a murdered man 'ere, that is to say—might I see the body?" His manner was deferential, but quite firm.

"Yes, of course—right in here," said Sir Denis. He opened the door to the séance room.

The lights were even brighter than when I'd left—there were several candles now burning in addition to the gas, and Dr. Parkhurst's body was clearly illuminated. Someone had poked up the fire, as well, and added a few lumps of coal to the grate. The policeman walked over to the body and looked closely at it, not touching it, then looked up at us. " 'E's been shot, all right. There won't be much work for the doctor. 'As 'e been moved at all?"

"Yes, he was over at that table when it happened," said Mr. Clemens. "We all were."

"Aye," said the policeman, turning around. He saw the drying blood on the carpet and nodded. "And where did the shot come from?"

"Damned if I know," said Mr. Clemens, scowling. "I was sitting right at the table with him, and I didn't hear any gun go off. Didn't see a flash, either. I'm getting up in years, but I didn't think I was going deaf and blind, yet."

"But there was an absolute racket of knocking and banging," said Sir Denis. "Whoever did the shooting must have picked his time for the noise to cover up the report. Still, I'm surprised I didn't notice it—I've been shooting since I was a lad, and I'd wager I've heard every kind of firearm made."

"Perhaps the shot was from a distance," I suggested. "Then it wouldn't have been as loud, would it?"

"How could it have been fired from any kind of distance, in a room no more than fifteen feet across?" said Mr. Clemens, raising his eyebrows. "Besides, the whole place was darker than the inside of a black cat—you couldn't see your hand before your face in here, let alone pick out one man to shoot at."

"Well, dark or not, the gentleman's got a bullet wound in 'is 'ead," said the constable. "You'll all 'ave to remain 'ere until the inspector comes to take your statements. Until then, I'll ask you please not to touch anything so as not to muddle up the evidence. And it 'ud be best not to discuss what you saw or 'eard so as not to confuse your stories."

"I don't have no story," said Slippery Ed McPhee. "I

wasn't even in the room when the shot went off—didn't even know about it till it was over. I wish you'd let me say a word to my little lady, though. She ain't used to rough stuff or gunplay, and I reckon she's mighty disturbed by all this happening right in front of her eyes."

"I don't know about that—" began the policeman, but he was interrupted.

"Yes, by all means let the poor fellow speak to his wife," said Sir Denis, putting a hand on the policeman's arm. "The rest of us are clearly suspects, but Mr. McPhee could hardly have known what was happening in here, what with being in the other room. And he's not spoken to his wife since the—er, unfortunate incident. It would be unnecessarily cruel not to allow him a word or two to comfort her."

"I suppose there's no 'arm in it, then," said the policeman, nodding. "But I'll ask you not to discuss what 'appened 'ere until the inspector's come. Is that understood?"

"Sure, sure," said McPhee, waving his hand dismissively. "Like I said, I didn't see none of what went on anyways, so you can stop worrying. I just want to make sure Miss Martha's all right."

Sir Denis went and tapped gently on the door to the room where the ladies had retreated, and after a moment his wife, Lady Alice, peered out. "Mr. McPhee wishes to speak to his wife," said Sir Denis. "Would she rather see him inside, or come out to meet him?"

"Best she come out, I think," said Lady Alice. "Mrs. Parkhurst is still quite distressed. Wisest not to disturb her further. Just wait a moment and I'll call Mrs. McPhee out."

The door closed; we waited perhaps a minute, then it opened and Martha McPhee emerged. She seemed to have regained most of her aplomb since the violent termination of the séance, although I detected a touch of dismay as she glanced at the doctor's body. "Edward," she said. "I'm glad to see you. Are the police here yet?"

"I reckon so—that big lug over there ain't a steamboat captain," said McPhee, indicating the constable with a nod. "We're just waiting for his boss to get here. Let's go set down someplace a bit more comfortable."

McPhee took her by the arm and led her into the little outer room, where they sat down next to each other. The rest of us followed, not so much to eavesdrop on their conversation as to get out of the room with the dead body. When they were seated, McPhee said, "How are you holding up, Martha? Are you all right?" That surprised me; it seemed out of character for McPhee to show concern for another person.

"I'm a bit shaken, I'm afraid," she said quietly. "I wish I knew what happened—everything is a blur."

"Well, I know even less than you, for once," said McPhee. "Ain't much a man can see through solid walls, you know. I guess the cops will sort it all out, and then we can go about our business."

"Not if the cops figure out what your business really is," growled Mr. Clemens. "More likely, they'll put you on the first steamer headed west, and none too soon."

"Sam, this ain't hardly a time for jokes," said McPhee, puffing up his chest. "I'll ask you to respect this here young lady's tender feelings, if nothing else." Whatever he was going to say next, a firm knock on the outer door interrupted, and the policeman went to answer it.

A thin-faced young man entered, dressed in civilian clothes—a heavy topcoat over a brown tweed suit, with a bowler hat. His fair skin and light brown hair made him look very young, but I thought he might be a year or so older than I. Even so, it was evident from the constable's deferential posture that this young man was of superior rank. "Hello, Wilkins," he said to the constable. "What's the matter here?"

"We've got a dead body in the next room, Sergeant," said the constable. "Bullet wound in the 'ead, but these gentlemen say they never 'eard a shot."

"Well, we'll have to see about that," said the detective, stepping through the door into the séance room. The rest of us began trooping after him, but he stopped abruptly a couple of paces into the room and turned around to face us—as it happened, Mr. Clemens was directly in front of him. "The body's been moved," said the young detective, waving an admonitory finger. From his expression, it might have been a crime equal to the actual shooting.

"Of course we moved him," said Sir Denis, who had just cleared the doorway. "There was a chance he might live, and we wanted to get him into a more comfortable position. I fail to see the harm in that."

The detective looked Sir Denis up and down, then wrinkled his nose fastidiously. "Don't see any harm, do you? For your information, you've just addled any clues about how he fell, or which way he was facing when he was hit. And the lot of you have been smoking those stinking pipes in here, as well."

"You're damn right," said Mr. Clemens, bristling. "Didn't know there was a law against an American smoking his pipe anywhere he damn well pleased. And who the hell are you?"

"Detective Sergeant Peter Coleman of the Criminal Investigation Division, New Scotland Yard," said the man, glowering at my employer. "There may be no law against smoking your pipe, but I wish there were. Now we've no way to tell which room the gun was fired from. Half the evidence is already gone, no thanks to you. The chief inspector won't like this one bit when he arrives—which should be any moment, now. Can anyone tell me how long it has been since the shooting?"

"Not quite an hour," said Sir Denis, stepping forward. "See here, Mr. Coleman, I know the smell of gunpowder as well as any man in England, and I can tell you without a shadow of a doubt that there was no odor—and no report, and no flash, either."

"So you say," said Coleman, looking down his nose at Sir Denis. "You may even be right, but I'd rather trust the scientific evidence—which you lot have gone and obliterated without a thought. Or, just possibly, you might have done it on purpose."

"Young man, I resent your implication," said Sir Denis. "Do you know to whom you are speaking?"

"To a homicide suspect," said the detective. "Has anyone left the premises since the shooting?"

"No one's left since I arrived," said Constable Wilkins. "I can't say what 'appened before that, Sergeant."

"Mr. McPhee and I went out to notify the constable," I volunteered. "Other than that, I believe everyone has stayed here the entire time."

"McPhee, eh?" The detective turned to the constable. "I assume you've noted down everyone's name, Wilkins."

The constable swallowed. "No, sir, I've 'ardly 'ad the chance. You got 'ere so quick, I'd just begun—"

"I see," said the detective, tight-mouthed. He pulled a small notebook and a pencil out of his pocket. "Well, we'll just have to start at the beginning and do everything properly. You there, what's your name and place of residence?" He addressed this question to my employer.

"Samuel Langhorne Clemens, of Hartford, Connecticut," said my employer. "That's in America, or was the last time I checked."

"Are you attempting to be facetious?" said the detective. His expression was stony. "I don't advise it—this is a very serious matter you're involved in, I'll have you know. Anything you say can be held against you."

"Really? I hardly noticed how serious it was, I was paying so much attention to that dead man over there," said Mr. Clemens, puffing vigorously on his pipe. "But I hope you won't hold it against me if I try to be facetious. It's what I do for a living, and they tell me I'm pretty good at it, by and large. Of course, being English, you might not be able to tell the difference."

"Exactly what do you mean by that?" the detective began, but he was interrupted by a knock on the outer door. "That'll be the doctor, likely enough, or maybe the chief," he said. "Be a good fellow, Wilkins, and see who it is."

"Aye, Sergeant," said the constable, moving to the door. After a moment, I heard the door open and the constable said, " 'Ullo, Chief Inspector. We've got quite a puzzle 'ere."

"It won't be such a great puzzle, once I've had a look at it," said the new arrival, striding energetically into the apartment. He was a short, athletically built man—something in his face reminded me of a ferret, but his manner was all bulldog. He didn't stop to remove his hat or overcoat, but came straight into the inner room where we were all standing.

"I'm glad you're here, Chief Inspector," said Sergeant Coleman, deferentially, although I noticed he looked askance at the new arrival's pipe, which gave off a particularly noxious odor. "I've begun interviewing the suspects, sir."

"Good man, good man," said the new arrival. "I'll just have a look around, and we'll soon know what's what." He walked over to the sofa where the body lay, knelt down, and grasped it by the chin to turn the face toward him. He looked intently at the wound. "This man's been shot," he said, accusingly.

"Yes, sir, so we believe," said Sergeant Coleman.

"Well, then, where's the gun?" asked the chief inspector, standing up and peering round the room. "I can't say I've ever yet seen a man shot without a gun, and I am no spring chicken."

"We haven't found the weapon yet," Coleman replied.

"Well, then, either it's hidden or it's been spirited away," said the chief inspector. "Where have you looked?"

"Well, sir, I'd just arrived, and I thought it better to get the suspects' names and—"

"Aye, so you told me. Well, you go ahead with that business." He stopped and looked at the rest of us for the first time. "Here now, I know that face," he said, staring at my employer. "Haven't I seen you before?"

"I reckon you might have," said Mr. Clemens. "I've been to London a couple of times before, and sometimes they put my picture in the newspapers and magazines."

"Do they, now? And what have you done to merit that?" asked the chief inspector. He was still wearing his coat and hat, and his pipe was filling the room with fumes even stronger than those coming from the other gentlemen's pipes.

"Oh, a couple of things," said Mr. Clemens. "Told the truth about kings and queens, and stood up against injustice, and took some people down a peg when I thought they needed it. Nothing anybody else couldn't have done, if they took a mind to."

"Now I've got it," said the chief inspector, brightly. "I did see you in one of the magazines. You're that American writer fellow, Train, Twain, something like that. Pleased to

meet you—Lestrade's the name, Chief Inspector Lestrade."
He pronounced it to rhyme with *played*.

"Always a pleasure to meet an admirer," said Mr. Clemens, shaking Lestrade's proffered hand. Then his expression turned serious as he continued: "But tell me, Inspector; my wife and daughter and some other ladies—including that poor fellow's widow—are in the next room, there. I reckon they'd be a lot better off in their own homes. How soon do you think they'll be able to go?"

"Ladies, eh?" said Lestrade, following Mr. Clemens's gesture toward the closed door. "Well, we certainly don't want to keep them here any longer than we need to, Mr. Train. This is an ugly bit of business, and no doubt about it. No place for a lady at all, really. But you see, we've got a murder on our hands."

"Yes, I'd noticed that," said my employer. "That's why we sent for a policeman. We didn't have much need for one before that."

"Good, I'm glad you understand, then," said Lestrade. "What we'll have to do is get everyone's name, along with a domicile or place of lodging, and statements from anyone who was present when this fellow was shot . . ."

"Well, that lets me clean off, sure as fire," said McPhee. "I wasn't in this here room at all when the hammer fell, and there's a dozen witnesses can swear to that."

"A dozen witnesses?" Lestrade's eyebrows rose. "What, were there that many of you in the place?"

"An even dozen including the dead man, yes—though he won't be much good as a witness," said Mr. Clemens. "In fact, it was dark enough that none of us really counts for much as a witness."

"Dark, you say?" asked Lestrade. He took off his hat and fanned himself with it. "Do you mean to tell me this fellow was shot while the lights were out?"

"Maybe we ought to begin at the beginning," said Sergeant Coleman, timidly.

"Yes, I think we had best do that," said Lestrade. He tossed his hat onto the table, and began to unbutton his overcoat. "This is a rum business," he said. "As much as I'd like to let the ladies go, I'm afraid we've got to get some answers before we can let anyone leave the scene. Now, I'm going to have Coleman take your statements out in that room while I have a look around for clues in here.''

"Yes, sir,'' said the younger detective. He turned and pointed to Mr. Clemens. "I'd just begun talking to this gentleman, and I think we'll just continue with him. Come along, please.''

Mr. Clemens and I began to follow Coleman into the anteroom when Lestrade turned and said to me, "Hello, young fellow, where do you think you're going?''

"I am Mr. Clemens's secretary,'' I said. "He may need my assistance.''

"I'm terribly sorry, but that's just the kind of thing we can't allow in the midst of a murder investigation,'' said Lestrade. "The sergeant will interview you one at a time, and I'll ask the rest of you to wait in the room with the ladies. Constable, will you see to it?''

"Yes, Chief Inspector,'' said Constable Wilkins. "Gentlemen, if you'll be so kind? You, too, ma'am.''

Politely but very efficiently, the constable herded us into the room with Mrs. Clemens, Susy, and the three other ladies, to wait our turn. Noting her husband's absence, Mrs. Clemens turned a searching look toward me. "Where is Samuel?'' she asked.

"They're taking his statement,'' I said. "I don't think he's in any trouble; they're going to ask us all to give statements.''

"Well, I can give you my statement right now,'' said McPhee. "I wasn't even in the room, and I didn't do nothing. They can't find any flies on Ed McPhee, this time.''

"I'll ask you to wait until you see Sergeant Coleman to speak of the case, sir,'' said the constable. "You'll all have your chance to talk, but until then, I must ask you to be patient.''

I did my best, but patience is hard to conjure up when one is waiting to be quizzed about a murder. At least, I was glad that they had taken Mr. Clemens first. He would have been extremely awkward company if he'd been forced to wait, and I was uncomfortable enough already—especially since I had every reason to believe that one of the people in the room with me was a cold-blooded murderer.

7 ～

Waiting is hard in the best of circumstances. Standing in a small room waiting to be questioned by the police about a violent crime that took place in one's presence would disconcert a saint.

With eleven of us in a small bedroom, there was not space for everyone to sit, even with a couple of chairs brought in from the outer room. And there was no room at all to pace. Cedric Villiers, McPhee, and I remained standing. I pulled out my watch for perhaps the third time to see how long Mr. Clemens had been talking to Detective Coleman. Half an hour. At that rate, it would be nearly four in the morning before the last of us had been questioned. Would they insist on interrogating the entire group before letting any of us go home?

At last, Mr. Clemens came stomping in the door, followed by Constable Wilkins, who looked round the room and asked, "Mrs. Parkhurst, would you be so kind as to come with me? And bring your purse, please. We'll be needing to search it."

The doctor's widow stood up from the edge of the bed, where she had been sitting. Her sister, who had sat consoling her, stood and threw her arms around her. "Be brave, dearest Cornelia," she said.

Mrs. Parkhurst nodded and squeezed her sister's hand. "This will not be hard, Ophelia," she said. "Believe me, the hard part is already over." She smiled bravely and followed the constable out of the room. The door closed behind her, and the rest of us turned instinctively to Mr. Clemens.

He looked around the room at ten anxious faces and spread his hands. "Well, the good news is that I convinced that brass monkey of a detective to interview the ladies first, and to let each of us go home once we've answered his silly questions. So at least some of us will be able to get to bed at a sensible hour. The bad news is that he intends to go through the whole list tonight, so the rest of us will have to wait until he's ready for us. Oh, and one more piece of news—a doctor came to look at the body while they were talking to me, and now it's official, Parkhurst's dead, shot by a person or persons unknown."

"That's hardly news," said Sir Denis. "Nobody could have lasted long with that head wound."

"Sure, but Scotland Yard can't settle for something that obvious," said Mr. Clemens. "That chief inspector's out there going over the place on his hands and knees, tapping on floorboards and picking up specks of dust. If there's been an ashtray spilled in that room anytime in the last week, I reckon he'll know the make of every cigar that was smoked there, and whether it was lit with a match or off the gas. That don't mean he'll catch the shooter, but if they give medals for diligence, I'd bet he's already got a bushelful."

"That's really brilliant," said Cedric Villiers, his voice dripping sarcasm. "The fellow putters about looking for clues, when he's got near a dozen eyewitnesses sitting here. Why doesn't he send out for another interrogator so as to speed things up? Or better yet, do some real work himself? I'll wager I'm not the only one who had other plans for the evening."

"Don't sell the police short," said Sir Denis. He sat next to his wife on the windowsill, which had been fashioned into a comfortable-looking bench, just wide enough for the two of them. I could have seen it as a pleasant spot for reading or conversation, in other circumstances. "I've heard of this

Lestrade from my friends in the Home Secretary's office,'' he continued. ''They call him one of the best men in Scotland Yard, an absolute terrier. Once he gets his teeth into a clue, he'll not let go until he's followed it home.''

Cedric Villiers snorted. ''That's not what I've heard. Word is, Lestrade's too bullheaded to be any use. He might have been a good man once, but he's let success and promotion go to his head. I can believe it, after what I've seen tonight.''

''We'll find out soon enough how good he is,'' said Mr. Clemens. ''Lestrade came in and listened some while that young puppy was trying to pry me open. He seemed to think it was important that nobody heard the gun go off. I reckon he's right, although I'm not so sure he has to look very far for the explanation. All that other noise—''

''Never mind the other noise,'' said Sir Denis. ''I know the sound of gunfire, and I'll swear there wasn't a weapon fired within yards of me tonight.''

''That ain't the half of it,'' said Mr. Clemens. ''Lestrade's right about one thing, if nothing else—if a man's been shot, there's got to be a gun somewhere. Where the hell is it?''

''I wonder . . .'' It was Hannah Boulton who spoke, her voice tremulous. She was sitting on the foot of the bed, wringing her hands. She looked to Sir Denis, as if asking permission to speak, and he nodded to her.

''Could it be possible that the shot was not fired in this world?'' she asked, her eyes wide. ''That would explain why we neither heard nor saw the weapon, and why it cannot now be found.''

''Good Lord!'' exclaimed Sir Denis, slapping his forehead. ''I've never heard of such a thing, but yes, it might account for the missing gun. Do you think it's possible, Clemens?''

''I wouldn't waste time on that idea,'' said Mr. Clemens, shaking his head. ''It's against all common sense, not that common sense is all that common anymore.''

''The spirits you heard tonight are real,'' said Martha McPhee, quietly. ''I know that as well as I know anything.''

''Maybe so, but that ain't the question on the floor,'' said Mr. Clemens, pointing downward. ''Even if there is a spirit world, and even if we heard voices from it tonight, you're going to have a pile of convincing to do if you want me to believe that some spook took a potshot at the doctor.''

''I'm surprised at your lack of imagination,'' said Cedric Villiers. ''Surely, Clemens, you aren't going to rule out the possibility of a supernatural agency without due consideration.''

''You're the ones who ought to be ashamed at your lack of imagination,'' said Mr. Clemens. ''You haven't even begun to look at all the perfectly natural explanations for what happened there tonight. Why, there must be dozens of ways it could have been done.''

''Name one,'' said Villiers, with a smile that conveyed no warmth at all. ''Will you be so kind as to elucidate the matter with one of your perfectly natural explanations, Mr. Clemens?''

''That's the police's job, not mine,'' said Mr. Clemens. ''If you're promoting the theory that Dr. Parkhurst was murdered by a spook, go right ahead. There's no law I know against spreading damn-fool ideas. But don't waste your breath on me—tell it to that Detective Coleman, when it's your turn to talk. I guess he'll give it all the consideration it deserves.''

''There, so much for his natural explanations. He as much as admits that he doesn't have one,'' said Villiers, turning to the rest of the room with a superior smirk.

''Now, I wouldn't sell ol' Sam short—'' McPhee began, but he was interrupted by the door opening to admit Chief Inspector Lestrade, followed by Constable Wilkins.

''Where's the fellow who says he was in the other room when the shot was fired?'' said Lestrade, looking at the group.

''That's me, sure enough,'' said McPhee. ''But I didn't hear no shot, no more than any of the others.''

''And I suppose you knew nothing about the peephole in the wall, did you now?'' Lestrade shook his finger under McPhee's nose.

''Peephole? Why, no, nothing at all about it,'' said McPhee, doing a creditable job of appearing surprised.

''How long have you occupied this flat?'' Lestrade continued. His gaze was fixed intently on McPhee's face.

"Five or six weeks, I reckon," said McPhee, shrugging. "Something just over a month."

"And you've been giving these spiritualist parties the whole time, have you not?"

"Well, off and on, you know. A nonstop party would get pretty tiresome, with all the goings-on—"

"Yes, the goings on must have been quite impressive," said Lestrade. "Did you install the apparatus, or was it all here already?"

"Apparatus? What in the world do you mean?" said McPhee, his face all innocence. I'd seen exactly the same expression when he'd claimed to have cheated me in order to teach me a lesson.

"I thought it was rather peculiar to find three bellpulls in the foyer of a little flat like this, and none anywhere else," said the chief inspector, a feral grin on his face. "What do you think happens when you pull them? Or perhaps you already know, don't you, Mr. McPhee?"

"I reckon a bell rings somewhere, is all," said McPhee, shrugging. "We're just regular folks, can't afford no servants, so we hardly even gave 'em a look, did we, Martha?"

"Why, no, we're not at all used to that sort of luxury," said Martha McPhee. "What exactly are you intimating, sir?"

"Why don't I just show you?" Lestrade said. "These people ought to know exactly what kind of chicanery you were up to so they can make up their own minds about your spiritualist rubbish."

"Inspector Lestrade, I am sorry to learn that you are so closed-minded," said Hannah Boulton, disapproval plain on her face. "I would have hoped that the police might have some concern for things beyond this earth."

"Rubbish I said, and rubbish I meant," said Lestrade. "Come into the next room, the lot of you, and I'll show you something to open your eyes."

Not knowing quite what to expect, I looked at Mr. Clemens, who shrugged. He took his wife on one arm and his daughter Susy on the other, and followed the chief inspector, who had spun on his heel and marched out into the main room. Along with the rest of those in the bedroom, I went with him, curious to see what the detective had discovered. I noticed, though, that McPhee and his wife exchanged a glance that to my eyes suggested quiet resignation to whatever the search had turned up.

Coming into the main room, I found it impossible not to glance at the couch where Dr. Parkhurst's body lay. To my relief, someone had found a large bedspread and draped it over the body. Even so, I found a macabre urge to peek at the huddled mass under the covering, imagining its posture and terrible expression . . .

"Now, the lot of you stand here while I go into that outer room for a moment," said Chief Inspector Lestrade, once we were all there in the main room. "Only this time, you'll have the lights on and the door open."

He strode through the door, and a moment later we heard a distinct rap from the vicinity of the table. "How's that?" crowed Lestrade. "Here's another!" And sure enough, there came another rap, just as predicted, from a different corner of the room.

Mr. Clemens strolled over to the doorway and looked through at the policeman. Behind him, I could see the faces of Detective Coleman and Mrs. Parkhurst, looking out at us. "Do that again, if you don't mind," my employer said. A pair of loud raps followed. Mr. Clemens turned and looked back at us, a mischievous smile on his face. "Well, Ed, I think I know why you had to leave the room after the lights went out," he said.

"Let's see what this one does," came Lestrade's voice, followed by the muffled ringing of a bell. "Oho, a regular orchestra we have here. But that's not even the best part of it. Watch here, ladies and gentlemen."

I was not quite certain where he meant, but it quickly became evident as a small oval picture on the wall swung quietly to one side, and Lestrade's face could be plainly seen peering out the opening. "Here's where your shot was fired from," said Lestrade. "You'll notice it's in a direct line with the chair the victim sat in. An easy shot, especially if you've lined it up in advance."

"That's all well and good," said Slippery Ed, who stepped

forward, ignoring Martha McPhee's hand on his elbow. "But I was in that room the whole time, and didn't nobody come in and shoot that fellow. I'd have seen him, sure as you're born."

"Perhaps you should look in a mirror," said Lestrade. "By your own admission, you were in this room when the shots had to have been fired. What's more, you were in a perfect position to make loud noises just at the right time to prevent the shot's being heard."

"Hey, I didn't shoot nobody," said McPhee, a hurt expression on his face. "I never even seen the poor man before this very evening, ain't that right, Martha?"

"What I'd like to know is, where did he put the gun?" demanded Cedric Villiers, strutting over to Lestrade. "There lies Dr. Parkhurst with a bullet through his head, so there must have been a gun. And yet, after searching the place from top to bottom, you've found no murder weapon. You haven't a notion where it is, do you?"

"Not yet," Lestrade admitted. "That's a detail, but we're good at piecing together details. This scoundrel may have had time to take the gun outside for disposal. Or—"

Whatever he was going to propose, he was interrupted by the opening of the outer door to admit a man I recognized as the one who'd been with McPhee on the doorstep when we'd arrived. "Hello, where's Mr. McPhee?" he asked, his voice somewhat slurred. Then his eyes took in the constable's uniform, and they opened wide for a brief moment before he turned and we heard his boots pounding as he beat a hasty retreat down the stairway. Constable Wilkins was after him in a flash, and I heard the constable's whistle blow as he thundered down the stairs.

"There's your answer, Villiers," crowed Lestrade, turning to the astonished dandy. "McPhee's accomplice took his gun away right after the shooting—by now, he's pitched it in the Thames, or stowed it somewhere for future devilment, just as like."

"A smashing bit of luck, what?" said Sir Denis De-Coursey, rubbing his hands. "You practically called your shot!"

"There's still something I don't understand," said Mr. Clemens. "Why the hell would that man come back here, if he'd just taken away the murder weapon?"

"Your common criminal is a pitiful sort, at best," said Lestrade, with an air of confidence. "Low mentality—you could see it written all over that man's face. That's why the criminal always returns to the scene of his crime, like a moth to a burning candle."

"Maybe so, but you've missed the point," said Mr. Clemens. "If he's the one that ditched the gun, he knew what it was used for, and he'd make himself scarce around here. If he absolutely had to come back afterwards, he'd have been ready for the cops to be here. He'd have had a bulletproof alibi all ready, and a face as innocent as any choirboy. But the way he bolted just now, he didn't have the faintest glimmer that he'd be walking into a roomful of constables and detectives—if he did, I'll buy every man in Scotland Yard a drink."

The chief inspector grimaced. "You'd lose that bet, or my name's not Lestrade," he said. "We'll learn the whole story when Wilkins fetches him back for questioning. But I don't think there's any more reason to detain you all—Coleman will note down your names and addresses, and we can come by tomorrow or next day to record your statements. It's as plain as the nose on your face, this fellow here pulled the trigger." He pointed triumphantly at Slippery Ed McPhee.

There was a stunned silence. Every eye in the room turned toward McPhee, and those nearest him took a step back—so that where we had all been bunched together, there was now an open circle around Mr. and Mrs. McPhee.

"You wait a cotton-pickin' minute, Mr. Scotland Yard," said McPhee. He took a step toward Lestrade, his fist raised. Then Martha, her face grim, touched her husband on the arm, and he regained his composure. "I ain't never pulled the trigger on a living soul," he said firmly, "and you can take that to the bank. You ask Sam here—killin' ain't Ed McPhee's style, no sir, and any man who says different is a bald-faced liar."

Mr. Clemens rubbed his chin, then nodded. "I'll grant him

that much, Lestrade. Don't get me wrong, now—I wouldn't lend Ed two cents if he gave me the keys to the mint for collateral. But I don't believe he's got it in him to shoot a man.''

''If you'd spent as many years as I have at the Yard, you'd not be so quick to think you know what a man's got in him,'' said Lestrade, shaking his head.

''That may be true,'' said McPhee, ''but I never laid eyes on that poor doctor before this very night. I swear, I never shot him.'' Suddenly I realized that as he spoke he had been edging closer to the half-open door out of the apartment.

Lestrade stepped forward and laid a hand on McPhee's shoulder. ''You'll need to do better than that, Mr. McPhee. You had the means and the opportunity, and if you didn't pull the trigger yourself, I wager you know the man who did.''

McPhee shook off the hand and turned suddenly toward the exit, but Sergeant Coleman had taken up a position between him and the door, and he seized McPhee unceremoniously by the arm, twisting it behind his back. ''Be still now,'' he said. ''I must advise you that anything you say may be taken down and used against you in court.''

''You go ahead and do that, see if I care,'' said McPhee, struggling. ''You won't find a single thing that'll stick to me. As for Terry, he was just out having a couple of drinks, is all. He's no more the accomplice than I am the killer.''

''His running away would seem to argue otherwise,'' said Cedric Villiers. ''Why flee so precipitously if he had nothing to worry about?''

''Well, from what I hear tell, over in this country an Irishman starts off with one foot in the hole,'' said McPhee, staring Villiers in the eye. ''Same as the colored back home. I guess Terry figured it was smarter to find out what the cops were after before he let 'em get their paws on him. I might have done the same, in his shoes.'' McPhee sounded defiant, but it was easy to see that he was shaken.

''A lot of good it'll do him,'' said Lestrade. ''Wilkins will fetch him back forthwith, and he'll have the worse time of it for his efforts. Aha, I'll wager that's them now.''

Sure enough, the sound of footsteps came from the stairway. We all turned to look, but even before they reached the landing, we could tell that only one person was climbing the stairs. "I'm right sorry, sir. The rogue gave me the slip in the fog," said a sour-faced Constable Wilkins, coming through the door. "I went over to the station to start the hue and cry, and then came back to lend an 'and 'ere."

"I knew Terry was a spry one," said McPhee, with something like pride in his voice. "Much as I wish he was here to back me up, I'm glad he's still free. He'll have a chance to get his wits about him before he tells his tale."

"We'll have the hue and cry on him before he's gone a mile," said Lestrade, his jaw jutting out. "Meanwhile, Constable, I'll ask you to place Mr. McPhee under guard. We'll take the names and addresses of these other ladies and gentlemen, and then we can let them go to their homes. We've got our murderer, or his right-hand man. We'll know which it is once we've had a little talk down at the station."

"You ain't got nobody!" bawled McPhee. "I'm an innocent man, for once!"

"So say you," said the chief inspector, with a superior smile. "So say they all. But the Detective Branch will learn the truth, or my name's not Lestrade!"

8

Once McPhee had been arrested, the rest of us gave our names and local addresses and made our way back home. The whole affair had taken a surprisingly short time, considering how much had occurred—the séance, the murder, the police investigation, and the arrest—the clock on the mantelpiece was pointing to just a quarter past midnight as Mr. Clemens and I led his wife and daughters downstairs to the carriage.

I noticed as I left that Martha McPhee had, for the first time in my memory, lost her composure. She sat, disconsolate looking, on the sofa in the little foyer, watching the sitters at her séance bundle up for departure. Nobody seemed to be paying her any mind. I took a moment to step over to her and offer a mild word of encouragement. "Be brave," I said. "If Mr. McPhee is innocent, the police will have to release him. I hope it won't be long."

She looked up at me with an anxious expression. "I hope you're right," she said. "He didn't do it, Mr. Cabot. I won't deny that Edward has been in trouble before, but he's never really hurt anyone. Even Mr. Clemens will tell you that."

"I'm sure everything will come out all right," I said. I would have said more, but Mr. Clemens nudged my elbow, and so I tipped my hat to Martha and we hurried downstairs.

When we were all seated in the carriage, Mr. Clemens said, "Well, I reckon we got more of a show than we bargained for."

"Rather more than I hope to see again," said Mrs. Clemens. She and her daughter Susy sat next to each other, huddling close in the chilly night air. "Dear Lord, if I'd known ahead of time what sort of dreadful business was about to happen, I'd never have set foot in that house. But who could have known that Mr. McPhee was inviting us to a murder?"

"I don't think he knew there was going to be a murder, Mama," said Susy. "It would be a very stupid man who would plan a murder and then invite a dozen witnesses."

"Slippery Ed ain't as smart as he thinks," said Mr. Clemens. "And he's got enough brass to start his own Marine Band and still have change left over. If anybody ever thought he could get away with it, it would've been Ed."

"If it wasn't he, who could it have been?" asked Susy. "It must have been someone in the room, mustn't it?" Her voice was surprisingly animated. I thought she sounded far less horrified than I at the bloody affair we'd just witnessed.

"That's the way to bet," said Mr. Clemens. "But I tell you right now, I've seen enough murder to last me the rest of my life. Somebody must have put out the word that Sam Clemens doesn't have enough to keep him busy, and whoever arranges these things decided to throw a few cadavers in my way. Well, I've hit my limit. It was bad enough finding that fellow dead on the riverboat, but having somebody shot right in front of me is more than I bargained for. I'm swearing off the detective business. Let that Scotland Yard man do his job, and leave me out of it." In the dim illumination from the street lamps outside, I could see him lift his eyes upward, as if addressing his words to a higher power.

"A wise decision," said Mrs. Clemens, reaching over to touch his shoulder. "Leave crime to the criminals, and rely on the police to bring them to justice. I shudder to think what might have happened had that bullet gone astray tonight. Terrible as it was to see that poor man lying there so grievously wounded, it would have been far worse had it been one of us. What if it had been you, Youth?"

"Don't you worry, Livy," said my employer. "Writing's my main line of business, and I mean to stick to it. I've dabbled a little at detecting, and I can't deny there were a couple of times I thought I was pretty good at it. But enough is enough."

I thought very much the same as we trundled along the streets of Chelsea, on our way to a long-overdue sleep that I fervently hoped would not be disturbed by images of poor Dr. Parkhurst with a bullet in his head. Surprisingly, I slept like a baby.

The next morning, Mr. Clemens was all business. If he had any further thoughts on the events of the previous evening, he kept them resolutely to himself. And apparently Mrs. Clemens had taken her daughters aside and forbade any discussion of those events at the breakfast table—although I had no doubt that Susy had regaled her sisters with the full story out of their parents' hearing. Little Jean squirmed, full of curiosity, but one stern look from her mother was evidently enough to convince her that silence was the wiser course this morning.

After breakfast, my employer and I went into his office, and we began to work on the manuscript he'd brought to England for publication. Mrs. Clemens had read it over and made several suggestions, my employer had given it a final polishing, and now all that remained was the proofreading before we took it into the publisher's offices.

We had gone through about a quarter of the manuscript, and all of a pot of coffee, when Mrs. Clemens entered, closing the door behind her. I could tell by her expression that she was not happy. "We have a visitor," she said.

"Send 'em away," said Mr. Clemens, gruffly. Then, catching something in the tone of his wife's voice, he looked up and saw her face. "Oh, damnation. Is it that detective again? I guess he's got some more fool questions."

"No, it's not the detective. I'd almost be happier if it were."

"Who, then?" said Mr. Clemens. He put down the pages he'd been working on and rose to his feet.

"It is Mrs. McPhee," said his wife. "I have already told her you would see her."

My employer's eyebrows moved upward half an inch. "I'd just as soon wash my hands of the whole swindling bunch of 'em. Be a blessing to humanity if the English just went ahead and hanged Slippery Ed, even if he didn't shoot that man. But if you think I should see her . . ."

Mrs. Clemens nodded. "I do, Youth. Of course you must make your own decision whether to do anything once you have heard her story."

"I can tell you right now what my decision's going to be," said Mr. Clemens. "I'll sit back down and finish reading this damned manuscript. But if you say I should talk to her, I will. Show her in here. Wentworth, why don't you stay and listen? You know her better than I do."

"Yes, sir," I said, and waited with heightened curiosity as Mrs. Clemens ushered Mrs. McPhee into the little office. I stood and let her take my chair, moving to an unobtrusive position near the fireplace.

As always, Martha McPhee was attractively dressed, and her face betrayed no outward distress; but it was obvious to anyone who had been with her the previous evening that she must have spent a harrowing few hours since then. She held her back straight as she took her seat, declined the offer of something to drink, and came straight to the point.

"Mr. Clemens," she said, "I am here in hopes of enlisting your help in clearing my husband of the allegations against him."

Mr. Clemens raised his hand to halt her. "Young lady, I hate to disappoint you, but you're talking to the wrong man. It don't agree with my health to go chasing people with guns. That Scotland Yard detective is the one you need to talk to."

"He's ready to send Edward straight to the gallows," said Martha McPhee. "I know very well that you believe you have reason to think ill of my husband, and perhaps he has in some ways deserved your opinion. But even you cannot suppose that he is a murderer."

Mr. Clemens wrinkled his brow. "Ed's a fraud and a swindler, even if he's not a killer. Why should anybody with the tiniest regard for the public welfare want to turn him loose to prey on unsuspecting innocents again?"

Martha bowed her head. After a moment, she said, "For simple justice, Mr. Clemens. I will not pretend that Edward has led a blameless life—nor have I, to tell the truth. But whatever my husband may have done in the past, surely you cannot want to see him punished for something he has not done."

"Hmm. What about imposing on respectable people with the idea of getting their money? I saw all those peepholes and bell ropes, and all that paraphernalia set up to make us think we were talking to spooks. Maybe there's no law against it in this country, but that don't mean it's right." My employer glared at Martha McPhee. "Come to think of it, you were up to your ears in that same business, weren't you?"

Martha McPhee blushed. "Mr. Clemens, I fear you have found the chink in our armor. Yes, Edward set up those bells and that gramophone and those other effects. He persuaded me that they were necessary to put on a good show, as he described it. But whether you believe me or not, I tell you that every voice you heard, every word they spoke, was true and authentic." I was almost ready to believe her, even knowing what I did of her.

Mr. Clemens wasn't. "Then why did you need all that foofaraw? If you were really in touch with the spooks, wouldn't that be enough?"

"Had I had my own way, we would have had none of it," said Martha, looking my employer straight in the face and speaking very quietly. "I *do* have a gift, one I cannot explain to you by rational argument. But it is an unassuming gift, hardly given to spectacular effects. Edward thought we should display it to better advantage so as to attract more sitters. He argued that unless we could bring in a steady string of customers, we would have had little choice but to return to our previous means of earning our livelihood. And I am not yet so desperate as to return to that life. I will not deceive you, Mr. Clemens."

My employer listened to her in silence, massaging his chin between his right thumb and forefinger. Finally he said, "Maybe you are telling the truth, young lady. Polishing up the apples is just Ed's style of business. But I don't think you need to worry about him. If he didn't pull the trigger, he'll find a way to slide out of jail, sooner or later, and not much the worse for it. Why, he'd probably slip right through the noose if they tried to hang him."

"Mr. Clemens," said Martha McPhee, looking my employer in the eyes, "I am in a strange country, with no resources and no close friends. The events of last evening have for all practical purposes destroyed my means of supporting myself—at the very least, until Edward is cleared of suspicion. Who will visit a medium whose husband is accused of killing a man?"

"I reckon the same kind of customer that comes to any other medium," drawled Mr. Clemens. "I'd be surprised if Ed couldn't parlay that shooting into some way to double your business."

"Youth!" said Mrs. Clemens, sharply. I thought she was about to say more, but before she could do so, Martha McPhee had risen to her feet. Her visage was stern, but I thought I saw her lip quiver for a moment before she spoke.

"Very well, Mr. Clemens," she said, rising from her chair. "I can see that I have been wasting my time, and yours, too. I did not really expect to find a friend here"—did she glance in my direction as she said that word?—"so much as an ally against injustice. I was evidently mistaken. I shall go my way and leave you to your own business."

"Now just a minute . . ." said Mr. Clemens, coming to his feet, but Martha McPhee brushed past him and was out the door before he could complete the sentence. He stood for a moment staring at the door, and then said, "Damn." I had never heard him get quite so much expression into a single syllable.

"Very well done, Youth," said Mrs. Clemens. "Now you need not exert yourself in the least. And if McPhee is hanged, why possibly he will have done something to deserve it."

"Hell, I reckon he has," said Mr. Clemens. "Besides, I

told you I wasn't going to play detective anymore. You acted as if you thought it was a good idea."

"I thought so last night, yes," said his wife. "That was before I heard Mrs. McPhee's story this morning—which you have managed to prevent her from telling."

"What the hell did she say?" My employer's scowl deepened.

"Oh, it hardly matters," said Mrs. Clemens, with a dismissive wave of her hand. "Besides, I could never tell the story as well as she could." She stood up and moved toward the door.

"Damnation!" said Mr. Clemens. "I can see I'm going to have to hear her out, after all—and eat some crow while I'm at it. Wentworth! Run and see if you can catch her before she's gone."

"Yes, sir." I hastened out the door and down the stairs, trying not to make too much noise. As I passed the parlor, I saw Susy and Clara Clemens sitting with books on their laps. They looked up at me with surprised expressions. "Did you see which way Mrs. McPhee went?" I asked them.

"She just called for her coat and went out the door," said Clara, pointing.

I threw open the door and rushed outside, where I saw Martha McPhee being assisted into a carriage by the man who'd driven us the other day—Jimmy, I remembered. "Mrs. McPhee—Martha!" I cried. "Please wait a moment."

She glanced back at me over her shoulder. "And for what reason, Mr. Cabot?" She stood with one foot in the carriage, showing her ankle, and turned to look down at me. "I thought Mr. Clemens made it quite clear he wanted nothing to do with me or my husband."

"Perhaps Mr. Clemens spoke too hastily," I said. "He appears already to regret his haste. Will you come back in and finish what you came to say? I will do what I can to see that he listens to you, this time."

A faint smile came to her lips as she contemplated my statement, then she said to the driver, "Jimmy, I'm afraid you'll have to wait a little longer. Mr, Cabot, will you help me down? If Mr. Clemens is ready to listen to me, I suppose

I must swallow my pride and go talk to him. I do not have an overabundance of allies.''

"Any port in a storm, eh, missus?" said Jimmy, grinning mischievously. I did not entirely like his expression, but he was not the one I had to deal with. I reached my hand up to Martha, helped her down from the carriage, and led her back inside to plead her case to Mr. Clemens.

Susy and Clara Clemens gave us curious glances as we went back up the stairs. There we found my employer by the fireplace, poking up the fire. To judge by his subdued expression, Mrs. Clemens had been making clear her opinion that his brusque manner with Mrs. McPhee was not consistent with the seriousness of the other woman's predicament.

"Young lady, I guess we need to start over," said Mr. Clemens, putting the poker back in its rack. "Tell me again why you think I ought to help get the cops off your husband's back.''

"That should not require any long explanation," said Martha McPhee, taking the same seat as before. "He is a fellow American, and an old acquaintance—if not exactly a close friend—and he is being unjustly accused. I heard you say last night that you did not believe him to be a murderer.''

"Well, maybe not a murderer," said Mr. Clemens, "but it wouldn't surprise me if he took a little bribe to let somebody use that spy hole last night.''

"Youth!" said Mrs. Clemens, but Martha McPhee raised her hand.

"Thank you, Mrs. Clemens," she said. "I appreciate your solicitude, but if we are all to work together, I think the time has come to speak frankly. After all, the police will undoubtedly be making these same accusations, and we had best be ready to refute them.''

"I'm glad you see it that way, young lady," said Mr. Clemens. "Now, both of us know Ed—you better than I, likely as not—and I think you'll agree that he has a sharp eye for a dollar, and a faster hand to take it. Why wouldn't he have let somebody else use that spy hole while he took a stroll around the block, if the fellow offered to pay him for it?''

"Because he'd have had to take the time to show the other person how to use the rest of the apparatus," said Martha. "We can never predict what spirits will appear, or in what order, so Edward always has to pay close attention to decide when to pull the rope that makes raps, or to play the gramophone. Some other person could not just walk in and take over those tasks. Edward would have had to stay—so he would have seen the shooting."

"You don't think he'd have snitched, do you?" said Mr. Clemens, leaning forward. "That don't seem like Slippery Ed."

Martha looked thoughtful. "It would depend," she said. "If a fellow professional were involved, probably not, unless Edward felt that he himself had been betrayed. Or if he'd taken a payment, he might feel bound to keep silent."

"Honor among thieves," suggested my employer.

"If you like," said Martha, spreading her hands. "But that isn't my point. Edward was as surprised as I was at the shooting, even half an hour later when I finally saw him. Believe me, Mr. Clemens, he could not have deceived me in that regard. I know my husband better than that."

"I'll concede that," said Mr. Clemens. "Ed can lie near as well as I can, but that didn't look like an act to me, last night. So where does that take us?"

"It seems very clear to me," said Mrs. Clemens. "If we postulate that Mr. McPhee was not involved in the killing, someone else must have been. And the inescapable conclusion is that it was someone in the room with us."

"Weren't me," said Mr. Clemens. "And it wasn't you or Susy. I reckon I'd have noticed if you'd pulled out a pistol and started taking potshots, since you were both right next to me. Wentworth, now, he's got a look about him—"

"I beg your pardon," I said. "Both my hands were being held at the time—one by your daughter, one by Mrs. McPhee here. I hardly had the opportunity to shoot anyone, even if I had been so inclined. And I assure you I was not."

"But then everyone else at the table has the same alibi," said Mrs. Clemens. "In that case, nobody could have done it. What do you think, Youth?"

Mr. Clemens furrowed his brow for a moment, then gave his head a shake. "Damnation," he said at last. "Here I've been swearing up and down that I was through with that detective business, and you were telling me I was right to leave it to the police, Livy. Now you're talking like you want to take it up yourself. Which am I supposed to listen to?"

"It's a woman's prerogative to change her mind," said Martha McPhee, smiling. "But your wife is an eminently sensible woman, Mr. Clemens. I suggest you listen to her. Of course, I say that with my own interest in mind."

"There must be a dozen good detectives here in London," my employer insisted. "Any of 'em would be a better choice than I am. Here I am, an old rascal who's fallen into the business by accident, with less experience than any new recruit to the police force. On top of that, I'm a foreigner— why, every twelve-year-old Cockney knows this city better than I ever will. Besides, I've got a book to work on, lectures to prepare, and way too many debts to pay. Why pick on me?"

"I can think of three reasons, actually," said Martha McPhee. "To begin with, hiring a professional detective is simply beyond my means. But perhaps you would help me out of a sense of justice. Secondly, any other detective would have to be told everything from the beginning—you were there, and saw it all with your own eyes. You are a witness."

"That's not necessarily an asset," said Mr. Clemens. "Somebody else might be more objective. But I can understand not having the money to pay somebody—I guess you know that money's been short in my household for a while, too. I haven't been charging anybody for my detecting, and I guess I won't start now. What's your third reason?"

Martha blushed, very prettily—I had had occasion before to wonder whether she could blush to suit her purposes. "Why, Mr. Clemens, because someone has killed a man right in front of your face. I should think you'd consider that a challenge, if not an outright insult. I'd think that would spur you to find out the truth for yourself—if only to show them they can't play you for a fool."

My employer's mouth fell open in astonishment, but then

he frowned and said, "You only say that because you want me to think Ed didn't shoot that man. What if I find out he did do it? Do you want the truth, or do you just want Ed out of jail? Because if I start mucking around in this mess, I'm going after the truth, whether or not anybody else likes it. And if that means I've got to find Ed guilty, then I will."

"I can accept that," said Martha calmly. "I already know that Edward is innocent, so I have no fear of anything you can discover."

Mr. Clemens looked from his wife to Martha McPhee, then back again, as if trying to decide how to answer. But before he could say anything, the sound of girlish laughter came from the half-open doorway, and he looked up to see his three daughters peering around the edge of the door, spying on our meeting. Realizing they had been caught, they boldly threw open the door and stepped inside. "You will help her, won't you, Papa?" said little Jean, running up to her father and throwing her arms around his neck.

"I don't see how I can get out of it now," he said. Then he looked at me, with a half smile. "Let this be a lesson to you, Wentworth. Beware of the ladies, because they'll surely run your whole life if you let 'em."

"Why, of course," said Mrs. Clemens. "Why shouldn't we? You men are very bright in your way, but you're perfectly hopeless when it comes to practical matters. You can hardly expect us to allow you to stumble along all by yourself when we know perfectly well what you ought to be doing." She smiled, and her two youngest daughters giggled.

"I guess it's settled, then," said Mr. Clemens, in a resigned tone. He reached over to his desk and picked up a pipe. "Now, do any of you oh-so-practical ladies have any idea how we poor men should go about catching this murderer?"

≈ 9

It did not take us long to decide where we ought to begin our inquiry into the death of Dr. Parkhurst. Martha McPhee suggested that Mr. Clemens and I return to her apartments and make our own inspection of the scene of the crime. "The police were quite thorough up to a point," she said. "But once Mr. Lestrade decided to take Edward into custody, that was the end of his search for clues. I think it's quite possible they left something unexamined."

"I am surprised you suggest that," I said. "Scotland Yard has the reputation of being very meticulous in their investigations."

"Having the reputation for something isn't the same as doing it," said Mr. Clemens. "I once got out of a duel by convincing the other party that I was a crack shot, which was about as close to the truth as Illinois is to China. But it served the purpose just fine. Now, I wouldn't put it past Lestrade to convince a judge that he's done a more complete search than he really has, and found all the evidence there is. So we'd better go over the place with a fine-tooth comb, and maybe a brush and a pair of scissors, too. Livy, do you think the girls have a magnifying glass we can borrow?"

"I have one!" cried little Jean Clemens. "I'll let you use it if I can come along!"

"Certainly not!" said Mrs. Clemens. "I am surprised that a young lady would be so anxious to visit a place where something so terrible has happened."

"Oh, Mama, the dead man won't be there anymore," said Jean, putting on her most persuasive manner. "And neither will the murderer, unless it's Mrs. McPhee here, and I don't think Papa would be helping her if she was. There's nothing in that place that can hurt me. You know that, Papa! Tell Mama I can come with you . . . please?"

Mr. Clemens frowned. His bushy eyebrows made his disapproving expression even more dramatic, although his eyes belied the attempt at severity. "Well, little angel face," he said, "I certainly appreciate the loan of your magnifying glass. But I reckon this won't be anywhere near as much fun as you're looking for. You said yourself that the dead man won't be there, and neither will the murderer—so we won't be catching anybody and turning him over to the police. We'll just be looking at the furniture, and the floors, and all the other truck in the place. You'd be bored before we'd been there twenty minutes."

"No I wouldn't!" said little Jean, pouting. "It's not fair. Susy was there last night, and she saw the whole thing—she told me and Clara all about it. Why can't I go see where it happened?"

"Because I forbid you," said Mrs. Clemens, with an expression that made it clear she expected no contradiction. "I shall have to speak very severely to Susy. I wouldn't be surprised if she gave you and Clara nightmares, telling you such stories. Murder is not a fit subject for young ladies to dwell on."

"It's not a fit subject for anyone to dwell on, but it looks as if somebody's been doing it," my employer said, laying his hand on his pouting daughter's shoulder. "Your mama's right, though, Jean. This isn't a game. If the man who killed Dr. Parkhurst figures out that I'm trying to catch him, I might be in danger myself—and anyone who's with me will be in the same fix. I can ask a grown-up like Wentworth to take that risk, but I'm not going to bring my little angels along for some villain to shoot at. Not even Susy, and she's a lot older than you. But you can help me, if you'll go find that magnifying glass. I promise to tell you if I find anything with it—that way you'll know you had a hand in solving this case.''

Having determined that she had gotten all the concessions she was likely to get, little Jean nodded solemnly and went to her playroom to retrieve the magnifier. After a few minutes, she returned with the instrument. After getting our coats and hats, Mr. Clemens and I accompanied Martha McPhee down to the street, where we mounted into her carriage and her driver Jimmy took us off to see the scene of the crime again—this time in daylight.

Martha's building looked considerably more ordinary in the afternoon sun than it had in the rain and mists of the previous evening. Then it had seemed uninviting, even a bit gloomy. Now it appeared little different from the buildings on either side, a blocky brick edifice that could have been transplanted to New York or Boston without attracting much notice. Jimmy pulled the horses up in front of it, and I hopped out to reach a hand to Mrs. McPhee as she descended.

Mr. Clemens stepped out and peered up at the windows of the apartment where the murder had taken place less than twenty-four hours ago. I thought he must be sharing my reflective mood, until he said, ''The room we were sitting in is on the other side of the building, isn't it?''

''Yes, it's in the back,'' said Martha. ''Did you want to see it from the ground?''

''Probably don't have to,'' said Mr. Clemens. ''I was trying to figure out if anybody from outside could have seen into that room last night—maybe the shooter wasn't in the room at all. But I can look out the upstairs window and get as good an answer to that as I could from ground level.''

''The curtains were all drawn,'' Martha reminded him. ''Besides, what could someone from outside have done? If the bullet had come from outside, one of the windows would have broken.''

''Not if it was left open,'' said Mr. Clemens.

"And if it had been open, we would have felt a draft," said Martha. "Besides, it could not have been done without my knowing it. But why are we holding this discussion out on the street, when we could be upstairs looking for whatever the police may have missed? Follow me, please, gentlemen." And she turned and led the way into the building, and up the stairs.

Inside the apartment, Martha lit the gas, then turned to my employer and said, "Where do you think we should begin?"

Mr. Clemens looked around the little front room, and said, "I'd like to get a closer look at all those trick bell ropes and spy holes that detective found last night. I always wondered how the spooks made all those noises people heard at séances."

A disappointed look came over Martha's face. "I can't see how any of that can help Edward," she said.

"I can't either—yet." Mr. Clemens walked over to the bell ropes and gave one of them an experimental tug. The sound of a clattering chain came faintly through the door to the other room. He flashed a smile, like a boy who'd found a hidden box of Christmas toys, then turned to Martha with a more serious expression. "But I think there's a good chance that the murderer knew what to expect. The shot seems to have been timed for when there was a racket to cover up the gunshot, and that suggests to me that the killer knew there was going to *be* a racket. Did anybody besides you and Ed know about these contraptions?"

Martha had kept a stoical expression as my employer spoke, but after he finished she gave him a pale smile, and said, "Oh, very well. If I really want you to help me, I can't reasonably hope to prevent you prying into dark corners. We had a man come in to do the actual work—Edward isn't very good at carpentry or the like, although he designed all the apparatus. He's very clever at things like that. But naturally the workman would have known about it."

"Figures," said Mr. Clemens. He reached over and gave a tug on another rope, which produced the sound like a distant church bell, then continued. "Ed's never been a man who'd do anything to put calluses on his hands, unless you can get 'em from a deck of cards. I reckon it'd be worth our while to talk to that worker. Did you hold on to his address?''

"Well, yes we did, but I don't think you're likely to find him there," said Martha. "It was Terry Mulligan, the man who ran away when he came back and saw the police here. He's most likely gone into hiding someplace—unless they've found him today and taken him in.''

"Damn," said Mr. Clemens. "I don't know whether I'd rather have him stay free or get caught, but either way, I guess we aren't going to learn anything from him before the police get it. We'll get his address and maybe look in there later, on the off chance we can find out something useful, but I'm not going to get my hopes up very high. Let's have a look through that spy hole. Where is it?" He turned and looked at the wall behind which the séance room lay, scanning the various picture frames and lighting fixtures there.

"Behind this," said Martha, indicating a small colored engraving of an outdoor scene. She lifted it up to reveal a brass plate about six inches in diameter, with several parallel slits, almost like a miniature gridiron. A hinged plate was mounted in the center, just about at eye level for a short man or a tall woman. Someone standing there could easily reach out and manipulate the bellpulls with the right hand.

Mr. Clemens and I stepped forward to inspect it more closely. There was a small hinge that let the circular piece flap down, revealing an opening through the wall. Mr. Clemens bent over a bit and put his eye to it. "I can't see anything," he complained.

Martha nodded. "You need to push that lever to move aside the picture in the other room. That's to make sure that no one in the other room will see the opening. We also keep this room dark so that no telltale light comes through."

"That's interesting," I said. "Mr. McPhee had the lights on, and was playing some sort of card game, when we came to tell him what had happened. Why wasn't he at the spy hole?''

"Maybe he was," said Mr. Clemens, looking at Martha. "I'd guess that Ed saw everything that happened and decided it was time for him to put on his poker face. I didn't hear everything you two talked about after the shooting—did he let on that he'd seen anything unexpected?''

Martha shook her head. ''Do you think I didn't ask him that? It was the first thing I wanted to know. But he didn't really bother to watch—he couldn't have seen much, in any case, once the lights were out. But he could hear everything that was said at the table. All he had to do was listen, and pull the appropriate rope from time to time.''

''Still, the lights were on in here,'' said Mr. Clemens. ''Wouldn't he have been worried that somebody at the table would see the gleam?''

''He didn't light the gas until after the . . . the *killing*,'' said Martha. ''He realized rather quickly that something had happened, and he knew that people would be coming here. So he quickly closed the peephole and lit the gas, hoping to prevent anyone from guessing about the apparatus.''

''Lot of good that did him, once Lestrade got here,'' said Mr. Twain. ''I suppose he had to give it his best try, though. Was he in this room the whole time?''

Martha shook her head. ''So he told me, and I believe him. If he had left, there would have been no one to work the apparatus.''

''I suppose that's so, unless Mulligan had stayed,'' said Mr. Clemens, nodding. ''Was Ed by himself the whole time? Did anybody come in and go back out during the séance?''

''I asked him that, as well. He was alone the entire time.''

Mr. Clemens looked her in the eye, then asked, ''You don't think he'd lie to you? Say, to protect somebody else?''

Martha raised her chin. ''He might try to, but I very much doubt he would have any success at it. I know Edward far too well for that.''

Mr. Clemens peered intently at her for a moment, then said, ''I guess you would, wouldn't you? We'll consider that settled, then. Let's take a look around the other room.''

''Fine,'' I said. ''What are we looking for?''

''Damned if I know,'' said Mr. Clemens. ''We'll just have to look for anything that shouldn't be here, or for anything that should be here and isn't, or anything at all that don't make sense.''

Chuckling at this description of our tasks, my employer led us into the room we were to search. The window shades were up today, and even though muted by lace curtains, the sunlight gave the room a far different aspect than it had had in gas- and candlelight (let alone in the darkness of the séance). I thought to myself that if I had been leading the police investigation, I would have sent my detectives back for a second search. Perhaps Lestrade felt he already had enough evidence to make a case against McPhee. But I thought it a missed opportunity—which we should take advantage of ourselves so as not to miss any clues that might remain.

After walking over and peering out the windows, Mr. Clemens looked around the room and asked, "Have you moved anything since last night, or taken anything away? Other than the body, that is—I can see that's gone. But I guess you didn't have anything to do with that."

Martha laughed nervously. "No, thank goodness. The policemen finally took the poor man away, though it seemed they waited forever to do it." She glanced involuntarily at where we had lain Dr. Parkhurst right after the shooting. My gaze followed hers, and I saw that a dark brown stain covered the cushions on one end of the sofa, a grim reminder of why we were here.

Mr. Clemens must have noticed our reaction, because he cleared his throat and asked, "Has anything else been moved or removed, as far as you know?"

"Well, of course I put a few of my own things away. And everybody took home the things they'd brought with them, their coats and umbrellas and the things they'd brought for the sitting. The police looked in all the coat pockets, of course, but otherwise they didn't greatly disturb things. I suppose it would've been different if they'd caught somebody trying to smuggle a pistol out the door."

"Yes, I reckon even Lestrade would have noticed that," said Mr. Clemens. He looked around the room again. "Time to begin, I guess. Wentworth, you start over by the doorway; I'll search by the big table, and Miss Martha can take the middle of the room. Sing out if you spot anything you think might be important."

I bent to my task—quite literally, examining the carpet and peering underneath the furniture. There was nothing worth "singing out" about, unless one considered dust a discovery of significance. I looked under and behind the large sofa, in case someone had dropped something there for concealment, and under the cushions of all the chairs. I looked behind all the pictures on the wall, and examined the knickknacks on a corner shelf. Nothing had been attached to the bottoms of the chairs or table, and if there were trapdoors or hidden compartments in the walls or floor, I did not find them. I even picked up a corner of the rug, but found nothing but bare boards beneath.

The one anomalous object I found turned out to be the picture that swung aside to uncover the peephole. Mr. Clemens came over to give it a cursory examination, then nodded and went back to his own search. Neither he nor Martha McPhee had discovered anything worth drawing attention to, either.

Finally, after about an hour of searching, Mr. Clemens got up off his knees (he had been prowling under the large table at which we'd sat for the séance), put little Jean's magnifying glass back in his pocket, and stood up. It looked very much as if he were favoring a crick in his back. He rubbed a spot just above his coattails and said, "Damnation! This whole silly Sherlock business is overrated. I've looked at a couple of acres of floor, and the underside of the table and every single one of the chairs, and tapped things and shook 'em and looked at 'em through the magnifier, and I haven't found so much as one Trichinopoly cigar ash, let alone anything to help me find a murderer. Hell, if I had to prove somebody's shot a gun off in here, I don't think I could. If the police can make a case out of dripped candle wax and scuffed carpet, let 'em do it. Sam Clemens is out of his depth, and not too proud to admit it."

Martha was down on her knees in the far corner of the room. She gave a sudden sneeze, presumably from the dust she had been inspecting. "Excuse me!"

She stood up and continued. "I haven't found anything, either. But I have a personal stake in this question, you know.

If this avenue is closed, there must be another open. What do we do to find it?''

"Perhaps we are wasting our time attempting to duplicate the work of the police," I suggested. "Their detectives perform searches all the time, and I would be surprised if any important physical evidence escaped Inspector Lestrade's notice—if it did, it is likely to be something small enough to escape our notice, as well."

Mr. Clemens paced a few steps back and forth, stretching out his arms to work out the kinks in his back. "I hate to admit that weasely-looking fellow might be smarter than I am, but I reckon you have a point, Wentworth. When it comes to searching a place, he's got years of experience and I'm a pup. So I reckon I've got to steer my own boat and see if I can get to the dock ahead of him. Let's go back to the beginning, Martha. Sit down and tell me everything that happened last night, just as you saw it."

"Very well, Mr. Clemens," said Martha, settling into one of the armchairs near the doorway. "But a great deal happened last night, as you know. Where should I begin?"

"Start with the guests arriving," said Mr. Clemens. He plopped himself in a chair opposite her, and gestured to me to take out my notebook. It looked as if we were in for a long session.

10

"**W**ho was the first to arrive last night?" asked Mr. Clemens. He had taken out his old corncob pipe and was scraping it with some sort of pipe-cleaning tool. I had grown to suspect that he enjoyed fiddling with the pipe almost as much as actually smoking it. It was an excellent excuse for a conversational pause, gaining him useful time to think.

"Cedric Villiers was first," said Martha McPhee. "He lives not far from here, and came over after supper. Next were Sir Denis and Lady Alice. They brought Hannah Boulton with them. The Parkhursts—and Mrs. Parkhurst's sister, Miss Donning—arrived about the same time as you and your family."

"Good, but let's not get ahead of ourselves," said Mr. Clemens. "I want to go through the guests one at a time. How did you meet Villiers? How did he get invited to the séance?"

"Cedric was one of the first people Edward and I met in London," said Martha, touching her chin with the tip of one finger. "He expressed a great interest in spiritualism, and that led very naturally to my telling him about my mediumship. Later, he introduced me to others who shared that interest, and in fact most of those who came to the sitting were people we met through his kind offices. He has been a great help to me.''

"Surprising,'' said Mr. Clemens, looking up from the pipe. "I'd have thought he was way too wrapped up in his own cleverness to much notice anybody else.''

"Oh!'' said Martha. "Cedric *is* a bit of a snob, isn't he? He and Edward have never really gotten along—as you saw last night, I think. But in spite of all that, he's been my entrée into English society''—she paused, and her expression turned sober—"though after what happened last night, I fear many of those doors will close to me.''

"Well, if we prove you and Ed didn't have anything to do with the murder, I reckon you'll be all right,'' said Mr. Clemens. "But let's stay on track, now. Villiers—did he help you any way besides introducing you to people?''

"Oh, yes,'' said Martha. "He found this apartment for us— a *flat*, he called it, and it took Edward a while to understand what he meant. We'd been living in a much less suitable place closer to the City, and he told us this one was available—I think someone he knows had looked at it, but ended up not taking it. And he let us borrow a few bits of furniture, too, so we could have enough chairs for all of the people we'd have in for a sitting, and candles, and other things to help us get properly set up.''

"Well, that makes sense,'' drawled Mr. Clemens. "Without the chairs, all you could have would be a standing.''

Martha McPhee smiled. "Now it is you who are straying off the track, Mr. Clemens. "What else do you need to know about Cedric Villiers?''

"I don't know,'' said my employer. He fished in his pocket, came up with a match, and struck it. "Did Villiers ever mention the doctor? That is, did he say anything to suggest he had some grudge against him, or some reason to kill him?''

Martha looked thoughtful while Mr. Clemens lit the pipe, then said, "No, nothing really. If I remember correctly, the only time the doctor was mentioned was when we were trying to see whom we might invite to our first sitting, and Cedric said that he knew some people who might be interested. Edward asked who they were, and Cedric mentioned a doctor—I don't remember if he told us the doctor's name, at the time—along with quite a few others. Not all of them ended up coming that first time, but I think most of them have come since. But in any case, we never met Dr. Parkhurst before last night."

"That's true of most of the guests, isn't it?" I interrupted, looking up from my notebook. "That you were meeting them for the first time just last night?"

"No, many of them came to the same spiritualist meetings where I met Cedric. Mrs. Parkhurst and Hannah Boulton attended regularly—I saw them every time I was there. Sir Denis and his wife were there at least once."

"What can you tell us about Hannah Boulton?" asked Mr. Clemens. His corncob pipe had gone out after only a couple of puffs, and he stared at it with irritation, then put it down on the table next to him.

"Not a great deal, actually," said Martha. "We met at the spiritualist society, but did not speak long. She lives out in Bloomsbury, not far from the museum. Apparently her husband Richard came from money, and they invested a great deal of it in art—Cedric tells me that she has a marvelous collection of French paintings. The poor dear lost her husband about a year ago, and it affected her deeply. I believe it was the reason for her seeking out a medium—to communicate with him one last time."

"Had she met the doctor before tonight?"

Martha turned her hands palms up. "I have no idea whether Mrs. Boulton knew the doctor," she said. "She certainly knew his wife from the spiritualist society, though I can't say whether they were particularly close."

"But she obviously knew Sir Denis and his wife, if they brought her here. It's beginning to look as if everybody here—except for my gang—knew each other before last night. So any one of 'em might have had some reason we don't know about to hold a grudge against the doctor." Mr. Clemens rubbed his chin, then continued. "What's your impression of Sir Denis?"

Martha said, "I haven't ever seen anyone quite like him, except perhaps some of the very rich southerners back home. He's on top of the world, and convinced it's his right to be there, and quite charming to speak to face-to-face. If he thought he had to kill a man, I'm sure he'd show no more compunction about it than at shooting a deer. I have heard that he is an expert shot with pistol and rifle, which would make him one of the more likely suspects."

Mr. Clemens nodded. "Well, that's something I didn't know before." He stood up and walked over to look out the window, then turned around and said, "I'd think Sir Denis would've had more reaction to the shooting if he'd been the one who pulled the trigger. He sure didn't show any sign that he'd just pulled off a difficult shot in near-total darkness. He was pretty cool, in fact—all common sense and practical suggestions."

"I suppose you're right—although I wasn't really *there* at the time," said Martha. "When the shooting happened I was in my trance, and when I woke up, everything was chaos, utter chaos. Before I could really get a notion of what was happening, the other ladies and I all went into the bedroom, trying to console Mrs. Parkhurst, poor thing."

"Now hold your horses, young lady," said Mr. Clemens, raising his hand. "Do you mean to tell me you were so deep in some kind of trance that you didn't see or hear anything? What am I supposed to make of an eyewitness who claims she didn't see or hear anything at all when a man was shot dead maybe six feet away from her?"

Martha looked him straight in the eye. "Make of it what you please, Mr. Clemens. You needn't swallow anything you don't wish to. What do you think I have to gain by trying to deceive you?"

My employer frowned. (I recognized this as a sign of deep thought, rather than displeasure.) After pacing back and forth for a few moments, he said, "I can think of a few reasons, but they're all based on either you or Ed being the guilty parties, or in cahoots with them. And there's no more evidence for that than for anything else, at present. Damnation— where does that leave us, Wentworth?"

"No worse off than we already were," I said. "We certainly don't have any shortage of eyewitnesses. You and I were there, after all, and so were your wife and daughter. And unless all the other guests were part of an elaborate conspiracy to murder Dr. Parkhurst, some of them should have seen or heard something that may help us."

"Of course," said Mr. Clemens. "And the police haven't been around asking them questions, either. At least, they hadn't come knocking on my door as of lunchtime today—I reckon they will, soon enough, if they can't squeeze anything out of Ed. And if Ed didn't have anything to do with it, there won't be much there for them to squeeze. I take it they haven't come to question you, either, young lady?" He turned toward Martha.

"No, I would have told you that," said Martha, shifting in her chair. "I doubt they would have been done with me in time for me to come ask your help this morning. I suppose eventually they'll want to search the apartment again, and they'll probably ask me some more questions then. It's a shame we didn't find anything worth our time, but I suppose that means they won't find much of anything, either."

"I would think that anything that escaped all three of us, as well as the police search last night, must be very small indeed," I pointed out.

"Very small, or very innocent-looking," agreed Mr. Clemens. He sat back down and leaned forward, propping up his chin with his right hand. "Let's go back a couple of steps and think about what we're looking for, and maybe that'll give us a better idea where we might find it. There are two big puzzles: how somebody shot the doctor without any of us hearing the shot, and where the gun went to afterwards. I'd guess it had to be done from outside, except the place was too dark to give the shooter a target—besides which, there's no broken glass and no bullet holes in the curtains."

"The rapping could have covered up the sound of the gun," I said.

"Yes, but nobody seems to have spotted the flash—it would have been mighty hard to miss in the darkness," said Mr. Clemens. "And we still don't know where the gun went to, since neither we nor the cops could find it . . . damn it all, Wentworth, I'm starting to think in circles.''

"We haven't disproved Lestrade's idea that Mr. McPhee admitted someone else to the premises, who fired at Dr. Parkhurst from the foyer, either through the peephole or with the door between rooms open just enough to take aim, and then removed the weapon when he made his escape," I said. Then a thought struck me. "I wonder, though—what if the killer meant to shoot someone else instead? Parkhurst may have been an accidental victim.''

"I don't even want to think about that," said Mr. Clemens. "We've got to assume the killer got the man he came looking for. Otherwise—" Whatever he was about to say, he was interrupted by a knock at the door. He turned in his chair and looked over his shoulder toward the entrance. "Well, I calculate that's Inspector Lestrade coming back to ask a few probing questions he forgot last night," he said. "Why don't you go let him in, Miss Martha?"

I thought Mr. Clemens was rather too confident in his prediction that the person at the door would be Chief Inspector Lestrade. But as it turned out, he was right. When Martha McPhee returned to the room where we waited, she was followed by two men—Lestrade and Sergeant Coleman, his younger assistant. "Good day, Mr. Mark Twain," said Lestrade, taking off his hat. "Fancy meeting you here!"

"Nothing fancy about it, Inspector," said Mr. Clemens, drawling more than usual. "I reckon you're here on business. Don't let me bother you, I'll set right here and smoke my pipe." He picked up the corncob pipe (which had gone out) and waved it at the two Scotland Yard men.

"I certainly am here on business," said the inspector, crisply. "The Queen's business, to be exact. Might I ask what brings you and your young friend here? This is hardly a place I'd expect you to return to, after what happened last night. Not unless you have some particular reason, that is."

"I guess you could say that my secretary and I are just being neighborly," said my employer. "We know this young lady and her husband from back home——not that we're par-

ticular friends, mind you. But when you're in a foreign country, and trouble comes a-calling, a familiar face can be a
comfort. Mrs. McPhee is real worried about her husband, and
so Wentworth and I came over to see whether we could be
any kind of help. But you don't have to pay me any mind—
go on about your business—I'll just smoke my pipe until
you're done." He gestured with the pipe again, still not making any attempt to light it.

"You realize, sir, that we are conducting a murder investigation," said Sergeant Coleman.

"Are you, now?" Mr. Clemens sounded utterly surprised
by this revelation. "Why, I wouldn't have known it unless
you told me so. Now you've got me all interested. Do you
mind if I watch? Maybe I can put some of it in a book sometime."

Sergeant Coleman turned red and began to sputter, but Lestrade smiled thinly and said, "Oh, you can do much more
than just watch, Mr. Twain. I expect you can assist us a good
deal with our investigation. Since you're right here, it would
be a fine time for you to answer a few questions while Coleman takes a look around the premises. We'll have a few questions for the young gentleman here, as well, and some for
Mrs. McPhee, of course. You see, you're all three witnesses
to the matter we're investigating."

Mr. Clemens raised his brows. "What, haven't you learned
anything from that fellow you took away last night? You were
talking as if he was the key to the whole business."

"Aye, that he is," said Lestrade. "But so far he's played
it close to his waistcoat—if you were to credit the rascal, he
didn't see anything, didn't do anything, and doesn't know
anything, either. Well, he thinks he's clever now, but he's
setting himself up to learn a hard lesson if he wants to try
that game against Lestrade."

"May I visit him?" said Martha, concern in her voice.

"All in good time," said Lestrade, unbuttoning his overcoat. "We'll let him sit a little longer in the lockup, and see
if his memory improves. For now, I'd like to ask you a few
questions."

"Why should I answer them, if you will not let me visit

my husband?'' demanded Martha. ''It is dreadful of you to take a man away in the middle of the night and throw him into jail like a common criminal. I tell you, Mr. Lestrade, Edward has not done anything to deserve such treatment. He is an American citizen, you know. If I get no satisfaction from you, I mean to bring this matter to the attention of our embassy, and I assure you they will not take it lightly.''

''Mrs. McPhee, I can assure *you* that the Metropolitan Police Authority does not take cold-blooded murder lightly,'' said Lestrade. He removed his coat and draped it over a chair, putting his hat on the seat. ''There may be a killer walking the streets, even as we speak. All your husband has to do is answer our questions. If he's done nothing against English law, he has nothing to fear from us. Meanwhile, you might think about this: if you can tell us something that helps us catch the murderer, then your man will be back with you that much the sooner.''

''I've heard that story before,'' said Martha, defiance in her eyes. ''I know better that to trust a policeman holding out empty promises.''

''Do you really?'' asked Lestrade. ''And have you and Mr. McPhee been in trouble with the police often before?''

Before Martha could open her mouth to answer, Mr. Clemens stood up and raised his hand. ''Hold on now, both of you. This little squabble is about as helpful as a dogfight in a canoe. We're all aiming for the same thing—finding out who killed the doctor.''

''You're assuming the lady's husband isn't the murderer himself, or an accomplice,'' said Sergeant Coleman, looking up from the floor over by the table, where he had begun an inch-by-inch search.

Now it was Lestrade who raised his hand. ''Wait a while, Coleman,'' he said. ''Mr. Twain, do I understand you to say that you are trying to find the murderer yourself? I fear you've bitten off more than you can chew.''

''Don't say that before you know how big my mouth is,'' said Mr. Clemens. ''I've done this kind of thing before, and had my share of luck at it.''

Lestrade peered intently at my employer before answering.

"I've had dealings before with private persons who fancied they were better than we are at catching criminals. From time to time, one of them stumbles across a bit of evidence before the police discover it, and helps us solve the case. But take my word for it, Mr. Twain, these things are best left to the professionals. I've been at Scotland Yard a dog's age and longer. I've seen everything there is to see. There's no substitute for practical experience, no matter how clever a fellow thinks he is."

"Well, I wouldn't argue with that," said Mr. Clemens. "And being a foreigner, of course I can't know your territory as well as you do."

"Yes, exactly," said Lestrade, nodding.

"Still, Ed McPhee and I have known each other a long time," my employer continued. "I have a pretty good idea what he'd do and what he wouldn't, and I don't believe he's got murder in his heart. I don't think he'd cover up a murder, either—not unless the other fellow had something mighty serious to hold over his head in exchange for his silence, that is. And I can't see how that could apply here."

"If you'd seen as many murders as I have, you wouldn't be surprised by anything," Lestrade said. "A man everybody knows and trusts can suddenly snap—because of money, because of a woman, because of a hundred things, Lord knows. This McPhee chap may have been under pressures you can't imagine."

"You're talking to a man who makes up stories for a living," said Mr. Clemens. "If I can't imagine it, it ain't worth the trouble. But never mind that; there's fresher fish to fry. I'm going to do what I can to figure out who killed Dr. Parkhurst last night. I don't have any axes to grind; if it turns out McPhee did it, you can hang him without me raising a finger—sorry, Miss Martha, but that's all I can promise you."

"No more than any honest man would undertake," said Lestrade, nodding. "But you're leading up to something, I can tell. What's your point, Mr. Twain?"

"I think McPhee may tell his 'old buddy Sam' things he wouldn't tell you," said my employer. "How about letting me in to talk to him—maybe giving him your promise that if you're happy with what he says to me, he can talk to his wife? You'll catch more flies with molasses than with vinegar, you know.''

Lestrade gave him a searching look, then said, ''Perhaps we can do business, then. But first I have a few questions for you three. If I'm satisfied with your answers, then we can consider letting you talk to McPhee. Do we have a bargain?''

''Well, I don't see how I've got anything to lose by it,'' said Mr. Clemens. He paused and looked at me, then at Martha McPhee. ''Of course, I'm only talking for myself. But if these two young folks are agreeable, I think we've got a deal.''

''I can't turn down any plan that lets me speak to my husband,'' said Martha. I added my agreement, and Lestrade took out a notebook of his own. Mr. Clemens reclaimed his chair, and we awaited the detective's questions.

11 ~

L estrade rubbed his chin, thinking, then said, "Let's begin with the young lady. When did you first meet the
deceased?"

"Last night," said Martha. "No more than twenty minutes
before our sitting commenced."

Lestrade squinted when he heard that. "Really! And if you
didn't know the gentleman before that, how did he happen to
be here last night?"

"His wife and I had met at a spiritualist-society meeting,"
said Martha. "She asked him to come. And to be quite frank
with you, I had the distinct impression that he was there only
to escort her and her sister. He showed very little enthusiasm
for the proceedings."

"So you say, but do you have any corroboration?" asked
the detective. He held the pencil poised above the blank page,
clearly waiting for her to answer.

"It doesn't seem particularly farfetched to me," said Mr.
Clemens, waving his unlit pipe. "I was here myself mainly
because my wife and daughter wanted to come. Otherwise,
I'd have skipped the whole thing, and probably been a lot
happier."

"I suppose I should resent that, Mr. Clemens," said Martha

McPhee, with a very faint smile. "But perhaps some good will come of your presence last night. One of your party may have seen or heard something that will help exonerate my husband."

"It would be even better if you could get the spirits to tell us who did the killing," said my employer; I could not tell from his expression whether he meant the suggestion to be taken seriously. "That might even make me decide there was something to the afterlife, after all."

"I wish it were that simple," said Martha. "Believe me, Mr. Clemens, I thought of that approach myself, late last evening. But my ability to see beyond this plane is very unreliable, and the spirits can be quite capricious. Nonetheless, I would be willing to essay the attempt."

"Well, if we can't get anything useful by the regular means, maybe I'll ask you to do just that for us," said Lestrade dryly. "But I doubt it'll be necessary. We at the Criminal Branch have our methods, and they have stood the test of time. Not many slip through our grasp, I can tell you that."

"What about that business out at Whitechapel a few years back—Jack, I think the fellow's name was . . . ?" said Mr. Clemens.

Lestrade's face turned red. "That devil!" he exclaimed. He gnashed his teeth, and for a moment his eyes flashed. Then, getting control of himself, he continued. "You're right, Twain, that's one villain who got away from us. If the people in charge had listened to what some of their men on the streets had to offer, things might have come out different. But the fellow's beyond our reach now—and getting a regular diet of brimstone, I daresay."

"You never found a body, did you?" When Lestrade shook his head to signify the negative, my employer continued, "These things never get wrapped up quite as neat as you'd like to think. Don't be so sure the killer's dead. But we're off the subject, aren't we? You had some questions for us."

"Yes, of course," said Lestrade. "Where were we?" He glared at Sergeant Coleman as if looking for a cue.

"You'd been asking about the deceased," Coleman

prompted, raising his head. He hit it on the edge of the table he'd been searching under, making a loud bump, and rubbed it, muttering. He picked up his pocket magnifier, which he'd dropped, and began searching again.

"Exactly," said Lestrade, nodding. He managed to convey the impression that he'd had the answer all along, and was just testing his assistant. He turned around and inched his chair closer to the one Martha occupied. "Now, did the deceased say or do anything to indicate that he might have an enemy here? Did he pointedly ignore anyone, for instance, or act annoyed to see someone here?"

"Not that I noticed," said Martha. "I thought his manner was a bit stiff and reserved, but he didn't ignore one person any more than the rest."

"Typically English, in other words," Mr. Clemens added.

"Not quite, though I know what you mean," said Martha, a small smile playing about her lips. "He appeared somewhat embarrassed to be seen patronizing a medium. Many respectable people act that way. And yet practically all my sitters come from the higher ranks of society."

"No surprise there," said Mr. Clemens. "They're the only ones with money to spend listening to spirits tell them a bunch of stuff they already ought to know. Not many mediums hand out free tickets to the street cleaners and stable boys in the neighborhood."

Martha's smile vanished and her back stiffened. "Mr. Clemens, you know very little of how I conduct my affairs. In any case, it seems unbecomingly small of you to accuse me of mercenary motives, considering that I invited you, your family, and your secretary to attend last night, all without charge."

"So you did," said Mr. Clemens. "I'm still not sure you weren't hoping I'd write a favorable article about you, and make you the talk of London overnight. You should have known me better."

Martha turned a sad face toward my employer. "I know you to be no great friend of spiritualism, but I allowed myself to hope that I might show you the shallowness of mere skepticism. To tell the truth, I had a much simpler reason for inviting you: to bring the number of sitters to twelve—a very powerful number. And I must say that, before the unfortunate incident, the rapport between myself and the spirits was unusually deep.''

Lestrade had visibly grown impatient with this digression, and now he stuck his face forward, close to Martha's, taking charge of the proceedings again. ''What about the others in attendance?'' he asked, pointing around the room with his pencil. ''Had any of them been to séances with you before?'' I fleetingly wondered whether he was seriously considering either Mr. Clemens or me as likely suspects or accessories to the murder.

''Only Cedric Villiers had been to any of my previous sittings,'' said Martha. ''I met him at the spiritualist society, and he did a great deal to help me make my way here in London. He helped me organize my first sitting, and attended another, as well.''

''What about the others? Did you find them at spiritualist meetings, too?'' His stance and tone were belligerent, as if he did not believe her statements.

''Many of them,'' said Martha, shrinking back slightly. ''Mr. Villiers introduced me to several of the others at the Spiritualist Society. I must have met twenty or thirty people there, more if I count those to whom I was briefly introduced without any extensive conversation. Of those, Mrs. Parkhurst, Hannah Boulton, Sir Denis and his wife, and of course Cedric were at the sitting last night.''

''What about the others?'' Lestrade pressed her.

Martha spread her hands, as if showing the detective she was not concealing anything in them. ''I met Mr. Clemens and his secretary in America some months ago, and his wife and daughter just the previous night, at their place in Tedworth Square. Dr. Parkhurst and his sister-in-law were the only two I had never met—Mrs. Parkhurst invited both of them.''

Lestrade had gradually inched his chair even closer to her, and was now no more than two feet away from her face. ''Are you absolutely certain you never met the doctor before?'' he said, unnecessarily loudly, I thought.

Martha sent an annoyed look at her interrogator. "You seem to be looking for some motive on my part. I assure you, Mr. Lestrade, I had nothing to gain by killing the doctor."

"Mrs. McPhee, I am a police detective," said Lestrade, with exaggerated patience. "I have to suppose that anyone connected to this case might be guilty—else I'm likely to miss something. I have been noting down what you say, and I'll read it over at my leisure when I'm back at the station. You can be certain I'll be speaking to the other witnesses. If their stories jibe with yours, all's well and good. If they don't jibe—"

"If they don't jibe, I may find myself in jail along with my husband," said Martha. "I accept that risk, Mr. Lestrade. You may remember that I am cooperating with you, in hopes that I can convince you to free my husband. Now, did you have other questions?"

"Yes," said Lestrade, leaning back just a bit. He glanced over at Coleman, who was examining the chairs around the table where the séance had been held, turning them over and looking under their seats. He nodded, evidently pleased at his assistant's progress, then turned back to Martha and continued.

"One last thing. We need to reconstruct, as best we can, where everyone was sitting last night. Once we know that, and measure the angle the shot came from, we'll have a good idea just who could have fired it."

"Maybe," said Mr. Clemens. "That's assuming the doctor didn't turn his head to one side or the other just before the shot was fired."

"Of course," said Lestrade, after a slight pause. "Still, I think we need to know who was sitting in what seat. Mrs. McPhee?"

"Mr. Cabot was to my left, and Cedric Villiers to my right," said Martha. "I believe—Mr. Cabot can correct me if I'm wrong—that Miss Susy Clemens was on his left, and Mr. Clemens next, followed by Mrs. Clemens."

"Very good then, we've half the table accounted for already," said Lestrade. Coleman, who had evidently finished his search of the floor, was busy with his notebook and pencil. "And what was the order of the others?"

"I think Hannah Boulton was at Cedric's right hand, followed by Mrs. Parkhurst, and then the doctor," said Martha.

"That doesn't sound right," said Mr. Clemens. "I remember Mrs. Parkhurst's sister being next to Villiers, then the doctor and his wife after that."

"So you think the doctor was between his wife and her sister?" asked Lestrade. He had been scribbling down notes, stopping to scratch out something as one or another of us changed our minds. He stared at his pad, then said, "That last bit can't be right—it doesn't leave any place for Mrs. Boulton."

The Scotland Yard man stood up and pointed in the direction of the table. "I'll tell you what—we'll go over to the table and see if we can sort this out better."

"All right," said Martha. She stood up and followed Lestrade to the large round table, which was still surrounded by a dozen chairs. "This is where I sat," she said, placing her hand on the back of one of the seats.

"Are you quite certain?" said Detective Coleman, who had rejoined the group. "I'm trying to draw a chart of the seating arrangements, and a mistake at the outset could throw the whole thing off."

"Oh, I couldn't possibly be mistaken," said Martha. "I always sit here, in case I need to signal to Edward in the other room."

"I knew there was some kind of trickery going on last night!" said Mr. Clemens, slapping the palm of his hand on the tabletop. "I should have taken that chair when I had the chance, but you bluffed me out of it. But that's not the worst of it. Twenty minutes ago, you told me you were in a trance the whole time, and now you say you were sending signals to Slippery Ed. Which is the truth?"

"Yes, I find that very interesting," said Lestrade. "Exactly what sort of information were you conveying to him?"

Martha sat down at the table and looked up at us with a perfectly calm expression. "My goodness, gentlemen, you are very quick to seize upon a quibble. I did not say I *was* sending my husband signals last night; I said I sat here in case I *needed* to. Surely you can see the distinction."

"I can see it all right, but I'll be damned if I can see how it makes any difference," said Mr. Clemens. "Were you in a trance last night, or not?"

"Yes, exactly as I told you," said Martha, looking at my employer with an expression of perfect innocence. "A very deep trance, in fact—so deep that I have no memory of anything that transpired between the beginning of the sitting and my being awakened by bright lights and frightened voices. But the trance is not always so deep, and sometimes it does not come very quickly, or last very long—and then I need to cue my husband to increase the sounds and other effects. I am sorry to say that most of my visitors are far more impressed by a rattling chain or a distant violin than by what the spirits have to say to them."

"Well they might be," muttered Mr. Clemens. I thought he was about to go on, but Lestrade stepped forward and took charge again.

"You were in this chair, then," he said. "And the young gentleman was to your left? Would you sit there, sir? And Mr. Twain, would you please go to where you sat last night."

I sat down next to Martha, followed by Mr. Clemens, who took a seat two places to my left and put his corncob pipe (still unlit) on the table in front of him. While I had not paid close attention to the exact seating arrangements the night before, I was sure the three of us were now in the same places.

"Very good," said Lestrade. "Now, we'll write the names of the rest of the party on slips of paper, and Coleman will match them to their seats."

This process took only a short time. Martha wrote out the names—I was somehow pleased to note that her handwriting was legible as well as graceful—and handed them to Sergeant Coleman to place around the table. It was only a matter of minutes before there were slips of paper in front of the remaining chairs.

"Now we're getting somewhere," said Lestrade. "But are you certain where the doctor sat? His body had already been moved when I got here."

"He was second or third to my left, I think," said Martha, though she didn't sound entirely certain.

"That sounds right," said Mr. Clemens. "He was pretty much straight across from me."

"Let's see, then," said Lestrade, moving to the side of the table they'd suggested. He looked down and said, "This is about right. There's a bloodstain on the carpet between these two chairs, so he must have been in one of them."

"It depends on which direction he was shot from," Sergeant Coleman pointed out. "If we could determine exactly where he was, that would give us a better idea which of the others shot him."

"Good thinking, Sergeant, but you've missed the main point," said Lestrade, with a smug expression. Coleman bowed his head, looking chastened.

"I reckon you're going to tell us what that is," said Mr. Clemens. "Or are you going to keep it up your sleeve to spring on the suspect when you get to court?"

"Oh, I don't mind telling you at all," said Lestrade. He pointed toward the door. "Whichever of these chairs the doctor sat in, he was directly facing that spy hole over there, and the door to the outer room. Any decent marksman could have potted him from that distance."

"What, in pitch darkness?" said Mr. Clemens, turning to look over his shoulder at where Lestrade had pointed. "If Annie Oakley's in town, maybe she could have hit him from there, but I'd bet against anybody else pulling off that shot."

"Yes, and the bullet would have had to pass directly between two other people at the table," I said, looking in the same direction. "Your marksman would have had to be completely confident of his aim—or not care at all whether he hit the wrong person. I frankly don't believe it."

Lestrade scoffed at our objections. "It doesn't matter whether you believe it. If the fellow had been standing, he'd have a clean line of sight over the heads of the people on this side of the table," he said, pointing to the spy hole again.

"That's assuming he knew where his target was going to sit," said Mr. Clemens, pointing to the far side of the table where the doctor had sat. "Nobody told any of us what place to take, so there's no way he could have known it in advance. Hell, we can't even figure it out right now, and we saw the whole thing less than twenty-four hours ago.''

"That's where Mr. McPhee took a hand in the proceedings," said Lestrade, walking around to our side of the table. "He saw everyone seated before he turned out the lights and left the room, so he could point out exactly where the victim was. And if the shooter had time earlier that day to inspect the room, he'd have had a very good idea where to aim to hit a person in any given seat.''

"Surely you can't believe that!" said Martha McPhee. "Edward and I were together the entire day.''

"Perhaps it was the day before, then," Lestrade said. "Or the day before that. Can you swear you were with your husband every minute of every day since you rented the flat? I thought not," he said as Martha silently shook her head. There was fear in her eyes, now.

Lestrade turned to Coleman. The chief inspector was all but crowing, now. "I think this erases any doubt that McPhee was an accomplice to the murderer. He let the killer in, he helped him spot his victim, and he aided his getaway. We'll keep after McPhee until he fingers the man who pulled the trigger.''

"Yes, Chief Inspector," said Coleman, who had been hanging on to his superior's words. "But I wonder—how come none of the others heard the report, or saw the flash of the muzzle?''

Lestrade waved away the question. "They've all said there was enough racket to drown out a shot. McPhee most likely made some extra noises to cover up the sound of the weapon—he had the noisemakers right at hand. As for the flash, it's probably just our bad luck that nobody was looking directly that way—half of them had their backs to it, in any case. The others likely had their eyes closed or their heads turned the wrong direction—probably toward Mrs. McPhee. And that reminds me." He turned and pointed a finger toward Martha.

"I haven't enough evidence to arrest you, Mrs. McPhee— not enough yet, that is," he said. "But I promise you will be watched very closely. Any attempt to leave the city will force me to place you under detention.''

"On what grounds, sir?" Martha held her chin straight up. There was a spark of defiance in her eye, but I thought I saw a quiver in her lip as she spoke.

"Suspicion of being an accessory to murder, before and during the fact," said Lestrade. He went over to the chair where he had placed his coat and hat, and picked them up. "Perhaps your husband acted without your knowledge, but I think it unlikely. If you had anything to do with this atrocity, Scotland Yard will find you out—have no doubt about that. And then you will learn how British justice treats a murderess. I believe we are finished here, for today; come along, Coleman."

"One moment, sir," said Martha, rising to her feet. "You promised I could speak to my husband. Are you reneging on that?"

"I said I might let you speak with him if I was satisfied with your answers—and with his," said Lestrade, doing up the bottom button on his coat. "But neither of you has yet given me wholehearted cooperation. Until you and your husband change your tune, he can continue to cool his heels." And with that, the two Scotland Yard detectives swept out of the room, leaving the three of us staring after them.

12 ⌒

There was a long moment of silence after Inspector Lestrade left the room, and then Martha sighed. "That man hasn't the slightest intention of looking at other suspects. He's got it fixed in his mind that Edward is guilty, and he's not going to budge from that." She turned a pleading look toward Mr. Clemens. To my surprise, a tear was running down her face. All her poise had completely vanished; I knew this was no act.

Mr. Clemens understood that, too. He stood up and walked over to her chair, placing a hand softly on her shoulder. "Now, now," he said, awkwardly. "We'll get this straightened out somehow, don't you worry." Then he signaled to me with a movement of his head toward the window at the far corner of the apartment. I understood that he meant me to follow him there, giving the poor woman time to collect herself. I quickly followed him there, where we stood looking out at the building across from us. There was a small garden below us, with a fence at the back, but for the moment my thoughts were elsewhere. Behind us I could hear Martha quietly sobbing, and I was completely at a loss for words.

"Well, Cabot," said my employer in a near whisper, "this is enough to convince me that the young lady couldn't have

known what was going to happen to the doctor. Even if Ed
was mixed up in it, I don't think she had any part in it."

This conclusion dovetailed with my own. "Do you still
think McPhee himself was involved?" I whispered back.

"It doesn't look good for him," said my employer, shaking
his head. "Martha must know that, too. Lestrade may be on
the wrong track, but it's a plausible track, and that may be
enough to convince a judge that Ed let the killer in—or even
that he pulled the trigger himself." He turned and looked
back at McPhee's wife, and I followed his gaze. Martha was
sitting up straight again, wiping her eyes with a lace handkerchief. It looked as if she had regained control of herself.

Mr. Clemens gripped my elbow and continued. "It looks
bad for Slippery Ed, but damn it, I know that old rascal thirty
years. Make no mistake about Ed. He's a skunk for sure—
but that's not the same as a killer, or a man who'd knowingly
help one. That's the thing Lestrade don't know, and I do."

My employer strode back over to the table where Martha
McPhee still sat. He pulled out the chair next to her—the one
in which I had been sitting—and sat down next to her, saying,
"Well, Mrs. McPhee, we've got to put our heads together if
we're going to get that husband of yours out of jail."

"You surprise me, Mr. Clemens," said Martha McPhee.
"Until a moment ago, I was under the distinct impression
that you considered my husband's guilt an even-money proposition at best. Now you talk as if you're convinced of his
innocence. Do you mind telling me what led you to change
your mind? Or are you merely annoyed at Chief Inspector
Lestrade, and taking your position contrary to whatever he
currently espouses?"

"Oh, I'm annoyed at the smug little weasel, all right," said
my employer. He fished in his pocket for a match, which he
struck and picked up his pipe to try lighting it again.

Martha pressed him. "And if your annoyance with the inspector passes, will you again decide that Edward might be
guilty? Or do you genuinely believe that he played no part in
this murder?"

"I see what you're worried about," said Mr. Clemens. He
shook out the burning match, his pipe still unlit. "You need

to know for certain I'm on your side, so if you have some piece of evidence that might make Ed look bad, you can tell me about it without my running to the police and blabbing. Is that it?''

She nodded. ''I might not have put it quite so baldly, but in a nutshell, yes, that is my concern. If I were to retain a lawyer, I would expect as much of him.''

''I guess I don't have to tell you I'm not a lawyer,'' said Mr. Clemens, frowning. ''That's to your advantage—for one thing, I'm not going to start spouting a lot of Latin words you don't understand; and for another, I'm not going to charge you a red cent for my time.''

''You underestimate me, Mr. Clemens. I do know some Latin, and a fair amount of law as well,'' said Martha, smiling now.

''I should have known,'' said my employer. ''Next you'll tell me you can play the trombone, ride circus elephants, and pilot a balloon, too. Maybe all three at once.'' Martha laughed at this incongruous listing of her possible accomplishments, and Mr. Clemens's eyes twinkled.

Then he held up a hand and said, ''But let's not get too far from your question—you do deserve a straight answer, even if you won't necessarily like it. Young lady, I've known your husband since before the Civil War—more than thirty years, in fact. He was a young swindler when I first met him, and he was still a swindler—although a good bit longer in the tooth—when we parted company in Memphis early this summer.''

''Yes, that describes Edward more or less accurately,'' said our hostess. ''I can't see any benefit in trying to deny something you know as well as I. Nonetheless, I think it is a long step from that to murder.''

''I agree,'' I said. ''But that doesn't address the main point of Inspector Lestrade's theory. He accuses Mr. McPhee not necessarily of firing the fatal shot himself, but of opening the door, after the séance had begun, to the person who did fire it. McPhee may not even have known what the other person intended, until it was too late.''

''So why didn't he spill the beans as soon as the cops got

here?'' countered Mr. Clemens. He walked over to the fireplace, which was banked low, and held out his hands to warm them.

"Possibly fear of reprisal," I said. "Perhaps the other person has some hold over McPhee, sufficient to convince him to bide his time in silence and wait out the investigation, confident he can't be implicated in the actual killing."

"You disappoint me, Mr. Cabot," said Martha. "I expected you to be more open-minded. Mr. Clemens, you may poke up that fire if you wish."

"No, I think Cabot *is* being open-minded, more than either of us have managed so far," said my employer, picking up the poker. "That's what I was trying to say before—for now, I'll work on the assumption that Ed is innocent, because I don't think killing is in his makeup. But I won't be satisfied until I have the whole truth. And that means I can't overlook any real possibility. The police won't be overlooking anything—well, maybe they will, if Lestrade's the best they've got. But we can't bank on it—and we sure can't bank on them making any efforts to clear Ed. As long as Lestrade's running the show, they'll be working on his theory, and that starts with the idea that Ed done it. So if anybody's going to find evidence that proves Ed might not have done it, it's going to have to be us."

"I suppose you are right," Martha admitted.

"All right, then, let's get down to brass tacks," said Mr. Clemens, turning back to face us again. He had still not done anything with the poker. "Have you seen any evidence that Ed may be under pressure, that somebody might be holding something over his head?"

"Not really," said Martha. "Edward has seemed entirely himself, as far as I could tell, except for having to explain himself to the police last night."

"I reckon that would disturb most people," said Mr. Clemens, leaning the poker against the bricks. "Ed's a pretty cool customer when he needs to be, though. I'd have thought he had enough experience with cops not to get too agitated at being questioned. But let's not harp on that."

"Why are you so reluctant to accept Lestrade's theory?"

I persisted. "Does it have some obvious shortcoming I haven't noticed—other than its origin, I mean?"

"My main problem with it is that I have trouble believing that the killer stood across the room, aimed between two people he didn't want to hit, and plugged the doctor right between the eyes, or close enough not to matter—all in a dark room. Maybe it isn't flat impossible, but it's damned unlikely. There's got to be an easier explanation for what happened." Mr. Clemens ticked off his points on his fingers as he referred to them. When he stopped and looked at me expectantly, I had to concede that his objections appeared valid.

"Good, I'm glad to hear it," he said, looking somewhat relieved. "I was afraid *I* might have gone off the track, when you didn't back me right away. You have a pretty good head on your shoulders when you decide to use it, Wentworth. If I can't convince you of something, it's time to stop and figure out what's wrong with it."

"I'm not certain whether I should take that as a compliment or not, sir," I said. "But more to the point, it seems to me that if we don't accept the explanation the police are offering, we're going to have to refute it if we wish to exonerate McPhee. Where do you think we should begin?"

"Well, Lestrade gave us a start when he brought us over to the table to figure out where everybody was sitting last night," said Mr. Clemens. "Let's make our own seating chart—I didn't get a look at the one Coleman made, so we'll have to do it from scratch. We can get Livy and Susy to help us remember who sat where, and maybe narrow down which of the people we know were in the room had an opportunity to make that shot in the dark."

"I have paper in the desk," said Martha. Mr. Clemens nodded, and she went off to fetch it.

"I don't see how anyone at the table really had the opportunity to shoot anyone," I said, returning to the subject. "Everyone was holding hands, remember? How could anyone have let go a neighbor's hand long enough to fire a weapon without its being noticed?"

"The same way they managed to cover up the sound and flash and smell of a gunshot in a closed room, I reckon," said Mr. Clemens. "If we can figure out the answer to any one of those, maybe the rest will come after it like baby ducks following their mama. Ah, thank you, Miss Martha," he said as she handed him paper and a pencil.

Mr. Clemens sat down in his old seat, and bent over the paper for perhaps two minutes, making a rough sketch of the seating arrangements. At last he looked up and said, "Here, both of you, tell me whether this matches what you remember."

The paper showed a rough circle, marked into twelve segments like the numerals on a clock face, representing the seats we had occupied last night. Each segment was marked with the name of the person in that seat. (Several of the names had queries next to them.) To the right of the chair labeled *DR. P. (?)* was a stick figure spread out on the floor, obviously marking where the doctor's body had fallen. At the corner of the paper, more or less opposite that figure, was an arrow pointing away from the table, marked *TO DOOR.*

"I'm not certain," I said. "I think you may have switched the positions of the doctor and his wife—but I could be wrong. I agree with all the ones you've marked as definite. That still leaves a few places in question, though."

"Let Miss Martha look," he said, and I passed the sheet to her.

She studied it a moment, then looked up and said, "It's right as far as I can tell. As Mr. Cabot says, you may have Mr. and Mrs. Parkhurst reversed, and I'm not certain whether Sir Denis or Lady Alice sat next to your wife—but Mrs. Clemens will remember that detail."

Mr. Clemens frowned. "Well, if both of you remember the doctor in the other chair, let's put him in it. We can change it if everybody else remembers different. But if we're going to go up against Lestrade, we need to know that for certain."

"How so?" I asked.

"Because it tells us where he was most likely shot from," said Mr. Clemens. "The force of a bullet knocks a body backward. If he was shot from over by the door, his body should have fallen to the left—his left, I mean. So if he fell to the right, that means the shot had to come from somewhere else."

"The shooter could have walked across the room to the other corner before he fired his shot," I pointed out.

"Sure, but why the hell would he do that?" said Mr. Clemens. "If he was right by the door, all he had to do was take his shot, duck back out, and go straight down the stairs. Walking over there, he'd have risked bumping into furniture in the dark, making it twice as hard to avoid notice—or to get away afterwards."

"He might have done it to confuse us," I said, realizing even as I did how improbable my explanation was.

"And he might have flown out the window over there and closed it behind him," said my employer, scornfully waving in that direction. Then his expression changed. "Damn—I never thought of that. There's not a balcony or a wide ledge, or anything of the sort outside that window, is there?"

"Not a balcony—I'm sure of that," said Martha. "To tell the truth, I've never looked to see if there might be a ledge."

Together the three of us traipsed over to the window in question, and raised the shade. The window overlooked a small garden, bounded by a low brick wall separating it from the neighbors' gardens. Martha undid the window latch and raised the sash—with some little difficulty, it seemed to me.

Mr. Clemens leaned out and looked down. "Well, there's a ledge," he said. "Maybe six inches wide; I wouldn't want to try to walk along it and open this window from the outside, but that doesn't mean somebody else couldn't have done it. So there *is* another way the killer could have gotten in."

"He'd have had to know in advance that the window would be unlocked," said Martha. "But it *was* locked, and as you just saw, it is not easy to open. I also think we would have noticed the draft as it was opened."

"Maybe," said Mr. Clemens. "But he might have had somebody inside open the lock for him. And maybe, over by the table, we wouldn't notice the draft if it was only open for a few seconds. Remember, there wasn't any wind to speak of last night."

"I don't deny that it was possible," said Martha. "As you know, I was not paying close attention to the external world at the time in question. But isn't it likely that one of us would have heard something, or felt the breeze, or seen light from the outside, when the killer made his entrance?''

"Well, it was pretty dark last night, so there wouldn't necessarily have been any light from outside," said Mr. Clemens. "As for the noise, well, we've already pointed out that there was enough other noise to cover it up. Don't get me wrong, now—all I'm saying is that, if the killer had help from somebody on the inside, and if he could get into one of the other apartments on this floor to get out on the ledge, and if he was fool enough to walk around it carrying a gun—'' He stopped with a sheepish look, then said, "Hell, that's a lot of *if*s, ain't it?''

"A few too many, I think," I said. "Nor should we forget that the ledge would have been slippery from the drizzle last night.''

"Maybe he came up a ladder from the garden down below," said my employer. He leaned out the window again, looking toward the ground below, then stood back up with a sigh, and pulled the window down again. "We ought to go down and see if there are any marks where a ladder might have set.''

"We can do that when we leave," I agreed. Then, after a moment's thought, I added, "I don't mean to reject your idea outright, but it seems to rely on too many improbabilities. It also assumes that the murderer was willing to risk being seen by a neighbor.''

"Mr. Cabot has a good point," said Martha. "The neighbors would very likely have sent for the police if they had seen someone on the ledge. At the very least, they would have remembered it this morning—especially after learning of the murder.''

"I reckon that if the cops are doing their job, they'll send somebody around to check on that," said Mr. Clemens. "Or maybe not—Lestrade seems pretty happy with his theory, so maybe he'll let things that might contradict it slide. But even if somebody did see our killer set up a ladder under that window last night, that doesn't help Ed, does it? In fact, it looks even worse for him—who had a better chance to make sure that window was unlocked?''

"I, for one," said Martha. "But I must tell you, this theory is just as farfetched as Mr. Lestrade's. Someone who wanted to murder the doctor would have been better advised to ambush him outside his home."

"That's the most sensible thing anybody's said," said my employer, with a wry expression. "The only problem is, the killer didn't do it the sensible way. If we're going to solve *this* case, we've got to find out what really did happen—and to do that, we've got to eliminate all the loose ends."

"Yes, I can see that," said Martha. "I agree that we ought to speak to the other tenants in the building, and to the neighbors on the back side, just in case one of them noticed a man on a ladder, or anything else that might further our investigation."

"I reckon you're the best one to talk to the others in your building," said Mr. Clemens. "Have you been here long enough to know any of them?"

"I've met a few in passing—coming in and out the door, or on the stairway landings," she replied. "They seem somewhat aloof to me, but that may be simply because I am a foreigner."

"Well, the English aren't the easiest people to get to know," said Mr. Clemens. "But by now, they'll all have heard about the murder. They'll talk to you, if only to pick up whatever gossip they can—they're worse than Americans when it comes to minding their neighbors' business. You can be pretty sure they'll let you in to talk. And they may tell a pretty young lady something they won't tell a police detective—or a white-haired Yankee writer." He paused, then added, "Of course, they're bound to talk all about you after you've gone."

"I long ago gave up caring what people say about me behind my back," said Martha McPhee, tossing her head—very prettily, I thought. "Given the life I have led, I should be extremely unhappy if I allowed gossip to get under my skin. Very well, then, I shall visit the neighbors and ask them if they saw anything unusual, and tell you anything useful I learn. What line of investigation do you plan to follow, Mr. Clemens?"

"First thing we're going to do is go down in that garden and see if there's any marks of a ladder," he said. He pulled out his pocket watch to check the time. "After that, we'll probably have time to visit at least one of the people who were here at the séance last night. Cedric Villiers lives here in Chelsea—I guess we'll look in on him first. Do you have his address?"

"Yes, of course," said Martha. "Let me go to my desk again."

She disappeared into the other room for a moment, and returned with a slip of paper. "Here it is," she said. "As I said, I will keep you informed of anything important I learn. Will you undertake to do the same for me?"

"I don't see why not," said Mr. Clemens. "It's your husband who stands to face a jury if we can't find something to clear him. I don't want to see him hang if he's not the killer. You'll hear from me—or Wentworth—about whatever we learn."

"Thank you, Mr. Clemens," she said, managing a weary smile. "I am glad to have you for an ally. Godspeed."

"Thank you, young lady," said my employer, with a little bow. "I hope you'll pardon my saying that if somebody had told me twenty years ago, I'd be trying to get Slippery Ed McPhee out of jail, I'd have called him a liar to his face."

"We all change, don't we, Mr. Clemens?" said Martha. "If you will only give Edward credit for the same ability to change as you find in yourself, perhaps all of us shall learn something form this sorry episode."

And upon that note, we took our leave of Martha McPhee and went downstairs to look for ladder marks.

13 ~

A t the bottom of the stairs, Mr. Clemens and I looked
for a way into the area behind the McPhees' apartment
building. The corridor had a numbered door on each
side, evidently other apartments. But there was no sign of a
doorway to afford access to the back gardens. "Damn," said
Mr. Clemens. "There's got to be a way out to the back. Our
killer can't have just marched through one of the downstairs
apartments with a ten-foot ladder and a gun. But that looks
like the only way to get there from here."

"This puts an end to the ladder theory," I said. "I didn't
think it was very likely to begin with, though."

"Don't give up too quickly, Wentworth," said my employer. "We haven't even looked to see if there's some easy
way to get to the garden without going through the house.
Let's take a walk around the block and see if there's an alleyway somebody could have walked down without being
noticed."

I saw a flaw in this proposition. "Even if there were, how
would someone get through the streets carrying a long ladder
without anybody seeing him? Surely he'd attract notice, just
as readily as if he came through a downstairs apartment."

"If he were dressed as a workman—a painter, say, or a

chimney sweep—nobody on the street would think twice about it, or even remember it the next day,'' said Mr. Clemens. ''It's not the same as barging through somebody's living room when they know they don't have any work for him to do. But let's not stand here jawing about it—we can settle the question in five minutes' time once we take a look out back. Come on.'' He headed toward the front door, and (having no alternative plan of action) I followed him perforce.

Out on the sidewalk, we looked in both directions. There seemed to be no obvious alleyway leading back between the buildings. ''We'll have to go all the way around the block,'' said Mr. Clemens, squinting in the afternoon sunlight. ''Any guesses which way is better?''

''None at all,'' I said.

''This way, then,'' said Mr. Clemens, and we started off to the left.

The block was on one of the oldest streets in Chelsea. Even so, the houses were cleaner, and surrounded by considerably more greenery and open space, than those in the more central districts of London. So, with the sun having decided to make another uncharacteristic appearance for this time of year, I found myself enjoying our little walk. In fact, when we rounded the corner, we discovered a delightful little park across the street. I must admit I found myself more interested in the trees and shrubbery than in our purpose. Thus, I was caught somewhat off guard when Mr. Clemens stopped in mid-block and said, ''Here's what we've been looking for.''

I turned and found that we were at the entrance of a narrow alleyway between buildings. An unpaved lane lay ahead of us, and, past the shadow of the buildings, I could see the garden walls on either side of it, the brickwork broken at intervals by wooden gates. ''We'll just stroll down here, and see what there is to see,'' said Mr. Clemens, and before I could say anything (not that anything I said was likely to change his mind), he was walking down the alley as nonchalantly as if he were the owner of the property, come to see what his tenants were doing with it.

The garden walls on either side were uniformly six feet high—just tall enough that I would have to stand on tiptoe to see over; my employer, four inches shorter than I, was at an even greater disadvantage. About halfway down the lane, he stopped and craned his neck toward the left side. After jumping up and down a couple of times, trying to see over the wall, he turned to me with a frown and said, "Damnation, all these buildings look the same from the back side. Can you tell which house is the one we're looking for?"

"I'm not certain," I admitted. The buildings on this block had evidently all been erected around the same time, and were very similar in both design and materials. "Do you remember how many doors it was from the corner? We could count buildings and find it that way."

"Seven, if I remember right," he said. "I wasn't paying close attention, though."

"Neither was I," I said. "Shall I go back around front and count, to be certain? It won't do us any good to look in the wrong backyard."

"That'll take too long," said Mr. Clemens. "Tell you what—give me a boost so I can peek over these damn fences. I bet I can figure out which house it is we want, once I can get a good look at 'em all."

"If you say so," I replied. He walked over to the wall, reached up, and put his hands on the top—which, fortunately, had not been covered with broken bottles as was the custom in New Orleans. I bent down and put my hands together to form a step, then lifted him straight up. Despite his being considerably shorter than I, he was by no means an easy burden—clearly, he had never stinted himself at suppertime.

After a few moments' pause—looking up, I could see him swiveling his head from left to right—he said, "As best I can figure, the one just to our right is Miss Martha's. I counted houses, and that's the seventh from the corner. Besides, it looks right."

"Looks right?" I said, lowering him back down. "I thought you said they all looked the same."

"The curtains on the second floor look right," said Mr. Clemens. "And I can see that ledge running under the window," he added. "It's got to be the place."

I stood on tiptoe, trying to verify his information. But the glare from the windows made it hard to see the curtains, and as far as I could tell, all the buildings on that side had the same ledge under the window. I told him as much.

"Well, I think it's the right place," he said, somewhat petulantly. "Let's go see if we can get in that gate."

We walked the short distance to the wall behind the building he had picked out. A green-painted garden gate (or, rather, a rustic wooden door that extended the full height of the wall) stood before us. Mr. Clemens tried to open it, first pushing, then pulling, but without success. "Locked," he said. "Or maybe it's just hooked from the inside. Boost me up again, Wentworth; maybe I can reach the latch and get it open."

Almost involuntarily, I found myself repeating a phrase that I had heard from my lawyer father far too often during my own youth. "That would be trespassing."

"Don't be silly, Wentworth," said Mr. Clemens. "We aren't going to steal anything, or hurt anybody. An innocent man could hang if we miss some important piece of evidence because we were afraid to open a gate. Now give me a boost—or would you rather go over the wall yourself?"

"Oh, very well," I said. But while I understood the need to gather evidence wherever we found it, somehow I felt like a timid young boy mocked by bolder playmates for not joining in their daredevil games. I had not felt like that in a long time. But when Mr. Clemens put his hands atop the gate, and lifted up his left foot, I obediently reached down and gave him a leg up.

After he struggled for a moment, he turned back to me and said, "There's a padlock on it, damn the luck. Let me back down a minute."

Back on the ground, he brushed himself off with his hands, then said, "We'll have to go over the wall. Can you climb it by yourself after you help me get in?"

"I should be able to manage," I said, looking at the obstacle. Nearly even with the top of my head, it would be easy enough for me to get over. Then, after a moment's thought: "But why do both of us have to go in? I could do it more quickly and easily by myself than the two of us can—besides, you're likely to ruin your suit, climbing over garden walls."

"It's too late to worry about that, I reckon," he said, casting a rueful look at his formerly clean pants and overcoat. Despite his brushing, they already showed signs of moss stain and brick dust where his knees and belly had scraped against the wall and gate. Mrs. Clemens would not be happy. "Besides, two pairs of eyes will be better than one—if somebody comes outside and catches you, I'll have a better chance of arguing us out of the pinch than you would alone. I guess I'm ready. Boost me up."

With a little straining and a couple of choice epithets, he was soon straddling the top of the wall, puffing a little bit. "The coast is clear," he said. "Follow me." He beckoned with his arm, then dropped over the other side.

I removed my hat and coat and tossed them over the wall, then pulled myself up and quickly vaulted over. Once inside, I saw a small vegetable plot (now past its season, and grown up in weeds), and two crabapple trees still bearing a handful of late fruit. Mr. Clemens pointed. "Look," he whispered. Following his finger, I spotted a wooden stepladder lying in the weeds along the left-hand wall.

"I don't think that's tall enough to reach the second story," I said. I retrieved my coat and hat.

"It doesn't have to reach the whole way," he argued. "If an agile fellow could get a good grip on that ledge, he could pull himself up to it."

"In the dark, and carrying a gun? I wouldn't want to try it, and I'm in better condition than most," I said, looking at the stretch. I might not be quite in the form I had kept up when playing football at Yale, but I had not slipped far from it.

"Well, maybe you're right," said Mr. Clemens, looking at the ledge again. "Let's take a look below those windows, and see if there are any marks that look like they're from a ladder. That's what we came for, anyhow."

Together we headed toward the building. I was conscious of the dozens of windows, in this and the neighboring buildings, from which we were clearly visible. In a sense, this gave me some encouragement; if the killer climbed a ladder from the garden, as Mr. Clemens postulated, someone might have

seen him despite the darkness and gloomy weather the previous evening. On the other hand, I had a guilty awareness
that anyone looking out one of these windows in the last few
minutes would have seen two men clambering over a wall
into a garden where they clearly did not belong. At any moment, I expected someone to challenge us, and I found myself
trying to decide whether, if caught, it would be wiser to run
away, or to stand my ground and let my employer try his
powers of persuasion.

Mr. Clemens interrupted my train of thought. "Now, which
window would have been the one he used?"

I craned my neck up at the building and pointed. "The
apartment was to the right when we came up the stairs, so
it'd be that one, wouldn't it? The window closer to the center
of the building."

"Yes, that looks about right," he said. He knelt down to
inspect the turf where a ladder would have had to rest to reach
that part of the building, and I bent down to look over his
shoulder.

The ground, though not quite muddy, was still damp, and
soft enough for me to feel it give under my feet as I had leapt
down from the top of the wall. As far as I could see, the
ground bore no impression at all, of a ladder or anything else.
After a brief inspection, Mr. Clemens straightened up and
said, "Well, if anybody used a ladder here, it wasn't last
night. I reckon that finishes that theory—not that I'm all that
sorry to see it exploded."

"Nor am I," I said. "An assassin from outside would be
ten times harder to find than someone from the group at the
sitting. I am just as glad not to have to expand our field of
inquiry to the entire population of London."

"I guess that's a blessing of sorts," said Mr. Clemens. "It
still leaves us trying to figure out how Parkhurst was shot,
and who might have had reason to do it."

"We haven't really looked at that last question at all," I
said. "I haven't any idea at all who his enemies were, if he
had any—I suppose he must have, unless the shooting was a
pure accident, or the murderer meant to kill someone else and
missed his target."

"If that's the case, then the original target is still in danger," said my employer. "We need to visit the other people at that séance—I reckon I can get most of them to talk. Somebody must know who had a grudge against the doctor—somebody besides the one who killed him, that is. I don't expect the murderer to come right out and brag about killing him, the way gunfighters used to in Nevada. London society's not quite as quick to set up a killer as a hero."

"Good Lord, I should hope not," I said. Then I realized that we were still standing under the windows while we talked, in plain view of anyone who happened to look outside. "Don't you think we ought to get away from here before someone notices us?" I said. "We've seen what we came to see."

Mr. Clemens glanced up at the building. "You're right, Wentworth," he said. "We can talk anywhere—let's get back over the wall before somebody calls the cops on us."

We turned and headed for the back of the property, but we had barely covered half the distance when a door behind us opened with a bang, and a gruff voice called out, "Come 'ere, you two! Wot d'ye think ye're doin' in me garden?"

For a fleeting moment, I thought about sprinting to the wall and vaulting over; had I been alone, I would have tried it. But that would have left Mr. Clemens alone to face the consequences of our trespassing. While he could undoubtedly take care of himself, it was not in my nature to abandon him. And so the two of us turned around to confront our accuser.

The man before us was almost a caricature of John Bull: his figure was short and squat, almost square, and his broad face was made even broader by his luxuriant muttonchop whiskers, which set off his clean-shaven chin and bald pate. His waistcoat was open and his shirtsleeves rolled up, as if in preparation for working in the garden—and indeed, he held a large garden fork in both hands. At least, I hoped he had brought it for digging, and not to use on trespassers. It might not be rapier sharp, but it could undoubtedly inflict a nasty wound.

" 'Ello, wot's this?" he said, when he got a look at us. His surprised expression made it clear that he had not expected to find two grown men, one with a full mane of white hair, in his garden. The usual run of trespassers was most likely small boys come to steal his apples. Then his eyes narrowed and he said, "I'd like to know wot you think you're doin' in me garden. A man's 'ome is 'is castle—that's the law. I don't know any honest reason for trespassin', but if you 'ave one you'd best tell me right fast, and if I don't like hit, you'll be talkin' to the constable next thing. There's been enough funny business 'ere already."

"There sure has," said Mr. Clemens, in a calm voice. "In fact, that's what we're here about. Are you the landlord, by any chance?"

"Lord, no!" said the fellow. Evidently deciding that my employer and I posed no immediate threat, he lowered his fork and rested the tines on the ground. "Do I look like a bloomin' duke? I'm the caretaker, and I gets my rent free and the right to plant this 'ere garden."

"Ah, then you're just the man we need to talk to," said my employer. "You know everything that goes on around here, don't you?"

"Aye, that's so. Wot's it to ye, now?"

Mr. Clemens lowered his voice and looked around as if making certain nobody was listening. "Well, then, you must know there was a fellow killed in that upstairs apartment last night. Mister—uh . . ."

"Johnson, Halbert Johnson," said the man, his own voice lowered to match my employer's.

"Well, I'm Sam Clemens, and this is my secretary, Mr. Cabot. We're trying to find out what we can about that murder." He signaled to me to take out my notebook and pencil, which I did, although I suspected he meant it more to impress Johnson than to record anything the fellow said.

"Ah me, wot a dreadful business! But I'm 'ardly surprised, I tell you, guv'nor. There was somethin' wasn't right habout them two Yanks—beggin' yer pardon, I know ye're Hamerican yerself, but I can see ye're a gentleman, and that Mr. McPhee, 'e *isn't*, if you know wot I mean. Wot with all the folk traipsin' in and out of the place it's a wonder somethin' didn't 'appen before."

"We've been keeping our eyes on McPhee for some time now," said Mr. Clemens, nodding. "He's got a reputation back in America, and not one to be proud of. Can you tell us what he's been up to since he moved in?"

"Well, 'e and 'is wife—a pretty little bit, don't know wot she sees in 'im—took the flat it must be six weeks since. Hit'd been hempty some months, and the landlord was pressing me to get hit let, so I didn't hask a lot of questions. Per'aps I should've hasked some more, lookin' back, but I didn't, seein' as 'ow they 'ad a character from a very proper gentleman, Sir Denis DeCoursey. But soon as they was hin, they started 'aving parties o' folk comin' hin and hout, halmost hevery hevenin'. Now, from wot I could see, the visitors wasn't riffraff or lowlifes, so I didn't say nothin', not until the noises began."

"Noises, eh? What kind of noises? You're writing all this down, aren't you, Cabot?"

"Yes, sir," I said, dutifully scribbling down what bits of the conversation I thought significant.

"Ah, the most ghastly stuff," said Johnson, glancing up at the second-story windows of the McPhees' apartment. "There was chains rattlin' and church bells tollin'—me and the missus would 'ear the din downstairs terrible late at night, y'know."

"Yes, that's what we've heard," said Mr. Clemens. "I reckon you asked them to stop making the noises. What answer did McPhee give to that?"

Johnson frowned. "McPhee allowed as 'ow 'e wasn't the one makin' the noises—'e blamed it hall on spirits, 'e did. Now, we'd never 'ad no spirits 'ere before, and I told 'im so to 'is face. 'Tell your spirits we doesn't want 'em 'ere,' I said, and I meant hit, too, guv'nor. But McPhee, 'e said 'e couldn't just horder 'em hout, like guests wot hoverstayed their welcome. 'Well then,' says I, 'wot if I turns you hout? Per'aps the spirits will go with you.' "

"And what did he say to that?"

" 'E said, 'We'll go hif you say so, but wot'll you do hif the spirits don't come with us? My missus says they was 'ere before we came, and she knows. She knows 'ow to make 'em be'ave, too, and I guess *you* don't—you hain't seen the pranks they can play when they gets frisky or hif they don't take a fancy to you. Noises hain't near the worst of hit. This place sat hempty near six months before we come and took hit—hever hask yourself why? Maybe hit was them there spirits.' And 'e 'ad me by the short 'airs, there, 'e did. Better a tenant wot gets halong with the spirits than none at all— not with the landlord comin' by and haskin' why hit hain't been let.''

"So you let him stay," said Mr. Clemens, with a sad but sympathetic expression. "Well, I reckon you didn't have much choice, so I can't blame you. The landlord won't hear anything about it from me, you can be sure. Now, about that business last night—did you see or hear anything unusual yesterday?''

"Not hif you don't call them 'orrible noises hunusual," said Johnson. "I saw McPhee and that Irish fellow wot works for 'im set hout for somewheres, just before teatime.''

"Did you notice when they came back?''

"No, sorry, guv'nor," said Johnson. "It just so 'appened I was on the step when they went out, I never saw 'em return. Then the noises started, the usual time, and hit seemed there was a bit more goin' hup and downstairs than usual. Me an' the missus, we shut our hears and went to bed, and then this morning we learn a gentleman was killed hup there. A sorry thing, says I.''

"How did you hear about the killing?" said Mr. Clemens.

"The constable came by this mornin', after breakfast," Johnson said. " 'E wanted to know hif we'd 'eard or seen anything, same as you gentlemen. We told 'im pretty much wot I've told you. And that's that, pretty much.''

"Well, I reckon we've found what we need to, then," said my employer. "Cabot, can you think of anything I haven't asked Mr. Johnson?''

I studied my notebook a moment, then said, "No, not at the moment. Perhaps we'll think of something when we've talked to some of the other witnesses.''

"Yes, of course," said Mr. Clemens. "Well, Mr. Johnson, we thank you for your cooperation, and we'll be in touch if there's anything else we think you can help us with. Can you get in touch with us if you think of anything you've overlooked? Give him our address, Cabot." I scrawled it on a sheet of notebook paper, tore it out, and gave it to Johnson, who took it and nodded.

"Now, we've got some other people to speak to today," said Mr. Clemens. "If you could let us out the front way . . ."

"Yes, sir," said Johnson, eagerly. He led us through a plainly furnished flat that smelled of boiling cabbage—I caught a quick glimpse of a dowdily dressed middle-aged woman, his wife I guessed—and showed us out at the front of the building. The door closed behind us, and Mr. Clemens and I looked at one another.

"I'll be damned," said my employer, staring back at the building. "I wouldn't have thought we could get away with it. I figured we were in real trouble when that fellow showed up with the pitchfork, but he turned out to be tame enough, didn't he? By the time we finished, I reckon he'd have given us the family jewels, if I'd asked him politely enough."

"Perhaps," I said. "Still, I'm just as glad he didn't call the constable—we'd have been hard-pressed to explain things to him."

"Well, we've bluffed our way out of that pickle," Mr. Clemens said. He brushed his hands together as if washing them, then pointed down the street to our right. "Now, let's go see if we can find Cedric Villiers at home—we've barely started, and there's still a killer to catch."

≈ 14

It was not quite fifteen minutes' walk from the McPhees' flat to Cedric Villiers's home—or it would have been, if I'd been walking it on my own. At Mr. Clemens's leisurely pace, it was closer to half an hour before we found ourselves outside Villiers's picturesque cottage on Godfrey Street, not far from Chelsea Green. Actually, to call it "picturesque" would be an understatement—the entire street was lined with homes that looked as if an artist had designed them. Given what I had seen of Villiers's tastes, this was exactly the kind of neighborhood where I would have expected him to live.

"This looks to be a very pleasant place to live," I said. "Something about it strikes me as particularly English."

"Yes, very clean and well kept up," said Mr. Clemens. Then, after a rueful glance down at his soiled trousers: "Better kept up than I am just this moment, I'm afraid. Maybe I should have gone home and changed clothes. But we're here, so let's see if he's home. Now that we've walked all this way, we shouldn't waste the opportunity."

We opened the little wooden gate in the boxwood hedge that fronted the house, went up a short walk to the front porch, and I rang the bell. After a short interval, the door opened and we found a long-nosed man in a dark old-fashioned suit with a supercilious air peering out at us. "Good day, gentlemen. May I help you?" he said, in a voice that could have been set up as a model of sheer hauteur.

"Yes, tell Mr. Villiers that Samuel L. Clemens would like to see him. I assume he's at home?"

"Perhaps, sir. I shall return directly," said the man. His glance fell upon the smudges on Mr. Clemens's coat and trousers, and his eyebrow rose a barely perceptible fraction. His eye lingered on the dirty clothes just a moment longer than necessary. Then he turned and disappeared within.

"Perhaps?" said Mr. Clemens. "Hell, if somebody who worked for me didn't know whether I was home or not when somebody came looking, I'd send him to have his head examined."

"I think he meant something else," I ventured.

"I know exactly what that long-snooted lackey meant. He meant that he didn't know whether his boss wants to see *me*. That's nothing new—there've been thousands of people who didn't want to see me, and just as many who I felt the same about. But anybody I'm paying to answer my doorbell will have better manners than to turn up his nose at people who come asking to see me. I know a wild-eyed Croatian inventor whose hair goes in all directions and who doesn't give a damn about pressed shirts or polished shoes. If I'd decided not to talk to him because my butler didn't like the way he looked, which he didn't, I'd have missed some of the most amazing stuff I've ever heard. The man's got better ideas than Edison, and I ought to know—I've met Edison, too."

"Sometimes I think you must have met everyone worth knowing," I said.

"I'd be disappointed if that turned out to be true," he said. "It's a big world, with a hell of a lot of people in it I haven't met yet. I'd hate to think that none of 'em are worth getting to know. It would take away half my reason for traveling."

I was not quite certain how to reply to this observation, but was saved having to do so by the return of the butler, who opened the door and said, "Mr. Villiers is at home. If you will please follow me." He accompanied this revelation with the most perfunctory bow imaginable.

Mr. Clemens responded by bending his upper body nearly parallel to the ground, accompanied by a florid gesture. "Lead the way, kind sir," he said. The butler made a yeoman effort not to alter his expression, but even I could see that my employer had nonplussed him. He turned on his heel without a word, and we followed him into the house. A glance at Mr. Clemens showed him doing his best to suppress a mischievous grin.

The butler led us down a short hallway, paneled in dark wood and lit with candles—a curious choice of illumination, I thought. Surely this well-to-do neighborhood had gas, if not electricity, available. What I had seen of London indicated that despite the venerable age of many of its buildings, it had adopted most of the modern conveniences to be found in the larger, younger cities of America. The hallway was lined with oil paintings, mostly portraits of gentlemen and ladies in the costume of a considerably earlier time, but we moved along far too rapidly to admit close inspection of them.

"In here, sir," said the butler, stopping outside a doorway leading off the right side of the hallway and gesturing toward the entrance. Mr. Clemens led the way in, and I followed. This room was also dark-paneled, with thick velvet curtains over the windows and numerous candles burning in tarnished brass sconces around the room. (Bright as it was outside, I would have thought the sunlight would have been welcome, if only to reduce the expenditure for candles.) A thick Persian carpet covered the floor. At a large table, piled high with books, sat Villiers, a large leather-bound folio printed in a black-letter typeface open in front of him. Two large and very ornate silver candelabra sat on either side of him, and a crystal decanter—containing tawny port, to judge by the color—occupied a tray on a side table. The tray also held goblets, of a style matching the decanter.

Villiers looked up as we entered, and rose to his feet, a thin smile on his lips. He wore a dark crimson satin jacket, the color almost matching the curtains and rug. "Mr. Clemens—what an outstanding pleasure to have you as a visitor. As perhaps you have felt, my home is devoted to works of the creative spirit. A visit from another man of genius is always an occasion to be celebrated.'' If he noted my presence, he did not consider it worth comment.

My employer bowed again, this time less ostentatiously than when he made his mock bow to the butler. "I don't know I'd call myself a genius, but I reckon it would be rude to contradict a man in his own home, especially when he's trying to throw a compliment in my direction. So I thank you, Mr. Villiers. I hope we haven't come at too inconvenient a time."

"Not in the least, Mr. Clemens," said Villiers. He gestured toward the book open before him. "You found me leafing though Sir Thomas Browne's *Vulgar Errors*—a volume I always find highly amusing, though perhaps I read it differently to most people nowadays. I find myself thinking that the title reflects as much on its author as on the ostensible subjects. Still, it remains an inspiration for my artistic endeavors. I wonder if you know it."

"Mostly by reputation," said Mr. Clemens (which was more than I could say). "Old Dr. Browne wouldn't believe anything he hadn't seen with his own eyes, if what I've heard is right. I guess we'd have found a few things to laugh about together, if he'd been born a couple of hundred years later. But I've never bothered to go dig up his book—I can usually find a month's supply of moonshine without going that far out of my way."

Villiers responded with a smile. "Yes, the fools are always with us, are they not?" he said. "But I am neglecting my duty as a host, Mr. Clemens—I hope you will join me in a glass of this excellent port."

"Yes, indeed," said my employer. "Cabot and I have been running all over town on one errand or another. I'm sure a taste would do both of us considerable good."

Villiers showed us to chairs, then filled three glasses and passed them around. I am not ordinarily fond of sweet wines, but the effects of this port on my nose and palate made me think I might acquire the taste. Mr. Clemens and I murmured appreciative words, and then my employer said, "You can probably guess what brings us here."

"Yes, I should think so," said Villiers, steepling his fingertips. "That unpleasant business last night, isn't it? It's a bit of a novelty to have a man shot dead five feet from me. But I suppose the police will sort it all out."

"Well, I guess they will eventually, but it looks as if they've started on the wrong foot," said Mr. Clemens. "I don't think Ed McPhee knows as much about it as I do, and that's precious little. I've told Mrs. McPhee that we'd see if we can find some way to spring her husband out of jail, so I'm talking to the others who were there to see if I get to the truth."

"Of course," said Villiers. "Mr. McPhee seems a bit of a crude chap, but I don't make him out to be a killer. Now, that Irish fellow who ran away may be another story."

"Maybe he is," said Mr. Clemens. He swirled the wine in his glass, then looked up at Villiers and asked, "What reason do you think he might have had to shoot the doctor?"

"There's the rub, isn't it?" said Villiers. "At a guess, he was taking revenge for some old insult. The Irish are hot-tempered, you know."

"That makes as much sense as anything," said Mr. Clemens, nodding. "You don't have any idea what that old insult could be, do you?"

"Nothing really," said Villiers, rubbing his chin. "I don't believe I've ever exchanged two consecutive sentences with the Irishman, so anything I ventured would be speculation. For all I know, he was a hired assassin."

"Well, that's as good as any other theory we've got so far," said Mr. Clemens. "Who do you think might have had enough of a grudge against the doctor to pay someone to kill him?"

"Enough to have him shot? Hard to say." Villiers put his fingertips to his chin. "Everyone has enemies, of course, and Parkhurst was no saint. Rumor has it that he kept a mistress—I'd look into that, if I were you."

"You wouldn't know her name, or anything about her, would you?" Mr. Clemens motioned to me to take out my notebook.

"Sorry, no," said Villiers. "Rumor is all I know, there. I'd ask his partner, Dr. Ashe—he'd be a good man to talk to, in any case. Talk to Parkhurst's son, too—Tony's said to be rather a profligate. I'd imagine he's the one with the most to gain from Parkhurst's death, if he owes as much money as everyone alleges.''

"Good, we'll do just that," said my employer. "But you haven't mentioned anyone who was there last night. What about them? Did any of them have reason to do him in?''

Villiers took a sip of his port, then set the glass back down. "I dare say Cornelia—Mrs. Parkhurst—had reason, if she'd learnt he had a mistress. I don't know that she had, of course. Hardly the question one asks a lady in casual conversation, is it?''

Mr. Clemens took a sip of his own port, then said, "I guess not. I reckon Scotland Yard will ask it, though. How well did you know the doctor and his wife, by the way? Mrs. McPhee said you and she were members of some spiritualist group.''

"I was Dr. Parkhurst's patient, not quite four years since," said Villiers, looking intently at my employer. "I met Cornelia more recently—late last year, when the Spiritualist Society began. At first I didn't realize who she was—he never came to meetings with her, and of course she hadn't been in his offices when I went there.''

"What were you seeing the doctor for?" asked Mr. Clemens. "He was a surgeon, wasn't he?''

"Yes; but he saw all sorts of patients," said Villiers. "It was the winter after I first came to town. Three or four of us were going to the opera, and getting out of the cab, my foot lit on a patch of ice. I took a nasty fall. It turned out I'd cracked my collarbone. Being new in town, I hadn't a doctor of my own—I came here straight out of university, you see. One of my friends recommended Parkhurst, and there you have it.''

"Had you seen him since?''

"Not at all regularly," Villiers said, wrinkling his nose. "I don't much like the smell of doctors' offices, and Parkhurst was not at all my notion of company. If his wife hadn't brought him along last night, I doubt I'd have seen him until the next time I needed his services.''

"What was your relationship to Mrs. Parkhurst?" asked

Mr. Clemens. "You were both members of the Spiritualist Society, you say. Did you just see each other at meetings, or were you closer than that?"

Villiers laughed—a harsh bark of a laugh that startled me. "I see what you're trying to get at, Clemens," he said, with a grimace. "I should tell you to mind your own business—but I have nothing to hide. If you really want the truth, Cornelia is rather too unimaginative and stiff to much interest me. Even if I were attracted to older women—married women at that—I promise you she would not be my sort."

"Sorry, I didn't mean to malign your taste," said Mr. Clemens. "Was there anyone else at the table last night you think might have had a reason to shoot the doctor, or to hire someone to shoot him for them?"

"Oh, indubitably," said Villiers, toying with his wineglass. Then, after a pause, he continued: "I'll wager Sir Denis was just practicing his marksmanship—though I fear he must have missed, and been ashamed to admit it, poor old duffer. Or perhaps it was your man here, Mr. Clemens—pray tell, my good fellow, what reason did you have for potting the doctor? Or did someone hire you to do it?"

Mr. Clemens gave a short laugh. "Well, I reckon I can tell when a man's done all the talking he's interested in doing. I'm sure those Scotland Yard boys will be by sooner or later to ask you a lot of the same questions, so you might as well be grateful for the chance to practice your answers. One more thing, and then we'll leave you alone."

My employer reached into his breast pocket and retrieved a folded piece of paper, which he handed to Villiers. "We're trying to make a chart of where everybody sat last night," he said. "Do you see any mistakes?"

Villiers unfolded the paper and peered intently at it for a moment, then shook his head and returned it to Mr. Clemens. "I think not," he said. "Unless someone changed seats in the dark, it's correct."

"Hell, I never thought of that," said Mr. Clemens, frowning. "Was everybody in the same place when the lights came back on?"

"The people on either side would have known if someone

had moved,'' I objected. ''We were all holding hands, re-member?'' Then I looked over to see Villiers smirking at us.

Mr. Clemens saw it, too. ''Never mind, Wentworth,'' he said, standing up. ''We've gotten what we came for, for to-day.'' He turned to Villiers and said, ''Thanks for the port, and for the tips about the doctor's mistress—and his son. We may come see you again, if we think of anything else you might tell us.''

''I shall tell Cathers to remember you,'' said Villiers. ''Good afternoon, sir.'' He touched a small bell on the table to his right, then, without standing, he extended his hand to Mr. Clemens, who shook it. He did not offer to shake my hand, and I was just as glad that the butler made his appear-ance and led us back out before the awkward moment grew too long.

Out on the street, Mr. Clemens looked back at the house and said, ''Well, that was a useful interview.''

''I can't really agree with you,'' I said. ''I don't believe a single word the fellow said. I doubt the son or mistress are worth talking to, either—they weren't even there, so how could they have killed him?''

''Maybe they were in cahoots with the one who did kill him,'' said Mr. Clemens. ''We can't leave them out of this, just yet. And we can't make too much of Villiers's evasions. Even the innocent ones are likely to have something to hide, something they're afraid makes them look guilty, and so they'll lie to protect themselves.''

''Villiers certainly appeared to be hiding something,'' I said. ''And at the end, he was most uncooperative. I wouldn't be surprised if he turned out to be the killer.''

''Sure, he's as good a possibility as any,'' said Mr. Clem-ens. We had begun walking at his usual leisurely pace back toward Tedworth Square, where my employer's family—and our dinner—were awaiting us. ''But I can't say I'm surprised that he got tired of playing along with us. Hell, there's no law saying he's even got to let us in the door, let alone give us straight answers. Not to mention the drinks.''

''But if we know everyone is going to lie about themselves,

how will we ever get to the bottom of this case?'' I wanted to know.

"Because they're likely to tell the truth *about each other,* which they'll do just out of sheer ornery human nature. And since we aren't the cops, they won't be as much on their guard. That's our main advantage, the way I see it. At the end, we take what they tell us, and compare it with the others' stories, and see what shakes out.''

I had no answer to that, and so we made our way in silence along the pleasant streets of Chelsea. At Tedworth Square, we were greeted by the aroma of roasting chicken, and that was enough to make me forget the day's frustrations for a while.

After dinner, Mr. Clemens asked his wife and his oldest daughter Susy to join us in his office. When we were all seated, he took out the diagram he'd drawn of the séance table and laid it out in front of them. "Here, both of you look at this and tell me whether I've got everything right. I'd like to be absolutely certain where everybody sat when the shooting took place. I especially need to know where the doctor was, so I can figure which way he fell when the shot was fired— which might tell us where the shooter had to be standing. The shot would have knocked him backward, you know.''

"You have everyone placed correctly,'' said Mrs. Clemens, after examining the diagram. "I have no doubts about it.'' Susy, looking over her mother's shoulder, added her agreement.

"Hmm,'' said my employer, pointing at the diagram. "I hate to say this, Wentworth, but my idea about the killer coming in the window is starting to look better again. The doctor's body fell to the right of his chair, which means he could have been shot from over in this corner.''

"That would make sense,'' said Susy. "But it doesn't mean the shooter had to be all the way back there. Anybody on this side of the room could have done it.''

"Meaning about half the people in the room, not including us,'' said Mr. Clemens, frowning. "Assuming nobody got up and moved in the dark, and that nobody came in without our knowing about it. That's a lot of assuming, if you ask me."

"Yes, Daddy, but if everything else is impossible, then what's left must be true," said Susy.

"You've been reading about Sherlock Holmes, haven't you?" said Mr. Clemens. His frown was deeper.

"Yes, of course," said Susy, straightening her back and raising her chin. "What difference does that make? I know you don't think much of those stories, but that doesn't mean it isn't true about eliminating the impossible."

"I never said it wasn't true," said Mr. Clemens, "but it sure ain't all that easy. I'm not impressed by a made-up character solving a case some writer has arranged to make the detective look like a genius when he solves it, and to make everybody else in the story look like an utter fool for missing the plain truth. Real life's a whole different kettle of fish. Real people don't act consistently or play by fair and square rules, and they don't leave around conveniently enigmatic clues that point to the one and only guilty person and to nobody else. Look at this case—we've got next to no clues. What the hell would Sherlock Holmes be doing here?"

"Your language, Youth," Mrs. Clemens admonished. "I'm sure these two young people have heard worse—probably from you, I'm sorry to say—but you shouldn't expose them to it continually. As for your question, I don't know what Sherlock Holmes might do, other than play his violin or light a pipe. Neither of those strikes me as a fruitful course of action. But if I were leading the investigation, I'd attempt to interview the people nearest to the victim when he was shot. That is to say, to Mrs. Boulton and Mrs. Parkhurst. I would be very surprised, in fact, if Inspector Lestrade has not already spoken to them."

Mr. Clemens nodded. "Hmm—you make sense, as always, Livy. Maybe they saw something nobody else saw. I *would* be surprised if Lestrade had talked to them, though. He's fallen in love with the idea that Slippery Ed was in cahoots with the killer, and he's riding it for all it's worth—which ain't much, if you ask me."

"I agree," said Mrs. Clemens. "Mr. McPhee would not be welcome in many polite homes, but that is far from making him a murderer. Well, then, you must make appointments to speak to Mrs. Boulton and Mrs. Parkhurst, tomorrow morning if possible—although we must allow for the possibility that Mrs. Parkhurst will be too distraught to speak to anyone quite yet. Except perhaps for the police—I suppose they will insist on it.''

''Hel—'' Mr. Clemens began, then caught himself *almost* before the entire word came out. His wife's expression remained calm, so he continued without further apology. ''You're right, Livy. Of course, those are two of the most important witnesses, and I meant to speak to them as early as possible—except I forgot to ask Martha McPhee for their addresses. I guess I'll have to send Wentworth back over there to find out where they live.''

''That won't be necessary,'' said his wife, complacently. ''I suggested that we ladies at the séance exchange addresses when we were sequestered immediately after the murder, and everyone agreed. And unless I misremember, several of them even have private telephones! I didn't know exactly how that information would be useful, but I was quite certain it would be.''

''I'll be g—'' Mr. Clemens stopped himself again, then said, ''I'll be grateful if you'd bring me those addresses and telephone numbers, Livy. I don't know what I'd do without you.''

''You'd undoubtedly be in a great deal of trouble without me,'' said his wife, smiling sweetly. ''Luckily for both of us, we are together. I'll be right back with the addresses. And then we shall spend some time with the girls—we've been neglecting them shamefully!'' And she stood and left my employer with his mouth half-open.

He finally recovered himself enough to say, ''Take my advice, Wentworth. Never take a woman for granted. It's the surest way I know of to make a fool of yourself.''

''Yes, sir,'' I said. It seemed the only possible reply. And I was quite certain that trying to expand upon it would get me in more trouble than even Mr. Clemens was capable of wriggling out of.

15 ⌒

The next morning Mr. Clemens went out early to find a telephone, our rented premises not having one installed. The landlady, Mrs. Taurcher, had directed him to a public house three or four blocks away where she thought there might be a phone. But when Mr. Clemens had not returned after nearly an hour, I feared that she had misdirected him. Finally, somewhat after ten o'clock, he returned. Anticipating that being sent on a wild-goose chase might have ignited his temper, I had gone to the office and busied myself with his papers and correspondence. Giving the appearance (at least) of virtuous industry might not entirely deflect his displeasure, but appearing idle was a very likely way to draw it down upon my head.

To my surprise, he was in an ebullient mood when he walked in the office. "Well, Wentworth, finish up what you're doing and grab your coat and hat. We've got a morning appointment up in Bloomsbury, halfway across town, and another after lunch."

"Yes, sir," I said. "Whom are we seeing?"

"Hannah Boulton first; she's the young woman who lost her husband a while back. Then Opheila Donning, Mrs. Parkhurst's sister. Mrs. Parkhurst has a phone, but nobody was answering it, probably on purpose. But if we can convince Miss Donning that what we're doing might help bring the doctor's killer to justice, maybe she'll be able to persuade Mrs. Parkhurst to talk to us." Mr. Clemens made a face, then added, "Assuming she isn't the killer herself, of course."

"Do you really think it likely?" I asked. "It would seem next to impossible for her to have shot the man at such close range, without our hearing the report."

"It keeps coming back to that, doesn't it?" Mr. Clemens said, opening one of his desk drawers and fetching out a fresh pipe to take along. "But there's no getting around it, until we know the real explanation. I'm ready to believe almost any damn thing, Wentworth—short of the spooks deciding to shoot him, that is. That would be one too many even for me."

"I should think so," I said. "I have enough trouble believing in spirits. That they might effect events in our world stretches credibility."

Mr. Clemens laughed. "If you could just learn to say what you mean in plain English, you'd be a wonder, Wentworth. But I'm distracting you. Let me know when you're done with those papers, and I'll go call our driver around."

"I think I can set them aside right now," I said, very truthfully. "We shouldn't keep Mrs. Boulton waiting, should we?"

Mr. Clemens gave me a knowing look. "Of course not. Besides, the papers won't run off while you're off with me, jotting down what pretty young widows say. I'll go call the driver, then." He winked, and headed downstairs.

I did not have the opportunity to reply to him, and perhaps it was just as well. While Mrs. Boulton was certainly very attractive for a woman of nearly forty, I could only assume that Mr. Clemens was making one of his jokes. I neatened up the stacks of papers I had been working on, then hurried to join him downstairs.

Bloomsbury, as it turned out, was in the same quarter of London as the British Museum. So our driver took us, in reverse, along the route I had taken after meeting Mr. and Mrs. McPhee at the museum. Mr. Clemens sat back, evidently lost in thought, and so we passed the journey in silence until the driver pulled his horse up in front of a plain-looking brick house on Gower Street, which is essentially the continuation of Bloomsbury Street to the north of Bedford Square.

At first glance, I thought the neighborhood distinctly unattractive. Although the street itself was wide and the houses appeared to be well kept up, the sameness of the buildings gave the impression of an arbitrarily imposed design—something I more readily might have expected in an American city than in the Old World. But inside Hannah Boulton's house, the climate was entirely different. Her servant ushered us into a sitting room where a warm fire was burning, and the gas was lit, making the room a bright sanctuary against the gloomy day outside.

Mrs. Boulton was dressed in mourning, as she had been on our previous meeting, but even her dark clothes and veil could not detract from the feeling of warmth in her home. She and her late husband had evidently been art collectors, for there were a number of fine modern French paintings and drawings on the walls, as well as several very good English pieces of the school of Rossetti and Holman Hunt.

The impression of aesthetic sensibility carried over to the furniture and general decor of the room. One wall was given over to bookshelves, filled with a bewildering variety of novels, collections of poetry, dissertations on art and architecture, and memoirs both ancient and modern. In another corner of the room was a pianoforte, and a music stand next to it, both bearing numerous sheets of music—evidently this was a home to all the arts. Even the fireplace was faced not with plain brick, as it might have been in America, but with ornamental tiles in light blue and white, like fine china.

Mrs. Boulton offered us tea and a bit of pastry, which we both accepted—I could have done without, but it helped to begin our meeting on a friendly note. We exchanged desultory small talk and admired the paintings—at least, I did, while my employer maintained a diplomatic silence—and she happily babbled on about where she and her late husband had acquired them. After a short interval, the servant arrived with the refreshments. Then, after taking a few sips of the excellent

English tea, Mr. Clemens got down to business.

"I told you on the telephone what this was all about," he began. "I don't think the police have the faintest idea who murdered Dr. Parkhurst—although they *think* they do. If I thought they were right, I'd leave 'em alone—I've got plenty of things more important than trying to teach Scotland Yard its business," he said. "So I hope you'll help me, so I can quit playing detective and get back to what I do best."

"That would appear to be to everyone's benefit," said Mrs. Boulton. "Mark Twain's admirers could hardly be pleased to learn that he is dabbling in police work instead of writing and preparing speeches. And I am certain that Mr. Samuel Clemens would be far happier spending time with his charming wife," she added, smiling.

"You can understand, then, why I want to get this whole mess out of the way," said my employer. "It would be easiest just to let the police do their job."

"Quite so," said Mrs. Boulton, leaning forward to put her hand on his forearm. "In fact, that is exactly the course I would urge upon you, Mr. Clemens. Why dirty your hands with this unpleasantness when there are experts working to find the murderer? I think we all know what Scotland Yard can do, when they set their bloodhounds on a trail—and Mr. Lestrade is one of their most experienced. I hope you will pardon my saying so, but his chance of finding this criminal is far greater than that of any private individual, especially one unfamiliar with British law or customs."

"In other words, an amateur and an American," said Mr. Clemens, looking her directly in the eyes. "I reckon I'm guilty on both counts, but don't expect me to be ashamed of it. I might have the advantage over Lestrade, if you get right down to it. For one thing, I was *there* when the doctor was shot. I don't care how smart Lestrade is, he didn't see what you and I saw. You were sitting right next to the doctor when it happened, weren't you?"

Mrs. Boulton sat up straight. "Yes, and I devoutly wish I had been elsewhere," she said, with a sideways glance and a shudder. "I don't mean that I would have wanted to miss the séance, and the wonderful opportunity to hear my dear departed husband's voice once again, you understand. I mean only that I wish I hadn't been sitting next to the poor doctor. But there's no changing that now, is there?''

Mr. Clemens's voice was gentler, now. "No, no more than you can change any other terrible thing that's happened. None of us can do that. But there is one thing you *can* do—one thing all of us who were there can do, if we put our minds to it.''

"You say *we,* but I think you really mean *me,* don't you? What are you about to ask me to do, Mr. Clemens?'' Mrs. Boulton looked at him with puzzlement on her face.

"Maybe you can save an innocent man from the gallows,'' said Mr. Clemens. "Lestrade and his boys think Ed McPhee is the guilty party, or at the very least his sidekick. And unless somebody proves they're wrong, they'll hang him, sure as you're born.''

"You need more faith in British justice,'' said Mrs. Boulton. "Mr. McPhee will not go to the gallows if he can prove his innocence in a court of law.'' She paused, a finger at the side of her chin. "And if he cannot prove his innocence, perhaps the world would be a better place without him.''

"We see it differently back home,'' I pointed out. "A man is not guilty until proven so.''

"At least, not a respectable-looking white man who can afford a good lawyer,'' said Mr. Clemens. "The rest take their chances. Now, Ed McPhee is a humbug and a swindler—and if Lestrade hasn't learned that, he will soon enough, if he sends a telegram to Pinkerton, or anybody else in America who keeps his eye on shady characters. But I know something Pinkerton doesn't: Ed's not a killer—and the longer Lestrade has his dogs barking up the wrong tree, the easier it will be for the real killer to cover his tracks and get away clean.''

"Mr. Clemens, I am not quite so certain that Chief Inspector Lestrade's men *are* barking up the wrong tree, if I understand your metaphor,'' said Mrs. Boulton, looking somewhat dubious. "But assuming they are, what would you have me do?''

Mr. Clemens tapped his forefinger on the rim of his teacup. "I want you to tell me about last night. When did you first realize something had happened to the doctor?''

Mrs. Boulton lifted her chin and stared into the distance for a moment, then began speaking. "Well, of course, I was very excited when I learned of the sitting. Mrs. McPhee seemed to have such a genuine gift—I cannot remember having seen one so luminous before. Cedric used exactly that word when she first came to the Spiritualist Society—*luminous*. And so I knew I absolutely had to go to the sitting. And of course when I arrived there, I was pleased to find you and your family—it made me think, 'If Mr. Clemens has come here, all the way from America, Mrs. McPhee must be even more gifted than I knew.' ''

Mr. Clemens glowered as he heard these words. "I should have put a gunnysack over my head," he muttered under his breath. "Now everybody in London will think I believe in that claptrap."

Mrs. Boulton glanced at him, but he gestured to her that she should continue, and she did. "Of course, when the lights went out and the spirits began to speak, I was hoping so that poor dear Richard would visit us. That was the real reason I went, you know. It has been so long without him, and I have been so lonely. And then, just as I was beginning to fear that Mrs. McPhee would not be successful, he came to us and spoke! I was thrilled beyond belief, Mr. Clemens. I know now that he is safe on the other side, at the end of all his pain, and that I can hope to rejoin him when my own time comes. He suffered so very much, and we had tried so many things—I wanted to take him to Lourdes, but he was too ill to travel, and then . . . then he was called away before we could make the journey. I still believe the waters might have saved him."

"Yes, of course," said Mr. Clemens, though his expression made it clear—to me at least—that his patience was wearing thin with her meandering about the subject. "But what about Dr. Parkhurst?"

Mrs. Boulton shook her head, a sad expression on her face. "Oh, Richard thought Dr. Parkhurst was the only man in London who could save him—the poor dear, if he'd only trusted in spiritual healing as readily as he did in doctors and hospitals, I know he'd be sitting here today. Of course medicine has come a long way, even in our lifetime, but it cannot treat diseases of the soul, can it? I tried to tell him exactly that, but—''

Mr. Clemens looked utterly baffled at this apparent digression until he realized—a moment before I did—what Mrs. Boulton was evidently referring to.

''Pardon me, Mrs. Boulton. I guess I didn't make myself clear,'' he interrupted. ''I didn't know Dr. Parkhurst had treated your husband. I was referring to the other night, when the doctor was shot.''

''Oh, how silly of me,'' said Mrs. Boulton, throwing up her hands. ''Of course you were! And now I've forgotten what I was getting at. What was it you wanted to know about the doctor?''

Mr. Clemens held up a hand. ''Well, first, I'd like to know whether you were satisfied that Dr. Parkhurst did the best he could for your husband.''

Mrs. Boulton sighed. ''Mortal medicine has its limits,'' she said with a resigned expression. ''I doubt whether the finest doctor alive could have done any more for him.''

My employer nodded, then returned to his previous question. ''Since you were sitting next to the doctor at the séance, I wondered if you remembered exactly when you realized something had happened to him. Or did you not notice anything until his wife cried out?''

''Let me think, now,'' said Mrs. Boulton. ''Of course, I was paying attention to what the spirits said rather than the other people at the table. With the room darkened, I only became aware of the others in the room as they spoke.''

She thought for a moment—I realized it was the longest she had kept silent since we had begun questioning her—then answered, ''It was just after your daughter asked the spirits her question about whether she or one of her sisters would marry first. I could tell that it disturbed them—they do not approve of frivolous questions.''

''Meaning any question the medium can't answer,'' Mr. Clemens muttered, loud enough for me to hear it from the neighboring chair.

Mrs. Boulton gave him a questioning glance, but she must

not have heard him clearly. He nodded, and she continued as if nothing had happened. "We were all holding hands, you will recall. And right after her question, the spirits began their rapping and rattling of chains, which of course meant that they were agitated. Right about then, I suddenly felt the doctor squeeze my hand very hard, and then he let go of it entirely. That broke the circle, of course—I was worried that it would break our link to the spirit world, and so I turned my head to look, although really it was too dark to see much of anything, and just at that point Mrs. Parkhurst let out a cry. What happened after that, I think you remember as well as I do."

"I guess so," said Mr. Clemens, rubbing his chin. "I may still have a couple of questions about it before we're done. But first—did you hear anything unusual or unexpected before he let go of your hand? Anything at all?"

Mrs. Boulton's eyebrows arched. "Really, Mr. Clemens," she said, "I am astonished that you need to ask such a question. If you stop a moment to reflect upon that remarkable evening, I think you will agree with me that *everything* we heard was unusual—to the highest degree."

My employer scowled, but then he nodded. "I'll have to grant you that much, even though I doubt much of it had anything to do with spoo—uh, spirits. I'm looking for something more down-to-earth, I guess. Did you see or hear anything that sounded like someone moving around the room, opening a door or window, cocking a gun—anything at all that might let us nail down when and how the murder was committed? Think hard; anything you can remember is likely to be a help—because, frankly, if evidence was gunpowder, I don't have enough right now to blow up a flea's outhouse."

Mrs. Boulton stared at him for a long moment before she burst out laughing. She composed herself and sat up straight, then said with a trace of a smile, "I really should take exception to your figure of speech, Mr. Clemens, but I suppose I have laughed entirely too much to convince you of the sincerity of my protest. So I shall pretend to ignore it."

"Thank you, ma'am," said Mr. Clemens, gravely. "You have my permission to ignore the metaphor, as long as you don't take it as a warrant to ignore the question it was attached to.''

''Oh, by no means,'' said Mrs. Boulton. She set down her empty teacup on the table next to her. ''In fact, I have thought about that very question ever since the . . . *incident*. I fear the answer will disappoint you. Until the moment when I realized the doctor was hurt, I noticed nothing in any way suspicious—and I can say that without qualification. Anyone who studies spiritualism knows that false mediums sometimes impose upon gullible sitters. I had no particular reason to suspect Mrs. McPhee, of course, but I was alert for any deception. If any of the things you suggest had taken place, I am certain I would have noticed it. In fact, I am more certain than ever of Mrs. McPhee's gift.''

''Hmm—that's what I was afraid of,'' said Mr. Clemens, clearly disappointed. ''I went there with plenty of suspicions, myself, but I didn't spot anything fishy before Lestrade uncovered Slippery Ed's bellpulls and peephole. Well, I'm going to talk to the others at the séance if I can, and maybe one of them spotted something that'll give me a clue. One more question, before Cabot and I go on our way. Is there anyone you know of—it doesn't matter whether they were at the séance—who might have wanted to see the doctor dead?''

''I know nothing of his personal affairs,'' said Mrs. Boulton, with a disapproving look. ''We moved in different circles. I knew his wife from the Spiritualist Society, but we had never spoken more than a few words to one another. As far as any enemies he may have made in the course of his practice, I cannot really say. Dr. Parkhurst had a very fine reputation, which is why my husband went to him for help—of course Richard and I knew nothing of medicine, so we could only judge by what we had heard. And, as I said before, the doctor's best was not enough. I am sorry to be so vague on these things, Mr. Clemens.''

''Not at all,'' said my employer, waving his hand. ''It's better to admit you don't know something than to pretend you do. At least I won't go chasing any wild geese on account of something you've told me. Well, then, I reckon you've told us everything you can—unless Cabot can think of anything I've forgotten to ask.''

"Only one thing, really," I said, putting down my notebook. "It's probably not important, but I'm curious to know how you happened to sit next to the doctor, if you weren't acquainted."

There was the briefest hesitation before she said, "Oh, it was entirely accidental. We were all about to sit down, when Cedric motioned to me to sit next to him, and so I did. And by chance, the doctor had chosen the seat on the other side of me. So you see, there was nothing sinister about it. Nothing at all, really."

"I see," I said. "Thank you, Mrs. Boulton, that's what I had guessed, but of course I wouldn't know if it were true unless I asked." I closed my notebook and returned it and the pencil to my breast pocket.

"Of course," she said. She leaned slightly forward and turned to my employer, smiling brightly. "I hope you'll be able to find your answers somewhere, Mr. Clemens. Please feel free to call me on the telephone if you have more questions."

"I'll do just that," he said, rising to his feet. "These modern inconveniences do have their uses sometimes, don't they? Thanks again, and we'll let you know if there's anything else you can help us with. Come along, Cabot—we've got another appointment to get to."

16 ⟋

We stopped for luncheon in a neighborhood public house just off Great Russell Street—I remembered it from my visit to the British Museum. The food was very plain, but filling: I had a large wedge of Cheddar cheese, a thick slice of brown bread, pickled onions, and some unidentifiable relish which (after one taste) I left uneaten. The ale, on the other hand, was rich and foamy, considerably better than what one would find in a local saloon back home. Mr. Clemens grumbled a bit about the undistinguished fare, but I decided that his complaints were strictly pro forma, since he cleaned his plate, including the relish. And he evidently agreed with me on the merits of the ale, quaffing two pints in the course of the meal.

"We're not making much progress, are we?" I said between bites of the sandwich I had made from my bread and cheese. "Unless somebody saw something that neither of us did, we haven't made even the first step toward clearing McPhee. Or proving him guilty, either."

"Well, we've got a few leads to follow," said Mr. Clemens. "I reckon we'll need to talk to Parkhurst's partner, and to his son—and to his wife, if she'll talk to us. The biggest problem is, I've got lectures starting next week, and that'll pretty much put an end to any snooping I can do. Luckily, the first few talks are here in town, so I won't have to give up entirely until we have to go on the road. But unless we're hot on the trail by then, I think we'll have to pack it in.''

"I thought we would learn more from Mrs. Boulton,'' I said. "But for the life of me, I can't think of anything she said that was the least bit helpful. Perhaps something will show up when I go over my notes.''

"I'm amazed you managed to fit them all in that little book of yours,'' said my employer, shaking his head. He took a bite of his cheese, then continued. "I swear, Wentworth, asking that woman a simple question is like asking for a glass of water and getting dunked in the river. You'd almost think she'd done it on purpose. But I guess a young widow must get anxious for people to talk to. Still, I think maybe there are a few leads to follow up in what she said. It's interesting that both Villiers and her husband were Parkhurst's patients. I'd never have guessed that from the way they all acted before the séance started.''

"Yes,'' I said. "You'd have thought they'd never have seen the doctor before that evening.''

"Or that they'd met him and didn't want anything more to do with him,'' said Mr. Clemens. "We'll have to see if he had a record of malpractice or incompetence. Maybe his ex-patients were all itching to pay him back for the way he treated them. And I mean that literally.''

"But we've heard that he was one of the best doctors in London,'' I pointed out. "Cedric Villiers and Mrs. Boulton both told us that he was recommended very highly. That argues against his being incompetent.''

"Recommendations don't mean a man's any good, just that he's popular,'' said Mr. Clemens. He picked up his tankard of ale and drained it. "He could've had a streak of lucky cures when he first set out, or he maybe he was just part of the right social set. The patients that die don't get a chance to run down the doctor's reputation.''

"No, but their families do,'' I argued. "Mrs. Boulton had the chance to damn him as a quack, if she'd wanted to. Perhaps she could have praised him more highly, but she certainly didn't accuse him of killing her husband.''

"Well, we'll try to find out what happened there," said Mr. Clemens. He picked up the napkin and wiped his moustache. "Well, I'm ready to get back on the case—how about you?"

I nodded—my plate was empty, except for the relish, and my tankard was dry. "I'm ready to go," I said.

"Good—let's go see what the doctor's sister-in-law says." He put twelvepence on the table—more than enough for our two meals, and we went out to find our carriage and driver.

Ophelia Donning lived in the Southwark section, which I had not previously seen. We crossed the river on Waterloo Bridge, and soon found ourselves in a somewhat older neighborhood. The streets were narrower than those of the Bloomsbury district we had just left, and the houses not as well kept up.

Miss Donning's home was on a small side street. Like the others on the street, it was clean and neat, although it had been some time since its last coat of paint. An elderly servant, who squinted at us in the afternoon light, opened the door to our knock. "Come hin," she said broadly, "Mistress 'as been hexpectin' you." She led us into the sitting room, where Miss Donning rose to meet us, and sent the servant off to stow away our coats.

As before, I was struck with Miss Donning's aristocratic bearing. Her golden-blonde hair was done up in a knot, without a single strand amiss, and her blue-gray eyes could have been taken from the portrait of a queen—or a general. She was unusually tall, and dressed in impeccable taste—just enough behind the fashion not to seem frivolous, but not dated either.

On the other hand, her house and furnishings suggested that Miss Donning—or her family—had seen more prosperous days. The chair I sat in was a design I had seen in my grandmother's parlor, one of a matched set. While it had undoubtedly been of the best quality in its time, now it showed signs of wear, as did the sofa on which our hostess sat. There were no new pieces in evidence. The room was slightly dim, as well, although the curtains had been opened all the way—perhaps to economize on gas.

After we were seated, Mr. Clemens cleared his throat and began speaking. "I'm glad you were able to see us today," he said. "I guess you have some idea why we're here—"

"Yes," she said, cutting him off with an imperious gesture. She was impressive despite the threadbare furniture and dim lights. "You want to find out who killed my brother-in-law—the swine. Well, I'd like to find the one who did it, too—to congratulate him. Or her, if it turns out that Cornelia summoned up her courage and finally did what she should have done years ago. I doubt it, though—the poor thing was more likely to have taken her own life than his."

Mr. Clemens's eyebrows rose. "You're telling me you were happy to see the doctor dead."

"I'm not the only one, I assure you," she said, with a smile that might have been attractive, had it not been so full of outright malice. "I tell you again that Oliver was a swine. London is a far cleaner place without him. I suppose I ought to tell you I didn't do it myself—not that you'll believe me, in any case. I *would* have done it, if I'd thought I could get away with it. But I must confess, I haven't the courage, any more than Cornelia does."

"You call the doctor a swine," said Mr. Clemens, gravely. "Would you care to explain that?"

"Why not?" she said, with a little laugh and a graceful toss of her head. "You'd learn it from someone else, if not from me. A moment, though." She stood and rang for the servant, then turned back to us. "I'm going to drink a glass of sherry while I talk. Would you gentlemen join me? My recital may take a while."

"Yes, thank you," said Mr. Clemens. I nodded my assent, as well—although I was not quite certain about accepting a drink from this singular woman. I had been in the presence of at least one probable murderess before, and in a voodoo woman's parlor, but never had I felt quite so uncomfortable.

The servant appeared almost at once, bearing a crystal decanter and three small wineglasses—I wondered whether she'd been listening in on us, or whether the sherry was prepared in advance. The glasses were filled, the servant disappeared (leaving the decanter behind), and Miss Donning took a judicious sip. I followed suit; the sherry was a dry and nutty Amontillado, the perfect drink for an autumn afternoon. "Now, where should I begin?" she said, looking at my employer.

"Seems to me you already began," said Mr. Clemens. "I'll ask you one more time. What did the doctor do for you to call him a swine?"

"Ask ten people and you'll get ten different answers," said Miss Donning, gazing coyly at us. It seemed as if, having opened the door a crack, she hesitated to open it the rest of the way.

"I can believe that," said my employer. "It's the usual run of things. But what's *your* answer, Miss Donning?"

Now a more serious look came to her face. "My sister and I are our parents' only children," she said. "Our father was the second son of a gentleman in the country, and so he had only a modest inheritance. Papa had to make his own fortune—which he did, retiring after a successful career in the East India Company. He had saved up a tidy sum, and although our mother died while I was still quite small, we were comfortable growing up. Being young and naive, we expected that our lives would continue to be comfortable."

"Yes, I can see there used to be money in your family," said Mr. Clemens, looking around the room. "And now your share of it's pretty much gone, if I know the signs. Are you telling me the doctor got his mitts on it, somehow?"

"You are perceptive, Mr. Clemens," our hostess said, with an appreciative nod. "Yes, in a nutshell, that is what happened. Oliver was a promising medical student when Cornelia fell head over heels in love with him. I remember him back then—he was handsome, and very persuasive, and he swept her off her feet. I was a very young girl, and I thought he was wonderful, too—little did I know."

"Were you jealous of your sister, for winning him?" Mr. Clemens asked. He was peering at her very intently, now, though she did not seem to notice.

"I suppose I was, in a girlish way. But that soon passed.

What I didn't understand until much later was that he was going to take away not only my sister, but practically everything else that was mine. And once he had that, he had almost no use for me—and even less for poor Cornelia, though she never really understood that.'' She stared into the distance for a moment, then looked down at her wineglass and started, as if noticing it for the first time. She took another sip, and then continued.

"When Oliver finished his medical studies, he needed money to set up in practice. Papa lent it to him—it came out of my dowry, and with my consent. Mother had died of cancer, and we all believed that helping a bright young surgeon to get his start in life was something she would have approved of. Oliver would pay it all back in a few short years, once he was successful. Perhaps he would have, if Papa had lived. But that was not to be.'' She paused again, looking down at the floor. "You see, there were no papers signed, nothing to document the loan—my father trusted Oliver implicitly. He had no way of knowing that, after his death, his beloved son-in-law would represent the loan as an outright gift, and leave me helpless to regain what was mine.''

"Was there anything irregular in your father's death?'' I asked.

"No, nothing,'' she said, with a sad look. "He was going to visit friends in the country, and the coach mired down. The passengers got out to help free it, and the effort burst his heart. He died almost instantly, we were told. Blame it on the bad road, and the bad weather—nothing more. I wish I *could* blame it on something more. It seems unfair.''

"I'm sorry to hear it,'' said Mr. Clemens, speaking very gently. "I lost my own father at a young age, so I know how it must have felt. But you were telling us about the doctor—please go on.''

Miss Donning sat up straight, and nodded. Her voice sounded bitter, now. "Yes, well, Oliver promised to see that I got my share, and to put it directly, his promise was worthless. He and Cornelia bought a fine house, he had fine offices and always the newest surgical equipment, and I got the old home and the hand-me-down furniture and seventy pounds a

year. There was an occasional dinner invitation, or a night a
the theater or the opera if Oliver and Cornelia were gettin
up a party and thought to include me. I suppose many woul
think Oliver had taken quite good care of his poor spinste
sister-in-law.''

"But you don't think so, do you?" said Mr. Clemens. H
stood up and took a few paces, then spun around suddenl
and asked, "There's more to it than just the money, isn'
there?''

Miss Donning lowered her glance again. "You are right
Mr. Clemens,'' she said. She picked up her wineglass an
drained it, then set it down next to the decanter. "Sometime
after my father's death, I understood that I had been cheated
and I confronted Oliver about it. I didn't want Cornelia t
know what I was about, so I went to his offices. I made m
little speech, and he sat there smirking. When I was done, he
suggested that I might *earn* back my dowry. I was a sheltere
young woman, Mr. Clemens, but I knew what he was pro
posing. I left the office in a cold fury, determined to have
nothing more to do with him.''

"I can understand why," I said. "Good Lord, what a mon
ster!''

"Monster indeed," said Mr. Clemens. He walked gently
over to our hostess and refilled her wineglass from the de
canter. "And yet you were with him just the other night
Why?''

"I did not go with him, but with my sister," said Miss
Donning. She picked up the glass and took another sip of the
sherry. "I have only one sister, Mr. Clemens. She may have
been married to an ogre, but she is still my flesh and blood.
And she needed me even more than I did her—after all, she
had to live with the beast for twenty-six years. I don't know
how she dealt with it, Mr. Clemens. If you will recall, Cor
nelia sat between me and him. I did not want to hold his
filthy hand, even in the name of evoking the spirits,''

"I am sorry," said Mr. Clemens. "It must be hard for you
to tell these things to a stranger.''

"I don't really know why I am telling them at all," she

said. "The city is better off with him gone—though I'm not sure my poor sister realizes that yet."

"You said before you didn't think she could have killed her husband," said Mr. Clemens. He sat back down again, but leaned forward as if to hear her better.

"That is my opinion, though she had more reason than anyone," said Miss Donning. "She knew of Oliver's infidelities—I wasn't the only one he approached in that manner, and some were more agreeable than I. She knew, and was powerless to prevent, his cheating me out of my dowry—and out of my chance at a life beyond this wretched house. She saw the beastly way he treated their son—he strapped the boy without mercy for the slightest infringement, real or imagined. Tony was never happier than the day he was sent away to Rugby School, and he was miserable every time he had to return home. "

Mr. Clemens leaned forward and said in a quiet voice, "Do you think the son could have killed him?"

"There were times when he would have, yes," said Miss Donning. "Once at dinner Tony attacked him with his fists. Oliver threw him against the wall and slapped him—and for a brief moment, Tony's eyes were those of a wild animal. They lit on the carving knife, and I knew as well as I know my own name that he was thinking about snatching it up and wielding it against his father. That moment passed—but there must have been many such, and Oliver did nothing to mend the rift between them."

"Do you happen to know where Tony is living now? Is he in London, or within reasonable distance?"

"I believe he is in town at present," said Miss Donning. "He shares apartments with two or three other young men— he moves from time to time, and I can never keep it straight just where he is staying. I will find you the current address before you leave; it is out in Chelsea, I think."

"Chelsea!" I said. "That is where the murder took place."

"That is correct," said Miss Donning, smiling pleasantly at me, as a teacher does at a schoolboy who has just recognized the answer to a simple problem. "I wouldn't attach too much meaning to the fact. After all, you are currently living in Chelsea, are you not? And nobody suspects you of the murder.''

"I reckon we ought to go see him," said Mr. Clemens. "Do you know whether he knew about the séance the other night?"

"Oh, of course," said Miss Donning, still smiling very broadly. "Cornelia made it a special point to invite him; he refused—rather violently, I believe—when he learned that his father would also be attending."

"The young man certainly seems to have had a motive," I noted. "But not being one of the séance party, it seems unlikely he could have shot his father. We've seen how hard it would have been for anyone to enter the room undetected."

"Well, maybe and maybe not," said Mr. Clemens. "Maybe you can help us with that question, Miss Donning. Did you see or hear anything that suggested someone might be in the room—besides those of us at the table, that is?"

"Nothing, really—unless you count the voices we heard. But I believe that Mrs. McPhee is the most likely source of those," said Miss Donning.

"So—you're not quite a true believer, are you?" asked my employer. From his expression, he had already suspected as much.

"Not at all," said our hostess, smiling. Then her expression turned anxious, and she said, "You won't tell Cornelia, will you? She's head over heels in the Spiritualist Society, and I think she'd have given them any money she had if Oliver hadn't stopped it. That may be the only subject on which he and I agreed. In fact, we had an unspoken covenant when we accompanied her to the séance, namely to prevent her from being cheated by those people."

"I see you have a better eye for character than most," said my employer. "I wouldn't trust Ed McPhee to make change from a penny, and I'm afraid his wife is just as crooked—a bit more presentable in good company, though. That séance was probably a hoax from start to finish. But that's off the point. You don't remember anything that suggested an intruder in the room?"

Miss Donning shook her head. "No, but I think a clever

ntruder would have avoided notice. Someone who had read he 'script,' so to speak, would find it rather simple to time is movements so the rapping or rattling of chains would over up the sound.''

Mr. Clemens grinned. "Yes, the noises came at pretty con-enient intervals, didn't they? I wonder if anybody besides 'd and his wife knew the 'script'?''

"Cedric Villiers had been to Mrs. McPhee's séances be-ore, but he's about as dangerous as a butterfly, in my opin-on,'' said Miss Donning.

"Really? He seems to cultivate a sinister air," I said.

"Yes, he dabbles in the occult and the forbidden—it is all he fashion with a certain set,'' she said. "He and poor de-uded Hannah Boulton have made themselves quite a repu-ation in spiritualist circles. It is rumored that they are omewhat more than friends—you notice she sat next to im.''

"She was next to Dr. Parkhurst, as well," said Mr. Clem-ns. "But you don't seem inclined to make anything of that.''

"Poor Hannah *is* rather good-looking," said Miss Don-ing—somewhat reluctantly, I thought. "Oliver usually pre-erred younger girls, though. Villiers's taste apparently runs n the other direction, possibly because some older women re easier to flatter.''

Mr. Clemens drummed his fingers on the chair arm. "Let's et back to Villiers, then. Why don't you think he could have one it?''

"Because he'd want to crow about it," she said acidly. 'He's so vain he'd couldn't bear to waste the effort to do omething at all difficult and then not be able to tell the world ow cleverly he'd done it. And he hasn't said anything, not word. I'd sooner suspect that Irishman who ran away when e saw the police. I would be greatly surprised if he didn't urn out somehow to be implicated in the whole affair. It vould be useful to know where he's vanished to.''

"Yes, that fellow's the missing link in the whole case," aid Mr. Clemens. "But I doubt we're going to see him unless he police bring him in. I'm too old to go looking for somebody who's gone into hiding in a city I don't know—not with a lecture tour starting next week.''

"Too old and too wise, I think," Miss Donning said. She paused, looking intently at my employer, then continued. "Consider what I am about to tell you, Mr. Clemens. Oliver Parkhurst's day is done, and the world is better for it. Had he lived, he would only have injured others. I know for a fact that he often entered the operating room in his cups—I saw him more than once lurch away from the dinner table after downing his two bottles, and go in to the hospital. Hannah Boulton's husband died under his care, and that was not the first patient he lost. Did his efforts hasten their demise? I suppose we shan't ever know. I will say that whoever killed Oliver may have committed murder in the eyes of British justice; but in the eyes of God, he was an avenging angel. Go home and let the police do their work, and go about your business with a clear conscience.''

Mr. Clemens peered at her for a long time before replying. "You know, Miss Donning, a man's conscience is the most unreasonable thing in the world. I've been trying to get mine to shut up for most of my life, and I haven't had a bit of luck at it. Maybe Dr. Parkhurst did deserve to die. But it ain't my place to judge, and I'm just as glad. All I know is that another fellow—a swindler named Ed McPhee—stands accused of killing him. I promised Ed's wife I'd try to find out the truth. Not so much because I believe he's innocent, but because if he *is* innocent, my no-good conscience just won't let me get a good night's sleep unless I try to save him. So maybe I'm not as wise as you think.''

Miss Donning picked up her wineglass again, tapping the fingers of her left hand against the bowl while her right hand grasped the stem. "You are a formidable man, Mr. Clemens," she said at last. "I am glad that I am not the one who killed Oliver, because I think you would not give up until you had found me out. I admire your desire to see justice done, and yet I cannot entirely bring myself to wish you success.''

"Then why did you consent to speak to me? You knew what I was coming here to ask about.''

A thoughtful expression came over her face, and instead of

answering directly, she stood and walked over to the fireplace, looking at the painting hung above it: the portrait of a fair-haired young man dressed in the fashion of an earlier day—her father, perhaps? After a moment, she turned again to face my employer. "You have heard my story—the story of a young woman who has been deprived of justice. And so, I cannot remain silent while another person may be in danger of a miscarriage of justice. I know that my sister did not do this, and I am willing to believe that your swindler Mr. McPhee did not. So it does me no harm to speak, does it? But I think I have said everything I should. Good day, Mr. Clemens. I will remember our meeting a long time."

"As will I, Miss Donning," said my employer, rising to his feet again. "One last request before I leave. Could you try to persuade your sister to see me? I realize that her sudden bereavement must weigh heavy on her, but she may have information nobody else can provide."

"I will ask her, Mr. Clemens, but I can promise nothing," said Miss Donning. "Cornelia answered the police's questions right after Oliver's death, which she could hardly avoid. That ordeal has left her at the end of her strength, and she has gone into seclusion. I hope you will understand if she does not wish to subject herself to questioning by a private person to whom she owes no obligation. As I say, I will ask—but I can promise nothing."

"I appreciate your promising to ask," said Mr. Clemens, with a small bow. "I understand your sister's feelings, and don't wish to make things any harder for her. But do tell her that I think her information could be valuable—and that I will do my best not to add to her distress. Thank you again for you time and your frank answers to my questions. I hope that when this ugly business is done, we can all feel some satisfaction in the outcome."

"I'll drink to that," said Miss Donning, and she drained her glass.

17 ⌒

Dusk was beginning to fall as we left Miss Donning'
house, but at last I felt that light had begun to penetrat
the darkness shrouding the murder of Dr. Oliver Park
hurst. We had a much clearer image of the man—of his vices
his habits, his enemies. The latter were somewhat more nu
merous than we had known before, but it was no longer suc
a mystery why someone would want to kill the doctor. In
deed, I could see possible motives for several of the peopl
who had been present when the shot was fired. Of cours
many details still needed fleshing out, but we were at last o
the path to some sort of answer.

Our driver had not yet appeared with the coach—the ser
vant had sent for him after Mr. Clemens and I were don
interviewing Miss Donning. This part of the city not being a
well lit as those areas we had previously frequented, I foun
myself peering first in one direction, then the other, hopin
to spot our driver. Luckily it was not raining, but the air wa
chilly, and a few wisps of fog were already gathering aroun
the corners of the houses.

At first, I paid no particular notice to a man I'd seen stand
ing across the street, a couple of houses to our left. I though
he was most likely waiting for his own driver to bring 'roun

a coach. I wondered whether our driver and his might be sitting in some warm public house, nursing a mug of ale together, while their masters stood on their doorsteps shivering. But as I glanced his way a second time, I had noticed that he was staring at us. Possibly he recognized my employer, as many people seemed to, wherever we went. Or perhaps seeing strangers in the neighborhood had piqued his curiosity.

Still, I paid him no mind—in my experience, staring back at someone is likely to be taken as rude. By rights, one could argue that the person who begins a staring match is ruder than the one returning the stare. But all too often, the person staring back is likely to be challenged with the ominous phrase "What are *you* looking at?" And after that, things usually deteriorate too rapidly for sorting out just who gave offense.

The third time I glanced his way I realized he was walking toward us. Something in his posture told me he was not merely strolling in our direction. While the light was not quite good enough to make out his features, I could see that he was about middle height, stockily built, and that he was carrying a stout walking stick under his left arm. I touched my employer's elbow and said in a low voice, "I think this fellow's going to be trouble."

"What fellow?" said Mr. Clemens, a bit louder than was comfortable with the stranger bearing down on us. I could now see his face, which was set in a scowl. At a guess, he was somewhat older than I, but still short of thirty. I thought he was dressed rather too well—with a top hat, patent-leather shoes, and fawn-colored spats—to be likely to have robbery in mind, but what else he might be after was anybody's guess. Still not certain what to expect, I took a step forward and interposed myself between the stranger and my employer.

At my motion, he pulled up short and looked me in the eye. I could see his face now; he had a prominent nose and deep-sunken eyes, with pouches underneath that suggested late nights and empty bottles. His chin thrust forward belligerently as he said, "You've no business here. Be gone with you!" His speech was slurred, and I realized that he had been drinking.

Before I could reply, Mr. Clemens spoke. "Well, we sure don't have any more business here, on account of we've finished what we came for. And we'll be gone just as soon as our driver shows up, so you don't have to fret about that, either."

"Think you're smart, do you?" said the fellow. From his accent he was an Englishman, of the educated classes—as his garb had suggested. He brandished his stick menacingly, and took a step toward me.

"I think you should keep your distance," I said. "We're minding our own business here, and you'd be best advised to leave us alone." He wasn't a big fellow, but he would be a real danger to me or to Mr. Clemens, if he began swinging his cane with intent to do harm.

"I've had about enough cheek from you," he bellowed, and rushed me, with the stick raised.

Almost by instinct I found myself ducking under the stick and taking him with a football tackle about the thighs. He let out a loud "Oof!" as he struck the pavement, but he held on to his stick and landed a blow across my back.

My football training did not extend to disarming the opponent, and there was no referee with a whistle to blow the play dead. So I knew I had to get the stick away from him before he could improve his aim, and I reached up blindly with my right hand, hoping to grasp his wrist. He took another wild swing with the stick, landing a glancing blow on my buttocks. I held him tight, thinking that as long as I could keep him down, he would be no threat to Mr. Clemens. Perhaps if I could pin his arms . . . if I could figure out how to do it without exposing myself to a direct blow to the head. I lurched forward, and got my upper body across his chest. I felt the air go out of him then, and it was only a moment more before I had his arms pinned. He tried again to hit me, but now there was no force in it. "Drop the stick," I said.

He cursed me in reply, and tried to wriggle out of my grasp, but I had both the superior position and a weight advantage. I was still trying to decide exactly what I was going to do with those advantages—I had no desire to injure this fellow, but I had no reason to believe he wouldn't renew his attack the minute I let go his arms—when a woman's voice behind me called out shrilly, "Tony! Stop that this instant! Behave yourself!"

It was Miss Donning, I realized as I heard the cane clatter to the ground. I turned my head to see my employer pick it up. "I've got it, Wentworth," Mr. Clemens said. "Let him up and let's find out what's going on here."

"Don't try anything else," I growled, taking my weight off the other fellow's chest. I got to my feet, then reached a hand to help my opponent to a standing position. He looked distinctly winded as he came up, but there was still fire in his eye, and I stood on my guard, ready to deal with any further attack. I sincerely hoped it wouldn't be necessary. It also occurred to me for the first time that the stick might not be his only weapon, and I felt a chill thinking of what I had just risked for my employer's sake.

"Tony, I never thought I'd find you brawling in the streets like a common ruffian," said Miss Donning, who stood beside my employer, a very stern look on her face. From the open doorway to her house I could see the maid peeping out, not making any particular effort to be inconspicuous. There were faces at two of the neighboring houses' windows, as well. And, to complete the scene, our carriage pulled around the corner, just a little too late to be of any help.

"You may call it brawling," said the young man, who I now realized must be Anthony Parkhurst, the murdered doctor's son. "I call it defending my family from police snoops."

"Mr. Clemens has nothing to do with the police," said Miss Donning. "He is an American who happened to be present when your father was killed. Really, Tony, you ought to learn what you are about before you set off on some lunatic escapade."

"Is that true?" said young Parkhurst, turning to Mr. Clemens. "Are you an American?"

"Yes, I am," said Mr. Clemens. "I'm Sam Clemens, and this fellow here with me is my secretary, Wentworth Cabot. We're trying to find out who killed your father"—so he had come to the same conclusion as I had—"and if we can do it without you two starting another rasslin' match, I'd like to talk to you about it. What do you say?''

"Oh, well, if you're not police then that's all right," said Parkhurst, with a shrug. "What do you need to talk about, and why with me? My aunt says you were there, so I guess you know more than I do about the whole business."

"Well, I don't want to talk about anything in the middle of the street with half the neighbors eavesdropping," said my employer, looking around at the nearby houses. "And I've already talked to Miss Donning, so I don't need to take up any more of her time. Do you know anywhere close where we can sit and have a smoke, and maybe a glass of something while we talk quietly? We can ride there unless it's right around the corner." He gestured toward the carriage, which had stopped in front of Miss Donning's home.

"That I do," said the young man, nodding. To hear his slurred speech, I was not surprised. "I'll take you to just the place—it's not ten minutes' drive from here. Aunt 'Phelia, I'll come by after a bit."

"You'll behave yourself, now, Tony," said Miss Donning. "I shall be very cross if I hear of your starting another row."

"Yes, Auntie," said Parkhurst with a sheepish smile. "I'll behave." He turned to Mr. Clemens and me, and gestured toward the carriage. "Shall we go, chaps?"

"Why not?" said Mr. Clemens, and climbed aboard. It occurred to me that young Parkhurst still had not apologized to either of us for his attack, and evidently he did not plan to. I did not relish sharing the carriage with such a thoroughly ill-mannered fellow passenger, but it would not be the least pleasant thing I had done in the line of duty. I waved Anthony Parkhurst aboard, and followed him into the carriage. A few words of directions to the driver, and we were off.

Following Parkhurst's directions, our driver took us to a small, dimly lit tavern not far from the river. The air reeked of stale tobacco smoke and sour beer, even though the place was nearly empty at this time of the afternoon. The bored-looking tavernkeeper took our orders: whisky and soda for Mr. Clemens, sherry for me, and brandy and soda for Parkhurst.

We sat at a table by a little window, where there was at least a little light. That was perhaps a mistake, for when the drinks came it was clear that whoever had washed the glasses had been less than meticulous. I did not find the place at all appealing, and mentally marked it up as another reason to dislike the fellow who had brought us there—not that I had any shortage of reasons for that opinion.

Mr. Clemens took a pair of cigars out of his pocket and offered one to Parkhurst, who took it with a perfunctory nod, as if it were his due. The two smokers took a few moments clipping the ends of the cigars, moistening them, and applying a match—with sips of liquor interspersed with their ritual. I toyed with my glass, not quite thirsty enough to drink from it. When the cigars were lit at last, Mr. Clemens said to Parkhurst, ''Your aunt told you part of the story—we were there when your father was shot. What she didn't tell you is that a man we know from America is being held by the police, and we don't think he did it. So we're trying to find out who did. Do you have any ideas?''

Parkhurst looked from my employer to me, with narrowed eyes, then said, ''Suppose I do. Somebody's just brought me into my inheritance a good ten years before I'd any right to expect it, you know. Why should I turn that fellow over to Jack Ketch? It seems a rotten way to pay back a rather large favor.''

Mr. Clemens shrugged. ''No more rotten than letting a man sit in the jailhouse for no better reason than to make the police look as if they're doing their job. Seems to me that if you let them hang a man who didn't do it, you're as much a killer as the one who shot your father.''

''Well, I didn't do that, at least,'' said Parkhurst. He picked up his glass and knocked back his drink in one gulp, then waggled a finger at the tavernkeeper to bring more before continuing. ''I can't say there weren't times I wished the old man would go ahead and die, but I never had the nerve to try and speed it up. It's not much use to inherit if you've a noose waiting for you.''

''I'm sure the police will ask you this, but I'll ask it anyhow,'' said my employer. ''Where were you the night your father was killed?''

''They asked already, and I told them: I was playing whist with some fellows at my club,'' said Parkhurst, grinning. ''For once, the cards were running my way—I cleared more than ten guineas, believe it or not. If I'd got cards like that every night, I'd had a lot fewer cross words with the old man, you know.''

''I already figured you two weren't best friends,'' said Mr. Clemens. ''Was it just on account of money, or was there other trouble, too?''

The tavernkeeper had delivered Parkhurst's second brandy—his second *here,* at any rate—and he took a sip before answering. ''Oh, we got along as well as you could expect,'' he said. ''The old man was always willing to give out a hiding if he didn't like what I was doing, but that's not so different to public school. In fact, I actually talked him out of it a few times, and I can't say I ever managed that up at Rugby.''

Mr. Clemens shook his head. ''That's not the whole story, is it, Tony? Your aunt said you and the old man fought all the time. Said she'd seen him put you up against the wall and slap you.''

''He did that once when I was a lad, yes,'' said Parkhurst. There was a smoldering light in his eyes; I'd seen something like it before, when he attacked me with his stick. ''If he'd tried it when I was big enough to fight back, I'd have killed him. He knew it, too.''

''And yet you say you didn't kill him.'' Mr. Clemens took a long draw on his cigar, waiting for Tony Parkhurst to answer.

The young man stared at my employer for an uncomfortably long time before looking aside. ''I said I didn't, and I have the witnesses to prove I was where I say,'' he said. Then he added in a sharper tone: ''A gentleman's word would be enough for anyone but a damned Yankee.''

''I don't pretend to be a gentleman except when it's to my advantage,'' said Mr. Clemens. ''But I judge you're telling the truth, as far as it goes. The boys at Scotland Yard can figure out for themselves just what your witnesses are worth. You still haven't answered my other question. Do you have any ideas—no, better yet, do you *know* who killed him?''

"It wasn't I," said Parkhurst, raising his chin slightly. "I doubt it was Mama, or Aunt 'Phelia, either—though Lord knows they both had reason. Who else was there that night?''

"My wife, my daughter, and Cabot here," said Mr. Clemens. "None of us had laid eyes on him before that evening, so we're not on the list. Mrs. McPhee, the medium, and her husband, the man who's in jail. They're not on my list, either—though they are on Scotland Yard's. The widow Boulton, and Cedric Villiers—we've talked to both of them, but they're not ruled out yet. And Sir Denis DeCoursey and his wife. That's the whole crew, unless there was somebody hiding under the table the whole time.''

Parkhurst curled his lip. "I've seen Villiers strutting about with his nose stuck into the air. He fancies he's far more clever than the other chaps about town. I've nothing against a fellow using his brains, but his playing the part of a great genius is very tiresome to watch.''

"A man can think he's smarter than everyone else and still not be a killer," Mr. Clemens said, leaning his elbows on the table and lowering his voice. "Or is there something else we ought to know about Villiers?''

Parkhurst's eyes shifted to one side, and I thought for a moment he was about to make some revelation. Then he shrugged and said in an offhand tone, "Nothing, really. I don't like the rotter, and that's all.''

Mr. Clemens was clearly not convinced, but he simply said, "OK, then, you don't like Villiers. What about the others— any reason to suspect any of them?''

"One thing," said Parkhurst. "When I heard that Sir Denis DeCoursey was in the room, I thought right away, 'He could have done it.' He's the best damned marksman in England, absolute aces. They say his wife's a good shot, too. But if there's a man alive who can pot a chap sitting across a table from him in a dark room, it's Sir Denis. Blind me if I can tell you *why* he'd want to kill my father, mind you—they'd met one another, but they weren't friends or anything.''

"Well, I guess that's worth knowing," said Mr. Clemens, rubbing his chin. "If nothing else pans out, maybe that's the answer. Or maybe he had some reason we just don't know about. We'll have to go talk to him."

"Possibly Sir Denis was acting for some party not present," I said, looking up from my notepad. "Being several miles away, possibly with a number of witnesses, would be an excellent alibi. Can you think of anyone who fits that description?" I had no trouble at all thinking of someone; in fact he was right across the table from me.

Parkhurst didn't rise to the bait, however. He thought for a moment, then said, "The chap who stood to gain the most from the old man's murder is Dr. Ashe, his partner. A sneaky rascal; I think his parents were foreigners. He was jealous of the old man for building up the practice, and I've heard him say he's the better surgeon. He and the old man were arguing, and I don't think they knew I could hear them. Now the practice is all his. He wouldn't have the nerve to pull the trigger himself, of course. But if he could get someone else to do it . . . no, it's impossible."

"What makes you think it's impossible?" asked Mr. Clemens. His eyebrows were raised, and the ash on his cigar looked about to fall on the floor.

"Why, suppose you were a crack shot and someone wanted to hire you to kill a man," said the doctor's son. "You wouldn't hire yourself out to just anyone, now—you'd have to trust the person, wouldn't you? Trust him not to turn you in, or to crack if he were questioned—otherwise, it's no good."

"I guess that makes sense, if you look at it that way," said Mr. Clemens. "And you wouldn't trust Dr. Ashe?"

"No, I wouldn't trust him, and neither would you if you saw him," said Parkhurst, surprisingly earnest. "He's not the right sort at all—a face like a stoat, and greasy little hands. He's bound to lose most of the old man's practice, once they realize they've got to let him touch them while they're asleep, especially with a scalpel in his hands. So you see, he couldn't possibly have done it."

"I'll be dipped in turpentine," said Mr. Clemens, turning

to me with a twinkle in his eye. "Just when I thought I'd heard it all, here's a brand-new one. He couldn't be the murderer because nobody would trust him?"

"Well, of course he could be, if he could have done it himself," said Parkhurst, warming to his subject. "If Ashe had been in the room, they'd be measuring him for a noose this very minute. But he wasn't—and that must mean he's innocent, you see. I doubt there's a killer in all of London who would trust Ashe to hire him."

At that, Mr. Clemens broke out into a loud guffaw, startling the tavernkeeper, who looked over at us with a baleful eye. I myself saw very little humor in the situation. As far as I was concerned, the single most likely suspect so far was the very person whose story Mr. Clemens found so humorous. All that remained was to figure out how he had done it. I found myself trying to do just that—but having nothing I could call success.

18 ⁓

The carriage ride back to Mr. Clemens's house at Tedworth Square was not pleasant. To begin with, I had several aches where Tony Parkhurst's wild blows with his cane had landed on my back and side. I suspected there would be bruises there when I got a chance to inspect my wounds. I had already discovered a large tear in the knee of my trousers, undoubtedly incurred while I was defending Mr. Clemens from the unprovoked attack. But more annoyingly, my employer nonchalantly dismissed my argument that young Parkhurst was almost certainly his father's murderer.

"Oh, he's rotten to the core, no doubt about that," said Mr. Clemens, waving his hand. "I don't have the slightest doubt that he was telling the truth when he suggested that whoever put that bullet in the doctor's head was doing him a favor. But he didn't do it, and I'll tell you why. He's too damned stupid. Hell, I've run across yellow dogs who are a good bit smarter."

"How long has a prodigious intellect been a requirement to becoming a murderer?" I demanded.

"It never has," said my employer, complacently packing his pipe. "If it were, we might have less of 'em—nobody with a lick of sense ever really thinks that murdering some-body will make things better.''

"You're contradicting yourself, now," I said. I rubbed my ribs along the right side, wondering if a soak in a hot tub would do me any good. I would have to get someone to heat up the water for me, since running hot water was apparently still a novelty to the British. "First you say the man's too stupid to have killed his father, then you say a smart man is less likely to kill anyone. Which is it?"

Mr. Clemens looked up from his pipe as if about to object to my quizzing him, but perhaps deciding that my annoyance stemmed more from my pain than from impertinence, he shrugged and said, "Tony's dumb enough to have thought that killing his father would solve his problems, no argument about that. But whoever killed the doctor did some thinking beforehand. That's all the reason I need to take Tony out of the picture; he'd have done it with the fireplace poker or maybe an empty bottle, most likely after emptying the bottle himself. I'd be utterly amazed if he could think ahead as far as supper before he got hungry."

"I think you underestimate him," I said. "All he really needs to be able to do is to hire a competent assassin, and leave the details up to him. It's no more demanding than going to the barber."

"Except an assassin doesn't have a red-and-white-striped pole outside his shop to help you find him," Mr. Clemens said, grinning broadly. "But I see what you're getting at. Well, I still think he's an unlikely suspect, but I promise not to write him off entirely, if that'll make you feel any better. But I reckon a couple of jiggers of whisky and an ice bag would do you even more good."

"I guess you're right," I said. "You didn't tell me when you hired me that this job would involve protecting you from hostile murder suspects. I suppose I should have guessed it, from the rest of what you asked about."

"Oh, you've already gone above and beyond the call of duty," said my employer. "Knocking down an Arkansas bully and fighting a duel in New Orleans are a good bit more than I'd have included in the contract if you'd asked me to write one up.''

"Does that mean I'm entitled to a bonus?" I said, not entirely facetiously.

"Hell, I'll do better than that. You've got a five-dollar-a-week raise, retroactive to when we sailed from New York. Remind me in the morning, and I'll give you the difference to date.'' Mr. Clemens struck a match, lifted his pipe to his mouth, then looked at me and said, "Don't try to tell me you don't deserve it, either. Plenty of people would stand back and solicit three cheers if they saw somebody coming after me with a club. I'd be a fool not to encourage the few people who still see some reason to take my side.''

"I think there are more of those than you give credit," I said, although I was not entirely certain who they were—or even, after my injuries, how solidly I myself was in that camp.

I had intended, once we were back at Tedworth Square, to forget the day's business and the entire murder case, but it was not to be. No sooner had my employer and I come in the front door of the rented house than Mrs. Clemens met us, saying, "That Chief Inspector Lestrade is here from Scotland Yard. He wants to question me and Susy, but I told him he'd have to wait for you to get home.''

"And now I'm here and it's my problem," said Mr. Clemens, shrugging out of his topcoat. "Well, let's get it over. Where is he?''

"Right here," said Lestrade, sticking his head out of the parlor. "I hope you don't intend to stand in the way of Her Majesty's justice.''

"I wouldn't stand in the way of a runaway turtle, right about now," said Mr. Clemens. "I'm about to have a glass of whisky, and my secretary needs one worse than I do. I'm going to offer you one, too, and I won't tell Her Majesty if you take it. What do you say?''

"By the rules I oughtn't touch a drop," said Lestrade. "But there's rules and there's common sense, and I doubt I'll need to subdue any felons in your parlor. Besides, I've got a sober constable along to note down what your ladies say, and he knows how to keep his mouth shut. So I'll take that drink, Mr. Twain.''

"Good, and maybe while you're here we can trade a few choice bits of information,'' said my employer, rubbing his hands.

"That's assuming you've anything worth trading,'' Lestrade shot back. "I doubt you've learned anything my lads can't find out by themselves.''

"Maybe not,'' said Mr. Clemens. "But unless you've changed your tune, you're so convinced that McPhee is your man that you probably haven't even looked at any other suspects. Why, I've talked to three of 'em today, and only one had talked to you—or if the other two had, they were doing a pretty good job of clamming up about it. in fact, I'm surprised to see you here. You've as much as admitted that none of my family is a real suspect. Odds are the doctor was killed by somebody who already knew him. So why are you about to waste your time and breath quizzing a bunch of people who met the poor buzzard less than an hour before he died?''

"Give me that whisky and I'll tell you,'' said Lestrade. "It's been a long day, and that blackguard we've got locked up hasn't said a blessed thing to make it any shorter for us.''

"I told you you should let me talk to him,'' said Mr. Clemens. He led us into the parlor and waved us to seats, then opened the liquor cabinet, talking the whole time. "I'll get more sense out of him in five minutes than your boys will all week, not that it'll be anything much.''

"He's a sly one, sure enough,'' said Lestrade, taking the glass of whisky my employer filled for him. "He's been behind bars more than once, or I don't know the type. Maybe I *will* let you talk to him; he might open up to an old friend— or at least that's what he claims you are. I take it you're of a dissenting opinion on that item. Cheers.'' He took a sip from his whisky and nodded appreciatively.

"I wouldn't lend him train fare to Timbuktu, if it was a nickel for a one-way trip, and no returns allowed,'' said Mr. Clemens, plopping himself down on the sofa.

"Aye, he's the sort would be back the next day asking for more,'' said Lestrade, with a chuckle. "Still, you seem friendly enough to that little wife of his. What were you doing at their place to begin with, if you weren't his friend?''

''I told you that already,'' said my employer. ''My daughter wanted to hear the spooks talk, and my wife thought it was a good idea, and so Cabot and I had to go along to make sure neither of them got swindled. Mrs. McPhee may be prettier and sweeter than her husband, but she's not much more honest.''

''Better not to have gone at all, then,'' said Lestrade. Then his face turned more earnest, as he continued. ''But you know, I've begun to think McPhee might not be our man. If he'd had aught to do with the killing, he'd have been working like a Trojan to convince us he was innocent. And he's not—he just takes it for granted, like. It doesn't occur to him that when all's said and done, we'll do anything but let him go. And until then, he knows how to spend his time in jail. He's already got the other prisoners into card games.''

''I'm not surprised,'' said Mr. Clemens. He took a sip of the whisky. ''Meanwhile the killer's had damn near two days to cover his tracks, or get clean away, if that's what he wanted.''

''Not so!'' Lestrade bristled, but then, evidently recalling whose liquor it was he was drinking, he calmed down. ''This isn't a common street killing, where some drunken ruffian stabs one of his fellows on the spur of the moment and takes to his heels. The whole look of it is different—there was planning went into this, or I'll eat my hat.''

''That seems clear enough,'' I agreed. I was starting to feel somewhat less put-upon, now that I'd had a chance to rest in a soft chair with a glass of something good to drink. ''But have you considered that the murder might have been the work of a hired killer? Let's say it was the doctor's son who wanted to be rid of him . . .''

Mr. Clemens laughed. ''We just tangled with the doctor's son,'' he explained when Lestrade looked puzzled. ''He's a rotten brat, and that's about the best testimonial I can give him. He came after me with a stick, thinking I was one of your men, and Cabot had to knock him down and sit on him until he remembered his manners.''

"I see," said Lestrade, looking at me. "Sergeant Collins questioned him this morning, and said his alibi looked good. Do you think he could have hired his father's killer?"

"Yes," I said.

"No," said Mr. Clemens, practically at the same time. He looked at me, and I glared back at him.

"I can see there's a difference of opinion there," said the Scotland Yard inspector, grinning. "I'll keep that in mind, too." He leaned forward and said in a quieter voice, "Now, here's a tip for you. Terry Mulligan is still missing—that's the Irish knave that came to the door of the place after the murder and ran away when he found the police there. McPhee claims he doesn't know where Mulligan lives, and maybe he's telling the truth for once. Said he used to meet him at a pub not far from his flat, a place called The Painted Woman. Nobody there claimed to know him when one of my lads went in. Maybe you'll have better luck. If you do, I'd appreciate hearing anything you find out."

"Is Mulligan a suspect?" I asked. I remembered the man's running away, but thought it a natural reaction. Anyone who associated with McPhee was likely to have good reason to avoid the police.

"Perhaps," said Lestrade, waving a hand. "Or perhaps a witness—he may have known something he didn't have a chance to tell McPhee, you know. We'll have a better idea when we've questioned him."

"Well, I don't know what we'll find out, but we'll go ask, anyway," said my employer. "Now, unless you've got something else important, why don't we call in the ladies and let you ask your questions. It's getting close to suppertime, and it's chancy trying to get a good meal out of this cook when we sit down at the right time. I'd hate to see what happens when things get thrown off schedule."

"Fine, call in the ladies," said Lestrade. "I'll tell my constable to come in and take notes." He drained his glass, put it on the table, and went to the door to call his man while Mr. Clemens went back to the sewing room to summon his wife and daughter.

.   .   .

"I'm afraid I can't tell you much of what happened between the lights going out and the discovery of the murder," said Mrs. Clemens. She and her daughter sat side by side on the sofa; Mr. Clemens had taken his position behind them, sitting on a windowsill with a refilled whisky glass. I thought he might have taken that position to assure Lestrade that he wasn't prompting his wife and daughter by his gestures or expressions. Of course, anyone who had spent as much time with any of the three as I had—and that was less than a week—would know the absurdity of such a notion. Mrs. Clemens had a mind of her own, as did her daughters, and Mr. Clemens was no more likely to dictate their answers than to order them to fly to the moon.

"Well, tell us what you do remember, before and after the séance as well as during it," said Lestrade, very patiently. "You never know just what might turn out to be important."

Given this opening, Mrs. Clemens embarked on a detailed description of the evening's events. I had not remembered—if, indeed, I had even noticed—what color vest Cedric Villiers had worn, or that Mrs. Parkhurst had worn garnets while her sister wore pearls. On the other hand, I thought I had a more exact recollection of what people (and in this case, the purported spirits) had *said*. I had previously been aware of my own ability to remember in great detail a conversation at which I had been present, but now I was surprised to learn how many details of people's appearance and manner had completely escaped my notice.

But looking at the evening as a whole, her memories of the séance differed from mine primarily in small details. She had recognized the melody the "ghostly" violinist had played—some air by Mendelssohn—and she recalled a scent of fresh flowers in the room at one point, where I had noticed nothing in the way of odors. And she had heard her husband mutter a few things that had not reached my ears, none of which were really germane to Mr. Lestrade's investigation. Lestrade asked her a few specific questions—had she seen or heard anyone moving about the room, had she noticed any sound that might have been the report of a firearm—both of which she answered in the negative. On the whole, it was evident that she had little of substance to add to what I remembered, and what the other witnesses we had interviewed had reported.

Then Inspector Lestrade turned to Susy Clemens, who had sat quietly, but with an interested expression, while her mother had answered his questions. "Now, young miss," he said, "I suppose you saw pretty much the same as your mother . . ."

"You may suppose so," she said, with a severe expression. "You may suppose whatever you wish, but you won't learn much if you've already made up your mind."

"Really, Susy, that's rather impertinent of you," said Mrs. Clemens, but Lestrade raised a hand. Mr. Clemens, for his part, was doing his best to keep from grinning.

"Mrs. Clemens, I've been given worse lectures by my superiors than I'm likely to get from your daughter," the detective said. "Anyhow, she's got the right of it. Any witness might have the one clue that will open up a hard case for us. But I'm wondering"—he turned to face Susy Clemens again—"what exactly prompted you to say that, young miss. Or was it just a general remark?"

Susy Clemens tossed her head scornfully. "You wouldn't be here if you had gotten anywhere with Mr. McPhee, and that means you've had the wrong man in jail all along. But you were so sure the night of the murder that he was your man that you didn't question any of us, when everything was fresh in our minds. Now we've all had two days to talk about the murder, and you'll never know whether I saw something myself or heard Papa mention it at breakfast. The murderer could be anywhere by now—on a boat to America, if he wanted. And it's all because you made up your mind that Mr. McPhee knew the truth, and ignored anything that pointed any other way."

"Perhaps you're right, miss," said Lestrade, doing a good job of keeping his calm. "The fact is, the Detective Branch have our own procedures, and we've a great deal of experience at solving crimes. A good bit more than even the brightest young American lady, I'd think."

"And you're still getting no place at all," said Susy. "Do you want to know what I saw that night?"

"Yes, perhaps I'd better," said Lestrade. "Just tell us what you remember about the séance, in your own words, and I'll stop you if I have questions."

"Oh, what Mother told you will do quite well for what I saw *during* the séance," said Susy, staring directly at the detective. "What you don't seem to be asking about is what happened afterward, between the time we found the doctor dead and the time you arrived. I knew as soon as the lights came up that somebody in that room had to be the murderer, and I made up my mind to pay particular attention to what everyone said and did. That wasn't as easy as I'd have liked, because of course we women were all shooed into the bedroom so we wouldn't have to look at the dead body."

"I had no hand in that," said the Scotland Yard man.

"Oh, I know that," said Susy. "But it did make it very hard for me to watch anyone who wasn't in the bedroom, which meant all the men, of course. Sir Denis came in briefly when Mr. McPhee wanted his wife to come out and talk, and Papa stuck his head in to see how we were doing, but for the most part they stayed out in the other rooms until the police came and sent the rest of them into the bedroom with us. Still, I tried to see if anyone was acting guilty, or not quite the way I'd expect after they'd just had someone killed in front of them."

"Ah, but you can never judge how someone will react to a murder," Lestrade said, in an unctuous voice.

"No, and of course I didn't really know anyone except Mama and Papa, and Mr. Cabot a little bit, so I hadn't very much to judge on. Mrs. Parkhurst did seem genuinely afflicted, and her sister was very solicitous—though I don't think Miss Donning was anywhere near as sorry to see the doctor dead as you might think."

"After talking to her, I'm not surprised," said Mr. Clemens, standing up and moving around the sofa. "She had a long-standing grudge against the doctor, from what she told me and Cabot."

"I can believe that," said Susy. "She seemed . . . not quite *happy* at the doctor's death—perhaps relieved would be the right word. She kept telling her sister everything would be all right now, which seemed not quite the right thing to say.''

"What about the others?'' asked Lestrade.

"As soon as we sat down, Mrs. Boulton started talking like a runaway train,'' said Susy. "I wondered if she was trying to distract Mrs. Parkhurst from what had just happened, or if she's always that way. But she didn't stop talking until the detective arrived. And Lady Alice sat over by the window and took a little book out and began to read. I thought that was a very sensible thing to do, and wished I'd brought along something to read. And Mrs. McPhee seemed almost dazed— it's as if she'd been asleep, *really* asleep the whole time and was just waking up, the way you do in the morning. I think she must have been in a genuine trance during the séance— I don't know how she would have shammed that convincingly.''

"Well, that's all very good,'' said Lestrade, with an indulgent smile. "I'll make certain to keep all that in mind—''

"I'm quite sure you will,'' Susy interrupted, ice in her tone. "But I'm not finished yet.'' Lestrade's smile vanished, and he nodded as she continued. "The men came into the bedroom after the police arrived and began their investigation. But just before they were all herded in, I stepped out into the larger room, just to escape all the crowding. And I noticed that several things had changed from when we were all there.''

"Ah, this promises to be interesting, then,'' said Lestrade. "And what had changed, young lady?''

"There were three large silver candlesticks in the room when we sat down. I thought they were for light, or maybe just for atmosphere, because the gas was lit when we came in. But nobody lit them until after the séance. Then I thought perhaps they were some of the things people brought to try to lure the spirits—remember, Mrs. McPhee asked us to bring something metal. But when I came out and looked around, there were only two of them. I thought at the time one of them must have been taken into the other room, except there were plenty of lamps in that room, too. But I didn't see it on the way out, and I *was* looking for it. Sometime between when the lights went out and the time the police arrived, one candlestick disappeared.''

''Are you certain of that? Might you have counted them wrong?''

Susy drew herself up straight and gave Lestrade a look I would not have wanted turned my way for all the money in England. ''I might miscount the difference between twenty and twenty-one, or even between ten and eleven. I do not think it likely that I would have mistaken two for three. And that was not the only thing different.''

''What else was different?'' asked the detective.

''There had been a book on the windowsill near the table— I had glanced at it when we came in, and saw that it was written by someone named Blavatsky, which I thought was an unusual name. It was missing, too.''

''Why, I saw that book, myself,'' said Mr. Clemens. ''She's one of those silly spiritualists who claims to know the secrets of the universe, but never tells you anything but a pack of lies and moonshine. I saw that book on the table when Wentworth and Sir Denis were moving the poor doctor to the sofa. Can't say I noticed it afterward, though. As for the missing candlestick, if someone brought it, they probably packed it up to take home with them.''

''Nothing else was packed up,'' she insisted. ''And I thought it was very suspicious that the chairs had been rearranged around that table, too.''

''Well, then, Miss Clemens—let's assume you're right,'' said Lestrade, leaning forward. ''Let's say there was a candlestick and a book gone missing, and chairs had been moved all about. What do you think all that means?''

For the first time, Susy looked uncertain of herself. ''Do you know, Mr. Lestrade, I've thought and thought about that. And after two days of asking myself that question, I'm afraid I have to tell you I haven't the faintest notion.''

⤳ 19

Naturally, after the visit from Chief Inspector Lestrade, the only subject the Clemens children wanted to discuss at dinner was the murder investigation. For most of the meal, Susy Clemens was the envy of her younger sisters, both for her lecturing the Scotland Yard detective and for her having noticed the items she claimed were missing or moved from the room where the murder had taken place. Mrs. Clemens tried (without much success, I fear) to steer the conversation to other topics, but inevitably someone would have something more to say about the murder case, and we would be off again.

The stickiest question was, if the various items really had vanished (an issue on which Susy would tolerate no dissent), who had taken them, and why. As one might well imagine, opinions varied wildly—especially among the two younger girls.

"I think Slippery Ed took the candlestick," said little Jean Clemens.

"Hush, child!" said Mrs. Clemens. "You should show more respect for your elders—call him '*Mister* McPhee.'"

Jean would not be dissuaded. "Papa always calls him 'Slippery Ed,' and I heard him say that man would steal the gold out of your teeth if you left your mouth open. So I think he's the one who stole the candlestick.''

Mr. Clemens had suddenly busied himself with carving himself another slice of the roast, and so he missed the look his wife sent in his direction, which managed somehow to combine long suffering and suppressed amusement. "Who wants some more roast beef?'' he said, innocence written on his face.

"I don't think Mr. McPhee stole the candlestick," said Clara Clemens, with the condescension older sisters reserve for younger. "Why would a man steal something from his own living room? Not even Slippery Ed is that stupid.''

"Maybe somebody lent it to him, and it was valuable, so he stole it," shot back Jean.

"I don't think so," said Susy. "He wasn't in the room during the séance, so he couldn't have stolen it then. And then he went with Mr. Cabot to bring back the police. And after that, the police were there. Nobody would steal something while the police were right there watching.''

"If they thought it belonged to him, they wouldn't know he was stealing it," said Jean, sticking to her guns. "After all, it was his place, even if he was renting it.''

"Well, that wouldn't matter once there'd been a murder there," said Mr. Clemens, having decided it was safe to emerge from the shelter of the roast. He put down the knife and fork and took a sip of his wine, then said, "If somebody tries to take something away, the police get very suspicious, because it might be a clue. Ed would surely know that. He's been in trouble with the police enough times to know that.''

"Then if he didn't steal the candlestick, who did?'' asked Jean.

"I think it must have been the murderer," said Clara, between forkfuls of peas and carrots. She put down her fork and added, "A person who would murder someone wouldn't think anything of stealing, too. But I think it's the missing book that's important, not the candlestick.''

"We're talking about somebody who shot a man in a room full of witnesses, without any of us hearing the gun go off,'' said Mr. Clemens. He wiped his moustache with his linen handkerchief, then continued. "I'm a lot more worried about that than sneaking off with a candlestick, or a book, or whatever else might be missing. But I suspect that Susy is overlooking perfectly good explanations for where those things went. They could have been brought to the séance by guests—remember, Mrs. McPhee told us that anyone who wanted to talk to a particular spook should bring something the person had used. The owners probably just took them home afterwards. Or maybe they were just pushed underneath the table, or moved to the other room."

"There was *nothing* under the table," said Susy, but there was a hint of doubt on her face. "I'm certain someone took away the candlestick. But I don't know why any more than you do."

"Don't forget the book!" Clara piped up. "I'll bet it was hollowed out, and the gun was hidden in it. I read a story where they used a hollow book to smuggle a gun into someplace." She smiled at her own cleverness.

Susy looked thoughtful at this suggestion, but then said, "I think the police would have checked for that, if they'd seen someone taking it away. It was a big, thick book . . . ."

"Tell you what," said her father. "Cabot or I will go over to the McPhee apartment sometime in the next couple of days and see if those things are there. Maybe Mrs. McPhee knows what happened to them."

"What if she's the one who took it?" said Clara, a bright look on her face again. "Who would have a better excuse to move something, right in front of the police and everything? She could have just put it in a closet, and nobody would have thought twice about it."

"I don't think she had the opportunity," said Susy. "She was in the bedroom with us the whole time until the police arrived, and after that they'd have been watching her."

"I bet it was the murderer," said Jean, waving her dessert spoon to emphasize the point. "He shot the doctor, and then he stole the candlestick!"

"Put your spoon down, young lady," said Mrs. Clemens. "We don't wave our silverware about."

"Papa does it all the time," said Jean, frowning. I could

see that this line of argument was a time-tested defense for such behavior. "Especially when he's acting like a bad, spitting gray kitten!" I had already heard the young ladies tease their father with this description when he got excited or lost his temper.

"Your papa should know better, and you certainly do," Mrs. Clemens said. "All this talk of murder has evidently gotten you too excited, if you forget your manners so easily. If you cannot save that spoon for its proper use, I shall tell Cook not to give you any pudding." This warning had the desired effect, and the spoon was returned to its proper place. And having finally gained control of the conversation, Mrs. Clemens turned it to subjects of her own choosing for the duration of the meal.

After dinner, Mr. Clemens smoked a cigar and enjoyed an evening of music with the family. Clara was an excellent pianist, and entertained her parents with a variety of pieces until little Jean's bedtime. I heard snatches of Brahms and Stephen Foster from upstairs, where I had retired to rest my weary limbs, and to inspect my bruises. At least, I had escaped broken bones or more serious injury—no thanks to Tony Parkhurst's cane. But my predinner drink, and a couple of glasses of wine with the meal, had at least dulled my awareness of my aching back and ribs. I was lying on my bed thinking about having Cook heat up some water so I could soak in a tub and retire early when my employer tapped on my bedroom door.

"Sorry to rouse you up again, Wentworth," he said, opening the door and peering in at me. "But I thought this would be a good time to go visit that place Lestrade told us about—you know, the pub where McPhee's Irish assistant used to wet his whistle. I'd like somebody with me if I'm going to walk into a rough workingmen's bar, preferably a big football player. I know you've taken your lumps already today, but do you think you could manage to get back on your feet for one more round?"

"You make it sound like a prizefight," I said. "I hope that's a figure of speech." He simply grinned, so I pulled

myself to my feet, with a deep sigh, and quickly girded my
loins to go back out on the town.

The place Lestrade had mentioned was within easy walking
distance, but in deference to my bruises, we took the carriage.
Not all the way: as Mr. Clemens pointed out, our clothes and
American accents were likely enough to make us conspicuous. Not wanting to emphasize that by pulling up in front of
it in even his modest rented rig, he had our driver drop us
off at the nearest corner, rather than directly in front.

Our destination, when we found it, was a shabby building
near the river. The street was not quite as brightly lit as other
parts of London I had seen, and there was a briny smell in
the neighborhood, reminiscent of a pickle barrel. The Painted
Lady's signboard was chipped and faded, hard to read with
the gas lamp all the way across the street. Below it was a
dilapidated flight of stairs leading to a stout wooden door. We
were the only ones on the street, but when we opened the
door we found a room full of smoke, noise, and brawny workingmen holding tankards of ale.

Every eye turned to inspect us, and there was a distinct
pause in the conversation—exposing the wheezing sound of
a concertina and an off-key tenor voice singing some oddly
familiar air whose words were lost in an accent too thick to
penetrate—then the denizens of the little pub gave a collective
shrug and returned to their amusements. Still, there was a chill
in the air around us as we made our way to the bar and leaned
against it, waiting for the tavernkeeper's attention. We were
by a considerable margin the best-dressed men in the place,
and both of us had decided to dress down for our foray into
Terry Mulligan's native habitat.

Finally the tavernkeeper—a broad-beamed fellow with
round spectacles and a waxed moustache—sidled over to us.
He looked us up and down, then said, "You gents might be
'appier in the Royal Harms, two streets over. This 'ere's just
a workman's pub, nothin' posh to hit. Gets a mite rough
sometimes, hit does." A big man next to Mr. Clemens nodded, scowling the whole time.

"We don't mind rough," said Mr. Clemens. "In fact,
we're here because we hear tell this is the right place to find

somebody that don't mind a little rough work. But I reckon the first thing we want is a couple of pints of your best bitter, if you don't mind drawing 'em for us.'' He slapped a pound note on the counter and waited.

The tavernkeeper stared at the bill as if it might be a ransom note—evidently folding money was not common hereabouts—but then he picked it up and went to draw the drinks. While he worked the taps, Mr. Clemens turned to inspect the crowd, leaning his elbows back on the bar. There were a few of the locals still eyeing us suspiciously—we were probably the only visitors the place had seen in weeks, other than the deliveryman for the brewery. Those who hadn't overheard my employer's Missouri twang were probably wondering if he was a plainclothes policeman, and what they had done to make themselves the object of his attention.

The tavernkeeper set the two pints to the side to let the foam settle, and came back over to our side of the bar; the scowling fellow had signaled him. The two leaned close together and whispered. The noise covered most of what they said, but the phrase ''bloody Yanks'' came through clearly enough. That, combined with the hostile glances the customer sent our way, was sufficient to convey the general tenor of their discourse. I remembered that Lestrade hadn't wanted to send his men in here, and I wondered how wise we were to enter someplace the police did not care to visit. I doubted whether any information we might find here was worth having to fight our way out of the place—a prospect Mr. Clemens seemed not to have taken into account.

Indeed, Mr. Clemens was scanning the room as nonchalantly as he might have an elegant parlor full of tea-drinking literary ladies. Most of the customers had gone back to whatever had occupied them before our entrance—a group was gathered around the concertina, others were playing cards or checkers, and many were simply talking, no doubt on very much the same subjects that would interest their peers in New York (or Singapore, for that matter). It would have seemed a perfectly ordinary place, except for the evident antipathy its regular denizens had for strangers.

Mr. Clemens broke my train of thought by nudging me and

saying quietly, "I don't think Mulligan's here, but maybe I don't remember him well enough to recognize him. Take a look and see if you spot him."

A quick look around revealed nobody resembling Mulligan, but the dim light and thick smoke and the fact that many of the men had their backs toward us made it difficult to say definitively whether he was here. "I don't see him," I said. "I wouldn't put a lot of faith in that, though. I'd have a better chance of recognizing him in daylight."

"Maybe we can just walk casually around the room and see if we spot him," said Mr. Clemens.

"Oh, I can see very well from here," I said, not wanting to encourage him in this idea. Standing by the bar, our intrusion was easily overlooked; walking around obviously looking for someone was likely to draw attention from someone hostile to strangers. I added, "Besides, I don't think he'd drink in one of his known haunts if he knew the police were after him, do you?"

"Don't be so sure of that," said Mr. Clemens. "If he gets thirsty enough, he might decide this is safer than someplace he doesn't usually go to. Here, at least, he knows there won't be many strangers." He craned his neck, peering here and there.

"Let's not make ourselves conspicuous," I said. "I'm beginning to think we shouldn't have come here."

"Hell, I've been in plenty of worse places," Mr. Clemens began. "When I was your age—"

Whatever he was about to say was interrupted by the arrival of the tavernkeeper with our pints, which he had topped off now that the foam had dissipated. " 'Ere's your pints," he hissed, shoving them across the counter at us abruptly enough to slosh some of the contents out of the glasses. "Hi'd had-vise you drink right up and be hon your way. We don't want no trouble 'ere."

Mr. Clemens picked up his glass and leaned forward. "We don't want trouble anywhere, but sometimes you get it when you don't want it." He took a sip, then added in a lower voice, "A friend of ours is in jail right now for something he didn't do. There's a man who comes in here sometimes who might be able to help us get him out.''

''Well, hif 'e drinks hin 'ere, 'e's no bloomin' barrister,'' the tavernkeeper said, his expression skeptical. ''What did ye say this bloke's name was, guv'nor?''

''I didn't yet, because the wrong people might hear it,'' said Mr. Clemens, lowering his voice to a barely audible growl. ''Scotland Yard's looking for him, and for all I know they've got half a dozen lousy snoops in here right now. Can you vouch for everybody in the place?''

The tavernkeeper narrowed his eyes and shifted them from one side to another, taking in the entire room in a single sweep. Then he shook his head. ''Not a soul 'ere but the reg'lars. Hi know the lot of 'em. Hexcept you and your fellow, 'ere.''

''That don't mean one of them won't go sell the cops every word he overhears,'' said Mr. Clemens. He had stuck a cigar in his mouth and was mumbling around it. It gave him an air of conspiracy, and I realized that he had somehow managed to make himself seem every bit as disreputable as the rest of the denizens of The Painted Lady. ''I reckon that's how they caught this fellow we know—he came in here a couple of times, I hear tell. Curly-headed fellow, wears a big hat and puffs up like a banty rooster. *McPhee's the name, Ed McPhee.*''

''Aye, that's the bloke to a tee,'' said the tavernkeeper, smiling for the first time at Mr. Clemens's imitation of McPhee's voice and accent. ''Jabbers and japes, just like that, honly louder. 'E's in the clink, you say now, guv'nor?''

''That's right,'' said my employer. He made shushing motions and lowered his voice again. ''Now, Ed came in here looking for somebody to help him with a job he was doing, I guess you know the kind of work I mean.''

''Maybe I does and maybe I doesn't,'' said the tavernkeeper, his face becoming suspicious again. ''Hit ain't wise for a man to blab heverythin' 'e might know.''

''That's the kind of man I thought you were,'' said Mr. Clemens, nodding approvingly. Just then there was an outbreak of raucous laughter from someone in the back of the room. We all peered through the smoke, trying to make out what was so funny, but whatever the reason was, we never learned it. After a moment, Mr. Clemens turned back to the tavernkeeper and continued.

"I like a man who finds out who he's talking to before he says something he might regret," he said. "I'm not here to ask a bunch of questions, anyway. There's just one thing maybe you can help me with. Ed hired a fellow name of Terry Mulligan, and we think Terry can help us get Ed out. Terry's gone into hiding, not that I blame him one bit. Now, I'm not asking you where he is—what I don't know can't hurt anybody. But if you knew somebody that might get the word to Terry that Ed's old pal Sam is looking for him—well, I reckon he can figure out how to find me if he wants to talk."

"Maybe I can do that," said the tavernkeeper. "I don't know if I remember Terry, or 'oo might know 'im."

"This might help you remember," said Mr. Clemens, and he passed a folded banknote to the man. "Just make sure nobody finds out who doesn't need to know."

"I'll think about hit, guv'nor," the barman said, slipping the bill into the pocket of his apron. He glanced around the room again, then said, "Now maybe you hought to drink up 'fore some of the lads get restless. Hif somebody recollects where Terry might be, I'll make sure 'e knows to get the message to 'im."

"Fair enough," said Mr. Clemens, and he handed the man another bill. "This ought to make sure the fellow knows to keep things under his hat." Then he turned to me and added, "Drink up, Cabot, we'll get out of the way so these good folks can drink without worrying about who's watching them."

Off in the darkness I heard a woman squeal, then say, with a giggle, "Keep yer 'ands hoff!" A chorus of male laughter followed her outburst.

"Yes, it's high time we got home," I said, reaching for my ale. I hadn't touched a drop of it, wanting to be ready for whatever might happen. Now I drained it in two drafts, though it was hardly the best quality. Mr. Clemens (who had a bit of a head start on me) finished his at almost the same time. I put my empty tankard on the counter and we turned to leave the disreputable pub.

" 'Ere, ye'll not go hout so heasy,'' said a gruff voice behind me, and a heavy hand fell on my shoulder. With a sigh I stopped and looked back over my shoulder. There stood the large man who had scowled at us while we waited for our drinks. His face was very red, and his shirt and trousers were soiled from whatever work he had done that day—perhaps for the last several days. From the look of his arms, the work involved a good bit of heavy lifting.

I tried to keep my voice calm. "Excuse me, friend, but I have had a long hard day. I think we would both be happier if I went on home and left you with your friends." It was exactly what I felt, and I sincerely hoped it would suffice to get us out of the place without any more trouble.

The fellow was not interested in being conciliated. He began railing at me, working himself up to a fighting furor. He was close enough for me to smell his breath, which reeked of fried fish and more ale than was healthy for him. "Too good for the likes of us, are you? You bloody toffs drinks your pint and shakes the dust hoff your feet, does you? We'll teach you to sneer at the workin' man.'' He cocked a ham-sized fist and took aim at my jaw.

" 'Arry! We'll 'ave none o' that,'' came a cry from somewhere behind him, but it was too late. I ducked under his drunken swing and planted three solid punches to his midsection before he could set himself for another assault. His eyes rolled up into his head and he went down like a rag doll.

I stepped back to give him room, but I could see that he was not about to get up for some time. "I'm sorry,'' I said, as much to the tavernkeeper as to him or to the now silent crowd. I held my hands out to my sides, palms open. "I would have walked away if he'd let me. You saw it. I don't pick fights, but a man has to defend himself.''

"That's hall right, Yank,'' said the tavernkeeper, who had come out to the front of the counter. "You done wot you 'ad to do, and nothin' more. 'Arry won't bother you, and won't nobody else, if they wants anythin' more to drink 'ere. You go your way, and that'll be that.''

I was about to say something more, but Mr. Clemens took my elbow and said, ''You heard the man, Wentworth. Let's get out of here while we still can.''

That seemed the best advice I'd had all day, and so I followed it.

20 ~

"Jesus, Wentworth! I didn't know you had it in you," Mr.
Clemens said for the third time since we had left The
Painted Lady. He looked sideways at me with an expression I could not quite read, though it seemed to contain
a large admixture of surprise. After my one-sided fight with
Harry, the barroom bully in the unsavory tavern, we had hurried away from the place—"That big ox doesn't worry me,
but he just might have friends," my employer had said, and
I needed no urging to put any possible pursuit behind me.
Any friends of Harry might not confine themselves to bare
fists. But we made it home without incident.

Mrs. Clemens and the girls had already retired. I had put
a large kettle of water to heat up on the kitchen stove, to fill
a tub for me to soak my weary and battered limbs before
retiring, but it would be some time before it was warm
enough. For now, we sat in the parlor, sipping Mr. Clemens's
whisky—mine liberally diluted with soda water. We thought
it might still be possible to make some sense of what we had
learned today—and to decide whether any of it pointed to
something useful.

"What do you mean?" I asked. "Are you surprised that I
managed to overcome that bully?"

"Not so much that," said Mr. Clemens. "You're a big man, but I never saw you *acting* like a big man. Until now, every time I saw you use your strength it was to protect me— like this afternoon, when Tony Parkhurst came at us with his cane. He wasn't after you, he was after me, and you just happened to be in the way. But tonight, that drunken igno-ramus wanted to take a bit out of your hide—and you put him on the floor before he could get started. I always won-dered when you would realize you can handle yourself in a fight, and now I've seen it twice in one day. I hope it isn't going to change you from the nice young boy I hired to be my secretary."

"I haven't changed, sir," I said. "To tell the truth, I was worried that the man I fought might come after you if I didn't stop him first. He wasn't looking for a fair fight, you know."

"Nor a clean one, either," he agreed. "You're lucky you downed him before he grabbed a broken bottle, or had one of his chums club you with a chair. And I'd probably have gotten bushwhacked if I'd done anything but watch 'em work you over. So I reckon I owe you my thanks again—that's the second time today. I'd give you a raise, except I already did that."

"I won't be greedy," I said. Then an idea struck me. "Do you think that man's sudden belligerence might have had something to do with your asking for Mulligan? Snooping around, as Tony Parkhurst might have put it?"

"That crossed my mind," said Mr. Clemens, with a nod. "But that Harry was giving us the evil eye before I ever mentioned Mulligan or McPhee. He was mad at us for being prosperous-looking foreigners, that's all. He's no more mixed up in the murder than the Throckmorton brothers."

"Good Lord," I said, remembering McPhee's old Arkan-sas cronies. "I certainly hope he hasn't brought them along with him."

"Coals to Newcastle, as they say over here," said Mr. Clemens. "Not even Ed's fool enough to pay those bullies' way across the ocean when he can go to any corner bar in London and find their like. There's no shortage of illiterate apes ready to do a little rough work, anywhere in the world.

If you're not too picky, you can get a whole crew of 'em for not much more than beer money.''

"That makes sense,'' I agreed. I took a sip of my drink, then said, ''I wish the rest of this case made half as much sense. We've ended today with twice as many suspects as we began with, and we still haven't the foggiest notion of how the doctor was killed.''

"You're coming at it from the wrong angle, Wentworth,'' said Mr. Clemens. He started to take a sip of his drink, then realized that his glass was empty, and made a face. He stood up and went over to the sideboard, where the bottle was sitting, then continued as he poured. ''We started off without any idea who might want to kill the man, or what for. Now we've got a barge load of suspects, most of 'em with first-rate motives. If that ain't progress, I don't know what is.'' He put another two fingers of whisky in his glass, then shot me an inquiring look.

I shook my head, declining the drink, then said, ''I'd be far happier if the killer had murdered the doctor in the middle of a railway station, in front of a thousand witnesses. Or almost anyplace else where you and I didn't have to get mixed up in it. There must be a hundred more convenient places to murder someone.''

"I doubt the doctor would have considered any of 'em convenient,'' said Mr. Clemens. He took a sip of his drink, still standing by the sideboard. ''But you're right, in a way, Wentworth. Whoever did this went to a good bit of trouble. I'd say that's one of our main clues. This murder took too much planning to pull it off. I reckon that's why Lestrade has Ed in the clink—the killer obviously had advance knowledge of how things were supposed to go that night, and Lestrade figures Ed must have tipped him off.''

"In that case, shouldn't he be trying to find out which of the suspects knew McPhee before the séance?''

"Hell, it looks like everybody except the victim knew him—or knew Martha, which amounts to the same thing,'' said my employer. ''You don't think they got that crowd there by putting an advertisement in the newspapers, do you?''

"Tony Parkhurst doesn't seem to have known McPhee,''

I pointed out. "And I'd doubt the victim's partner, Dr. Ashe, did, either—at least, not unless we can find some connection."

"Well, we'll talk to Dr. Ashe," said Mr. Clemens. "We can fish around for that connection then. But I think it's more important to talk to the other people in that room—they're the ones who had the best opportunity to shoot the fellow. And they had the best chance to see or hear whoever did it. I'm especially interested in finding out what Sir Denis De-Coursey has to say."

"Why, I would have thought he and his wife were the least likely suspects of all," I said. I put down my empty glass on the table next to the well-padded armchair I was in. I felt tired enough to fall asleep right where I sat. "Or are you interested in him because he's reputed to be a sharpshooter?"

He walked over to an armchair and perched on the arm, holding his drink, before answering. "Reason enough, don't you think? Tony thought of him right away when he learned he'd been there, and Villiers suggested he might have done it, too—though I doubt he meant it seriously. But I've got a better reason to see him. Back in New Orleans, when we had two people killed by poison, we talked to a woman who knew all about herbs and poisons. Now we've had somebody shot— why don't we talk to a firearms expert? Maybe he can tell us how to shoot a gun and keep it from going *bang*."

"You keep coming back to that," I said, yawning. "But why didn't he offer some explanation at the time? We were all commenting on how we hadn't heard the gunshot. You'd think he'd have said something then."

"We'll ask him that," Mr. Clemens said. "Lestrade's probably not going to ask it, so we get that job. Luckily, my name opens a few doors—even in England."

Another thought crept up from the back of my sleepy mind. "What if Tony Parkhurst's right, and Sir Denis is the murderer?"

He muttered something in reply, but I didn't hear it clearly. In fact, I heard nothing at all until I realized he had his hand on my shoulder and was saying, "Wentworth? Are you awake?"

"I suppose I am," I said, blinking at the light. "But I think it's time for me to take my hot water upstairs and soak my bruises—and try not to fall asleep in the tub. It's been a long day."

"That's the truth," said my employer. "And unless I miss my guess, tomorrow will be even longer. Try to get some sleep, and we'll see what we can do when the sun's up again."

Whether from exhaustion, or the nightcap, or the warm bath, I slept as soundly as I can remember. (Indeed, I did nearly fall asleep in the tub, and had to make a distinct effort to drag myself out of the warm water into the chilly night air.) In any case, when I finally opened my eyes, it was almost nine o'clock. I jumped out of bed—quite aware of my strains and bruises—quickly shaved, threw on my clothes, and rushed downstairs, where I learned that Mr. Clemens had already gone out to use the telephone again. Mrs. Clemens forced me to sit down with a bowl of oatmeal and a cup of American-style coffee (she had brewed a pot herself, the English cook's attempts at that beverage being undrinkable). I tried to focus my attention on a newspaper while I awaited my employer's return from his errands.

As luck would have it, the paper had an article on the investigation of Dr. Parkhurst's murder, under a headline reading MARK TWAIN WITNESSES A MURDER. While the details of the case were reported fairly accurately, most of the article was given over to Mr. Clemens's presence at the scene of the crime. Much was made of the person detained for questioning (McPhee) being a previous acquaintance of Mr. Clemens. The writer even ventured to speculate whether, given his recent successes as an amateur detective, the murderer had chosen this occasion to "cock a snook at the famous American," as the reporter put it. Chief Inspector Lestrade was quoted as being confident of a breakthrough at any minute, although there was no hint of what might have inspired that confidence.

I was just mulling over the final paragraphs of the article when Mr. Clemens came strolling in, almost as unobtrusively as one of his lecture-stage entrances. "Oh, good, Wentworth, you're up," he said. "All your parts seem to be in working order?"

"As far as I can tell," I said. "Did you see this article on the murder?"

"Yes, the usual pack of lies," he said, waving his hand. "Those vultures don't have any real news, so they jump on the details they figure might sell some papers. And Lestrade's playing right along with them. He must figure that making a big deal about me trying to solve the case will make him look even better when *he* arrests somebody, and of course the public will eat it up, their Scotland Yard man versus the foreigner. It's a rare newspaperman who can resist pandering to local prejudice, and when he does, it's usually because he's calculated he can boost circulation by pretending to be impartial when the competition ain't."

"Still, you'd think they'd try to get their facts straight," I said, standing up and tossing the paper onto the table.

"Well, they did get one thing right," said Mr. Clemens. "I'm getting more and more annoyed that the murderer decided to shoot that fellow right under my nose. It's a damned insult, and it's only made me more determined to find the rat who did it."

"Why, we weren't even invited to the séance until the day before. The murderer could hardly have contrived anything as elaborate as he appears to have done in that short a time, just to spite you."

"I reckon you're right as far as that goes," said Mr. Clemens. "But here—you haven't heard my news yet. Sir Denis doesn't have a phone, but I sent him a telegram and got the answer back in jig time. Take a look." He handed me a piece of paper, slightly different from the familiar Western Union messages, but recognizably a telegram. I picked it up and read: TODAY SUITS. TAKE NOON TRAIN. WILL MEET YOU AT STATION—DECOURSEY.

"Today? Noon?" I said, surprised.

"Sure enough. The old coot doesn't waste any time," said Mr. Clemens. "So if you're all done with breakfast, we'd better get down to work and see how much we can get done before we have to go out to catch the train. Don't want to keep an English baronet waiting at the station, do we?''

Somewhat to my surprise, we actually managed to finish a reasonable amount of work before donning our overcoats and calling the carriage around front to take us to Waterloo Station, whence we would take the railroad out to Sir Denis's country estate in Kent. The train station, like those I knew from my travels in America, was a large building full of bustling crowds and the noise and smell of steam engines.

But while the trains and tracks were familiar enough in design, it was easy enough to tell that we were not in any American train depot. For one thing, there were hardly any Negroes in sight. The porters, the vendors of snacks and reading material, even the shoeshine boys and the old codger pushing a broom, were all white. In fact, most of those I saw were of very similar type—there were very few of the olive skins that bespeak Mediterranean origins, nor of the sturdy, round-faced Dutch and German stock, nor of the tall Scandinavian blonds one sees in Minnesota—and if there were any Creoles or Indians in the place, they were keeping well hidden. I did see one Scotsman, sporting fiery red whiskers and a plaid tam-o'-shanter, but he was the only exotic specimen in the place.

And while there was a remarkable diversity of accents and idioms, they were all British—there were none of the gutturals of a native German, none of the extra vowels that an Italian would have added to the ends of words, let alone any of the more esoteric inflections one might hear in a large American city. Still, as odd as the lingo of New Orleans or Minnesota sounded to my New England ears, purebred Cockney or Oxonian drawl sounded more *foreign*. And there were voices here that I could barely understand—though enough recognizable English words came through to show that they were really speaking the same language as I—at least, in name. I wondered whether the British had as much trouble understanding their neighbors as I did—and, for that matter, whether they could understand me.

The enormous station was laid out according to some plan

that made absolutely no sense to me—unless it were designed to hold a Minotaur. We stopped and asked directions at least three times before finding the right platform for our train, and in the end we barely made it aboard in time. To add to the anxiety, as we pushed through the crowd toward the platform where our train was loading, we were jostled every two or three steps. "Keep a hand on your wallet," said Mr. Clemens, at my elbow. "A crowd like this is a pickpocket's delight, and London is the closest thing you'll find to a Yale College for the dip artists."

"Dip artists?" I said, instinctively reaching down to pat the pocket where my wallet resided. "I never heard of such a thing."

"It's what the other criminals call pickpockets," my employer explained. "Well, at least that's what they called 'em in America, last time I talked to somebody that knew. They may call 'em something different here—but that don't mean there's any shortage of 'em." He pushed ahead, I followed, and finally we found ourselves at the track where the train to Kent would be leaving. There, the crowds thinned out somewhat. As we stood waiting, a nearby newsboy began his chant, enticing the crowd to buy his papers. His Cockney accent was so thick that it took me several moments to understand what he was saying; but suddenly it became crystal clear: "Murder by a ghost! Read all about the murder by a ghost!"

Mr. Clemens recognized its significance at the same time I did. "Go get one of those papers, Wentworth," he said. I fished the change out of my pocket, handed it to the newsboy, and brought the paper (*not* the *Times*) back to Mr. Clemens. He scanned the front page rapidly, then sputtered, "I should have known better than to get involved with those scalawags! Look at this hogwash!" He shoved the paper at me, and I dutifully examined the front page.

The headline read, SPIRITUALISTS VOW TO INVESTIGATE MURDER AT SÉANCE; ACCUSE GHOST OF KILLING DOCTOR. Underneath was a drawing of several men and ladies sitting at a table. Above them was a hand emerging from a dark cloud, firing a pistol at one of the number. One of the sitters bore a distinct resemblance to Mr. Clemens—a bit taller and thinner than my employer, but not in the least unflattering. "Actually, it's not a bad likeness," I said, hoping to calm him down.

"To hell with the likeness, look at the story!" he said, his voice indignant.

I looked back at the paper. The pertinent sections of the story read:

> Sir Ellington Tichbourne, secretary of the London Spiritualist Society, told our reporter that the Spiritualist Society believe the murder weapon to have been an ectoplasmic pistol extruded by an evil spirit. He further revealed that the Spiritualist Society have plans to convene another sitting to call up the same spirits and confirm this finding ... Asked whether the spirits had actually fired the deadly shot, Sir Ellington said, "That is what we mean to discover. Scotland Yard are welcome to send representatives to interview the spirits." He added that a sufficiently powerful medium should be able to prevent a recurrence of the tragedy ... The American writer Mark Twain, who witnessed the murder, and Inspector G. Lestrade of Scotland Yard, who is leading the police investigation, were not available for comment ...

"This is preposterous," I said, looking back at Mr. Clemens.

"You have a remarkable gift for understatement, Wentworth," said my employer, shaking his head. "The damned newspaper never even tried to get my comment, or I'd have told 'em the whole thing was a pack of moonshine."

I opened my mouth to reply to this, only to be interrupted by a station attendant announcing the arrival of our train. We joined the rest of the passengers pressing to the front of the platform, and boarded one of the carriages in plenty of time for our departure.

I had not previously been on an English train, and I was surprised to find that the train was divided into a number of separate compartments, each seating four to six passengers.

If an American train car was modeled on an omnibus or streetcar, this arrangement had more in common with a stagecoach. Mr. Clemens and I found an empty compartment, and as luck would have it, when the train left the station shortly after, we two were still the only ones in it. This unexpected privacy was a pleasant change from an open train car, where one could hear and be overheard by passengers several seats away—not to mention having to smell their tobacco or perfume, or other less pleasant aromas. I suppose a bawling infant would have made its voice heard even through the partitions, but we were fortunate enough not to have that supposition put to the test.

It seemed a good opportunity for me to ask my employer's opinion on a subject that had been on my mind since our first discovery that Martha McPhee had set up as a medium. Now the newspaper story had brought it back to my attention. Mr. Clemens might not be the ultimate authority on questions of spiritualism, but he unquestionably had strong opinions, and hearing them might help me make up my own mind on this puzzling subject.

"It's amazing to think that all this affair came of my chance meeting with Martha McPhee," I said. "Was that the first séance you had been to?"

Mr. Clemens turned to peer at me—he had been looking out the train window at the backs of buildings we were passing—and snorted. "Not the first," he said. "Not the first by a long margin, though it's probably the first one where anything the least bit interesting happened. And that was the murder, which I don't think Martha or her 'spirits' can take any credit for, despite what that nincompoop said to the newspaper."

"I doubt she wants to take credit for that," I said. "Do you really mean to say that none of the séances you've been to were genuine, in your opinion?"

"I reckon that depends on what you mean by genuine," Mr. Clemens drawled. "I won't go so far as to claim that all mediums are deliberate frauds. I couldn't prove that, even if I believed it. Hell, it's as plain as the nose on your face that McPhee and his wife were trying to pull the wool over our eyes, but until Lestrade found those trick bellpulls, I couldn't have told you how they were doing what they did."

"That was rather disappointing," I conceded. "I had a hope that Martha really had found some sort of inner gift, though I suppose I should know better than to place much faith in anything McPhee is involved with."

"You're learning, Wentworth," said Mr. Clemens, with a wry smile. "If Slippery Ed told me the sun was going to rise in the east tomorrow morning, I'd check with Greenwich Observatory to make sure he didn't have an eclipse up his sleeve somewhere. So when his wife claimed to be setting up as a medium, I figured it was bogus from the start. Gave me a good bit of satisfaction to find out I was right."

"I suppose it would," I said. "But surely you don't take the McPhee's séance as the typical case. By now, there must be hundreds of reports of mediums, many of them observed by very reputable witnesses . . ."

He waved away my protestations. "Sure, though a reputable witness ain't necessarily a smart one. That's what's wrong with the Society for Psychical Research that's been looking into these questions over here. They've had some of the best-known men in the nation as members over the last decade or so—Tennyson was one, and so's Ruskin, fine upstanding folks. But I wouldn't give either one of 'em an even chance to spot Slippery Ed palming a card in broad daylight, with advance notice. And they're miles smarter than this stupid Spiritualist Society with its cock and bull about an ectoplasmic pistol. What it boils down to is, a lot of these mediums are nothing more than glorified sleight-of-hand artists. Enough of 'em have been caught cheating to prove *that*."

He gazed out the window a moment, then turned back to me and continued. "Still, maybe a few of 'em really do have some of the powers they claim. I've heard that Daniel Dunglas Home did things that have never been explained away, and if anybody ever caught him rigging any of his tricks, I haven't heard about it. But Slippery Ed, or that Blavatsky woman, or the Fox sisters, who started the whole fad by learning how to crack their toe joints, are a lot closer to the run of the mill. Frauds from start to finish, though some are smoother at it than others.''

Just as I was about to answer, the train lurched, then plunged us into darkness for a moment as it entered a short tunnel under a block of buildings. When we emerged into the light again, I said, ''Set the proven frauds aside—they're not at issue here. What about Daniel Dunglas Home? You admit that his feats appear to have been genuine—levitation in front of large crowds, not on a stage but in private homes where he couldn't set up apparatus or tricks in advance. What do you make of him?''

Mr. Clemens tapped his fingers on the window glass for a moment, then answered. ''Home's a tough case. Maybe he was smarter than the rest—or just luckier. There are supposed eyewitness accounts of him levitating, even lifting heavy furniture with him. He got run out of Italy when they got a hint that he was trafficking with spirits. So *they* took him seriously. But a lot of lot those witnesses *wanted* to believe, and that's the first step to being fooled.

''I don't think he ever got caught with his pants down, though. Browning saw him and thought he was a fake, and said so in a poem, but that's no better proof than what his supporters put forward. My main objection to him is the same as to all the others: even if they're real, they're dull as dishwater. I wouldn't walk across the street to see the best of 'em. Hell, I wouldn't have gone to see Martha McPhee's setup if Susy hadn't asked to go see what it was about.''

''How can you call it dull? I'd think word from the world beyond would be the most exciting news we could have.''

''That's what you'd think, ain't it?'' He rested his chin on his right fist, peering at me. ''Remember what Horatio tells Hamlet: 'There needs no ghost come from the grave to tell us this'? That describes every single thing I've heard of the spooks saying at a séance—or at least, every thing *I've* heard them say. It's all drivel, not worth a minute of a grown man's time.''

''I'm not sure I follow you,'' I said. ''Isn't the evidence of a life after this one a significant fact?''

''I guess it would be, if it were a fact,'' said Mr. Clemens.

''But as far as I can see, the jury's still out—even if you ignore the obvious hoaxes. I went to a séance some years back, where the medium called up a fellow my friends and I had known pretty well, a real hell-raiser off the riverboats. We asked the medium all kinds of questions, and we kept getting the same kind of answers: 'We are very content here,' 'We are at peace,' 'We want for nothing here.' *We* knew damn well that the first thing our buddy would have asked for at the Pearly Gates was the way to the best saloon in the place. The spook didn't cuss like him, it didn't crack jokes or laugh at 'em, it didn't even know how he had died—which was spectacular enough that I think he'd have remembered *that*. I finally asked if there was any way of life I could adopt to guarantee that I'd end up someplace other than where he was, because if that was Heaven, I didn't want any part of it.''

''I suppose that is consistent with your opinions,'' I said, unable to repress a smile. ''But isn't it possible that death so transforms us that all these mortal concerns lose their meaning?''

''Sure it's possible,'' he growled. ''It's also the easiest way for the medium to dodge any test that could prove or disprove the whole business. All we ever get are generalities. Or if an actual fact ever gets mentioned, it's something the medium could have found out with a little research from local newspapers, or even from a bit of gossiping. As for the advice the spirits give . . . If all they have to tell us is to put on our woolen caps and mittens when the weather's cold, why don't we just let the poor things rest?''

He took out his pipe and tobacco pouch, and I could see from his expression that he had said all he was about to say on the subject. So I turned to the window and the English countryside, and let the matter drop.

⇌ 21

Our train gradually left the built-up areas of London behind, and we found ourselves in the English countryside. For once, it was not raining, though the sky was overcast and there was more than a hint of chill in the air. The train made stops in several towns along the way, letting off the occasional passenger. Not many got on to replace them, no real surprise considering we were going away from rather than toward the metropolis.

For the most part, our view was green fields and bare autumn trees separated by hedgerows, with a thatched roof and a smoking chimney occasionally visible in the distance. When we stopped in the villages, we got a glimpse of quaint-looking cottages and an occasional stone church of evident antiquity. Once or twice I spotted a manor house or some such larger residence, usually surrounded by a substantial greensward and stately trees of considerable age. But English cattle and horses looked much like American cattle and horses, I thought to myself.

Finally, the conductor knocked on our compartment door and announced that we were pulling into Varley, where Sir Denis had promised to meet us. Mr. Clemens and I put on our overcoats and made our way to the door at the end of the car just as the train began to slow down. Through the window, Varley appeared much like the other little villages the train had passed through, with tidy-looking houses, a few small shops, and an unpretentious train depot. The train came to a stop, and Mr. Clemens and I stepped out onto the platform and looked around.

A porter stepped off the train onto the platform ahead of us, ready to assist any passenger with luggage. Another fellow in uniform was handing down a heavy pouch from one of the rear cars—the day's mail, I surmised. A couple of other passengers had gotten off the train at the same time we did; a young woman with a small boy. An older man—her father?—met her, picked up the boy in one arm, and took them off to a waiting carriage. I expected to find Sir Denis, or possibly one of his servants, waiting for us; but there was nobody I recognized on the platform. "I hope we haven't been stood up," I said, remembering Mr. Clemens's urging me not to dawdle in fear of keeping Sir Denis waiting.

"Well, maybe he's been delayed," my employer said. "Let's go in the station and get out of the cold. I reckon he knows to look inside if he doesn't see us out here." He pointed to the building at the end of the platform, and the two of us began walking in that direction.

Near the track was harnessed a horse and a cart very much like an American buckboard. A lanky fellow with a long face and a dark knitted cap pulled low on his forehead sat on the driver's seat, his hands thrust into the pockets of his long overcoat. "Hold on a second," said Mr. Clemens. "Let's see if this fellow's rig is for hire, in case Sir Denis doesn't show up."

The man looked up at our approach, and gave a sort of salute. "Need a ride, sirs? Yer can't do better nor Ned Perkins, no sir," he said. His accent was distinctly different from anything I had heard on the streets of London.

Mr. Clemens said, "Good to know that. The man we're visiting said he'd meet us at the train, but he's not here yet. Do you know where Sir Denis DeCoursey lives?"

"Aye, that I do," said Perkins. "Took hanother gen'l'man hout that way just this mornin'."

''Good,'' said my employer. ''About how far out of town is he? We may have to hire you if he isn't here fairly soon.''

''Oh, vive or six mile, thereabouts. 'Alf an hour or so to Sir Denis's vront door. I'll take the pair of ye vor a shilling, seein' as how ye've no baggage.''

''Well, that's good to know,'' said Mr. Clemens. ''We'll give him a little longer to get here, and if he doesn't show up, we'll ride with you. If he meets us on the way, we'll pay you the full price.''

''Vair enough, sir,'' said the driver. ''Won't be another train for an hour, noways, so I can wait.''

''Tell you what,'' said my employer, reaching in his pocket and tossing the man a small silver coin. ''Here's something to hold the ride. If Sir Denis comes for us after all, you can go ahead and keep it to cover your waiting time.''

Perkins caught the sixpenny bit and saluted again. ''Right decent of you, sir. I'll be waitin' if you needs me.''

Mr. Clemens waved back to the driver, and then we turned and headed for the station house again. But we had not gone more than a few paces when a loud report rang out, and I almost instinctively dodged behind a wooden bench on the platform. Mr. Clemens gave a jump, but then stood looking around for the source of the sound. I peeked up over the top of the bench and called to him, ''Get down, for God's sake! For all you know, they're shooting at *you*.''

''That didn't sound like a gun to me,'' he said, peering off toward the main street of the little town, Sure enough, the loud noise seemed to be coming from that direction—some sort of mechanical noise, I realized as I stood up, feeling rather foolish. The source of the sound became obvious as an outlandish contraption pulled into view: a bright green motorcar, the first I had ever seen actually running. The machine veered around the corner into the station at what I thought was an irresponsibly high speed, and came to an abrupt halt a short distance from where we stood. Ned Perkins had hopped off the seat of his rig and was holding his horse's head, glowering at the machine, but the animal seemed to have calmed down quickly enough, after his initial startlement at the machine and its noise.

One of the two men in the front seat stood up and waved in our direction. "Clemens!" cried a familiar voice—I now recognized Sir Denis DeCoursey despite the large goggles and muffler obscuring his features. "Jolly good to see you here!"

"I'll be damned," muttered my employer, wrinkling his brows. "I've never ridden in one of those things before in my life. Looks like today's the day, whether I feel like it or not."

Sir Denis clambered up to the platform, grinning broadly. He shook hands with both of us, chattering all the while. "Sorry not to be here earlier," he said. "The silly thing has its own mind about when it wants to run, especially when the weather's a bit cool. But she'll be fine, now she's warmed up. Climb aboard, I'll show you how she runs."

"How fast does this thing go?" said Mr. Clemens, walking off alongside Sir Denis. For a moment, I was left standing on the platform. What little I knew about motorcars suggested that they were unreliable, and prone to spectacular smashups along the roadway. It was one thing to rip along at high speed on well-maintained railroad tracks, but quite another on a rutted country road, barely wide enough for two wagons to pass. On the other hand, it did look like an exciting way to get from one place to another, providing one did get there . . .

Then Mr. Clemens turned and looked back at me. "Come on, Wentworth, you'll miss all the fun," he said in a jocular tone. "Or would you rather play it safe and ride with old Ned?" I snapped out of my moment of indecision, and followed my employer toward Sir Denis's machine.

Sir Denis introduced Mr. Clemens and me to Osmond, his driver and mechanic, who favored us with a few mumbled words that I could barely make out over the noise of the engine. We climbed into the seats, and Osmond adjusted a button similar to one of the stops on an organ, pushed on a large lever, and the vehicle gave a mechanical cough and lurched backward. At first I thought this was some kind of mistake, but the driver had turned around to look behind the vehicle, and so I decided it was probably intentional. The car abruptly came to a halt. Osmond threw the lever into a different position, then reached out and squeezed a rubber bulb on the right side of the car, which made a raucous horn blare out, startling Ned Perkins's horse yet again. Paying no attention to the poor animal, Osmond took off with another lurch, this time in the forward direction.

We rolled past the houses and shops of the little village at an astonishing rate. The inhabitants were evidently already used to seeing this contraption on their main street—we passed several people who barely spared a glance at us. Two local dogs did decide to make it their business to chase us out of town—at least, I assume they weren't actually trying to catch us. Then, almost before I could get a proper look at the town, we were on a country lane, whizzing past fields and little groves of trees.

The road out here was much rougher than in town, and we were kicking up far more dust than a horse-drawn vehicle would have. I felt that I might be thrown loose at every curve. Fortunately, there was a sturdy brass rail mounted on the back of the front bench of the motorcar, and I held on to it as if my life depended on it—which it quite possibly did. But for sheer dread, nothing matched the moment when we crested a hill only to see an enormous farm wagon and a straining team of oxen on the road directly in front of us. To this day, I could not tell you how we missed it—I fear my eyes were closed tight at the crucial instant—but when I opened them, I found that either by Osmond's skill or by the grace of God, we were still alive. I knew then that the future held no further terrors for me. I had ridden in a motorcar driven by a madman, and I had lived to tell the tale. Not even the prospect of returning to town by the same conveyance could intimidate me now.

Shortly after that, the driver slowed down and made a turn between two rugged stone pillars into a tree-lined lane. Sir Denis turned around and shouted something at us, but I could not make out what he said. Then I looked where he was pointing, and between the trees I could make out the front of a large stone building directly ahead of us. His home, obviously—and the closer we got, the more impressed I was.

Finally, we cleared the trees, and I could see the entire

building. It was symmetrical, three stories high in the center and two on each wing. It was made of a reddish stone, perhaps sandstone, with a slate roof and numerous light pink chimney pots. In front, there was a large greensward, with boxwood hedge cut into fanciful geometric patterns. The driveway curved around the central lawn in a large circle, broad enough for three coaches to pass. The windows were large and numerous, set off with slate-gray shutters. To judge from the number of windows, the center portion was three rooms wide, and the wings the same (though a bit smaller). A gilded weathervane in the shape of a hunter aiming his gun decorated the central portion of the main roof. And, despite its rural location, a line of wooden poles carried electrical service to the house. I had seen plenty of fine homes in America, but nothing quite so impressive as this. And I could not help but think—if this was where a baronet lived, what must a duke's palace be like?

The driver took us around the driveway in a clockwise direction, and came to a stop near the large front door. This was in proportion to the rest of the building—in other words, of a size I associated more with public buildings than with private homes, with heavy brass hardware and a knocker shaped like a bearded Turk's head. Osmond touched a button and the sound of the engine died. The sudden silence was as startling as the noise had been when first I heard it. Two large dogs—pointers, I thought—had come loping around from the side of the building to meet us, and stood waiting eagerly for Sir Denis to descend from the car.

"So, Clemens, how do you like her?" cried Sir Denis, turning around to face us. "Isn't this a smashing way to ride about?"

"I guess so!" said my employer, with an enthusiasm I did not entirely share. "I'd buy one of these babies in a minute if I was in my home in Hartford. Where'd you get this thing, anyhow?"

Sir Denis patted the engine housing and said, "The mechanical part's German-made, by a fellow named Daimler. He's supposed to be a wizard—I read about him in the *Times,* and ordered up a motor and all that. It came in five different crates, and Osmond had to put it together from odd little pieces. But I wanted good British workmanship for the body—there's a carriage maker down in Ashford who does wonders with wood and metal, and I gave him some drawings out of a magazine. It took a couple of tries before he and Osmond got everything fit together just so, but it was worth it. In ten years, everybody will have one of these, I'll wager, but I've got mine *now*.''

Mr. Clemens laughed. "I know how that feels," he said. "I was one of the first men in America to have a telephone in my house, back in 'seventy-four. The damned thing was more a nuisance than any practical good—there wasn't much of anybody I could call, at first—but I had it before anybody else, and that sure felt good."

"Well, I don't hold with telephones," said Sir Denis firmly. "I don't want to make things too easy for just any rascal who takes the notion to try to sell me something, or badger me some other way. If someone's going to waste my time, I want him right here where I can give him a good kick in the arse when I get tired of his jabber. But we needn't stand here in the open—come on in, and we'll have a nip of something to take off the chill."

He turned and led the way toward the doors. They opened into a wide oak-paneled hallway, where a butler took our coats. The hall was lined with portraits of ladies and gentlemen in the dress of periods dating back as far as Restoration times. In between the portraits were cases with antique firearms of various sorts, many very ornate, others distinctly unpretentious and workmanlike. A stairway at the end led up to a paneled second floor, but Sir Denis took us into a door to the left, and we found ourselves in a very comfortably appointed sitting room, with a large bookshelf at one end.

Under the window sat a tray with glasses, a liquor bottle, and a siphon. Sir Denis gestured and said, "I thought whisky would be the thing on a cold afternoon like today, but I've sherry if you'd rather. Or I can have Cook make something warm."

"Whisky's fine," said Mr. Clemens, and (not wanting to make special trouble) I followed suit. Sir Denis poured, we saluted one another and took a sip, and then Mr. Clemens continued. "We don't want to be like those fellows who make you want to kick 'em, so I'll come right to the point. People tell me you know as much about guns as any man in England."

"Oh, hardly," said Sir Denis, but I could see that he was flattered. "I'm just an amateur, you know—I've put a bit of a collection together over the years, starting with some things my father left me, and his father before that. I'm rather proud to say that every single piece I own is in working condition— I've test-fired them all myself. But I won't pretend to know half what some other chaps do, especially on the military side. Still, if there's something I've found out that might be of use, it'd be my pleasure to share it with you. What's the question?"

"You ought to be able to figure that out," said Mr. Clemens. "In fact, I reckon you can give me a lot better answer than any of those other chaps you were talking about, because for this one you don't have to rely on somebody else's story to know what went on. What kind of gun doesn't make any noise when you shoot it—and then vanishes into thin air?"

≈ 22

"A gun that doesn't make a noise?" Sir Denis DeCoursey wrinkled his forehead, and stared at Mr. Clemens over his whisky glass, then suddenly exclaimed, "By Jove! I see what you're after, Clemens. Of course, that dreadful business at the sitting."

"Yes," said my employer. "We all assumed that the noise of the séance covered up the bang of the gun. But there's another explanation, which is that the gun didn't make any bang."

"I think you're onto something," said Sir Denis. "I was so caught up in the rush of events—seeing poor Dr. Parkhurst shot down, right there at the table—that I didn't ask the question at the time."

"Well, it's not to late to ask it," said Mr. Clemens. "If you can answer it, you may help us find the killer. I don't think the police are likely to find it. They're still barking up the wrong tree. But let's assume it's not a regular gun—what are the possibilities?"

"Well, those are two different points," said Sir Denis, rubbing his chin. "As for the first, a gun needn't use gunpowder, so there needn't be any great bang. Gunpowder gives the most speed and distance, but it's not essential. And for the second, there are probably as many ways to conceal a gun as there are guns. Let me show you what I mean.''

We followed him across the hallway to another room, full of gun racks and display cases. I'd never seen so many fire-arms in one room, with the possible exception of the armory in Boston, which one of my uncles had taken me to visit when I was a boy. Sir Denis took us to a wooden case in which were displayed several military-looking weapons—rifles, I as-sumed. He pointed to a large one in the middle of the case. ''See that great ugly piece? As deadly as anything you'll see here, but it barely makes enough sound to startle a sleeping baby.''

My employer leaned over to look at the weapon. ''That thing? Jesus, it looks like a cannon. Tell me about it.''

''That's an Austrian weapon from Wellington's time. It was a sniper's weapon—quite accurate for its time, practically inaudible even at short range, and smokeless, too, of course. The Frenchies used to execute any soldier they caught carry-ing one, on grounds that he must be an assassin.''

''I'll take your word for it,'' said Mr. Clemens. ''But how's it silent? Or smokeless, for that matter.''

''There's no smoke and no report because it doesn't use gunpowder,'' said Sir Denis. ''This is a compressed air rifle, about fifty caliber—they used a large bullet to make up for the slightly lower velocity.''

''Compressed air!'' Mr. Clemens peered at the weapon more intently. ''Sure, I should have thought of that myself. There was an air-rifle factory in Hartford until just a few years ago, when they switched from making rifles to making bi-cycles. It wouldn't surprise me if the damned bicycles killed more people than the rifles.''

''I've seen those Hartford air guns,'' said Sir Denis. He took a sip of his whisky, then continued. ''Shouldn't rightly call them *rifles,* since they're smoothbores, but very respect-able workmanship. Small-game weapons, though, not up to military standards. Now, here's another air gun in this next case . . .''

He showed us two or three more compressed-air weapons, ranging in size from the Austrian sniper gun to very compact air pistols. "A lady could have one of these in her purse and nobody'd be the wiser," he pointed out. "Of course, any kind of search would spot it in a flash. But let me show you some other items here . . ."

He went to a cabinet on the far side of the room, took a key from his pocket, and opened a drawer. "I keep these locked up, because they're just the sort of thing I wouldn't want to get into the wrong hands. A regular gun's dangerous enough, but at least if you see somebody with a gun, you're on your guard. Now I'm going to show you some *real* assassin's weapons . . ."

He took out a leather-bound book, and I thought he intended to show us an engraving of some weapon until I saw the title: *Ovid's Metamorphoses* Surely this could have nothing to do with firearms. Imagine my surprise when he opened the cover to reveal that the insides had been cut away to make room for a small pistol! "Clever, eh?" he said. "You could walk right up to anyone, carrying this. And if you press the center of the capital *O* on the spine, it drops the hammer."

"I'll be tarred and feathered," said Mr. Clemens, laughing. "It's Clara's book! I'll have to tell her she may have been right after all."

Sir Denis looked at him with a perplexed expression, and Mr. Clemens went on to explain. "At dinner last night, we were speculating about the murder, and my daughter Clara suggested that the killer might have smuggled in a gun into the séance in a hollowed-out book. I threw cold water on the idea, and of course, now you shove one right into my hands! That'll teach me." He paused a second, then added, "Maybe I'd better be careful next time somebody comes up to me with a book to sign, too!"

"Oh, nobody would be such a philistine to hollow out the pages of anything you wrote," said Sir Denis, smiling. "Now, if it were some socialist tract, it would be a blessing to humanity . . . but you can see what I mean. Now, have a look at this." He took out what looked like a stout walking stick with several silver ferrules.

"Don't tell me there's a gun in that," said Mr. Clemens.

"Yes indeed," said Sir Denis, touching one of the ferrules.

A small hatch popped open. "Here's where you load it." He touched another point, and a recognizable trigger dropped into view. He then reached up and unscrewed the end ferrule with a quick twist, and revealed the end of the barrel. He handed it to Mr. Clemens, who examined it, holding it to his shoulder as if sighting.

"This is the damnedest thing," he said at last, shaking his head. "I notice it takes a little time to get it set up, though." He handed it over to me, and I inspected it.

"Yes, good point," said Sir Denis. "They call this a 'poacher's stick.' A fellow can't carry a gun into the woods without people taking notice, but a walking stick looks harmless enough. Of course, any clever game warden knows to look for them, nowadays. But an assassin could bring this into a theater or a lecture hall and very few would blink an eye at him. Its main shortcoming is poor accuracy at any range much over twenty yards. He'd want a steady rest for the barrel to hit a target at any range beyond that. But if he had time to set up unwatched—say, in a private box—it'd serve the purpose. It's absolutely illegal to have one of these, you know. Even I could get into a spot of trouble for owning this if I weren't a recognized collector."

While he was talking I had put the cane to my shoulder and sighted down the barrel. I touched the trigger, and there was a loud click. "Don't do that!" Sir Denis snapped. His jovial expression vanished.

"Why not?" I said. "It isn't loaded."

He wagged a finger at me sternly. "You shouldn't take my word for it," he said. "Always inspect the weapon yourself before you touch the trigger, and never point it at anything you don't wish to shoot. You shouldn't pull the trigger indoors, in any case. I don't know how many men have been killed, or badly hurt, by guns somebody thought weren't loaded."

"I'm very sorry," I said contritely. "I really haven't much experience with guns. I'll know better, now."

"I hope so," said Sir Denis, somewhat mollified. "Just remember, never touch a trigger unless you want to shoot something—or someone."

"I'm beginning to see the possibilities for our killer," said Mr. Clemens, returning to our original subject. "If somebody disguised one of those air guns as something else . . ."

"There you have it," said Sir Denis, nodding. "But there's another way it could have been done." He pointed to the table in the center of the room, where there were several leather-bound books held together by a set of heavy antique brass bookends, a pen and inkwell, and a pair of ornate silver candelabra. A tastefully carved wooden chair with a cushioned seat sat by the table. "See if you can find a gun there."

Mr. Clemens went over to the table and picked up one of the books. "You showed us one book with a gun inside it, so that'd be my first guess," he said. But when he opened the covers, it was an ordinary book, with engravings of various firearms accompanying the text.

"Never mind the books," said Sir Denis, chuckling. "They're part of my reference collection. I won't keep you in suspense any longer—lift up the chair cushion."

"Really?" said Mr. Clemens, picking it up. Under the cushion there was an inlaid wooden seat. "Now what?"

"Watch," said Sir Denis. He pushed down on one side of the inlay, and it opened to reveal a small cut-out depression—in which a pistol rested. "It's an exact copy of an Italian piece from the last century. The original is in Bologna, at the home of a minor nobleman."

"What is the use of such a thing?" I asked. "Did the Italians make a custom of inviting their enemies to dinner and dispatching them there?"

"I believe this was a defensive weapon in the main," said Sir Denis. "In those days it was wise to have a few hidden assets, and the local *duce* who commissioned this is supposed to have had weapons concealed all over his villa. The idea wasn't original with him, I assure you—I've several pieces you can see later if we've time, some very clever. The joke is, the pistol did him no good in the end—the silly fellow fell into a lake and drowned himself."

"But there's another point I wanted to make," he said, pointing his forefinger at Mr. Clemens. "Your ordinary criminal wants his victim to know he's armed, to intimidate him and discourage resistance. But your assassin needs to get close enough to the victim to take him off his guard, and that's where hidden weapons like the ones you've seen here come into play.''

Mr. Clemens nodded. ''That makes sense. So whoever shot the doctor went to a hell of a lot of trouble. Which means somebody with a long-standing grudge.''

''I still find it hard to believe that any sort of gun could have been fired within a few feet of us without anyone hearing it,'' I said. ''Wouldn't even one of these air guns make enough of a pop for us to hear it in a closed room?''

''Well, seeing's believing,'' said Sir Denis. ''Or I suppose it's hearing, in this case. I've got a bit of ammunition for that big Austrian air gun. Let's take it out to my target range and shoot it off so you can judge for yourself.''

''Good idea,'' said my employer. ''Then all three of us can decide whether we heard anything like it the night of the murder.''

''We'll do it straightaway,'' said Sir Denis. ''Tell you what, I'll have Smollett fetch the coats while you go finish your drinks. Brace yourselves against the chill, you know? I'll take a moment to run a cleaning rod through the air gun before we shoot it, just to be on the safe side. Then I'll join you directly.''

''Fair enough,'' said Mr. Clemens. ''I can't say I've ever seen whisky go bad from sitting around, but who wants to take the chance?''

''There's a man after my own heart,'' said Sir Denis, with a laugh. He clapped Mr. Clemens heartily on the back, then led us back to the sitting room where he had poured us drinks. He took a moment to finish his own drink, then went out for a few minutes. When he returned, he was wearing a shooting jacket and carrying the big air rifle. ''Ready when you are,'' he said.

My employer and I put on our coats, which the butler had brought us during Sir Denis's absence. Then we followed Sir Denis down a long hallway to the rear of the building. On the way, we got a more extended look at the building and its furnishings. I must say it was everything I expected of an English lord's home. He gave us a bit of running commentary on some of what we saw, mainly the portraits of some of his ancestors. "That's Sir Roger, who was at Charles Second's court. Used to go out drinking and wenching with Rochester, they say—not that I consider that any great distinction."

"No, since half the court apparently did it," said Mr. Clemens. "But perhaps your ancestor at least had enough sense not to write poetry about it."

"If he did, he was sensible enough to keep it out of print," said Sir Denis, with a wink. "For all I know, there's trunks full of it somewhere around the place. If any turned up, I expect I'd have it burned. Can't always trust posterity to have good sense."

"I reckon you can't," Mr. Clemens agreed. "It's a rare enough commodity at present. No guarantee the next generation will have any more than we do now. Though I suppose I'm lucky; my girls seem to have more sense than their father."

"Ah, I envy you," said Sir Denis, shaking his head. "We lost poor little Emily quite a few years ago. Alice was heartbroken; she hasn't really been the same since. That's partly why she began to take an interest in spiritualism, to get in touch with the hereafter."

"I'm sorry to hear that," said Mr. Clemens quietly. "Livy and I lost a son, little Langdon, not long after our marriage. A terrible thing to lose a child."

"Yes, so you can understand," said Sir Denis. "Now, we'll go down this stair—this was rebuilt in George Second's time, after a fire. Luckily it was put out before it spread. The portrait up there is my great-great-grandmother, Lady Caroline, by Joshua Reynolds. She was quite a beauty in her day, as you can see . . ."

We went downstairs to a less ornately decorated part of the home, out into a sort of shed. It was full of dirty boots, riding gear, and other outdoor items. Despite its humble function, even this room showed a quality of craftsmanship and finish far superior to what one would expect in an American home. How many generations of DeCoursey baronets and their re-

tainers had used this room to dress for riding or hunting? It
was almost beyond my imagination.

Outside, we followed a gravel path through a perfectly
groomed lawn. We passed a bit of garden, followed a path
that led behind the stables, and found ourselves at last in a
roughly rectangular area about fifty yards across, bordered on
one side by an apple orchard and on the other by woodland.
At the far end was a steep gravel bank, and at various dis-
tances in front of that were wooden frames for tacking up
targets. In the near corners were spring-loaded catapults for
hurling clay pigeons into the air for target practice. Sir
Denis's shooting range, obviously.

"Here we are," said Sir Denis. "This'll be fun—I've not
had the chance to fire this one for some years, now. Give me
a minute, and let's put up a target or two so I can check its
sights, while we're at it." He pulled a few pieces of folded
paper out of his pocket.

"I'll put those up if you'll tell me where," I said.

"There's a good lad," said Sir Denis. "Why don't you put
one up at twenty-five yards—that's the first stand, there—and
another at fifty. That'll be long enough to find out what I
want to know today."

I walked down the range, attached the targets to the stands
(there were small metal pins there to hold them in place), and
trotted back to join the two older men. Sir Denis nodded and
said, "Perfect! Now I'll ask you two to stand off a few feet,
and I'll try a shot or two."

Mr. Clemens and I stepped back a pace or two, and
watched Sir Denis pump a long lever that I assumed must
compress the air the weapon used. After three or four
pumps he was evidently satisfied; he said, "Heads up,
ready on the firing line," lifted the air gun to his shoulder,
and pointed it at his target. There was a moment of anticipation while he sighted, then I heard a soft sound like a
wine bottle being uncorked. The *thwack!* as the bullet hit
the wooden frame, twenty-five yards away, was almost as
loud as the report of the gun.

"That *is* quiet," said Mr. Clemens, clearly impressed.
"Still, I think I might have heard it if there weren't some

other noise to mask it. What do you think, Wentworth?''

"I probably could have heard it if I'd known what I was listening for," I said. "Not expecting it, I can't say for certain I'd have noticed it."

"It's almost completely quiet compared to a regular gun, I can tell you that," shouted Sir Denis. "Let me pump it back up and try another. You two can have a go, too, if you'd like."

"I'll pass," said Mr. Clemens. "I found out long ago I couldn't hit a church with a gun, unless maybe I was inside it."

Sir Denis chuckled, working the lever to recompress the air cylinder. "Maybe so, but a good instructor could set you right up," he said. "Come out some morning when the weather's a bit milder, and I'll make you a sharpshooter in no time at all."

Whatever Mr. Clemens was about to say, he didn't get the chance. Off in the woods to our right there was a loud *crack!* and almost at the same instant a spurt of dust kicked up mere inches from my shoe tip. "Bloody hell, someone's shooting," cried Sir Denis. "Get down!" He followed his own advice, flopping on his belly like a small boy sledding down a hill.

But Mr. Clemens craned his neck and looked toward the woods. For a brief moment, he was an excellent target, until I took two steps, hit him from behind, and knocked him as flat as any man I'd ever tackled on the football field—just as another shot rang out. I did my best not to land on him with my whole weight, but even so he landed with a loud "Oof!" He lifted up his head to glare at me. "Jesus, Wentworth . . ."

"Stay down," I said, breathlessly. I put my arm across his back to enforce my order. "That last shot might have been aimed right between your eyes."

"Where the hell is the shooter?" said Mr. Clemens, still sounding more annoyed than concerned. "I hope to God he's out of bullets."

"I can't see the blighter," said Sir Denis, working the lever of his gun again. He was lying prone, peering toward the woods whence the shot had come. Even as he spoke, there came a third *crack!* and I heard something whiz overhead.

"Sh—t!" said Mr. Clemens, flattening himself out even more. There was no mistaking the fear in his voice, now.

"Just stay down," I said, trying as much as possible to shield my employer with my own body, while at the same time wishing I could do something to make myself very small. We had almost no cover here.

"There you are!" said Sir Denis, and I heard the air gun make its soft sound again. There was a high-pitched cry from the woods, and then I heard someone thrashing through the brush. Had Sir Denis hit his target, or simply frightened him off?

Almost without thinking, I jumped up to pursue. Mr. Clemens reached out and tripped me. I fell flat on my face. "Damn fool, stay down yourself," Mr. Clemens said in an angry voice. "Let the son of a bitch get away. I don't need you getting shot."

"Yes, better keep heads down," said Sir Denis. "It might be worth your life to pursue—that's an Enfield if ever I heard one. The blackguard can get off four or five rounds to my one—though he doesn't seem to fancy getting shot at in his turn. He could turn and make a stand even if he's wounded. I suggest we get back to shelter."

"*Shelter* is the sweetest word I've heard today," said Mr. Clemens. "What do we do, jump up and run for it?" He looked back toward the orchard, some twenty yards away.

"You can't run," I pointed out. "If he's still out there shooting, it'd be suicide."

"Here's what we do," said Sir Denis. "I'll stay here and do what I can to suppress the blighter's fire. You two crawl back to the orchard—the trees should give us enough cover to get to the stables, and from there I think we'll be safe."

"I hope to hell we're safe a long time before I get there," said Mr. Clemens. He got up on his knees and elbows, and I did the same—trying very hard to keep a low profile—and crawled to the orchard. It seemed to take forever, though it probably took only a few minutes. Our clothes were badly soiled by the time we got there, but that seemed preferable to getting bullet holes in them.

We reached the shelter of the trees, and looked out to see Sir Denis crawling toward us on hands and knees. He made rather good time, I thought, considering that he was still carrying the gun. He rose to a crouch when he reached us, and said in a low voice, "There haven't been any more shots. I think the rascal left when he realized I was returning his fire."

"Well, let's get out of here before he comes back," said Mr. Clemens. We got gingerly to our feet, and dodged through the trees, trying to make as much speed as possible without exposing ourselves too much. I, for one, kept looking over my shoulder, worrying that someone might be drawing a bead on me at any moment. But we reached the shelter of the stables without further incident.

There, we were met by a slow-looking old fellow in dirty overalls pushing a wheelbarrow full of manure. " 'Ullo, Sir Denis," he said, with a jovial salute. "Been 'avin' a bit of a shoot?"

Sir Denis shook his head. "Look here, Blevins, we've got a poacher out there, or maybe something worse. Have you seen anyone with a gun on the property? Anyone who doesn't belong here, I mean?"

"Why, not at all, Sir Denis," said the servant, with a bewildered look on his ill-shaven face. "I been inside muckin' out the stables, and I didn't even know you was out until I 'eard the shots. Vigured it was target practice and nothin' else."

"Well, keep an eye out," said Sir Denis. "Somebody just fired in our direction. I think we frightened him off, but I wouldn't be too sure. I'd stay close to the house and stables, if I were you. I don't want my people getting shot any more than I do my guests, you know."

"Aye, Sir Denis," said Blevins, a worried look on his face. "I'll not stick out my neck too var, you can be sure o' that."

"Good lad," said Sir Denis. "If you see or hear anything amiss, let someone at the house know right away."

We walked quickly across the garden to the main house, still doing our best not to show any more of ourselves than necessary. I was safely inside Sir Denis's walls, with a stout oak door closed behind me, before I ventured to stand up to my full height. And even then, I found myself reluctant to stray too close to the windows. The house had seemed cheerful enough before we went out, but now it seemed like the front lines of a battlefield. It was not at all a welcome change.

⮢23

Back at Sir Denis's house, Mr. Clemens and I took off our overcoats and trousers and gave them to the servants to get the worst of the dirt brushed off. We sat by the fire in borrowed flannel robes—mine several sizes too small—warming ourselves (and repairing our shattered nerves) with hot toddy. I would have thought it a very cozy way to spend an afternoon at an English gentleman's country house if we hadn't just been shot at in his woods.

After a while, Lady Alice came in, trailed by a maid with a little tray of cakes. Lady Alice made a fuss over us while Sir Denis paced and muttered to himself. The baronet seemed almost more annoyed that someone had been trespassing on his private property than at having had shots fired past his head.

At first, Lady Alice pooh-poohed the idea that the gunman had been aiming at us. "It's bound to be a poacher," she said. "It wouldn't be the first time we've had trouble with that sort. Likely enough, he took to his heels as soon as he realized he'd shot at a man."

"I'd agree if he'd fired only the one shot," said Sir Denis. "But he squeezed off two more after we'd gone to earth. A poacher would've come to see what he'd hit. This blackguard was after one of us, no two ways about it.''

Lady Alice's expression turned to one of alarm. ''In that case, we must tell the sheriff at once.''

Sir Denis nodded agreement. ''We can't allow these people on our property,'' he said firmly. Not having a telephone to call the police, he was ready to hop into his motorcar and rush into town to inform them of the incident. But Lady Alice objected that the person who had fired on us might be waiting along the road for a chance at another shot. This gave us pause. Finally Sir Denis decided that he could safely drive into town by a back way and drop us at the train station on the way to talk to the authorities. ''This gunman's not likely a Kentish man,'' he said. ''He won't know where to wait for us.''

''I don't know how you can be sure of that,'' Mr. Clemens growled. ''The no-good skunk found his way into your woods easily enough.''

''I just remembered something,'' I said, slapping my knee. I set down my mug of toddy and continued, ''We were talking to that driver at the station—Ned something—and he said he'd driven someone out here earlier today. Do you think that could've been the man who shot at us?''

''Aha,'' said Sir Denis. ''There's a bright lad—the sheriff will want to hear about that, for a certainty. With luck, old Ned will be able to describe the rascal, and then we'll have a notion whether it's someone from these parts.''

''Well, maybe he's not a local, after all,'' admitted Mr. Clemens, rubbing his chin. ''But if it wasn't some poacher with bad eyesight, who was it? And why was he shooting at us?''

''I'm afraid it's *you* he was shooting at,'' said Sir Denis, pointing at my employer. ''I think it's someone trying to keep you from finding out who shot Parkhurst. Good thing the bastard's no marksman—unless he was just trying to scare you off. But I don't think he'd have fired three times, if scaring you were all he wanted. I'd keep my eyes open, if I were you.''

''Keep my eyes open?'' Mr. Clemens reached up with his

fingers and pantomimed propping up his eyelids. "Hell, if I could grow another pair in the back of my head, I'd keep *them* open, too. You're right about one thing, though. If all this two-legged rattlesnake was trying to do was scare me, one shot would have covered the tab. Three is downright exorbitant."

"You should be safe enough back in London," said Sir Denis, with a heartiness I hoped wasn't false reassurance. "But do be careful, old man. We can't afford to lose Mark Twain over something like this."

Mr. Clemens was quite subdued during the motorcar ride back into Varley. The road we took was narrow enough for two men on horseback to have brushed knees as they passed. It was somewhat less harrowing than our earlier ride, since Sir Denis's driver kept the machine at a slow pace. I was just as glad; I'd had enough near misses today to last me a lifetime. At least I got a chance to enjoy the Kentish scenery, which was quite charming. I asked Sir Denis about the quaint beehive-shaped structures I saw here and there in the fields. He told me they were *oasts*—special sheds for drying hops, an important local crop.

Finally, we reached the station without undue incident, a few minutes before the London train was due. There were two or three others on the platform, none of whom looked the least bit dangerous. "The train will be here directly, now," said Sir Denis as we got out of the motorcar. "Don't you worry, you're probably safe now."

"Shouldn't we go with you to the sheriff?" I asked. "Won't he need to talk to us, as well?"

"Come along if you'd like," said Sir Denis, with a shrug. "Only thing, there's not another train into town till half ten tomorrow morning. I'm sure Alice would put you up at our place overnight. We've plenty of extra beds, and there's always room for guests to dinner. And then we'd put you on the train tomorrow."

"Well, I appreciate the offer," said Mr. Clemens. "But after what happened this afternoon, I can't wait to get back to the city, where being knocked down and stomped on is more likely than being shot. If the sheriff needs to talk to us, I'll come back out. But not tonight—tell him I want to get inside my own front door and lock it.''

''I don't think he'll need you back,'' said Sir Denis. ''Nobody saw the blighter, unless it's the fellow Ned drove out my way. So I can tell him as much as you. He'll pay attention to me, I can promise you that. Now, here's your train coming—don't miss it! I'll tell you anything I learn.''

We got up on the platform moments before the train pulled to a stop, and next thing we knew we were on our way back to London. I tried to gather my thoughts about the events of the day, but I must have been more fatigued than I thought. My mind began to wander, and I must have dozed off almost immediately, because the next thing I recall after leaving the station was Mr. Clemens tapping me on the shoulder, saying, ''Wake up, Wentworth, we're here.'' I opened my eyes, and sure enough, we had returned to London.

We took a hansom from the station out to Tedworth Square. For a short while, the only sounds were the horse's hooves and the rattle of the wheels. But at last, Mr. Clemens was ready to talk about the shooting incident. ''I thought about things a good bit while you were napping on the train,'' he said. ''First, I don't want you to talk to anyone about this unless you know I've told them already. That especially includes the other suspects in the case. But it also includes Livy and the girls.''

''You're not going to tell them about it?'' I asked.

''I'll tell Livy after the girls have gone to bed, when I can talk to her in private,'' he said. ''I trust her advice, and it wouldn't be fair not to let her know this. But I won't tell the girls until this thing's over—one way or another. They don't need to worry that their father's going to get shot at every time he goes outdoors.''

''Do you really think that's likely?''

Mr. Clemens thought a moment before answering. ''No— well, I sure hope not, anyway,'' he said. ''I do think the shooter wanted to scare me off, not to kill me. If he was trying to hit me, he'd better go out for some target practice before he tries again.''

"That may not be necessary, if he can get you in closer quarters," I said. "If it's the person who killed the doctor, we know he can hit a man between the eyes at short range, and in the dark. That's either very good accuracy, or even better luck. But there's another thing that doesn't jibe. How did the gunman know you were going out to see Sir Denis today? You only made the appointment first thing this morning.''

"Hell, that's no mystery," said Mr. Clemens. "Haven't you noticed that half the time when I visit somebody, all their friends and neighbors contrive to come over for a little visit just at the time I'm there? Not because they're psychic—it's because the host has bragged to everybody within earshot that Mark Twain is coming to visit. I bet that between them, Sir Denis and Lady Alice told half the county I was coming.''

"Very likely, but half the county doesn't want to shoot you," I said.

Mr. Clemens chuckled. "I reckon there've been times and places you could've gotten up a pretty sizable collection to buy a rope to hang me, but I take your point. Still, these things spread like dandelions—only faster. You tell your friends a funny story, they tell it to somebody else, those people tell all *their* friends, and next thing you know, they're laughing at it in Australia.''

"True enough," I admitted. "Still, I think we should find out to whom Sir Denis mentioned our coming.''

"Yes, first thing tomorrow," said Mr. Clemens. "It's damned inconvenient he doesn't have a telephone. I'll have to send a telegram again. It does worry me if somebody was determined enough to follow me all the way out to Kent. If they did that, it's a good bet they're watching our house, as well. And I don't like that idea one bit—it puts Livy and the girls too directly in the way of trouble. But if I let somebody scare me off . . .'' His voice trailed away.

"I take it you don't intend to drop the case," I said, after a long silence.

"Wasn't that obvious?" said Mr. Clemens. He struck a

match to light a cigar—I hadn't noticed him taking it out, in the dark cab—and I could see the determination on his face. "If the bug-eating speckled lizard who shot at us thought he was going to scare Sam Clemens off that way, he was dead wrong. I was mad enough before, when he hadn't done any more than kill somebody right in front of me. Now he's *really* got my back up. By the time I'm done with him, he'll wish he'd kilt me when he had the chance. At least there's one good thing that came out of this."

"What's that?" I asked. The sulfurous odor of the match was replaced by the complex aroma of cigar smoke.

He took a puff and then replied, "Now at least I know for sure it wasn't Slippery Ed shooting at me out there. Unless Lestrade has changed his mind, Ed's still in jail—and for once, I reckon he'll be glad that's where he was."

"You don't think McPhee would shoot at you even if he could, do you?"

"It ain't his style, not one bit," he drawled. "Ed would steal your belly button if you left your shirt open, but he was never one to tote a gun, let alone use it. Of course, Lestrade doesn't know that, and he's probably right not to take anybody's word for it. For a while, even I had a nagging suspicion that Ed might've done it—he did have as good a chance as anybody. Now I'm almost willing to scratch him off the list."

I was surprised at his qualification. "Almost? I'd think he'd be eliminated altogether."

"Well, pretty near," said Mr. Clemens. "There's just two things I'd like to be sure of. First, did Lestrade suddenly change his mind and let Ed out today? And second, did Ed have any chance to learn where I was going today, then send a message to somebody to get out to the country and take a potshot at me? He might not be a gunman, but that don't mean some of his pals aren't. That Terry Mulligan might be one, for example."

"Yes, he's an important missing link, isn't he? But I suppose he's keeping himself well hid. Unless Lestrade's men can find him, I doubt we'll ever know what his part in this was—if he had any part at all." The cab swayed as we rounded a corner, the springs creaking as the weight shifted. The driver said something to his horse, but the words did not quite penetrate inside to my ears.

"Well, he may turn up," said Mr. Clemens. "If he does, we'll find out what he knows. For now, that's not my main problem."

"What's that?" I asked. "Are you worried that the gunman may come back?"

"No, not really," said Mr. Clemens. "I don't expect he has anything against me personally, and coming after me makes it more likely he'll get caught. If one try won't scare me off, I doubt he'll try again."

"I hope you're right," I said. "Those shots were closer to me than to you, I think."

"I told you the worthless jackass couldn't shoot straight," said Mr. Clemens, laughing. "But what I'm really worried about is Lestrade finding out about the shooting. He'd probably use that as an excuse to order me to stop trying to solve the case, or at very least to send a bobby to protect me—and incidentally to see that I don't go anyplace he doesn't want me to. So we won't tell him about it, and he'll leave me alone."

"Don't you think he'll learn it on his own?" I asked. "I'd think that Scotland Yard would keep in close touch with other jurisdictions. Or the sheriff in Kent may want to ask you about the incident."

I could see him shrug as a streetlight briefly illuminated the passing cab. "I guess Lestrade will find out about it eventually," he said. "But police the whole world over are jealous of their own jurisdictions. Lestrade is the kind of cop who probably thinks the country police are too dumb to clean their own boots. So he may pretty much ignore their reports unless he's bored. And the same may be true of the Kentish sheriff— he may prefer coming directly to me than to asking Scotland Yard's help. That may give us enough time to get something done before Lestrade decides it's too dangerous for me to be involved."

Perhaps it is too dangerous for us to be involved, I thought. But Mr. Clemens had made up his mind to go forward, and

that settled the question. It was my job to go where he went—
dangerous or not. I hoped my own worries were unfounded.
But I was not about to shrug them off. I found myself wondering where Martha McPhee had been this morning. She
certainly knew that we planned to visit Sir Denis eventually.
Had she gotten word to her husband, or some other confed-
erate, that we were interviewing all the witnesses to the murder? Then I remembered her breaking down in front of us,
and I felt a twinge of guilt for even considering Martha as
possibly having set up the shooting incident.

Mrs. Clemens and her daughters had already eaten before
we got home, but the cook had left a big pot of hearty chicken
soup simmering on the stove, and we ate it with great chunks
of buttered bread while Mrs. Clemens and the two older
girls—little Jean had already gone to bed—listened to Mr.
Clemens give a somewhat selective account of the day's
events. Luckily, our clothes had cleaned up well enough to
pretend that nothing worse had happened to them than a tramp
through the woods and a bit of kneeling on the damp ground
at Sir Denis's shooting range.

But as we were finishing our dessert, the maid came into
the room and said, "Pardon me, Mr. Clemens, but there's a
man at the back door says 'e wants to see you."

"Oh? I wonder who that could be," said my employer,
starting to stand up. Then he caught the tone of her voice and
her disapproving expression. "What's wrong?" he asked.

" 'Tis a great bloomin' Irishman, and 'e's polite enough,
but you'd think 'e'd find time to wash before 'e come to visit
respectable folk." She sniffed.

"Irish, is he?" Mr. Clemens's face lit up. "Well, don't
keep the man waiting. Bring the fellow in, bring him in here."

"If you say so, sir," said the servant, and she went back
into the kitchen to admit the mysterious visitor.

"Irish," I said. "Do you think—"

"I reckon we'll know in a minute," said my employer.
"But I'd lay odds it's the man we went looking for the other
night."

The door opened again, and in walked a man whose face

I recognized, though I had seen it only briefly. "Terry Mulligan, right?" Mr. Clemens stood up and extended his hand to McPhee's assistant, who took it in both of his and shook it.

"Aye, that's the name," said the man. Then he peered at my employer for a moment. "I saw your picture in the paper."

Mr. Clemens growled. "I wonder if there's any way to sue those bast—" Then, with a glance at his wife, he remembered his manners. "I guess you can understand why a fellow might not want his face to become too familiar. Come on in and have a seat," he continued.

"Thank you, sir," said Mulligan, and took a chair. His clothes were dirty and rumpled, and he sported several days' growth of beard. He cast a sidelong glance at the empty soup bowls on the table. It seemed clear that he had been in hiding ever since the murder.

Mrs. Clemens saw him look at the table, too. She stood and asked, "Have you eaten? There's good soup hot, and plenty of bread and butter. And I can bring you tea."

"Or something stronger, if you'd rather," said Mr. Clemens.

"Soup and bread would be grand, mum, if it's not a trouble to you," said Mulligan. "And a spot o' tea would be perfect right now." He had a warm baritone voice with a less pronounced brogue than I would have guessed.

Mrs. Clemens smiled and nodded and went into the kitchen. A few minutes later she returned, carrying a tray. She set a soup bowl and a mug of tea in front of Mulligan, handed him a napkin and silverware, and said, "If there's anything else, please let Cook know. Now, girls, I think it's time we went upstairs."

Susy and Clara were clearly unhappy at being deprived of the chance to observe a key witness in the murder investigation, but they followed their mother without complaint, leaving me and Mr. Clemens to watch Mulligan eat his soup and bread, which he did without wasting breath on conversation.

Mr. Clemens sat back in his seat and looked at Mulligan.

After he judged the man had had sufficient time to take the edge off his appetite, my employer said, "There's a bunch of people besides me looking for you, you know."

"Sure, and I'd have to be stone blind not to know that, wouldn't I?" said Mulligan, wiping his mouth with a napkin. "But most of 'em are bobbies, and I never got along with them. Mickey over at The Painted Lady said two of Mr. McPhee's friends were lookin' for me. I guessed that might be you, and I'm hopin' you're not after callin' Scotland Yard to take me in."

"Scotland Yard does its own work, and I do mine," said Mr. Clemens. "But McPhee's in jail, and if you know something that'll get him out, you might tell it to me. I can pass it on to the cops without saying anything to put them on your trail."

"I understand you," said Mulligan. "Sure, then, I can't say I know aught that might help Ed McPhee, but ask away, and if I can give you the answer, it'll be yours."

"Fair enough," said Mr. Clemens. "Let's start at the beginning. What kind of work did you do for McPhee?"

"Handy work of one sort or another," said Mulligan. "Mr. McPhee had a need for a man that was good with his hands, and he asked about and found me."

Mr. Clemens smiled broadly. "Where I come from, if you say a man's 'good with his hands' it can mean all sorts of things. Maybe he's a good man in a fight. Or something else—I don't know if you've ever seen Ed with a deck of cards . . ."

Mulligan gave a long-drawn-out whistle. "Enough to know not to play him for money. That's not my line, though, nor fighting neither, though I can take care of meself if it comes to that. Nay, it's making different devices that's my work, crafting this thing or that, whatever folk have need of."

"I see," said my employer. He gestured toward the teapot, and Mulligan reached over and refilled his cup. After he'd taken a sip, Mr. Clemens asked, "And what exactly did Mr. McPhee have you make for him?"

"Things to make sounds in the sittin' room," said Mulligan. "The main job was a set 'o bellpulls. One dragged a bit o' chain across a tin plate so it'd rattle good and loud. Another was hooked to a mechanical hammer that knocked on a hollow block of wood. Another made the sound of bells. There was a hidden gramophone, too—one of those American music boxes—that played a fiddle or an accordion. Then he had me cut a peephole through the wall, and hide it behind some pictures. And a few other things of the like. Nothin' fancy—'twasn't near as tricky as some jobs I've done. And then, when he found out I needed a little steady cash after, he kept me on in odd jobs, watchin' the door when folk were arrivin', and such.''

"So, you weren't doing anything actually illegal—is that right?'' asked Mr. Clemens, leaning forward.

"Not a bit, unless there's a law against bein' good with your hands.''

"Then why'd you run when you saw the police?''

"Sure, and wouldn't I run from a mad dog when I saw it comin'?'' said Mulligan. "I'd gone out to take the edge off me thirst, and when I returned, first thing me eyes lit on was that big bobby. I knew right then it was no place for Terry Mulligan to be, and so I put my legs to work. Next day, when I learned a man'd been shot there, I knew 'twas the right thing I'd done. You don't look like a fellow who's had aught to do with the police, but any Irishman'll tell you tales enough.''

"So would any Chinaman in California,'' said Mr. Clemens, nodding. "I guess I don't blame you for skipping out, but I wish you hadn't, because that complicated everything. For starters, it gave McPhee a few nights in jail that he didn't deserve.'' Then, after a pause, he added, "Or maybe he *did* deserve 'em for some of the other stuff he's done. But never mind that. It's the shooting we're worried about today. You were standing by the door as everybody came in that night. Was anybody carrying something suspicious?''

"Oh, they had all sorts of things along,'' said Mulligan. "Mr. McPhee told me folk'd be bringin' the odd bundle to the sittin's, and so they did, every single night. But 'twasn't my charge to inspect 'em, and I didn't.''

"When you were doing your work in that place, did you

see any sign of a hiding place—something big enough to hold
a gun, set up so somebody could get it quickly and then hide
it again?''

"Not a bit," said Mulligan. "If there was aught of the sort,
'twas someone else put it there, not Terry Mulligan."

"Nothing in the walls? Nothing in the furniture?"

"Why, there could have been most anything in the furniture, for 'twas all borrowed," said Mulligan. "That Mr.
McPhee and his little lady hired the place empty, with not a
stick in it. Saved a pretty penny, they said. Then the young
lady went 'round to all their posh friends, that baronet and
Mr. Villiers—I did some work for him, once or twice—and
a lot more, and got the loan of everything—carpets and chairs
and beds and lace curtains and teacups and paintings for the
walls. I never saw the like—she has the gift o' blarney, same
as her husband. But if there was a hidin' place in anything,
I never got wind of it, and I helped carry the most of it
upstairs."

"So much for that angle," I said. "Another door slammed
in our face."

"I think not," Mr. Clemens said. "If Ed and Martha borrowed all their furniture, there might have been a hidey-hole
in almost any piece of it. The killer could lend it to them,
wait until he knew the doctor was coming to the séance, then
bring along a gun, knowing he'd have a place to hide it after
the shooting. If we can find a hiding place, we'd know that
the person who lent that piece is the killer. That's assuming
there *is* a hiding place."

"The police searched very thoroughly," I reminded him.
"Remember Sergeant Coleman looking under the chairs? We
did our own search, and didn't find anything. I have a question for Mr. Mulligan, though. You say you did some work
for Mr. Villiers—what kind of thing did you do for him?"

"Funny thing you should ask," said Mulligan. "I just now
remembered, it was just the kind of thing your boss was as-
kin' about—furniture and the like with secret hidin' places. I
made that cane of his—'tis all hollow, with a glass phial
inside—he never said what he meant to keep in *there,* and I

thought better than to ask. Anyhow, you'd never fit a gun into that.''

''What about the furniture he loaned? Were any of your pieces among it?''

''Nay, I'd have remembered that,'' said Mulligan. '' 'Twas all just plain wooden chairs, and a little wooden side table, nothing at all fancy.''

''Well, there's some food for thought, at least,'' said Mr. Clemens. ''I don't know what it means yet, Wentworth. Maybe it doesn't have anything to do with the murder. But I know there's an answer to be found somehow, and I'm going to find it.''

''I hope you do,'' said Mulligan, standing up and picking up his cap. ''Because until this case is wrapped up, I'll have to dodge every time I see a bobby, and that's no picnic. So the sooner the better, says I. And if there's aught I can help with, you let me know.''

''I'll do that,'' said Mr. Clemens. ''Tell Wentworth how to get a message to you, and you'll hear from us if we need your help.'' He shook hands again with Mulligan, and I showed the Irishman out the back way again. But I thought to myself that I had never seen Mr. Clemens so discouraged.

24 ⌒

Next morning I was up early, but not before Mr. Clemens, who had gone out to use the telephone yet again. He stuck his head into the dining room, where I was just finishing my toast and marmalade with tea, and said, "Hurry up and finish your breakfast, Wentworth, we've got more work today."

"I'll be up to the office directly I finish this," I said, waving the last half slice of toast.

"No, this isn't inside work," he said, walking into the room. He was still wearing his overcoat. "I've spoken to Dr. Milton Ashe—Parkhurst's junior partner, and from what he said on the phone, he's got a mouthful to talk about with us. I want to go see him before the patients start lining up in his waiting room so he can give us the whole story with no interruptions."

I put down the toast, unfinished, and pushed back my seat. "In that case, let's not tarry." I had no idea what Dr. Ashe had told him over the phone, but it had clearly recharged his enthusiasm for the murder investigation. He was champing at the bit, and it would take a braver man than I—or a far more foolish one—to try to hold him back.

• • •

Dr. Parkhurst's surgery was located on Thomas Street not far from Guy's Hospital, where he had taught in the medical school. This was a good distance from Chelsea, but Mr. Clemens's driver took us there by a quick route along the Thames. We crossed the river at Westminster Bridge, and cut through the Borough to our destination. Mr. Clemens was in a reflective mood, and I took the opportunity to watch the river traffic, which was as varied as that of the Hudson or Mississippi—though here the boats were mostly smaller, and the city was much more built up on both banks than along either of those great American rivers.

Our destination turned out to be a modern building that housed the offices of several physicians. The rooms occupied by the late Dr. Parkhurst and Dr. Ashe took up a corner suite on the first floor. From the paneling in the entryway and the tasteful rows of framed engravings along the hallways, the building had more the air of a first-class hotel than of a medical office—certainly in comparison to the rooms of the family doctor I had gone to in New London. I wondered whether Dr. Ashe would be able to retain enough of his senior partner's patients to maintain himself in such lavish style. But the waiting room was already beginning to fill up, and (to judge by their dress) charity patients were in the distinct minority. Perhaps Dr. Ashe would be able to keep up the rent, after all.

A stern-faced woman in a plain but well-tailored dress sat behind a desk guarding the entryway; I judged her to be just the other side of thirty years old. She looked up with a mixture of annoyance and pity as we entered, but when my employer announced himself, she nodded and said, ''Oh, yes, Mr. Clemens, the doctor said to show you right in. This way, please.''

One well-padded man with a fringe of white hair around the pink globe of his balding cranium gave us a scathing look as she whisked us past him. I wondered how long he had been waiting for the doctor. In fact, with this many patients to attend to, I wondered how long it would be before the doctor could spare any time for us.

This part of the suite had evidently been Dr. Parkhurst's personal office, for his framed diplomas (from Cambridge and

Edinburgh) were still on the wall behind the desk—itself an
impressive expanse of dark polished wood, with only a few
tidily arranged piles of paper atop it. A floor-to-ceiling book-
case full of medical tomes filled the wall to our left, while a
pair of windows, giving a view of the hospital itself, occupied
the right wall. There was a faint whiff of carbolic acid, and
some other chemical odor I could not identify. Mr. Clemens
and I sank into two overstuffed, leather-covered chairs, and
waited for the doctor.

I was just beginning to wish for something to read when
the door opened and in walked a short middle-aged man. His
face bore a few wrinkles, and his dark brown beard had begun
to collect a few silver hairs. His complexion was sallow and
his features somewhat coarse, and his shoes needed shining.
But his eyes were a warm brown, and his smile as he saw
my employer was the genuine article. "I never thought I
would find Mark Twain sitting in my office," he said, shaking
hands with both of us. "I gather you're not here on account
of your health." His hands were long and thin, as I would
expect a surgeon's to be, and there was an unmistakable
strength in his grip.

"That's right, Dr. Ashe. I told you on the phone we wanted
to see you about some unusual business," said Mr. Clemens
after we had resumed our seats. The doctor had taken his
place behind the big desk, and sat with his fingers steepled
in front of his lips.

"You are investigating my partner's murder," said Dr.
Ashe, his face a blank page. "Naturally, I have a strong interest in seeing justice served. But perhaps you will pardon
my asking just how my answering your questions will advance the cause of justice in this particular matter."

"Well, to tell you the truth, maybe it won't," said Mr.
Clemens. "The police have a fellow in jail already, and they
think he's going to tell them the answers they want. Except
he hasn't yapped, so far. Anyways, the suspect's wife asked
me to find out the truth, and I reckon I can at least try."

"So you believe that the police are wrong, and that the
man in jail is innocent." The doctor's expression did not
change.

"I wouldn't swear to either one," said Mr. Clemens. "If the murderer had laid for Parkhurst in some back alley and shot him there, I'd probably never even have heard about it. But he didn't. Instead, he decided to do it right in front of me—and in front of my wife and daughter, too. I can't help but take that kind of thing personally. I'll take a certain measure of satisfaction to know I helped catch the killer. It may be petty of me, but I won't apologize for it. Are you going to help me?"

Dr. Ashe looked my employer in the eye for a long moment, then shrugged and averted his eyes. "Of course, Mr. Clemens. If I weren't going to help you, I wouldn't have invited you to my office." He leaned down and opened a drawer in the desk, and took out a small stack of dossiers. He put them on the desktop between us, leaving his right hand resting atop the stack. "These are patients' records. I don't know how much medical terminology you understand, Mr. Clemens. But I think you will find much of what you need in here. I do hope you understand that normally these records would be shown only to another physician, and I trust you to keep anything not relevant to this case in confidence."

I glanced at the stack, and saw the name on the paper at the top: Richard Boulton. Hannah Boulton's late husband—yes, of course, he had been one of Parkhurst's patients. How many of the others who came to that séance had loved ones who had been under the doctor's care—who had died in his care?

Mr. Clemens must have read my thoughts, for he raised his hand and said, "Dr. Ashe, I appreciate all this. To tell the truth I'm likely to understand the medical lingo in these papers about as well as a Bulgarian sermon. So before I go digging through them, maybe it would make things easier if you could answer a couple of questions for us."

Dr. Ashe nodded. "I can spare you a few minutes more, Mr. Clemens, but please remember that there are others who have a claim to my attention. Especially now that my partner is gone . . ."

"I understand," said my employer. "But murder is a matter of life and death, as well as medicine. Especially medicine as practiced by Dr. Parkhurst—I've heard hints that his surgical skills were a bit erratic.''

Dr. Ashe grimaced and spread his hands. ''That is a delicate way to put it,'' he said slowly. ''My colleague's training was of the highest caliber, and I believe he was a fine surgeon when he began practice. But in his later years he did not keep up with advances in the science, and I fear his hand was no longer as steady as it had been. This is often true of older surgeons, I am sorry to say. Younger doctors often make it a point to look out for them, or for those who have drunk too much, and to take over for them—for the patient's sake.''

''But sometimes nobody stops them,'' said Mr. Clemens, raising an eyebrow.

''No one *could* stop Dr. Parkhurst when he was determined to do something,'' said Dr. Ashe, and for the first time I thought I detected a note of bitterness in his voice. ''One of the unavoidable facts of medicine is that patients often choose doctors for reasons having nothing to do with their competence. Dr. Parkhurst's social standing guaranteed him a following among the best people in London—at least, so they would consider themselves. And he was sufficiently aware of his own limitations to take me on as a partner. I was fresh out of school, with good recommendations and plenty of prospects. But there are limits on what someone of my religion can achieve, Mr. Clemens. The average Briton does not like to put himself into the hands of a Jew—not even when his life may depend upon the skill of his surgeon.''

''Damn fools, if that's true,'' said Mr. Clemens. ''But I reckon it's not much better in America, or anywhere else. There's always somebody who sets himself up as better than the rest, usually for no good reason. The only thing we've done in America is make it easier for a man to advance on his merits—most of the time. But that's not the point, right now—you were talking about Dr. Parkhurst.''

''Yes,'' said Dr. Ashe. ''My partner recognized that his eroding skills jeopardized his ability to keep his following, and so he took on the best young surgeon he could find—or so I flatter myself. He would interview and examine the patients, he would be the physician of record—but more and more, when the ether took effect, it was I who stood there to do the real work. Many patients believed he had operated on them, when in fact he had left the surgery after seeing them go under the ether. He had the reputation, he had the following, he had the rewards of his position. And I remained the junior partner, behind the scenes, to be ordered about and reminded of my inferior status almost every day.''

"And you resented it, didn't you?''

"It would take a better man than I am not to, Mr. Clemens,'' said the doctor, spreading his hands. "But all of us have our price. To do work that benefits society, to support my parents in their old age, to give my wife and children a good home—to me, those things were worth the price I paid for them. And now, if I do not let the opportunity slip, perhaps I can gain for myself some of the recognition Dr. Parkhurst denied me.''

Mr. Clemens looked the doctor straight in the eye. "You didn't do anything to hasten the arrival of that opportunity?''

Dr. Ashe clenched his fist. "There were times—oh, yes, there were times,'' he said, and there was steel in his voice. Then he relaxed, and said, "There were times I could have cut his throat with a scalpel to keep him out of the operating room. We had very harsh words over that issue on more than one occasion. Luckily, I usually managed to persuade him to let me perform the operation in his place.''

"But not invariably,'' said Mr. Clemens.

"No, I am afraid not,'' said Dr. Ashe. "Even then, he was often lucky—or perhaps it was the patient who was lucky. But the luck sometimes ran out. There were . . . tragedies. You will find a brief summary of them—the ones I think are relevant to your inquiry, at least—in the records there.''

"Thank you, Dr. Ashe,'' said my employer. "One last question, and then I'll let you return to your work. You had as much reason as anyone to benefit from the doctor's demise—not that I think you did it, mind you.''

"I appreciate your faith in me,'' said Dr. Ashe. "But if you want something more solid, I can produce several very credible witnesses who can testify to being in my presence the evening of the murder. Although one of them was under anesthesia, and is probably unable to swear that he saw me the entire time.''

''I looked into that before I came to see you,'' said Mr. Clemens, smiling. ''I like to know that kind of thing in advance. But what I wanted to ask was whether you had a strong reason to suspect any of the people in that room. I take it you know who was there.''

''Oh, yes, I read the newspapers,'' said Dr. Ashe. ''I must say that your name would have caught my eye even if the victim had not been my partner. But the rest of the list was full of very familiar names, as well—Cedric Villiers, for example.''

''Ah, yes, what about him?'' Mr. Clemens leaned forward in anticipation.

''A pathetic case,'' said Dr. Ashe. ''He originally came to us for a broken collarbone, which Dr. Parkhurst set. When he complained of persistent pain, my partner prescribed morphia—to which Villiers became addicted. He began to haunt the office on a regular basis for several years, begging for more. Dr. Parkhurst finally had the good sense to stop supplying him—but not before Villiers made a dreadful scene, out in the waiting room. There were threats—''

''How long ago was this?''

''Something under a year since Dr. Parkhurst cut him off,'' said Dr. Ashe. ''I remember we'd had the first snowfall of the season.''

''Hmm,'' said Mr. Clemens. ''Maybe Villiers would nurse a grudge that long, or maybe not. And maybe he got another source for the stuff.''

''It's long enough for him to do the kind of planning the killer did,'' I added.

''A determined addict can usually find someone willing to sell him what he wants,'' said Dr. Ashe. ''I am afraid that some of my colleagues are less scrupulous than they should be in prescribing opiates.''

Mr. Clemens picked up one of the dossiers. ''Richard Boulton—what do you remember about him?''

The doctor wrinkled his brow a moment, then said, ''Mr. Boulton had a cancer of the bowels. I examined him and was of the opinion that he had only a few months to live no matter what we did. His wife wanted to attempt a pilgrimage to Lourdes. I myself recommended palliative measures—anything to make his last days comfortable, but Dr. Parkhurst overruled me and persuaded them that an operation might save him. Boulton died in the recovery room—in his weakened condition, the operation was more than his system could bear. Perhaps, in the long run, that spared him a great deal of suffering. But I think Mrs. Boulton saw things otherwise. I myself felt he could have lived at least six months longer, possibly a year or more. Only at the very end would he necessarily have been an invalid.''

Mr. Clemens flipped over another dossier and I saw his eyebrows rise. "Emily Marie DeCoursey. Is she who I think she is?"

"She was the daughter of Sir Denis DeCoursey and Lady Alice, if that is what you mean," said Dr. Ashe. "She was visiting her mother's sister in town, and complained of violent stomach pain. This was, if I remember correctly, seven years ago. The family doctor prescribed a laxative, but to no effect. When Dr. Parkhurst saw her, he diagnosed her condition as acute appendicitis, and urged an immediate operation. She died of a secondary infection several days later. Perhaps my partner did something to cause the infection, or perhaps the family doctor's misdiagnosis gave the septic agents time to spread through her system before the operation. I cannot say for certain—all this happened when I myself was ill with a fever, and in no condition to see patients. I do know that Sir Denis was in the office a few days later, asking several very sharp questions."

"I'm beginning to see a pattern," said Mr. Clemens. "Everybody at the séance seems to have had a grudge against the doctor. Not to forget his wife—his sister-in-law makes it clear that he was no model husband."

"Ah, yes, Miss Donning," said the doctor. "Normally I would advise taking her remarks with a grain of salt—she is a very bitter woman, quick to find fault and to impute blame, whether or not there is cause for it. In this instance, however . . ."

"So I gather," said Mr. Clemens. "She gave us a fairly long bill of particulars on damn near everybody in the case, including herself. Is it true the doctor was seeing another woman?"

"Until quite recently, yes," said Dr. Ashe. "He cut the relationship short just over a month ago. But I don't believe she can be considered a suspect. I know for a fact that she was out of town when Dr. Parkhurst died."

"What, do you know her?" Mr. Clemens's eyebrows were raised again.

"Oh, yes. May I depend on you to be discreet?" Mr. Clemens and I nodded, and Dr. Ashe continued. "You already saw her in the outer office. It was our secretary, Miss Ellsworth."

Now Mr. Clemens thought he scented the quarry. "She continued to work here after he broke off the relationship?"

"No, in fact she gave notice the very day he broke up with her," said Dr. Ashe. "It was the worst thing that could have happened, as far as the office was concerned. We had some young creature in here trying to do Miss Ellsworth's work, and the poor girl was hopeless. Or course, it was unthinkable to bring Miss Ellsworth back as long as Dr. Parkhurst was here. But after his death, I made efforts to locate her. From the family friend who had originally recommended her to us, I found she had gone back to Bath—she was from there, originally. Luckily, I persuaded her to return. This is her first full day back at work."

Dr. Ashe picked up a pencil from the desk and twiddled it in his fingers a moment, then looked out the window as he spoke. "What Dr. Parkhurst did to that poor woman is far from the least of his sins," he said. "She was an innocent girl from the West Country, completely new to London, when she first came to us. She fell under the spell of his power and position—he could be quite charming when he wished to, Mr. Clemens. When he moved to take advantage of her admiration, she was powerless to resist."

He shook his head, and let the pencil drop upon the desk, then looked at us with pleading eyes. "She should have been meeting people of her own age, eligible young men. She should be married, with a family of her own, by now. But she wouldn't look at another man; she believed Oliver when he told her that his wife was deathly ill, that he would soon be free to marry her. Of course that was a lie. In the end, he abandoned her in her turn, leaving her ruined and too old to find a husband. And it was I who inadvertently exposed her to his snares, hiring her upon the recommendation of one of my best friends. I feel a debt to her, Mr. Clemens. It is the least I can do to give her a new chance.''

My employer and I exchanged glances. ''Very good of you to take her back into your employment,'' said Mr. Clemens quietly. I silently agreed. I felt sorry for the poor woman, but she must have known what she was doing. Naturally, I could understand Dr. Ashe's desire to keep word of this from his patients—it would only prejudice them further against him if it were known that he gave a loose woman employment in his office.

Dr. Ashe shook his head. ''Oh, no, it was quite selfish of me. She may have made a very bad mistake, but that does not change the fact that she is extremely good with figures and organization, and very good with the patients. Do you need to talk to her? I have already advised her that you may need to, but I hope you will be gentle with her. She is more sinned against than sinning.''

''You can trust me,'' said my employer. ''I will want to ask her a few questions, but first let me try to plow through these papers. I don't want to waste her time asking about details of these cases if I can find the answers here.''

''Good, then I'll leave you alone for now,'' said the doctor, getting to his feet. ''Tell Miss Ellsworth if you need me again, and I'll try to come back when I've a moment free.''

''Appreciate your help, Doctor,'' said Mr. Clemens, shaking his hand, ''Maybe the answers will be here—I sure hope so.''

The doctor nodded and hurried out to see his patients, and Mr. Clemens and I sat down to look through a stack of medical files.

25 ~

Reading through the records of Dr. Parkhurst's patients was slow going. I knew nothing of medical language, other than the names of a few common diseases, and Mr. Clemens knew little more than I. From time to time one of us would ask the other what something meant; the answer was usually "I don't know." Still, it was clear that practically everyone at the séance had some reason to feel animosity toward Dr. Parkhurst. "I reckon we're lucky we didn't know the fellow any better," said Mr. Clemens, at last. "We'd have ended up wanting to shoot him ourselves."

"That's a sorry observation, but perhaps a true one," I said. "So much for thinking we could narrow the number of potential suspects. At least, the doctor's secretary was evidently out of town at the time of the killing, and Dr. Ashe seems to have a good alibi. So there are two we don't have to worry about."

"Still, it looks as if the secretary had motive enough," said Mr. Clemens. "She may have had friends or family who knew her story and wanted to avenge her. Besides, she'll know more than most about the doctor's doings. We'll talk to her before we go."

I went out to ask the secretary if she could speak to us,

and found her busy with an accounts book. "Excuse me, ma'am," I said, and she looked up at me with a trace of annoyance at the interruption. But when I added, "Mr. Clemens would like to speak to you, if it is convenient," she quietly put down the book, and followed me into the back office.

My employer stood as she entered, and said, "I'm sorry to take you away from your work, young lady. Have a seat, and we'll try to waste as little of your time as we can."

"Dr. Ashe told me you are looking into Oliver's murder," she said, taking the chair behind the desk—the one Dr. Parkhurst had probably used. Her voice was low and melodious, and her expression became more animated as she spoke. For the first time, I could see how the doctor might have found her attractive. "Has he told you that Oliver and I were . . . ?"

Mr. Clemens nodded in answer to the unfinished question. "It was actually Miss Donning who gave us the first hint of that," said Mr. Clemens. "Dr. Ashe merely confirmed what we already knew."

"Miss Donning," she said, and a hint of a sneer came to her lip. "Ah, yes, the estimable Miss Donning must have given me a fine character."

"She didn't mention you in particular, just the general fact of the doctor's . . . uh, affairs," said my employer. "She did manage to tear just about everybody else's reputation to shreds, so I reckon you got off light. Now, most of what went on between you and the doctor isn't my business."

"I'm glad you see it that way," said Miss Ellsworth. "It saves me telling you so myself." Her face flushed red, whether from anger or shame—or possibly both—I could not tell.

"Then we understand each other," said Mr. Clemens. "That'll save us both some aggravation. Just a few questions, then. Was it you or Dr. Parkhurst who broke off your relationship?"

She looked him in the eye, and for a moment, I thought she was not going to answer. Then she looked downward and said, "It was he, of course. Oliver grew tired of me; he let me know that I had become inconvenient, and that it would be best for me to leave his employment. And so I did, until Dr. Ashe called me back.''

"You say he grew tired of you," said Mr. Clemens. I could see that he was somewhat uncomfortable to talk to a young woman about the most delicate of subjects. "Is that the whole story? Or did something else happen—like his wife finding out about you?"

"Cornelia knew about me quite some time ago," she said, raising her chin. "Oliver never much cared what she knew about, once he had secured the benefits of her social position and her fortune. After that, she ceased to be of much interest to him. She was certainly never a threat to me."

"I see," said Mr. Clemens, tapping a forefinger on the desk. "But could•she have finally resented his behavior enough to kill him—or to conspire with someone else to have him killed?"

"Perhaps ten years ago she might have," said Miss Ellsworth. "I didn't know her then. But Oliver broke her spirit long since. I doubt she could find enthusiasm for anything but her spiritualism, now. Unless perhaps it is the sherry decanter. At one time I despised her for her weakness. I felt sorry for Oliver, being bound to her. Now . . . now I understand many things."

There was an awkward pause, then Mr. Clemens turned to a different subject. "What about other enemies? Can you think of anyone else who wanted him dead?"

"Dozens, probably," she said, in a tone that chilled my blood. "To know Oliver was eventually to learn how little he cared for anyone but himself. Even I came to hate him in the end—it was a relief when he told me it was over between us. And those records Dr. Ashe has given you will tell you how many enemies he made among his former patients."

"Yes, that's so," said Mr. Clemens. "One last question. You know who was there the night he was shot?" She nodded in the affirmative, and he continued: "If you had to pick one of them as the most likely to have killed him, who would it be?"

She answered almost immediately. "The most likely was one who wasn't there—that would be his son. Tony has all his father's worst qualities, and none of the ability that made Oliver a man to reckon with. In his cups, I think he would have killed his father without blinking. Other than he . . .'' She nibbled a forefinger, then said, "Cedric Villiers, most likely. I used to hear him screaming at Oliver when he wanted his morphine—that door was closed, but the sound came through. I could believe anything of him."

"So could I," said Mr. Clemens. "Except when he's crowing about his own genius. I give that about as much credence as a testimonial for hair-restoring tonic."

Miss Ellsworth smiled faintly. "I think you take him too lightly, Mr. Clemens. He may appear harmless to some, but I can tell you from personal experience that there is a dangerous beast behind that foppish exterior. I pity the world if ever it gets loose."

Mr. Clemens shrugged. "Well, I hope you're wrong, but I'll watch my back around him. I think that's everything I wanted to ask—unless you can think of something, Cabot."

"One thing," I said, trying to think how to phrase my question delicately. "I don't believe you fully answered Mr. Clemens's question about why Dr. Parkhurst lost interest in you. Do you know the reason he did so?"

"I believe he had found someone younger," she said, acidly. "At least, that is the best answer I have for his behavior. I suppose I should be resentful, but at least I have learned one lesson: a man who will betray one woman is not likely to remain faithful to another."

"Do you happen to know who the woman was who replaced you?" I asked.

"I have no idea," she said. "Quite frankly, I see no benefit to myself in pursuing that question. Certainly not now—I would just as soon forget him and everything about him."

"Thank you, Miss Ellsworth," I said, not quite sure what else to say. I settled for, "Good fortune to you." Miss Ellsworth only smiled ruefully.

We thanked Dr. Ashe for letting us peruse the records, and for answering our questions, but when we left the doctor's office, I was convinced we had made no progress at all. Again, we had increased our stock of information—but without any clearer idea of what it meant. We called our coach around and started on the long ride back to Tedworth Square. "I'm beginning to think we're doomed to failure on this case," I said. "Everything is contradictory, and all the promising leads turn into blind alleys."

"Well, we got a few clues from the doctor," said my employer, rubbing his hands together to warm them. "I just wish we had more time—I need to start working on my lecture series. I've barely got time to prepare an impromptu talk, let alone a real lecture. But if I spend much more time on this murder case, I may have to find out whether I can be facetious with no rehearsals at all."

"It's a shame we can't get the benefit of rehearsals and return engagements in solving this mystery," I said. "I can follow so much more the second or third time I hear one of your talks. It would be such an advantage if we could reenact the murder of Dr. Parkhurst, with the advantage of knowing in advance what was to happen."

"Maybe we can arrange just that," said Mr. Clemens, brightening up. "Wentworth, start a fresh page on your notepad. We've got a lot of plans to make. First thing we have to do is to convince Lestrade to go along with us . . ."

In the end, Chief Inspector Lestrade had no choice but to go along with us. He admitted that he was at an impasse in his own investigation. But when Mr. Clemens said, "Once we get all the suspects together, I'm pretty sure I can tell you who the killer is," the Scotland Yard man's first impulse was to threaten to take him into custody for questioning unless he revealed all. As for myself, I wondered whether my employer could possibly back up this seemingly preposterous promise.

"You know where that'll get you?" said Mr. Clemens. "It's one thing to throw Slippery Ed McPhee in jail—the embassy would probably pay you a few bucks to hang him, so he can't go back home to swindle any more innocent citizens. But I've got a few more friends than he does, and you'll find that out when you try to tell your bosses you want to lock me up as a danger to the realm. Meanwhile, if he's smart, the real killer can go catch a steamer for South America. But consider this: if my idea doesn't work, you're no worse off than you are now. If it *does* work, you've solved your case— and you can take your fair share of the credit. Hell, you can have *all* the credit, as far as I'm concerned. It ain't as though I need to see my name in the newspapers anymore.'' The two men stood face-to-face for several seconds. The tension between them was almost palpable until at last the policeman backed down.

''It's highly irregular,'' Lestrade argued, waving his pipe. ''Besides, we'll never get the entire lot together at the same place and time.''

''We did it once already, for the séance,'' said my employer, obviously pleased that he had won a standoff, however minor, with the Scotland Yard man. His pipe was smoking, too, and there was an unusual pungency to the atmosphere from the clash of the two men's tobacco preferences. He continued: ''An invitation delivered by a uniformed policeman carries a good bit of weight. I doubt anybody will plead a prior engagement if you're the one throwing the party.''

''In appearance only,'' said Lestrade, in a grumpy tone. ''I'd be a lot happier with the whole affair if you'd tell me what you intend to prove.'' I had to respect him for trying; Mr. Clemens had outargued him at every turn, but he was not going to give up without a fight.

''I mean to identify the person who killed Dr. Parkhurst, of course,'' said Mr. Clemens. ''Isn't that what you've been trying to find out for most of the last week?''

''Of course,'' cried Lestrade. ''What I don't understand is why you won't just tell me, if you really know, and let my men go about their work. A murder investigation is no place for a private person to stick his oar in. Why, you'll be endangering everyone else in the place, yourself and your family included. Do you want that daughter of yours exposed to gunplay?''

Mr. Clemens reflected on this point a moment, but then shook his head. ''Not at a simple reenactment of the séance. For someone to pull out a weapon would be tantamount to confessing. Whoever it is will have to bluff it out. Besides, you'll have your men here—they can search the apartment and all the suspects as they arrive. That includes me and my family, if you want.''

''You're dealing with a murderer,'' Lestrade insisted. ''You can't be certain he won't snap—perhaps attacking his accusers, perhaps trying to take a hostage to cover an escape.''

''No, you forget that this is almost certainly a revenge killing,'' said Mr. Clemens, shaking a finger. ''The killer had a grudge against Parkhurst, something strong enough to turn a normal person into a murderer. But Parkhurst is dead, and the grudge is satisfied—and unless I miss my guess, the killer will be feeling a good deal of remorse.''

I myself was not quite certain how easy it would be. After all, someone had taken shots at us at Sir Denis's estate. What guarantee did we have that it would not happen again—even with policemen in the room?

But Chief Inspector Lestrade rose to his feet and said, ''Very well, Mr. Twain, we'll try your experiment,'' he said. ''But pray that everything goes smoothly, because if it doesn't, the Home Secretary will make my life very miserable. And I intend to pass along that misery to the person responsible for talking me into such a reckless scheme.''

''Don't start whipping your mule until he balks,'' said Mr. Clemens. ''You take care of your part of the preparation, and I promise you this will all come out as smooth as butter.''

''I'll hold you to that,'' said Lestrade, putting on his hat and making his exit. Privately, I wondered if he might not be right. Mr. Clemens was staking a great deal on a belief that the murderer would give up quietly. I hoped he had not miscalculated this time—because I had no desire at all to find myself looking down the barrel of a gun. I had already had enough of that experience.

Inevitably, the impending meeting of suspects and witnesses became the central topic—indeed the only topic—of dinner-table conversation that evening. Mrs. Clemens did her best to quash the subject as soon as it reared its head, but Clara and especially little Jean were not to be shushed. The youngest of my employer's daughters was particularly insistent that she be allowed at the meeting as a spectator.

"Absolutely not," said Mrs. Clemens, with an expression that would have turned back a battleship. "Your father believes that one of the people in that group shot a man dead less than a week ago, and I will not have any child of mine exposed to that danger."

"Oh, Mommy, murderers don't shoot little girls," said Jean. She scooped up a small pile of boiled carrots on her fork, then held it midway to her mouth as she thought of an even better argument. "Besides, the police will make sure nobody brings a gun with them, won't they?"

"Of course they will," said Mr. Clemens. "I'm going to be there myself, and I sure don't want any shooting. But your mother's right. This is serious business, not entertainment for little girls. Not even smart ones like you. What if the murderer decides to try to escape, and takes one of you hostage?"

"Mommy and Susy will be there," Jean said, lowering her fork. "What if the murderer takes one of *them* hostage?"

"Wentworth and I will do our best to prevent that," said Mr. Clemens. "Are you going to eat those carrots?"

Jean put the carrots in her mouth, which gave her mother a chance to get a word in edgewise. "Believe me, if my opinion had been asked, Susy would not have been included in your father's plans. I am willing to face whatever danger there may be—and I sincerely hope there will be none at all—but I should have liked being consulted in advance, considering that our daughter's welfare is at risk."

"Don't be so worried, Livy," said Mr. Clemens. He wiped his mouth with his napkin and continued. "I don't think there's any real danger. Besides, if we don't have the whole group there, it might alert the murderer that we're close to solving the case. It has to look as if this is Lestrade's idea, and that he doesn't have the faintest ghost of idea who did it. He's even going to let Slippery Ed out of jail for the occasion."

"Won't that look suspicious?" asked Clara. "After claiming he's the main suspect, why would he let him out and give him the chance to escape?"

Mr. Clemens chuckled. "Oh, I reckon Ed will be handcuffed to a guard, or maybe he'll be wearing a pair of leg irons, to allay any suspicions on that ground. It'll do my heart good to see the old scoundrel properly trussed up. Then again, he'll probably raise enough ruckus about it to make me wish he would *escape,* but I reckon I'll just have to harden my heart." He picked up his coffee cup and took a sip.

I pointed out, "The remedy to that is to remind him that, but for your efforts on his behalf, he'd probably still be languishing in an English jail—if not actually dangling from the end of a hangman's rope."

Mr. Clemens toyed with the coffee cup. "It's a shame, in a way," he said, leaning back in his chair. "Here's one of the best chances I'll ever have to rid the world of that nuisance, and I'm committed to saving him—at least, if he's innocent, which I'm starting to think just might be true. Of course, it'd be a sight more useful to get rid of a few other scoundrels in the same line of work—a few kings, for example. But Ed would be a start, and I reckon a good preacher could work him up as an example to the rest. Still, I guess I've given my word to try to find the truth, and that's what I've got to do. It's a blasted inconvenience having principles, sometimes. But I guess there wouldn't be any virtue to it if it was always easy."

"You're always such a wonderful example to us, Papa," said Clara, a twinkle in her eye. "It's a shame we won't get to see you bring the murderer to justice. I'm sure it would inspire us to ever so many brave deeds of our own."

Her father gave her a wary look. "You wouldn't say that if you weren't trying to butter me up," he said. "The answer is still no. Your mother and your sister have to go because they were witnesses to the real murder. The whole plan depends on all the witnesses being there. But you're going to stay home, and be good girls."

"You will look for the missing book, won't you?" said Clara.

He made his fiercest face at the two girls and said, "Yes, and I'll make sure the chairs are all arranged exactly the way they were, and that Slippery Ed doesn't steal anything more, and that nobody is wearing a hollow wooden leg with a cannon inside it. And that's the last I want to hear about it.''

Of course, it wasn't, but in the end Mr. Clemens got his way—although he might have thought the price in aggravation was far too high.

26

As Mr. Clemens had hoped, Chief Inspector Lestrade's invitation to a reenactment of the séance at which Dr. Parkhurst had been shot was accepted (if not necessarily with good grace) by all parties who had been at the original. Not that the Scotland Yard man hadn't had to twist a couple of arms. Lestrade told us that Cedric Villiers had at first pled a previous engagement. The doctor's widow had also begged to be spared such an emotion-wrenching scene. I think I would have understood it had he made an exception for that poor woman—but Lestrade had stood his ground, and Mrs. Parkhurst had given in more easily than he had expected.

The atmosphere as we all gathered in Martha's parlor was far different from our first meeting, barely a week ago. To begin with, Lestrade had scheduled this meeting for the late afternoon, rather than after sunset. (This was primarily to allow his men to keep the place more easily under surveillance—both to prevent outside interference and to intercept anyone who might attempt to escape, once the purpose of the meeting became clear.) But more significantly, the events of our previous meeting had cast a cloud over everyone's mood. The minute I stepped into the parlor, I found my gaze drifting toward the table where we had sat that night—where the doctor had sat when he was struck down by his assassin.

Mr. Clemens, his family, and I had been the first to arrive, except of course for Martha, who still occupied the apartment. I was surprised that having a man murdered under her roof had not driven her to seek other lodgings, and told her so. She looked at me with incomprehension. "Why? We've paid for this apartment to the end of the month. We'd lose the entire rent, and still have to pay for the new place, if I moved out now."

"Perhaps the landlord would make an exception, under the circumstances," I said.

Martha shook her head. "Under the circumstances, I consider myself lucky the landlord hasn't thrown us out," she said. "It's just as well. I don't think I need to add apartment hunting to my list of troubles, right at present."

"I suppose you're right," I said, thinking of her husband still in police custody—in a foreign jurisdiction, no less.

Mr. and Mrs. Clemens had only just taken their seats when Inspector Lestrade arrived, along with his assistant, Sergeant Coleman and two other officers. Apparently others were stationed in the street below and in the back alley. Also with them was Ed McPhee, under the close attention of a stalwart constable. "Hello, Martha," he said, smiling sheepishly. She gave him a brief hug and a kiss on the cheek, which the constable (to his credit, I thought) did nothing to inhibit. Then McPhee turned to my employer and nodded. "Sam, it's good to see my pal here. I hope you can help straighten these birds out about old Ed McPhee."

"Ed, if I told them the truth about you, they'd never let you out," drawled Mr. Clemens, although there was enough warmth in his voice to soften the words.

McPhee guffawed and slapped his knee, saying, "Durn, there you go with them jokes again! You're enough to make a feller split his sides, Sam!" For all his demeanor betrayed, he might have spent the last few days in a fine hotel, rather than penned up by the London police. I wondered whether he was really so little disturbed, or simply putting up a good front out of sheer habit.

"Mr. McPhee, I'll ask you to take a seat until the others

are all here,'' Chief Inspector Lestrade said. ''I don't mind if you talk with the others, as long as you stay put. Constable Waters, you know your duty.''

''Yes, Chief Inspector,'' said the bobby, in a gruff voice. He was probably three inches shorter than I, with a physique like a wrestler's. I would not have wanted to tangle with him. Slippery Ed chose a small love seat as his perch—I wondered who had lent it to the McPhees. With the bobby's nodded permission, Martha sat down next to her jailbird husband. She leaned close and began to speak to him in a low voice—just low enough that I would have had to walk over to hear what they were saying. I took one step that way, but a glance from Martha made it clear that this would not be welcome, and I stopped, embarrassed at being caught. After all, with all the police in attendance, there was little they could do to cause trouble—if that was in fact what they had in mind.

Lestrade went back downstairs to see to the disposition of his other men, and while he was gone, the rest of those who had been present at the fatal séance began to arrive. Cedric Villiers, who lived within walking distance, was the first. This surprised me; a late entry would have been more in character with his nonchalant dandyism. Under his arm was a bundle—presumably whatever objects he had brought along to the séance before. I wondered briefly if the real killer would be arrogant enough to bring the weapon that killed Dr. Parkhurst. Or had the killer already disposed of the weapon? I thought I would have done so, had I been the guilty party.

Villiers nodded to us, set down his bundle, and went over to a vacant chair. He sat down, looked around the room with a smirk, and said, ''Well, the ravens begin to gather! What sort of feast does the famous Inspector Lestrade intend to offer us?''

''I reckon we'll find out soon enough,'' said Mr. Clemens. ''The others ought to be here soon enough, and then the show can start.''

''Yes, but who will play the part of the unfortunate doctor?'' asked Villiers, tapping his ebony cane upon the floor. ''We can't do a proper reenactment of the sitting without him, can we? Or does the inspector intend to bring him back for an encore?'' He grimaced at his own wit.

"That is hardly a pleasant topic," said Mrs. Clemens, wrinkling her nose. I thought perhaps she found the speaker as unwelcome as the subject, but we did not have the luxury of choosing our own company this afternoon. Otherwise, I would hardly be planning to spend the day with two known swindlers, a team of policemen, a sneering poseur, and (most probably) a very dangerous murderer.

Almost as if he had read my thoughts, Villiers answered her, "I fear there will be few pleasant topics before us this afternoon, Mrs. Clemens. I had planned on visiting the opening of an art exhibit this afternoon, but Inspector Lestrade would not hear of it. Pity—the organizers have got work from some very innovative people. I was so looking forward to speaking with some of the artists. Well, the paintings will be there tomorrow, even if the artists aren't.'' He lolled in his chair, the very image of elegant and idle aristocracy.

"You're probably just as well off to miss the artists," said Mr. Clemens. "At least the paintings won't get drunk and insult you, or try to borrow money from you."

"Ah, one must make some allowance for artists," said Villiers, smirking again. He evidently managed to hold himself superior to the general run of humanity, though as far as I could tell he had never deigned to prove it by accomplishing anything noteworthy.

I thought that Mr. Clemens was about to reply to this latest sally, but the moment passed as the door opened to admit two more guests: Mrs. Parkhurst, the doctor's widow, and her sister, Ophelia Donning. They were accompanied by Mrs. Parkhurst's son, Tony. I thought of the unfortunate encounter Mr. Clemens and I had had with Tony Parkhurst after our interview with Miss Donning, and found myself resenting his presence.

"Why, Tony, I didn't know you were invited to this little party," said Villiers. "I fear there won't be much in the way of diversion."

"I wish I were invited," said young Parkhurst, scowling. "That blockheaded bobby downstairs tried to keep me out until I told him I meant to escort my mother and aunt upstairs. I suppose they'll make me leave before the pantomime starts.''

"Oh, that'd be a shame," said Villiers. "It should be quite diverting. We were just trying to decide who should take your father's place at table, and of course you'd be perfect for the role. Don't you think so, Mr. Clemens?'' He raised an eyebrow and favored my employer with a sardonic smile. The murdered man's son glared at him, but held his temper in check. Apparently he was sober this afternoon.

Mr. Clemens shrugged. "I don't see why Tony shouldn't stay, if Lestrade doesn't think he'd be in the way. Scotland Yard's running this show, after all.''

"I'm sure Tony won't be in the way," said Miss Donning. "If he could stay, it would be a particular help to his mother.'' She indicated Mrs. Parkhurst, who was dressed in the deepest mourning. A thick veil covered her features, and the unremitting black of her garments reminded us what occasion had brought us all together. Somehow, it made Villiers's levity seem even more distasteful.

"Well, then, I'll stay until I'm told to leave," said Tony Parkhurst. "I don't suppose there's anything to drink?''

"I can offer you tea, or soda water," said Martha McPhee, "I haven't got anything stronger. I thought it would be best for us all to keep our wits about us. This is a police investigation, after all.''

"I didn't know Scotland Yard had started running temperance meetings," muttered Tony Parkhurst. I thought he was about to say more, but a sharp look and hissed admonition from his aunt changed his mind. He closed his mouth and wandered over to peer sullenly out the window overlooking the back garden.

An awkward silence fell upon the room at Martha's reminder of the true purpose of this meeting. All of us were too aware of what had taken place the last time we had all gathered here. Previously their faces had shown an anticipation of what might come of our attempts to communicate with spirits from another world. Now I could sense each of them asking themselves, "Which one of the others shot the doctor?'' or just as likely ''Do any of them think I am the murderer?'' Of course, unless Mr. Clemens's guess had gone far astray, one of them *was* in fact the murderer.

If I had nourished any hopes that we might avoid a long and thoroughly unpleasant afternoon, they had now vanished. Perhaps things would be somewhat improved if Lestrade decided to eject Tony Parkhurst. On the other hand, the chief inspector might well consider it useful to have this additional suspect on hand. The victim's son certainly had as good a motive for the murder as anyone here, although as my employer had pointed out, it was by no means clear that he had the patience or ability to carry out the sort of complex planning this murder had obviously entailed.

For his part, Mr. Clemens was packing a pipe, carefully avoiding looking anyone—including his wife and daughter—directly in the eye. I hoped he was using the brief respite to collect his thoughts. He was likely to need his full powers of concentration and observation once we were all seated at the séance table. And, needless to say, it was imperative upon me to be alert, as well. I knew that, for all his theories and hunches, he still did not know for certain who had fired the shot.

The door opened again, this time to admit the final three of our original party: Sir Denis DeCoursey, his wife Lady Alice, and Hannah Boulton, whom they had given a ride (as they had the night of the séance). I assumed that they had taken the railroad into town, and a cab from the station—first up to Bloomsbury, then out to Chelsea. I doubted they would trust the motorcar for such a long journey; even with a mechanic aboard, a breakdown might mean a serious delay. When one actually needed to travel, a good horse still had all the advantage over the motorcar—which might have a great future, but for now was still a rich man's toy, expensive and unreliable.

''Heigh-ho, are we all here?'' said Sir Denis, bouncing through the door. He was surprisingly cheerful considering our macabre business today. He wore a bright red cravat, with matching spats, inevitably clashing with the somber hues worn (for very different reasons) by the widow Parkhurst and

Cedric Villiers. Lady Alice, for her part, ventured a timid smile, but said nothing.

"All but Lestrade," said Mr. Clemens, looking up from his pipe. "I reckon he'll return directly."

"Good, good, can't wait to get started," said Sir Denis. "The sooner we get on with this, the sooner we can each go about our own business. I don't mind coming into town every now and then, but twice in a week is a bit of an imposition, don't you think?"

"Some of us live here, you know," said Cedric Villiers. "I suppose a man who inherits an estate and a title must play the country squire, and do his duty by his loyal country tenants, but I'd soon wither away if I had nothing to do but cavort with rustics. I believe London to be the only milieu for a true man of culture."

"Meaning fellows like yourself, I suppose," said Sir Denis. His raised eyebrow suggested that he might have said more on the subject, but we were deprived of his remarks by the arrival of Chief Inspector Lestrade.

Lestrade walked a few feet into the room, then stopped and looked at the assembled group. He was accompanied by Sergeant Coleman and a uniformed bobby. I recognized the latter as Constable Wilkins, whom McPhee and I had fetched from the square the night of the murder. The two men spread out to either side and slightly behind him, forming a sort of blunt wedge. "I see we're all here," said Lestrade, removing his hat. "Shall we begin?"

"Sooner begun, soonest done," said Sir Denis, but Hannah Boulton stood up and faced the Scotland Yard inspector.

"This is disgraceful," she began. "I hardly expected Scotland Yard to attempt to stoop to stealing the Spiritualist Society's thunder."

"Beg your pardon, ma'am?" said Lestrade, clearly caught off guard.

"Don't pretend you didn't see Sir Ellington Tichbourne's announcement of a séance to call up the spirits that perpetrated this tragedy," she said, waving a finger in his face. "There is the only sure way to discover this murderer. This mock séance is a waste of our time and yours, Chief Inspector.''

''Mrs. Boulton, I hope you'll let us be the judges of how best to employ our time,'' said Lestrade.

Mrs. Boulton would not let him off so easily. ''Do you have any intention of being present at the sitting Sir Ellington will hold tomorrow night?''

''Why, if nothing comes of today's meeting, I suppose it can't hurt,'' said Lestrade, backing off a step.

''Which of the spirits do you think shot the doctor?'' asked Mr. Clemens. ''If I remember right, you husband was the only one who might have known him. Do you think he was the murderer?''

''You obviously know nothing of the spirit world,'' said Mrs. Boulton, turning red. However, she had nothing further to reply to this sally, and Lestrade seized the opportunity to regain control of the assembly.

''Very well, then, let me explain why I've asked you here,'' he said. He paused a moment to look around the room, and his eye lit on Tony Parkhurst. ''I didn't ask *you* here,'' he said.

''No,'' said Tony, scowling. ''But you asked my mother and my aunt, who didn't have a blessed thing to do with shooting the old man. I'm here to see they get proper respect.''

''And to make sure nobody gives evidence against you, I suspect,'' said Hannah Boulton, latching onto a new victim. ''If the police had any sense, you're the first one they'd have taken in.''

''Tsk, Hannah, you should remember the old saying about glass houses and stones,'' said Ophelia Donning. ''I seem to remember that you were sitting next to the doctor when he was shot. Might you have had something to do with it?'' She threw a malicious look at Mrs. Boulton, as if daring her to respond.

Mrs. Boulton raised her eyebrows and gave a short laugh that conveyed no humor at all. ''If we're judging guilt by proximity to the deceased, there's another person here who was just as close on the other side,'' she replied, with a significant stare toward the doctor's widow.

''You old witch, who appointed you a judge?'' said Tony Parkhurst, shaking his fist. I remembered his violent temper, and worried for a moment he might actually attack the poor woman.

''We're not quite ready to declare anyone's guilt,'' said Lestrade, flushing angrily. ''But I will remind you all that the police are present, and that any statements you make here will be noted as evidence. Mr. Parkhurst, I didn't invite you but I suppose you might as well stay, if you promise not to cause any further interruption. Now, the fact is, we are here to reenact the séance, so as to determine the exact sequence of events on the evening of the murder. Has everyone brought along the things they had with them then?''

There was a general murmur of assent. Lestrade nodded, then said, ''Excellent, then to begin with, why don't each of you take out the things you brought, and show us where you put them that night.''

The bundles came open. Miss Donning had a large silver bell, which she set in the center of the table—it clearly jingled as she set in down. Even if a weapon had been concealed in it, it would be almost impossible to move without a telltale sound. Villiers had an ancient-looking book, which I recognized as the copy of Sir Thomas Browne's *Popular Delusions* that he had been reading when we visited his home. That certainly appeared to be genuine, unless he had a duplicate copy. Then I saw what Lady Alice DeCoursey was setting out. It was the silver candlestick that had been on the table during the séance. But I was certain I had seen it again, since—on the table of the room where Sir Denis kept his weapons collection!

Susy Clemens recognized it, too. ''That's the candlestick that disappeared after the shooting,'' she exclaimed. ''I knew I didn't just imagine it!''

''Why don't we have a look at that,'' said Mr. Clemens, stepping forward and holding out his hand.

''What on earth do you mean?'' said Lady Alice, looking around at the group.

But Sir Denis grinned. "Oh ho, I see what you're after, Clemens! By all means—show him, Alice!"

His wife turned a thin smile toward the group, picked up the candlestick, and handed it to Mr. Clemens. He held it with the candle toward the ceiling, pushing and prying on several of the ornately carved bosses and ornaments at the base. "Nothing happens," he said, looking accusingly at Sir Denis.

"I say not, old man," said Sir Denis. "This couldn't hurt a fly—well, if you swatted the beggar with it, of course, but short of that, no."

"What the devil is going on?" said Lestrade, stepping forward to look at the candlestick.

"You can fry me for a catfish if I know," said Mr. Clemens. "I saw this candlestick, or one just like it, in Sir Denis's home, right at the time we were talking about disguised weapons."

"Well, not everything an amateur thinks is a clue turns out to be one," said Lestrade. His smirk was a fraction less obnoxious than the one on Villiers's face, but not enough to make it any more pleasant. "Now, will you all please take a seat—exactly where you were the other night?"

"One moment, please, Inspector Lestrade," said Martha McPhee, raising her hand. "Mr. Clemens, what is the significance of the candlestick, if I may ask?"

"I can answer that," said Sir Denis. "I was going to bring it up myself, in any case. This candlestick is a replica of a very clever assassin's weapon—a nonworking replica, I should add. Mr. Clemens saw it in my collection, which is undoubtedly why he thought it significant. Would the inspector object to my showing it to everyone?"

"An assassin's weapon?" said Lestrade, his face taking on an eager expression that emphasized his resemblance to a ferret. "I'd like to see that, yes."

Sir Denis picked up the candlestick and held it in both hands. "As I say, this is a copy I had made, fixed so it won't shoot. But look here . . ." He pressed a raised section of the casting, and a small hatch opened. "You have to know exactly how to work it. Here's where you'd insert your bullet.

Now, this part of the foot is a lever to compress the air . . .''
It turned out to be hinged, and he pumped it a couple of times.
"And the face of this angel is the trigger." He held the piece
in both hands, pointed it toward the ceiling, and pressed the
button. There was a slight hiss, but no other effect.

"Let me see that," said Lestrade. Sir Denis handed it to
him, and the Scotland Yard man inspected the concealed
weapon. "Heavy little thing," he said. "Wouldn't be much
good at a distance, but I suppose that's not what it's designed
for, is it?"

"Just so," said Sir Denis. "I've never fired the real one,
myself, but I understand it could hit a man-sized target within
ten or fifteen feet. Good enough for the work it's designed
for."

"And good enough to have done the job the other night,
too," said Lestrade. He peered intently at the baronet, then
asked, "What exactly was your reason for bringing it here?"

Sir Denis smiled. "It does appear suspicious, doesn't it?
But I assure you, this doesn't work and never could have been
made to work. Your weapons experts are free to look it over
to verify that it doesn't shoot—naturally, I'll expect it back
afterward."

"We'll do just that, you can be sure" said Lestrade, firmly.
"Now, why did you say you brought it with you?"

"We brought it because it had been in my daughter Emily's
room while she was young," said Sir Denis.

"Yes," said Lady Alice, a wistful smile in her eyes. "The
dear girl loved the angels on it, and was fascinated by its
secret history. Later, she took it with her to school."

Sir Denis nodded and continued. "So you see, it fit Mrs.
McPhee's request to bring a metal object that a departed one
had used—and it was large enough that it would be unlikely
to go missing in the dark. I'd heard of spirits who decided to
take rings and necklaces back to the other side with them,
and all the medium could do was act surprised when the lights
came on and the jewelry was missing. No offense, Mrs.
McPhee, but one hears stories—and one would be a fool not
to learn from others' misfortune." He bowed apologetically
to Martha, who did not look at all pleased.

"But there was another point to bringing it, as well," he added. "It was a test for the medium's knowledge. Unfortunately, we never got to try it out this time. It has long been my practice to bring to a séance something that only I know the true nature of—something with a secret history, as it were. Then, at an appropriate point, I challenge the spirits to reveal the secret of the object I have brought."

"I see," said Lestrade. "Naturally, we just have to take your word for it—"

"Oh, no," said Hannah Boulton, "I can recall him asking a similar question at least twice at previous séances I have attended. He's even brought the same candlestick before, though I never knew what it signified till now." She shook her head disapprovingly. "I fear Sir Denis has less faith in the spiritual world than many of our members."

"I can vouch for that, as well," said Villiers. "It's silly to go about asking trick questions of the spirits, in my opinion. If a medium is trying to deceive the sitters, the spirits will simply refuse to answer such questions. And there's no reason to believe the spirits are omniscient, in any case."

"Still, a positive result would be so interesting, don't you think?" Sir Denis said, rubbing his hands together. "A diamond hunter doesn't expect to find a gem in every pebble—but when he finds one, it repays all his unsuccessful tries."

"Are you saying you don't think my little lady has the real gift?" said McPhee. "I can't say I take that very kindly."

"Don't be silly, Edward," said Martha McPhee, before Sir Denis could reply. "Sir Denis is justified in taking a scientific attitude—I'm certain Mr. Clemens was even less inclined to take the events at the sitting at face value. For my part, I'm sorry Sir Denis was prevented from asking his question—I cannot say for certain, but perhaps some of my spirits would have given him his answer. If little Emily had come through, of course she would have known the secret of the candlestick."

"We'll never know, now, will we?" said Lestrade dryly. "But let's move ahead with our little demonstration. Now, Mrs. Boulton, what did you bring for the spirits? And Mrs. Parkhurst, did you and your husband bring anything?"

Quietly, Mrs. Parkhurst opened her handbag and took out a man's gold pocket watch. She laid it on the table and sat back.

"What's the significance of that?" said Lestrade, peering at it.

It was her sister, Miss Donning, who answered. "It belonged to our father," she said. "He was given it as a young man, before he went out to India, and always carried it with him."

Everyone nodded at this, but Mr. Clemens and I exchanged suspicious glances. The item was small, but I was almost certain it had not been among the objects on the table at the original séance. But before either of us could say anything, Hannah Boulton gave a little sigh and slipped a ring from her finger. "This was Richard's wedding ring," she said. "I wore it then, but did not see the need actually to put it on the table." There was another awkward moment of silence as she added it to the items on the table.

With all the items accounted for, Lestrade took charge again. "Very well, then we'll get on with it," said the Scotland Yard man. "Will everyone please take their places at the table, sitting in the same chairs as they were the night of the murder?"

We moved to the large round table, and took our seats in the same order as before. Martha took her place with her back to the corner, facing more or less toward the corner where (as we now knew) there was a peephole allowing Slippery Ed McPhee a view into the room. Cedric Villiers sat to her right, then Miss Donning next to the empty chair where the doctor had sat. On the other side Mrs. Parkhurst took her place, with some show of reluctance. I felt sorry for her, imagining how it must distress her to take part in this reenactment. Next to her sat Hannah Boulton, then Lady Alice and Sir Cedric. Completing the circle were Mrs. Clemens, my employer, Susy Clemens, and I, just to the left of Martha.

"All right," said Lestrade, looking around the circle. "This is exactly where you all were? And all the things you brought are in the same places as then?"

I could see everyone looking around to verify the details,

and there was a general murmur of agreement.

"Who's going to sit in Oliver's seat?" asked Miss Donning. looking somewhat warily at the chair next to her. From where I sat I could not tell whether it might display blood-stains or other reminders of the grisly events it had seen. For the two ladies' sake, I hoped not.

"I hardly think we need anyone there," said Lestrade. "The point is to get everyone seated as they were the night of the crime. Now. Constable Waters—"

"Oh, I think it does matter," said Susy Clemens. Everyone looked at her, somewhat surprised. "After all," she continued, "we were all holding hands when the—the murder took place. Shouldn't we be doing that today?"

"I don't think—" began Lestrade, but he was interrupted again.

"Yes, I think it would be a very good idea to repeat everything exactly as it was," said Martha McPhee. "I will do my best to get in touch with the spirit world again. Who knows? Perhaps we will find an answer there when human agencies have failed."

"If you're going to do that, you'd better get Ed out where he can pull on the bell ropes," said Mr. Clemens, in an impatient tone.

"You know that ain't fair, Sam," said McPhee. "I had to miss the whole show the last time, and now you say I have to miss it all over again. Why don't I stay here so's you can see what Martha can do without any help from me? That way you'll know there ain't no tricks being pulled."

"Really, McPhee, we're attempting to find the killer, not to test the veracity of your wife's mediumship," said Villiers. "I fear that's already discredited, sorry as I am to say so. I did have hopes for her at first. But I would prefer to bring this little charade to an end and be about my business." He leaned back in his chair with an expression that suggested he'd just discovered an insect in his drink.

"As would everyone, I'm sure," said Lestrade. "Especially the killer, I would think. Actually, I believe there might be some merit to an exact reenactment—I'd like to judge how loud the noises were. And for that, Mr. McPhee, you'll have to go to the other room. Anthony Parkhurst, would you please sit in the seat your father occupied?''

''I suppose so,'' said Parkhurst. ''I shan't feel any sillier than I already do.'' He walked around the table and pulled back the chair his father had been sitting in.

''Hang on,'' said Mr. Clemens, suddenly standing up. ''There's no need for anything more today.''

''What on earth do you mean?'' said Lestrade. ''We've barely begun—''

''No, it's all over,'' said Mr. Clemens, waving his hand. ''I know exactly who the murderer is.''

27

"**K**now who the murderer is?" Chief Inspector Lestrade laughed. It was a dry laugh, not in the least a pleasant sound. "I say, Twain, I know you've a reputation as a humorist to uphold, but a police investigation is hardly the place for it. Now, if Mr. Parkhurst and Mr. McPhee will take their places—"

"No, I think this could be diverting," said Cedric Villiers. "Mr. Clemens has actually solved a few murder cases, or so I've heard. Let's hear his theories—they shouldn't take long, and they may be amusingly phrased, after all. When he's done—and I trust he won't occupy us excessively long—Scotland Yard can proceed with its usual methods."

"Hear, hear," said McPhee. "Sam's got a way with words, and he ain't half as ignorant as he makes out sometimes. Let him spin his yarn so at least I have somethin' to chaw on when you put me out in the waiting room."

Three or four other voices chipped in with similar sentiments, with only Mrs. Boulton overtly disdainful. So, putting the best face on things, Lestrade said, "Very well, Mr. Twain, please explain your theory. Mind you, though, British justice works on proven fact, not theories. You may have a very clever notion, but without facts to back it up, it's all hot air."

"Hot air's usually my stock-in-trade," said Mr. Clemens. "But brass tacks is what's called for now, so here's what I've got. I realized as we sat down to the table that the key to the murder was *how it had to have been done*. That was the puzzle all along, of course. There were a dozen people in the room, and another watching the door, and yet the killer managed to shoot the doctor without one of us seeing or hearing a thing—or admitting it, if they did."

"That's easily explained," said Lestrade. "McPhee was in league with the killer; he let him into the room after the lights were down—he'd darkened the outer room, too, so none of you would notice the door opening. After the fellow's eyes got used to the dark, he took his bead, shot the doctor, and escaped."

"That's a mighty fine theory, except it didn't happen," said McPhee, indignantly. He stepped forward, and the constable put out a hand to restrain him, which McPhee shrugged off, saying, "Say what you want about Ed McPhee, he ain't never been mixed up in killin', and that's the truth."

"Well, Ed, that's the way I see things," said Mr. Clemens. "But these people can't just take you at your word. In fact, Lestrade's right about one thing—the killer can't have been in this alone, because it's too hard for one person to pull off. The killer needed help to get to the doctor without any of us seeing him. Now, Ed could've let him in the place before the séance even started. After all, none of us went in the bedroom until after the doctor was killed. So the fellow could've been hiding there all along."

"I don't like the way all these theories keep pointin' the finger at me, Sam," said McPhee. "Jokes is one thing, but this feller here wants to put a noose around my neck."

"Relax, Ed," said Mr. Clemens. "I'm not pointing any fingers yet—just listing possibilities. The problem with that theory is that Martha would've had to know in advance what was going to happen. That young lady's poker face is near as good as yours, but I swear she was caught off her guard when the doctor was killed, and I don't think she could've pulled that off if she'd known. Besides, I've got better cards to play."

"I hope they're better than what you've shown so far," said Tony Parkhurst. "These two needn't have known the fellow they let in meant to kill my father. They might have thought it was all for a prank—or perhaps that he meant to rob the party."

"Good thinking, Tony, but still not the whole story," said Mr. Clemens. He stood up and leaned his hands on the table. "There are problems with the idea that McPhee let in some outsider to kill the doctor, or just to play a prank. When Wentworth and I first started working on this case, we thought maybe somebody had come in the back window and shot him from there—either coming along a ledge from one of the other apartments, or coming up a ladder from the ground."

"We looked into that," said Lestrade. "The other flat on this floor is occupied by a vicar and his wife. They were at home the entire evening. I think we can be quite certain nobody used their windows to gain entry here. As for climbing up from the ground, we've checked the back garden. There was no sign of a ladder being used, and the ground was soft—a ladder would have left marks."

"What about the front window?" asked Sir Denis. "A ladder wouldn't have left marks on the paving."

"That would've been noticed," said Lestrade. "This is a busy street, you know. A person climbing a ladder up to a front window is irregular enough for one of the neighbors to have noted it—not to mention a passing constable. We've looked into those possibilities, and we're satisfied it had to be an inside job."

"Good, I'm glad you did something sensible," said Mr. Clemens. There was an appreciative chuckle from Villiers, along with a malicious grin. For his part, Lestrade gave my employer a nasty look but held his tongue when Mr. Clemens hastened to add, "Actually, that's not fair. You've done a lot of sensible things, and they've narrowed down the field a good bit. You just haven't taken the next step, which is to see what's left after you've eliminated all the impossibilities."

"That's the problem with you amateurs," said Lestrade. "You always want to discount common sense in favor of some notion so esoteric it needs an Oxford don to puzzle it out. Well, your criminal mastermind is a creature of bad fiction. The real article is usually an ill-bred fellow whose main thought is for his next tot of gin and a girl of his own sort. That lot's not going to devise some complicated way to kill a man.''

"True enough," said Mr. Clemens. "But there *are* murderers who don't fit your image. And I think we've got one here. Just the choice of setting shows that this killer was more resourceful than the average. In fact, that's one of the things that exonerates Ed and Martha, in my mind.''

"I'm not certain we should take that as a compliment, Mr. Clemens," said Martha. "But if it leads to my husband's release, I will take no offense at it.''

"Take it however you want," said Mr. Clemens. "My point is, whoever killed Dr. Parkhurst had a long-standing grudge against him, and time to cook up a remarkably complex plot. How long have you been in the country, Mrs. McPhee? Not even long enough to meet the doctor—it was the first time he'd even gone to a séance, and that was at his wife's urging. Am I right, Mrs. Parkhurst? Did your husband ever even meet Ed or Martha before that night?''

"Certainly not to my knowledge," said the widow. "Of course, I did mention the new medium, Mrs. McPhee, to him when Ophelia and I were urging him to come. And it is possible that one of them visited his surgery, of course.''

"If they did, his partner didn't know about it," said Mr. Clemens. "My point is, they hardly knew him well enough to have any grudge against him—or even to sympathize with somebody else's grudge. They're both too mercenary to get tied up in somebody else's problems with no profit to themselves.''

"You don't know that," said Lestrade. "They may have been promised money when the whole affair blows over. Except we're here to make certain it won't.''

"Well, Martha's staying in the place where a man was killed because she'd lose the month's rent if she moved out," said my employer. "That isn't how somebody acts when she expects a lot of money to be coming in. But let's get back to how the murder was committed.''

"Yes, by all means," said Cedric Villiers, in his usual bored tone. "And could you try to make it more amusing than you've been so far? I'm having to forgo a very promising art opening, you know."

"Don't worry, there's a stinger at the end of it," said Mr. Clemens. "Let's get rid of the outsider theory once and for all. The biggest problem for an outsider coming in here after the lights were off is that they wouldn't know where the doctor was sitting. Even if their eyes were adapted to the dark, it would take a long time to figure out where he was—especially when he didn't say anything to give away his position.''

"What if the doctor was tricked into taking a prearranged seat?" asked Lestrade. "Then the assassin could simply fire at a known position. Trick shooters can hit a target blindfold.''

"Sure, I've seen Annie Oakley do that," said Mr. Clemens. "But she knows exactly where those targets are before she puts the blindfold on. We sat down pretty much at random that night—I even offered to trade chairs with Martha, to see if she might have had anything special rigged to her seat, and she was willing to let me sit anywhere I wanted. So that idea's got a couple of strikes against it.''

"I see where you're going," said Mrs. Parkhurst. "Only those of us who were in the room when the lights were still on could know for certain who occupied which seat. So the killer must have been one of us here—how dreadful!" She looked around at the others at the table with genuine worry.

"McPhee was here when the lights were on," growled Lestrade. "He could have told somebody in the other room."

"You're still barking up the wrong tree," said Mr. Clemens. "There's still another wrinkle to the story, one I didn't figure out until just a few minutes ago. You see, knowing where the target is is only the first step to hitting it. You still have to aim the gun and pull the trigger."

"Now, that's instructive," said Lestrade, with a sneer. "I thought you were going to tell us that your clever murderer had somehow concocted a weapon that aims and fires itself.''

"That might work in Jules Verne's books," said Mr. Clemens. "But we don't have to worry about that here. No, what I'm saying is that the killer had to have both hands free."

"But that's impossible," said his daughter Susy. "All of us were holding hands with our neighbors on either side . . ." Then she paused, and looked around the table and said, "Oh, my!"

"Yes, I think you see it," said Mr. Clemens.

"Well, I don't," said Lestrade. "Either the killer was holding hands or he wasn't. I don't see what you can make from that."

"My father means that the killer had not one but two accomplices," said Susy Clemens, looking around the room. "One person on each side who wouldn't say anything about the circle being broken right before the doctor died. So now we have to find three people . . . but how are we going to do that?"

I saw what the problem was. The killer had to trust the people on both sides of him not to reveal him to the rest of us. I knew who had held both my hands at the séance, and certainly Mr. Clemens knew whose hands *he* held—and could trust both of them to notice and report any such irregularity. That meant that Martha McPhee, who held my hand, was not the shooter, nor was Sir Denis, who held Mrs. Clemens's other hand. Presumably the dead man had not shot himself . . .

I snapped out of these thoughts as I noticed the others at the table looking around and making similar calculations of guilt, drawing from knowledge I did not possess. If my employer was correct, three of them had been in league to murder the doctor. But which three?

Cedric Villiers was the first to break the silence. "Damned brilliant of you, Clemens," he said. He leaned forward and peered 'round the circle at the others. "Thus begins a delicious game of Whom Do You Trust? It will be amusing to watch everyone writhe in anticipation. Of course, both *my* neighbors will testify that I held their hands the entire time, so I won't bother to offer that defense for myself."

"Two of the three married couples had a third relative present,'' said Lestrade. Now his face had an alert look, as my employer's hypothesis sank in. ''Mrs. Parkhurst had her sister along.'' He stared significantly at the widow and Mrs. Donning. Then he turned toward my employer. ''Not to forget that you, Mr. Twain, were here not only with your wife and daughter, but with your secretary. In fact, the five foreigners at the table were all sitting together.'' I could almost see his mind beginning to calculate his next move.

''Both of which make me and my family and my secretary look like prime suspects,'' said Mr. Clemens.

''Yes, if you remember that the victim didn't shoot himself,'' said Lestrade. ''And he sat with his wife to one side.''

''Don't be so certain he didn't shoot himself,'' said Villiers, his smirk back in place. ''How do you know Cornelia wouldn't agree to let go Dr. Parkhurst's hand if she'd known he was going to shoot himself?''

''Or perhaps she connived with you to shoot him, Villiers,'' said Tony Parkhurst, a nasty look on his face. ''Unless I'm badly mistaken about you and her, she had every reason to think she could trust you—''

''Anthony!'' said his mother, beginning to sob. ''Cruel to the last! You know I loved your father.''

''I know you'd say so to anybody who didn't know better,'' said her son. ''I drew a different conclusion.''

''You apologize to your mother,'' drawled Mr. Clemens. ''It just so happens you're wrong, and I can prove it.''

''I may apologize if you *can* prove it,'' said Tony Parkhurst. ''Perhaps Cedric the Great is the killer, over there. Perhaps he was in league with dear doting Hannah and our little medium, you know—she's his protégée, after all, and perhaps her silly old husband hasn't heard about Cedric's long line of conquests among the spiritualistically inclined ladies.''

''That's a better theory,'' said Mr. Clemens, stepping away from the table and leaning forward on the back of his seat. ''Still wrong, but I guess I can excuse it because you don't know Martha McPhee. She'd have talked way before now. Accomplices can hang, and she's an accomplice if she stays mum. She might have stayed mum for Ed, but never for Villiers."

"She might for enough money," said Lestrade. He motioned to his assistant, who moved to a spot between the table and the door—clearly to block the way, in case someone tried to bolt. The other policemen were also alert, their eyes darting from one person to the other, ready to move at need.

Mr. Clemens shook his head slowly at Lestrade's remark. "I already told you—if Martha was getting .that kind of money, she wouldn't have stayed here until the end of the month to avoid losing the rent. And she'd have hired herself the best lawyer in London instead of asking a jackleg writer from Missouri to outsmart Scotland Yard." He had to raise his voice to say this, since several of those at the table were beginning to mutter to one another after seeing the constables move to block the exit.

"You haven't outsmarted the Yard yet," said Lestrade, raising his own voice. "If she was in it, McPhee had to be as well. Now I know why he was so tough to crack—he was protecting his wife." He began to move toward Martha McPhee.

"Don't jump yet, Lestrade. You're still going after this thing the wrong way," said Mr. Clemens, speaking loudly enough so that all voices fell silent, and the whole company turned their eyes toward him. He let the silence ring for a moment, then pointed across the table and said, "The murderer is Lady Alice DeCoursey."

"Impossible!" said Ophelia Donning. "She held my hand the entire time."

"That's what you say, Miss Donning," said Mr. Clemens. "But it ain't so." He walked slowly around the table in her direction, speaking as he approached her. "You're in this, too—you let go Lady Alice's hand, knowing exactly what she planned to do—and you covered up for her afterwards. When I came to see you, you ran down the whole list of grudges everybody had against the doctor—all the reasons anybody had to kill him, including yourself, your own sister, and her son, your nephew. The only two people you skipped were Sir Denis and Lady Alice. But they both had a grudge against the doctor—and you didn't say one word about it. Their daughter died under Dr. Parkhurst's hands, and over the years they came to believe that he had botched the operation badly. Not without reason—Hannah Boulton lost her husband the same way, and Dr. Ashe, the dead man's partner, makes no secret of the fact that Oliver Parkhurst didn't think anything of getting drunk as a lord before going in to cut some poor soul open.''

''That's Papa, all right,'' said Tony Parkhurst. ''Mama used to try to stop him from drinking before he had to operate, but it was no use. But do you actually believe that Aunt Ophelia had anything to do with this? She'd talk all day long about how she hated Papa, enough to curdle your blood—but she'd never fire a gun herself. Too likely to get her hands dirty.''

''She didn't have to,'' said Mr. Clemens. ''Lady Alice took care of that, and your aunt just covered up for her. Sir Denis may not have known just what his wife was going to do, but he's no fool. He must have known immediately what had happened when he saw that the doctor had been shot. His wife had let go his hand shortly before it happened. A quick look at the candlestick and he would have known—this wasn't the harmless replica, but the deadly real thing. I'll bet you'll find another candlestick just like this in his gun room. It's the one that shoots, and they brought it here that night. Search their home and you'll find it, Lestrade.''

''Nonsense, I've told you this is a harmless replica,'' said Sir Denis. ''The police experts will verify that.''

Mr. Clemens shook his head. ''Maybe this one is, but you told me the other day that every piece you had was in working order—and that you'd fired them all yourself. I'm betting you've got the real one at home, and that's the one that killed the doctor.''

''I hate to point this out, Clemens, but you've overlooked something rather elementary,'' said Sir Denis, as if lecturing a dull child. ''Remember being shot at when we were out looking at that Austrian air gun? Someone was trying to stop you from talking to me—from finding out the truth. It must be an outsider. A damned poor shot, too, I must say.'' He seemed unnaturally calm—hardly what one would expect from a man whose wife has just been accused of murder.

"No, that won't wash. First of all, your shot—with a gun you'd just hit the bull's-eye with—went way high, as if you were making sure you missed. This was after the third shot fired at us—so right then it made most sense to think the other party would keep shooting. But you shot high, aiming at the branches."

"Yes, of course," said Sir Denis. "The blighter deserved at least a sporting warning. If he knew there'd be return fire, he might decide to slink away, you know."

Mr. Clemens shook his head. "You don't give a sporting warning to somebody who's trying to kill you, let alone with a weapon the enemy can't even hear twenty feet away. But soon as you pulled the trigger, the shooter let out a yell and skedaddled for the deep woods. It was pretty convincing until I figured out it had to be Lady Alice shooting at us, and aiming to miss. With a crack shot like her, missing by just enough to scare me shouldn't be too hard. The only thing she—and you—didn't figure on was that I might not scare so easy."

"Nonsense," said Sir Denis. "Even if it were some sort of pantomime of shooting, I would hardly have sent my wife out to do it. It would be far too dangerous."

Mr. Clemens shook his head. "No, because you two were the only ones shooting. There wasn't much chance of somebody being hurt by accident with two experts doing all the shooting—especially two experts who trust one another. I hear tell she's nearly as good a shot as you. You two might have thought you had reason to kill Dr. Parkhurst, but you couldn't bring yourselves to kill somebody that hadn't hurt you."

"Really, Clemens, you've let your imagination run away with you," said Sir Denis. "You're so anxious to see your friend go unpunished that you strike out wildly and hit everything but the target. This is silly, old boy." He laughed, and waggled his hand as if to dismiss the very idea. But the laugh sounded forced, and there was a thin line of sweat on his brow.

"There's one more detail you forgot," said my employer.

He turned to Chief Inspector Lestrade. "You can check this yourself as soon as you get to a telephone. When Sir Denis dropped us off at the train station after the shooting, he said he was going to go tell the sheriff. He never did—and yet, not half an hour ago, he claimed the sheriff was pursuing the matter and even told me a few clues he'd found. But the sheriff didn't find any clues at all. I know, because I telephoned the fellow myself, and he swore that Sir Denis never reported any shooting on his property. Sir Denis never dreamed I'd call the sheriff on the telephone—because he doesn't have a phone himself."

"That's queer, no two ways about it," said Lestrade. "Still, it doesn't prove the lady is our murderer."

"That's right, you must have talked to the wrong man," said Sir Denis, hotly. Now he rose, his hands pushing on the tabletop. "See here, it must be an underling you spoke to. Let's go talk to the sheriff; he'll set you straight." He took a step toward the door.

"Never mind, Denis," said Lady Alice. "You can't keep asking everyone to lie for us." She looked around the table at each of us. "Dr. Parkhurst *deserved* to die before he killed more innocent children—and innocent men, like poor Mr. Boulton. None of the other doctors would speak against him as long as he was alive. He was too powerful, too rich—he all but ran the hospital, even though he was a butcher in the operating room." Her face was sad, and yet peaceful, as if a great weight was off her conscience.

"Pay no attention to her," said Sir Denis, putting a hand on her shoulder. "My poor wife is distraught by all these wild accusations. Alice, calm yourself. You haven't done anything."

She shook off his hand, then stood up and continued. "Dear Denis! It's no use. The world is a better place without Dr. Parkhurst. I saw what needed to be done, and I did it. I am not sorry, and I will not ask anyone to lie for me. I will answer to my Maker for what I have done. I do not think He will judge me harshly." She looked straight ahead, her chin high.

There was a shocked silence. Lestrade finally broke it: "He

will judge us all," he said, soberly. "But for now, Lady Alice, I must ask you to come with me. Sir Denis, Miss Donning, I fear you are under arrest as well. I warn you that anything you say may be noted down and used against you in court. Coleman, call the other lads up here." The assistant nodded briskly and turned to go down the stairs.

Sir Denis shook his head. "I feared it would come to this," he said. "I must tell you, neither my wife nor Miss Donning had anything to do with the killing. I let go Alice's hand in the dark, as I sometimes do at séances to test whether the medium can sense it. Then, with one hand, I fired the shot that killed Dr. Parkhurst. I am an expert shot with either hand; everyone in England knows it. It was I, and I alone who killed him."

At this, Lady Alice started to speak. Sir Denis hushed her with a finger to her lips. "No, my dear, I can't let you take the blame for what I have done. But I shall always remember that you were ready to do so. Hush, my dear, we must neither one say anything more."

We all sat there in a state of shock; even Cedric Villiers seemed for once to be at a loss for words.

"I shall have to take you all before the judge," repeated Lestrade. He gestured to Coleman and the constables, who had begun to file into the room from downstairs.

"In that case, I shall let my barrister speak for me," said Sir Denis in a crisp voice. Ophelia Donning simply sat there with a stunned look on her face; she had said nothing since Mr. Clemens had linked her to the conspiracy. For a brief moment the tableau was frozen; I realized that Mrs. Parkhurst was crying softly.

Then: "I'll just get my wrap," said Lady Alice, with a brave smile. She stepped lightly into the bedroom, disappearing almost instantly, since she had been sitting only two or three paces from the door. Then several of us must have remembered the same thing at once: the coats were hung on the rack in the foyer. I got to my feet, as did Miss Donning on the opposite side of the table, and started for the door. Lestrade realized it a moment later; he motioned to Constable

Wilkins to follow Lady Alice. "Quickly, man," he said, and the urgency in his voice was clear.

It was only a few seconds' delay—surely no more—before the constable pushed through the door Lady Alice had closed behind her, but it was just long enough.

There was a dull report and the constable gave a cry. "No, ma'am! My gawd!"

Lestrade followed his constable, with Sir Denis hot on his heels, and everyone else crowding after them. Then, after a glance into the doorway, Lestrade turned and blocked it. "I don't think you gentlemen need to see this," he said firmly. He took Sir Denis, who had turned white as a ghost, by the arm and firmly propelled him back to his seat at the table as we all stood and gaped. Sir Denis said not a syllable, but his face spoke volumes.

"Sit back down," said Lestrade. "Everyone sit down, please." For once, the authority in his voice was compelling, not arrogant. Then he turned to his assistant. "Coleman, tell headquarters we've a shooting. And call a doctor."

"Is she dead?" asked Tony Parkhurst, trying to peek past the Scotland Yard man.

"Everyone stand back," snarled Lestrade. "I wouldn't be calling a doctor if she were, now, would I?"

I think he already knew that he was lying to us.

28 ⌒

"I still can't believe that nice old lady was the murderer," said Susy Clemens. She drew her coat up around her throat and gave a shiver against the autumn chill of London. "But I guess she didn't leave any question about it. It's very sad, really."

It was several days since the dramatic scene in the McPhees' flat, where in front of the reassembled séance group, Mr. Clemens had named Lady Alice DeCoursey as the one who had shot Dr. Oliver Parkhurst. That she could be the murderer had at first seemed incredible to me, as well, but Mr. Clemens had summarized the evidence irrefutably—as Lady Alice had finally proven by taking her own life before anyone could prevent her. It was a shocking end to a disturbing case, in which very few of the principals had managed to escape untainted.

"I suppose she preferred ending things herself to facing the gallows," I said, raising my voice to be heard over the clatter of the wheels on the paving stones. Mr. Clemens's family—and I—were on our way home from a visit to the Tower of London. "I can't condone her murdering the doctor, but I do have to admire her courage at the last."

"Foolishness rather than courage," said Mr. Clemens. He

had been gazing out the window at the Thames ever since we got in the coach, but now he turned back to face us. "If she'd gotten the right lawyer, he could probably have saved her. Even the sternest British judge is likely to draw back from sending a baronet's wife to hang—it goes against everything he believes in."

Mrs. Clemens touched her husband's arm and said, "I think you're overlooking one possibility, Youth. What if she killed herself not out of fear of the gallows, but out of a conviction that she deserved punishment—for killing a man even though she believed him to be a danger to society?"

"I guess she might have believed that," said Mr. Clemens. "Half the murderers in the world—probably more than half— think they're justified. But that's a judgement no single person can make—not even one with a title hitched to her name. If Dr. Parkhurst was a danger to society, Lady Alice could've stopped him short of murdering him. Shooting herself didn't wipe the slate clean, either. The only way to do that would be to bring him back."

"And only the Lord could do that," said Mrs. Clemens, in a tone that rang of finality.

"Certainly not the likes of Martha McPhee, much as she'd like us to think she can," said Mr. Clemens. "I reckon she's no worse than the run of the mill in her line, but that's like saying one pickpocket's no worse than another."

Little Jean broke in. "I liked Mrs. Boulton's idea about the ectoplasmic pistol," she said. "I wish that had been true."

"Thank the stars it wasn't," said her father, shuddering. "The last thing we need is spooks shooting at people."

"I feel sorry for Sir Denis and Ophelia Donning," said Clara Clemens. "Both are being charged as accessories to murder. Yet neither did much more than allow Lady Alice to get her hands free to fire the shot, did they?"

"There's more to it than that," said my employer. "I don't think Sir Denis knew in advance his wife was going to kill the doctor, because he'd have stopped her—or done his best to help her come up with a more practical plan. The way she did it wasn't all that hard to figure out, once I studied the evidence. If he'd helped plan it, it would've been much harder to trace back to her. Now, Ophelia Donning will have a tougher row to hoe, in my opinion. She may convince a jury that *she* didn't know in advance what Lady Alice was going to do—but I think she was the one who really convinced the victim to come to the séance, to escort her and her sister. And once the doctor was shot, they had to know for certain who had done it. They both did everything they could to steer suspicion from Lady Alice, including Sir Denis confessing to cover up for her. They may not hang for it, but neither one will get off scot-free, either—not unless the jury is full of nincompoops.''

"I wonder what happened to Mr. and Mrs. McPhee?'' said Susy Clemens. "They certainly took everyone by surprise at the end, there.''

That was undeniably true. In the hubbub following Lady Alice's shooting herself, as all the police officers gathered in the bedroom, Slippery Ed and Martha McPhee had somehow managed to make their way down the stairs and disappear. The constable posted on the doorstep claimed he'd never even seen them. Lestrade had been furious, of course, but by the time anyone realized they were gone, it was far too late to do anything but put out a bulletin for their arrest. They still had not been found.

"I hope they get away,'' said little Jean. "I liked Mrs. McPhee. And Papa's stories about Slippery Ed are funny, too.''

Mr. Clemens chuckled. "Well, they've gotten away so far,'' he said. "The ground was getting a little too hot under their feet here in London, and I reckon it's not the first place they've left in a hurry. Lestrade's mad as a hornet, of course, but he's not likely to catch them if he hasn't by now. I'd bet they've moved on to someplace where their reputation hasn't arrived first—most likely in some other country. Maybe they'll set up as mediums again, or maybe they'll find another racket to start on. But however it falls out, I can't imagine either of them taking up honest work.

"And speaking of honest work, I'm just as glad this whole case is wrapped up. I've finally had time to get ready for the lecture series,'' he said. "And I've had a few more days to spend with my little angels before I go on the road again. I'd been neglecting you girls shamefully with all this murder business.''

"Oh, don't feel so bad, Papa," said Clara, with a saucy laugh. "The murder is the most exciting thing we've had to talk about in ages. It's almost a shame it's solved—now we'll have to find some other amusement."

"Amusement?" said Mr. Clemens, raising his brow in mock horror. "Are these the same three girls I was calling 'my little angels' just a moment ago? Where exactly did you get the idea that talking about a man being shot dead is some kind of amusement?"

"I cannot imagine where such a morbid fascination comes from, Youth," said Mrs. Clemens, with a little smile. "Certainly nobody on the Langdon side of the family ever had such unsuitable thoughts."

"Hmmph!" he said, making a mock-ferocious expression. "I resent that implication. The girls must be getting these ideas on their own. They're probably reading some sort of low-class stuff about detectives, like those Sherlock Holmes stories. I'll soon put a stop to that. We'll start a course of improving readings soon as we get home—"

But little Jean burst out laughing. "Oh look, Mama, the bad, spitting gray kitten has come back! We've been ever so lonely without him." She reached up and stroked her father's hair.

And at that, even my employer had to let a smile onto his face as the carriage took us home through the twilit streets of London. Life had returned to normal—or as close to normal as it ever got in Mr. Clemens's company—and I was just as glad.

If you enjoy the MARK TWAIN
mystery series,
you will also want to read

THE DUMB
SHALL SING

by STEPHEN LEWIS

Catherine had just come out into the garden with Phyllis to see what vegetables might be gathered for supper when she heard a confused cacophony of voices rise from the road that skirted the hill on which her house sat. She and Phyllis hurried around to the front, and there she saw a crowd heading toward the northern edge of Newbury, where the town ran abruptly into the untamed woods. The voices seemed to carry an angry tone. She turned to Phyllis.

"Catch up with them, if you can, and see where they are going, and to what purpose."

She watched as the girl hurried down the hill and trotted toward the people, whose voices were becoming less distinct as they moved farther away. Catherine strained her eyes, keeping them focused on the white cap Phyllis wore, and she saw it bobbling up and down behind the crowd. The cap stopped moving next to a man's dark brown hat. After a few moments she could see the cap turn back toward her while the hat moved away, and shortly Phyllis stood before her, catching her breath.

"They are going to the Jameson house. They say the babe is dead. And they want you to come to say whether it was alive when it was born."

She recalled holding the babe in her arms and seeing that he was having trouble breathing. She had seen that his nose was clogged with mucus and fluids, and she had cleared it with a bit of rag she carried in her midwife's basket for that purpose. The babe had snorted in the air as soon as she removed the cloth and then he had bellowed a very strong and healthy cry. The only thing out of the ordinary during the birth that she could now remember was how the Jameson's Irish maidservant eyed the babe as though she wanted to do something with it. Catherine had seen dozens of births, and usually she could tell when a babe was in trouble. This one had given no indication of frailty.

"Come along with me, then," she said to Phyllis. "Just stop to tell Edward to watch for Matthew."

Phyllis did not respond, and Catherine motioned to the tree under which Massaquoit had slept.

"You know," Catherine repeated, "Matthew."

"I see, yes, he should wait for Matthew," Phyllis said.

"Edward need not think about going to lecture."

"He does not think about that anyway," Phyllis replied.

"Be that as it may, I do not think there will be lecture tonight," Catherine said. "Now go along with you."

The Jameson house was a humble structure of two sections, the older little more than a hut with walls of daub and wattle construction, a plaster of mud and manure layered over a substructure of crisscrossing poles. Henry Jameson had recently built a wing onto the back of the house to accommodate his growing family, and this new room was covered in wooden shingles outside and was generally more luxurious inside, having a wood plank floor and whitewashed plaster walls.

It was in this room that Martha had delivered her babe. Catherine remembered that the Irish servant girl had a little space, not much more than a closet, for a bed so that she could be near the infant's cradle, and that the parents' bedroom was in the original portion of the house. She also remembered how the girl had fashioned a crude cross out of two twigs, tied together with thread, and then hung it over her bed until Henry had found it there and pulled it off. He had taken the cross outside and ground it into the mud with the heavy heel of his shoe. There was a separate entrance to this side of the house, which gave onto a patch of wild strawberries, and it was before that door that the crowd had gathered.

As Catherine shouldered her way through the crowd, she felt hands grabbing at her sleeve. She was spun around, and for a moment she lost sight of Phyllis. Someone said, "I've got her," but Catherine pulled away. Phyllis emerged from behind the man who was holding Catherine's arm. A woman placed her face right in front of Catherine. She was missing her front teeth, and her breath was sour. She held a smoldering torch in one hand, and she brought it down near Catherine's face.

"Here, mistress," the woman said, "we've been waiting for you, we have."

Phyllis forced herself next to Catherine, shielding her from the woman.

"Go," Catherine said to Phyllis, "to Master Woolsey, and tell him to come here right away."

Phyllis pushed her way back through the crowd, which was advancing with a deliberate inevitability toward the house. Catherine moved with the energy of the crowd, but at a faster pace, so that soon she reached its leading edge, some ten or so feet away from Henry and Ned Jameson, who stood with their backs to their house. Ned had his arm around the Irish servant girl, flattening her breasts and squeezing her hard against his side. She held a pitcher in her hand. It was tilted toward the ground and water dripped from it. The girl's eyes were wide and staring as they found Catherine.

"Please," she said, but then Ned pulled her even harder toward him, and whatever else the girl was trying to say was lost in the breath exploding from her mouth.

The Jameson girls, ranging from a toddler to the oldest, a twelve-year-old, were gathered around their mother, who stood off to one side. Martha's gown was unlaced and one heavy breast hung free as though she were about to give her babe suck. Her eyes moved back and forth between her husband and the crowd, seemingly unable or unwilling to focus.

The toddler amused itself by walking 'round and 'round through her mother's legs. The oldest girl seemed to be whispering comfort to her younger siblings. Then the girl turned to her mother and laced up her gown. Martha looked at her daughter's hand as though it were a fly buzzing about her, but she did not swipe it away.

Henry was holding the babe, wrapped in swaddling, and unmoving. It was quite clearly dead. He took a step toward Catherine and held out the babe toward her. His face glowed red in the glare of a torch.

"Here she is," he shouted. He lowered his voice a little. "Tell us, then, if you please, Mistress Williams, was this babe born alive?"

"Who says nay?" Catherine asked. She looked at Martha, who stood mute, and then at the Irish servant girl, who did not seem to understand what was happening. Always the finger of blame, she thought, lands on some poor woman while the men stand around pointing that finger with self-righteous and hypocritical arrogance. She recalled how Henry had asked first what sex the babe was before he inquired as to his wife's health. "Henry will be glad," Martha had said as Catherine had held the babe in front of her so that she could see its genitalia. And then Martha had collapsed onto the bed, a woman exhausted by fifteen years of being pregnant, giving birth, suffering miscarriages, and nursing the babes that were born, and always there had been the poverty. She had not wanted to take Ned in, for there was never enough food.

"Just answer the question," Henry insisted. "We have heard how soft your heart is for a savage. How is it with this babe? Here, look at it, which is not breathing now who was when it was born. Was it not very much alive when you pulled it out of my wife's belly not three days ago?"

A voice came from the back of the crowd, strong, male, and insistent.

"An answer, mistress, we need to know the truth."

Catherine turned toward the voice, but she could not identify the speaker. It came from a knot of people that had gathered just beyond Ned in the shadow of a tall tree.

"The truth," the voice said again, and then was joined by

other voices, male and female, rising from the group beneath the tree, and then spreading across the surface of the crowd like whitecaps in a storm-tossed sea. "The truth," they clamored, "tell us the truth."

"What says the mother, then?" Catherine demanded. "What says Goody Jameson?"

"Nothing," came the response from the group.

Catherine turned back to Henry.

"Your wife, Henry, what does she say?"

"Nothing," Henry repeated. "She no longer speaks. She came to me not an hour ago, holding the babe in her arms, and handed it to me, and she does not speak."

Catherine studied Martha's face. Its expression did not change as her children moved about her. She did not seem to see that her husband was holding her dead infant in his arms, and she did not hear the insistent cries for the truth. It was as though she were standing in a meadow daydreaming while butterflies circled her head. Every moment or two she extended her hand toward the toddler that clung to her knees, but the gesture was vague and inconsequential, and her hand never found the child's head.

Catherine stepped close to Martha, close enough to feel the woman's breath on her face.

"Martha, you must speak," Catherine said, and Martha's eyes now focused on her, as though she had just returned from that distant meadow. She shook her heard, slowly at first, and then with increasing agitation. Catherine took Martha's shoulders in both hands and squeezed and then the nodding motion stopped. Still Martha did not speak.

"My poor wife is distracted by the death of our babe," Henry declared. "Can you not see that? Mistress Williams, you must answer for her."

"Well, then," Catherine said, "if Martha Jameson will not attest to the truth, I needs must say that this babe was born alive, and alive it was when I left it. Truth you want, and there it is."

A murmur arose from the crowd. It pushed toward Catherine.

"It is surely dead now," somebody said.

"If Goody Jameson won't speak, we have ways," said another.

"Yes, press her, stone by stone. She will talk, then, I warrant."

"You will leave her alone," Henry said, and the crowd, which had come within several feet of the clustered Jameson family, stopped. Henry held out the babe toward his wife.

"Tell them, Martha," he said. He thrust the babe toward her, but she did not hold out her arms to take it. He shook his head. "She brought the babe to me. It was dead. She said she had been asleep, and when she woke she saw the servant girl leaning over the babe. When she picked it up, it was not breathing. Then she brought it to me. That girl, she did something while my wife was asleep."

Catherine felt the anger rise in the crowd toward the servant. She remembered once, when she was a girl in Alford, how a crowd just like this one had fallen upon a little boy whose family was Catholic, and how they had beaten him with sticks until he lay senseless in the road. She strode to Ned and grabbed his arm.

"Let her go," she said.

"You are now interfering with my household, mistress. Leave be."

"Step away, mistress," a woman in the crowd said. "You have told us what we needed to know."

"She," Henry shouted, "standing there with the pitcher, ask her what she was doing with our babe."

The servant girl turned her terrified and starting eyes toward her master. Their whites loomed preternaturally large in the failing light of the early evening.

"A priest, it was, I was after," she said.

Ned pushed the girl forward so she stood quivering in front of the crowd.

"That is it," he said, "that is how we found her, practicing her papist ritual on our babe, pouring water on its innocent face, and mumbling some words, a curse they must have been."

"Its poor soul," the girl muttered. "There was no priest. I asked for one. So I tried myself to save its precious soul."

Henry looked at his wife, whose eyes were now studying the ground at her feet. Then he stared hard at the girl, his face brightening as with a new understanding.

"You drowned it, for certain," he said. "Or you cast a spell on it so it could not breathe. What, a papist priest? In Newbury? You have killed our babe and driven my poor wife mad."

"Try her, then," came the voice from the knot of people, still grouped by the tree. "Have her touch the babe. Then we will know."

The crowd surged forward and Catherine found herself staggering toward Henry, who dropped to one knee against her weight. Henry threw one hand behind him to brace himself, and Catherine reached for the babe so as to stop it from falling. As she grabbed for it, its swaddling blanket fell. The babe's skin was cold. Henry regained his balance and wrapped the babe tightly in the blanket.

"Try her," again came the cry from the crowd.

"Surely not," Catherine said. "Magistrate Woolsey is coming. This is a matter for him."

"We need not wait for the magistrate. We will have our own answer now," shouted one.

"Now," said another.

"Right," said Ned. "We will try her now."

Catherine turned to face the crowd and to peer over it to the road, where day was giving way to dusk. She thought she say two figures approaching.

"The magistrate is coming even now," she said.

Henry looked at Ned, and the boy pushed the servant girl toward him.

"Touch the babe," Ned demanded.

"Yes, touch it," Henry said. "If it bleed, it cries out against you."

"There is no need for that," Catherine said. "Talk of the dead bleeding. It is surely blasphemy."

"The blood will talk," came a voice from the crowd.

"Yes," others confirmed, "let the poor dead babe's blood cry out against its murderer."

The girl clasped her arms in front of her chest, but Ned

pulled her hands out. She struggled, but he was too strong, and he was able to bring one hand to the exposed skin of the babe's chest. He pressed the hand onto the skin, and then let her pull her hand back. Henry peered at the spot she had touched, and then lifted the babe over his head in a triumphant gesture.

"It bleeds," he said. "It bleeds."

He held the babe out for the crowd to see. Catherine strained her eyes as Henry and the babe were now in the shadows. Henry turned so that all could view. Catherine was not sure she saw blood on the babe's chest, but something on its back caught her eye, and then she could no longer see.

"Blood," cried voices in the crowd. "The babe bleeds! Seize her!"

There was a violent surge forward, and Catherine felt herself being thrown to the ground. She got to her feet just in time to see rough hands grabbing the servant girl and pulling her away. . . .

PETER J. HECK

DEATH ON THE MISSISSIPPI

"A thoroughly enjoyable period mystery with Clemens and
Cabot forming an uneasy alliance that possesses elements of
Holmes and Watson as well as Wolfe and Archie. A very
pleasant debut that will have readers eagerly awaiting the
next entry."—*Booklist*

__0-425-15512-9/$5.99

A CONNECTICUT YANKEE IN CRIMINAL COURT

"An enjoyable tour of 1890s' New Orleans...Twain can take a
bow for his performance. Heck takes a colorful city (New
Orleans) and a colorful character (Mark Twain), adds a murder, a duel, some voodoo and period detail and conjures up
an entertaining sequel to *Death on the Mississippi*."
—*Publishers Weekly*

"Irresistible...a perfect mix of history, mystery, and wit."
—*Alfred Hitchcock Mystery Magazine*

__0-425-16034-3/$5.99

EARLENE FOWLER

introduces Benni Harper, curator of San Celina's folk
art museum and amateur sleuth

❏ **FOOL'S PUZZLE**　　　　**0-425-14545-X/$5.99**

Ex-cowgirl Benni Harper moved to San Celina, California, to
begin a new career as curator of the town's folk art museum. But
when one of the museum's first quilt exhibit artists is found dead,
Benni must piece together a pattern of family secrets and small-
town lies to catch the killer.

❏ **IRISH CHAIN**　　　　**0-425-15137-9/$6.50**

When Brady O'Hara and his former girlfriend are murdered at the
San Celina Senior Citizen's Prom, Benni believes it's more than
mere jealousy. She risks everything–her exhibit, her romance with
police chief Gabriel Ortiz, and her life–to unveil the conspiracy
O'Hara had been hiding for fifty years.

❏ **KANSAS TROUBLES**　　　　**0-425-15696-6/$5.99**

After their wedding, Benni and Gabe visit his hometown near
Wichita. There Benni meets Tyler Brown: aspiring country singer,
gifted quilter, and former Amish wife. But when Tyler is murdered
and the case comes between Gabe and her, Benni learns that her
marriage is much like the Kansas weather: unexpected and bound
to be stormy.

❏ **GOOSE IN THE POND**　　　　**0-425-16239-7/$6.50**